Praise for *Shattered*

"Questions of loyalty and trust, thwarted and unrequited love, and even addiction are addressed in this nifty contemporary fantasy."

—*Booklist*

"An exciting read that will leave science fiction and fantasy fans hanging in suspense."

—*VOYA*

"An entertaining, high-octane read."

—*RT Book Reviews*

Praise for *Scorched*

"Tense and action-packed. It's a brave new world and I reveled in every page!"

—Sophie Jordan, *New York Times* bestselling author of *Firelight*

"*Scorched* is fun, fast, and greatly entertaining…a heart-pounding, twisty, time-travel fantasy with delicious dragon mythology!"

—Melissa de la Cruz, *New York Times* bestselling author of the Blue Bloods series

"A smoking triptych of time traveling, dubious double crossing, and enough dragons to sate the hungriest of gamers and fantasy fiends."

—*Kirkus Reviews*

"Exciting and original."

—*School Library Journal*

"Mancusi grabs readers and drags them into this fantastic world full of time-travel paradoxes, mythical creatures, and romance. The beginning of a trilogy you won't want to miss!"

—*RT Book Reviews*

"Fantastic, witty, fun… *Scorched* is an exhilarating, intriguing, and adventure-filled fantasy. Mancusi leaves the reader hanging, even dangling, in all the right places…"

—*Desert News*

More Praise for Mari Mancusi

"So worth reading, with dark humor, a distinctive voice, and a protagonist clever enough to get herself out of trouble. Thank you, Mari Mancusi, for a great ride."

—Ellen Hopkins, *New York Times* bestselling author of *Tilt*, on *Boys That Bite*

"Delightful, surprising, and engaging—you'll get bitten and love it."

—Rachel Caine, *New York Times* bestselling author of the Morganville Vampire series, on the Blood Coven series

ALSO BY MARI MANCUSI

Scorched
Shattered

SMOKED

MARI MANCUSI

sourcebooks
fire

Published by Sourcebooks Fire, an imprint of Sourcebooks, Inc.

P.O. Box 4410, Naperville, Illinois 60567-4410

(630) 961-3900

Fax: (630) 961-2168

www.sourcebooks.com

Library of Congress Cataloging-in-Publication Data

Mancusi, Mari.
  Smoked / Mari Mancusi.
     pages cm
  Sequel to: Shattered.
  Summary: "When Team Dragon finally rescues Emmy--now a full-grown dragon--they think the future is safe. Until Emmy reveals a secret: she's laid two dragon eggs, and her offspring may bring about the fiery apocalypse they've all fought so hard to prevent"-- Provided by publisher.
  (13 : alk. paper) [1. Adventure and adventurers--Fiction. 2. Supernatural--Fiction. 3. Dragons--Fiction.] I. Title.
  PZ7.M312178Sm 2015
  [Fic]--dc23
                                            2015009889

Printed and bound in the United States of America.
VP 10 9 8 7 6 5 4 3 2 1

To Mark and Ana Beach, for your continued dragon-sized support and love! You are the best in-laws a girl could have and I feel privileged to have you in my life.

PART 1:

ASH

Prologue

Year 190 Post-Scorch

E mergency. Emergency. Dragons incoming. Please proceed calmly to the nearest flame shelter. This is not a drill. I repeat: this is not a drill."

Sixteen-year-old Connor Jacks watched as the hallway erupted in chaos, doors bursting open, bodies spilling out everywhere, not a single soul seemingly interested in proceeding with any level of calm whatsoever. Instead, hands were clawing and eyes were bulging as howls of panic nearly managed to drown out the warning sirens above. All around, red lights flashed angrily, effectively capturing the mood as neighbor shoved neighbor, friend trampled friend.

In the dragon apocalypse, it was every man, woman, and child for themselves. A crush of the worst humanity had left to offer.

"Dragons incoming. Estimated arrival time: fifteen minutes," droned the computerized female voice over the loudspeaker, not exactly helping matters. "Fourteen minutes fifty-nine seconds. Fourteen minutes—"

"Move, damn it!"

Large hands shoved Connor in the back, out of the doorway he had been standing in and into the violent sea of people who crashed over him in waves and knocked him off balance. His hands slammed against the concrete floor first, followed by his knees, and he oomphed in pain as heavy boots trampled his fingers without apology. Biting his lower lip, he struggled back to his feet, grudgingly allowing himself to be swept along with the mob.

He felt a pulse at his side, a slight heat indicating an incoming message on his transcriber. His eyes darted around the hall, finally settling on an empty doorway a few feet ahead. Lunging forward, he managed to traverse the mob and dive through, landing in the entryway of a now-empty home of some Strata-C family. Like most Strata-C homes, this one was small, carved out of rock, and contained only the most basic of belongings. A crude kitchen table and chairs. A few cabinets. Hammocks to sleep in. Only a small, pink plastic teddy bear, abandoned in the middle of a concrete floor, gave any indication of the makeup of the family who might have called this place home.

Well, that and the giant full-color poster of Connor himself, one of the limited edition "Dragon Hunter Heroes" series that the Council had released a few months back and given to school children under the age of ten. He made a face. The artist had exaggerated his physique to the point of caricature, as well as the size of the gun-blade in his hands. The caption read *Hasta La Vista, Dragon Spawn!*—which they'd embarrassingly assigned as his catchphrase even though he'd protested that he'd never say anything so corny in real life. But the Council had insisted catchphrases increased morale, and so what could he do? Whatever gave these poor people hope, he supposed. Though if the fate of the known world really was relying on catchphrases, the world was totally screwed.

He pulled his transcriber from his belt, running his fingers across the smooth side. A hologram popped up, and an image of his friend and fellow Dragon Hunter Troy looked back at him, his face pale. "Jacks!" he cried in a hoarse voice. "Where are you? Are you anywhere near Subterra A? Damien up at the watchtower counted five headed your way, and we're all stuck over at E, working the peace rally you bailed on. We're headed back now, but we won't be there in time." Troy scowled, and Connor couldn't help but remember his friend's catchphrase—*You feeling lucky, dragon punk?* "The Council is recommending nukes."

Connor cringed. Of course they were. He pressed the record button to send a reply to his fellow soldier. "Tell them to stand down," he barked. "I'm not far. I'll handle it."

He sent the message then reattached the transcriber to his belt. Brushing his hair from his eyes, he exited the home and stepped back into the hallway. The once-crowded passage was eerily vacant now, with all the people of Strata-C hopefully safe and sound in the flame shelters below. Waiting for him to get the job done so they could get back to their everyday lives.

Connor ran down the hallway, his footsteps pounding to the rhythm of the flashing red lights as he made his way to the surface 'vator that would take him where he needed to go. But as he took a corner too quickly, he found himself nearly tripping over something on the floor. He looked down.

Make that some*one*.

The little girl couldn't have been much older than six, and her grubby face was stained with tears as she sucked on the end of a messy pigtail. She looked up at Connor with wide, awestruck eyes.

"Are you one of them?" she asked in a tiny voice. "Are you a Dragon Hunter?"

Suddenly her fear seemed forgotten as she rummaged through her filthy backpack, pulling out a trading card–size version of the poster Connor had seen in the house. She studied it for a moment, then looked back up at him. "It *is* you!" she cried excitedly. "Can you sign my card?"

"Where's your family?" Connor demanded. He needed to get moving. But he couldn't rightly leave the girl out here, exposed and unprotected and alone. These quarters weren't far from the Surface Lands and could go up quickly if the dragons weren't stopped.

Or worse—if the Council did pull out the nukes.

The girl dropped her hand, looking dejected. "We got separated. And then they closed the 'vators," she warbled in a thin voice. "They wouldn't let me down."

"What?" Connor frowned. This was, of course, completely against protocol. The 'vator operators were supposed to do a complete head count before closing down to make sure everyone in the strata was accounted for. But that didn't mean it always happened, especially during a major panic like this one had been.

"What's your name?" he asked.

"Salla," the girl whispered. "My name is Salla. And I'm scared." She stuck a grubby thumb into her mouth.

"Okay, Salla, I'm going to get you to a shelter." Connor

scooped the girl into his arms then switched directions, once again traversing the empty hall with as much speed as he could manage. Thankfully the girl was a light load.

He grabbed his transcriber with his free hand, pushing on it to call Damien above. "I'll be there in a second!" he told the Watcher.

"Hurry," Damien's voice crackled back. "It's bad up here."

It's bad down here too.

They reached the 'vator, and Connor lowered Salla to her feet so he could rummage for his key card to summon it. Soon the two of them were shooting down into the earth below. When they reached floor negative 23, containing the last flame shelter one mile beneath the surface of the earth, the doors slid open, revealing two guards standing watch.

Seeing Connor and the grimy girl, they barked, "No room."

But there was plenty of room, Connor saw. In fact, he had never seen a more roomy emergency shelter in his life. The people inside, dressed in finery, sipping sparkling beverages, chatting as if they were at the social event of the season, not hiding out from monsters. He thought about some of the other shelters he'd seen a few levels up, where there was barely room to turn around. He'd heard rumors of these places—where guards accepted bribes and turned others away. It made him sick to his stomach to see it for himself.

He reached into his shirt and whipped out the badge that hung from a chain around his neck. He didn't like to pull rank, but at the moment, he didn't have time to screw around.

The guards' eyes widened as the badge flashed under the fluorescent lights. They looked at one another and then back at Connor, nervous grins erupting on their faces.

"So sorry, sir. We didn't recognize you," babbled one.

"Of course you can come in. Anything you need. It's an honor to—"

He waved them off angrily. "This girl is under my protection," he stated, forcing his voice to stay even. "Take her and make sure she has water and something to eat."

"Of course! Of course!" the first guard assured him hastily. "I'll treat her as if she were my own daughter." He reached for the girl. Salla looked back at Connor with terrified eyes.

"Don't leave me!" she cried. "Please, Mr. Dragon Hunter!"

"You need to be brave, Salla," Connor commanded, hoping he sounded cool and confident and not the least bit afraid. "I've got to go. I have to fight the dragons and make things safe for you."

Salla thankfully seemed to get this. She smiled at Connor. "Hasta la vista, dragon spawn!" she cried, raising her fist in a cheer.

He smiled back weakly, then forced himself to repeat it, trying not to blush too hard as he did. Then he gave her a last salute before running back to the 'vator.

It was time to go slay some dragons.

Chapter One

Present Day

"Come on. They should be here by now."

Sixteen-year-old Trinity Foxx glanced down at the clock on her disposable cell phone, then over at Connor, who was sitting next to her, in the driver's seat of the delivery truck. He turned to her, a sympathetic look on his face.

"Yes, you've mentioned that," he said wryly. "About fifty times in the last five minutes, I believe." He reached over and squeezed her hand. "Don't worry, Trin. They'll come."

Trinity nodded absently, still staring out the grimy windshield. The wind had picked up, and the sand on the desert floor was swirling around like a living, breathing thing. Her gaze traveled to the large, gray building squatting in the distance, and she narrowed her eyes at it. As if the architecture itself were to blame for all their misfortune. "Well, they'd better get here soon if this is going to work."

And why do you think it will work this time? an ugly voice inside her head jeered. *When it's never worked before?*

It was, unfortunately, a valid question. In fact, it'd been nearly six months since her dragon, Emmy, had been captured and brought to this secret government lab buried deep in the Mojave Desert. Six months since Trinity had started receiving distress calls from Scarlet, who had surrendered along with her. Six months since they'd started formulating and acting out rescue plans that had failed to free either girl or dragon. Why should this one be any different?

"Oh, Emmy," she whispered. "Are you still in there? Are you okay?"

The worst part was, once upon a time, she would have known the answer to those questions. Would have heard the answer—straight from the dragon's mouth. Well, her subconscious whisper, anyway. Since before Emmy had even hatched from her egg, she and Trinity had shared a special bond. *Fire Kissed*, they called it. It allowed them to talk without speaking, share thoughts and feelings over thin air. And when they combined their powers together, they could bend people's minds and wills. At times, Trinity had been sure there was nothing she and her dragon couldn't do—if they did it together.

But that bond had long since severed. Dragon and Fire Kissed were now as separate as two beings could be. Back then, Trinity had believed the de-bonding was the best plan of action—the only way to keep Emmy safe from those who sought to capture her and use her for their own gain. But each day since, the screaming emptiness in her head had become more and more unbearable. And while once upon a time she might have been grateful to be spared the burden of being a dragon's guardian, now she was pretty sure she'd sell her very soul if only she could get her best friend back.

But that would never happen. Because Emmy belonged to Scarlet now. Scarlet, who should have never gotten involved in any of this in the first place—she was now Emmy's keeper and protector. A fact that, most days, made Trinity want to bash her head against the wall. She knew she should be grateful that Scarlet had willingly stepped in at that final moment. After all, if it weren't for her, they wouldn't have any idea where Emmy had been taken. That, in and of itself, was worth everything.

But that didn't mean Trinity had to be happy about it. She'd lost her dragon in more ways than one, and even if they did manage to stage a miraculous rescue, things would never be the same between them.

She reached out, searching for Scarlet now. When she'd first convinced the girl to surrender to the enemy—in order to keep tabs on Emmy—she'd used her gift of mental telepathy to open up a sort-of back door in her mind—a mental homing device to help them lock down Scarlet's location and put the rescue plan in place. At the time, Trin had figured it would be a short-term thing. They'd break Emmy and Scarlet out of their prison and that would be the end of it. She had no idea that the government would thwart their efforts for nearly half a year. And her heart ached as she imagined what they'd been doing to her dragon all this time, deep in their labs. Experimenting on her. Abusing her.

This had to work. It just had to.

"Look," Connor said, interrupting her tormented musings, his finger pointing down the road. Trinity followed it, heart in her throat. Sure enough, a parade of cars now stretched out before them, as far as the eye could see, winding down the dusty dirt road, toward the facility's front gates. Old cars, beaten-up cars, cars that looked brand-new. All colors, all

11

sizes, all coming their way. Connor rolled down the window, and Trinity's ears picked up the distant bass of the latest Two Sad Boys tune drifting through the air.

Her pulse kicked up. They'd come. They'd actually come!

The walkie-talkie sitting in the cup holder crackled to life. "Did someone order a flash mob?" asked the voice on the other end.

Trinity grinned, grabbing the walkie and pulling it to her mouth.

"Luke! Oh my God. There're so many! How did you get so many?"

She could hear the smile in his voice as he replied, "Yeah, well, that's the interwebs for you. Though they're going to be mighty disappointed when they find out this well-sourced rumor of a secret show is just that," he said with a laugh. "But hopefully you'll be in and out and long gone by then."

"Absolutely," she replied, watching the cars surround the facility, parking everywhere as a mob of colorfully dressed raver kids spilled out of every available door. Insta–Burning Man, just add water. "You did good."

As she set down the walkie-talkie, she could hear Connor's *hmph* beside her. She turned to him. "Come on, dude. You have to admit, this is pretty genius."

Connor shrugged. He'd made it clear he didn't trust Luke and his two friends, the gamer geeks from Fauna, New Mexico, who had dubbed themselves the Dracken and ran an Emmy fan site online. And Trinity supposed she couldn't entirely blame him for that. After all, for him, this entire thing was a strange sort of déjà vu. Where he came from—two hundred years in the dragon-scorched future—the Dracken had been the bad guys. The ones who had started this whole dragon apocalypse to begin with…by breaking into a government facility and letting the dragons free.

In other words, exactly the same thing they were doing now.

The Dracken, Connor had argued, shouldn't exist in this new time line. Not if Trinity had truly stopped the apocalypse. But somehow here they were. Not only here—but contributing to the exact same mission that had led to catastrophe in the first place.

Trinity had tried to convince him that things weren't the same this time. That these so-called Dracken were gamer geeks, not the trained animal rights activists the original Dracken had been. Heck, just their daily hamburger consumption alone should have clued him into that. Not to mention, this time, they'd formed on their own—without Trinity's help. And way earlier in the time line than the first time around.

But no matter what she said, Connor remained unconvinced. In fact, she knew if he had his way, they wouldn't be rescuing Emmy at all. She would already be dead—dragon apocalypse permanently averted.

But he hadn't killed Emmy when he'd had the chance. Because Trinity had asked him not to. And as much as he hated dragons, he loved her more.

She shook her head, trying to clear her thoughts. Right now, none of that mattered. The point was, they were here. They were going to rescue Emmy. This time it would work.

It *had* to work.

"Look," she said, pointing to the road again. "Here come the delivery trucks."

"Excellent. That's our cue."

13

Connor turned the key in the ignition and stepped on the gas, pulling their own vehicle into line with the others, heading around back, toward the facility's loading dock. Trinity swallowed hard, her heart pounding in her chest as they followed the other trucks into the belly of the beast. There was no turning back now.

By the time they entered the dock, chaos reigned. Which was exactly their intention when they'd set this plan into motion. Through the website, Luke had rallied a bunch of his followers into placing massive delivery orders of every kind—to be delivered at this very moment. Now, while music fans caused a scene in the front of the building, distracting all the guards, the loading dock would be assaulted from the back with pizzas and furniture delivery and Amazon orders, all arriving at once.

Luke had explained it was like a DoS—denial-of-service—attack on a computer, but in real life. Overwhelm them, knock out their resources, and slip inside unnoticed to stage the rescue. It truly was a brilliant plan.

And this time, it had to work.

Connor placed the truck into park. A harried-looking man with a clipboard ran up to them, sweat beading on his forehead. Connor rolled down the window and gave him his best annoyed look. "What the hell is going on here?" he demanded. "I just need to drop off a box. I'm already way behind schedule."

The man shook his head. "Hell if I know. They never tell us anything." He glanced over at the loading dock entryway, where more trucks were arriving. "Seriously, they do not pay me enough to deal with this." He groaned loudly. "Drop your box wherever you find room. I'll be back to sign off on it in a minute." He ran off to talk to the next driver. Connor turned to Trinity, his mouth quirked to a grin. Even if he didn't like the idea of this plan, she could tell the soldier in him liked the way it was working.

"Okay, Fire Kissed," he said. "It's showtime."

Together they jumped out of the truck, slamming the doors behind them. Connor ran around the back, rolling up the door and pulling out a huge box. Trinity helped him heave it onto the loading dock.

"Are you okay in there?" she whispered to the box.

"Perfect," Nate assured her from inside. "You guys go on ahead. I should be close enough now to hack into their security cameras and get them offline." He paused then added, "Good luck. Just don't forget about me once you have your dragon."

"Never," Trinity assured him, patting the box. Then she rose to her feet and approached Connor. "Ready?"

"As I'll ever be."

With confident, casual steps, they strode up to the guard, who was propped in a chair by the elevator, his feet up, nose in a book, completely ignoring the chaos around him. Guess deliveries weren't in his job description. Connor gave him a small smile. "We need the elevator," he informed him.

"Yeah, well, I need my ex-wife to get off my back," the guard said lazily, snapping his gum. "We've all got problems."

Connor's eyes zeroed in on him. "I don't think you under-stand," he said. "We *need* the elevator. We *need* to get upstairs. You *need* to let us in."

Trinity drew in a breath, watching him work. She had to admit, Connor looked particularly hot when he was working to manipulate people's minds. It was like he got this look in his eyes—those blue, glowing eyes of his—like he was some kind of Jedi Master or something. Truth be told, it kind of made her want to jump his bones. Not that this was the time or the place.

Pushing the inappropriate thought down, she turned back to his victim. Sure enough, the man's face had gone slack, and he was staring up at Connor with vacant eyes. "You need the elevator," he droned. "You need to get upstairs. You need me to let you in."

Then, to Trinity's excitement, he slowly rose to his feet, walked over to the elevator in question, and inserted his key. Just like that. A moment later, the doors yawned open. The guard looked at them expectantly.

Trin flashed Connor an approving look. *You didn't even need my help for that one,* she teased.

Yeah, well, it's all you from here on out, he shot back, but he looked pleased by the compliment all the same. She wondered how normal people who didn't have psychic powers managed rescue attempts. It was hard enough *with* the gift.

They stepped into the elevator, and Connor turned to her expectantly. "What floor?"

She closed her eyes, searching for Scarlet in her mind. "Three," she said after a moment. "She's on three."

Of course she would have much preferred to go straight for Emmy, rescuing her before even thinking about spring-ing Scarlet. But because the connection between her and the dragon had severed, there was no way to know precisely where they'd stashed her, and they didn't have time to waste wandering around. So they'd decided it was best to rescue Scarlet first and then have her lead them to Emmy.

Connor pressed the button, and the elevator grumbled loudly as its doors slid shut. As they shot up to the third floor, the walkie burst to life again.

"I've disabled the security cameras," Nate whispered from the other end. "It was ridiculously easy, actually. For a government lab, their security kind of sucks."

"Or maybe you're just kind of awesome," Trinity suggested, finally allowing herself to smile. For once, everything was going exactly to plan, and she was starting to feel hopeful that they could really pull this off this time. "Now stand by, okay? We may need you again."

"I'm taped up in a U-Haul box, remember?" Nate snorted. "I wasn't exactly planning on going out for cigs." He laughed. "Just don't leave me hanging too long. My legs are already starting to cramp up in this thing."

"Well, we were planning to swing by the cafeteria for a leisurely brunch, but I suppose we can expedite for your circulation's sake."

Trinity stuffed the walkie in her back pocket, then looked at Connor expectantly. He sighed. "Yeah, yeah," he said. "He did good, okay? What do you want, for me to give him a Medal of Honor?"

"If we pull this off, I'm buying everyone medals," she declared as the elevator doors slid open. "Maybe even full-on trophies."

They stepped out into a white hallway lined with doors fitted with barred windows. Thankfully there didn't seem to be any guards on duty—maybe they were all dealing with the music fans out front. She and Connor's gift to bend minds was vital to the mission, but it was also in limited supply. Too many minds and they'd end up out of spark. And they'd have to start taking out guards the old-fashioned way.

Trinity closed her eyes, seeking Scarlet again as they headed down the hall, Connor guiding her by the arm so she wouldn't walk into any walls. Halfway down the corridor, she opened her eyes, turning to one of the nondescript doors. She peered into the window.

"It's her," she whispered to Connor. "At least I'm pretty sure it is."

With a trembling hand, she reached for the door handle. But, of course, it was locked. She grabbed her walkie again. "Can you find the security system for the third floor?" she asked Nate. "We need to open cell door…" She scanned the area for a number. "Fourteen."

"Hm," Nate replied, and she could hear him typing furiously on the other end of the line, which couldn't have been easy to do from inside a box. "I don't think the doors unlock remotely. But I could cut power to the floor. It'd only be for a few seconds—before the emergency backup kicks on. So you'd have to move fast."

"Okay," she agreed, her eyes darting nervously down the hall. She didn't know how long they had left before the guards stationed on this floor returned. And she didn't want to be caught in the dark when they did. Drawing in a shaky breath, she wrapped her hand around the handle again. "I'm ready."

"Wait!" Connor hissed. "I think someone's—"

The lights cut out before he could finish, leaving them in total darkness.

"Hey!" a voice cried out. "What the hell?"

Startled, Trin let out an involuntarily squeak. Connor grabbed her hand—squeezing it tight, a signal for her to keep still. Her heart slammed against her ribs—so loudly she was almost positive the man in the hallway would be able to hear it.

What should we do? she sent Connor silently.

You get that door open, he returned. *I'll deal with this guy.*

He let go of her hand, and she felt him move; he was sneaking down the hall in the direction of the shuffling sound at the other end. It was then that she remembered how good his eyesight was—from a lifetime of underground living—and felt a little better.

She turned back to the door, pushing down on the handle slowly, so it wouldn't make a noise and alert the man to their presence. Fortunately, Nate's trick seemed to have worked, and the door gave way easily. Unfortunately, it let out a loud groan when it did, despite her best efforts. A groan that echoed through the hallway.

"Who's there?" the man called out. "What do you think you're—"

Before he could finish, the emergency power kicked in, just as Nate had predicted, and the hall burst back into light. Trinity whirled around, just in time to catch sight of the guard—and Connor, who had managed to sneak up behind him. The Dragon Hunter slammed his laser pistol down onto the back of the man's head, and he crumpled to the floor on impact, out cold. Trinity let out a breath of relief. Guess the old-fashioned way was pretty effective too.

Connor toed the guard, making sure he was truly unconscious. Then he looked back up at Trin. "Please tell me you
were able to open the door."

She grinned, bowing low and presenting him with the
now-open cell. Connor raced back to her, and together they
stepped inside. The emergency lights had only come on in the
hallway, so the interior of the cell was still pitch-black.

"Who's there?" a girl's terrified voice rang out through the
darkness. "Please don't hurt me!"

Trinity's heart flipped in her chest. It was Scarlet. It was
really her!

"Scarlet, it's me, Trinity," she said, keeping her voice low, in
case any more guards were lurking nearby. "Connor's with me.
We're here to rescue you."

Now that her eyes were adjusting to the darkness, she
could see the outline of the prisoner. Scarlet looked thin.
Much thinner than she'd been the last time Trinity had seen
her. And as she took a step forward, wobbling on pencil-thin
legs, Trinity felt an unexpected rush to her gut. The last six
months, she'd been so preoccupied with what Emmy must
be going through, she hadn't given much thought to Scarlet's
well-being.

You sent her here, the nagging voice reminded her. *Whatever
she's suffered is all because of you.*

"Trinity? Connor? Oh my God, is it really you?" Scarlet
cried. "I was beginning to think you'd forgotten about us."

Trinity winced at the unintentional jab, the guilt again
twisting in her gut. She wanted to protest—to explain they'd
been trying desperately, this entire time, to stage this rescue.
That she hadn't had one moment of rest since Emmy had

been taken away. But what would that matter to Scarlet? Scarlet who had been stuck in a dark, dank cell, waiting for the rescue that had been promised and—up until this moment—not delivered.

And what about Emmy? Had her dragon given up on the idea of rescue too?

"Where's Emmy?" she demanded. "We need to—"

A booming sound drowned out the rest of her question, followed by a flash as the fluorescents flickered back on. Someone must have hit the override. Now, in better light, Trinity could clearly see Scarlet standing before them, dressed in a dirty blue jumpsuit and brown slippers. She was definitely skinnier—almost gaunt—and her arms and legs were covered in track marks and bruises. She was pale too, her copper skin now faded to beige, as if she'd lost a good deal of blood. And her once-shiny, thick hair was dull and matted.

Nausea rose in Trinity's throat. What horrors had this poor girl been through? And if this was how they'd treated her—a fellow human being—what more had been done to her dragon?

Scarlet blinked, as if trying to adjust her eyes to the sudden bright light. "They keep Emmy on the other side of the facility," she told them. Her voice sounded hesitant. Strangely... reluctant. "I can take you there. I know the way."

A rush of relief crashed over Trinity. She hadn't allowed herself to consider, until this moment, the very real possibility that Scarlet wouldn't know where Emmy was being held. Or that Emmy had already been moved somewhere else. Or—she shuddered—that Emmy wasn't even alive to be rescued at all.

No. She's alive, she assured herself, her gut wrenching again. *She's alive and Scarlet's going to take you to her now. In just a few minutes, you'll see her again.*

This had to work this time. It *had* to.

She shook herself. "Great," she said, making her way to the door. "Then let's go."

She stopped at the doorway, realizing Scarlet wasn't following. She turned back impatiently. "Well?" she asked. "Aren't you coming?"

Scarlet stared down at her feet, shifting her weight from left to right. "Yes. Of course," she said in a slow voice. "But first, well, I think there's something you should know."

Trinity frowned. They were wasting time they didn't have. And yet Scarlet didn't look as if she were willing to move until she'd had her say. "What is it?" she demanded. "What is it you think I should know?" Even as she asked, she wasn't sure she wanted the answer.

Scarlet suddenly looked up, her eyes meeting Trin's for the first time. Large, frightened eyes that sent a shiver tripping down Trinity's spine. Whatever she was about to say—well, it wasn't going to be good. Trinity swallowed hard. "Scarlet, what is it?"

"It's about Emmy."

Chapter Two

A bout Emmy?

Trinity bit her lower lip, her heart thudding violently in her chest. She could feel Connor's hand find her arm, trying to calm her down, but she shook it off. They didn't have time for this. The guards could realize they were here any second now and sound the alarm. "Scarlet, what is it? What should I know about Emmy?"

"It's just...well, I think you should prepare yourself. I don't want you to be shocked when you see her," Scarlet said in a voice so low Trinity could barely make it out. "Emmy's...I don't know...different now."

Cold dread gripped Trinity with icy fingers. Suddenly, it was all she could do to keep standing upright. "Different?" she managed to repeat. "What do you mean, different?"

Scarlet let out a slow sigh, still not moving from the spot they'd found her. "I don't know. Maybe it's best if you see it for yourself."

"Well, I'd love to," Trinity volleyed back before she could stop herself. "If you'd ever get around to showing us the way."

Scarlet's face crumpled at this, and Trinity immediately regretted her harsh words. After all, Scarlet wasn't responsible for any of this mess. She'd only done what Trinity had asked her to do. And she'd suffered for it. By the looks of it, she'd suffered quite a bit.

"Sorry," Trin amended quickly. "I'm just a little on edge right now. Go ahead. We'll be right behind you."

Scarlet nodded, pushing past her to exit the cell and head down the hallway. Trinity and Connor followed close behind, stopping only to drag the unconscious guard into Scarlet's cell, closing the door behind him. They didn't need any evidence lying around for others to find.

"Come on," Trinity urged. "We've got to hurry."

They picked up their pace, making their way down the elevator, through the halls, trying to be as quiet as possible. For all they knew, there could be a hundred armed guards lying in wait around any corner, and Trin's adrenaline spiked at every turn.

Suddenly Nate's voice crackled over the walkie-talkie. "Are you guys almost done? It's getting pretty hairy down here. I'm not sure how long I'll be able to stay in this box."

"We're on our way to Emmy now," Trin told him. "Just hang in there, okay?" She could feel Connor giving her a look but refused to turn to meet his eyes. No way was she going to bail now—not when they were so close. She reached for the walkie again. "If you need to get out, take the truck with you," she told Nate. "We'll have Emmy fly us over to the rendezvous spot once we get her out, and we can regroup from there."

"Roger that," Nate said, sounding relieved. "See you on the flip side."

Trin stuffed the walkie back in her pocket as they reached the end of the corridor, blocked by a heavy metal door. Scarlet grabbed Trinity's arm, stopping her in her tracks. "There," she whispered. "That's the testing facility. That's where they keep her locked up."

"Hey! What are you doing in here?"

The three of them whirled around at the sound of the gruff voice. A man dressed in a scientist's white lab coat stormed toward them, fury on his face. "Scarlet? Why aren't you in your cell? And who are these people?"

Crap. They were totally busted. Trinity shot a look at Connor, then stepped into the guy's path. "We're no one," she told him, using her gift to push him as hard as she could. "No one at all. Maybe you should just walk away."

Walk away, walk away, walk away, she chanted in her head. She could feel Connor, joining her in the push. *We are no one. Just walk away.*

But unlike the guard down at the loading dock, the scientist didn't seem phased by the attempted mind manipulation. Trinity creased her brow, worry threading through her. Some people were natural resisters—or maybe the Dracken, Mara, who was currently working with the government had trained him somehow.

"You can't be here," the scientist continued. "This is a highly classified area. I'm going to have to call security."

He stalked over to a control panel by the far wall, where an intercom blinked green. Trin watched in horror as he made to press the button that would bring on the reinforcements. Her heart pounded.

They'd be discovered.

They'd be caught.

They'd be killed.

They'd fail Emmy one last time…not to mention the rest of the world.

No. This time it had to work. It *had* to.

Trinity dove for Connor's pistol, grabbing it from the holster and squeezing the trigger as hard as she could.

The bullet sang true—torpedoing into the scientist's back—and he staggered backward, a crimson stain spreading across his lab coat at an alarming rate. Screaming, he made one last-ditch effort to reach the intercom, but Connor grabbed him, wrestling him away and shoving him to the ground. There, the man writhed in agony, gasping for breath as blood dripped from his mouth. With a grim face, Connor put him out of his misery.

Trinity turned away, her stomach wrenching, the gun falling from her hand and clattering to the floor. Connor scooped it up, stuffing it back in its holster. Then he grabbed her by the shoulders, shaking her until he held her attention.

"You did what had to be done," he told her in a gruff voice. "You very well might have just saved the world."

She forced herself to nod, swallowing the bile that had risen to her throat. She didn't want Connor's worry for her to interfere with the mission. But as he turned away from her to concentrate on the door lock, she was forced to grab on to a nearby counter for support.

He was right, she tried to tell herself. This one death could lead to millions of lives saved. Millions of innocent lives. Emmy's life.

And yet—her stomach roiled again—could there have been another way? From the very start, from that first day Emmy's egg had arrived at the museum, there had been so

26

much death. So much pain and suffering—so many on both sides lost. Was this scientist an evil man who deserved death? Or just an innocent researcher caught in the wrong place at the wrong time? Was he out to destroy the world? Or just put food on the table for his wife and kids?

She stifled a sob, remembering Connor's repeated mantra from the very beginning. *Sacrifice one to save the world.* But how much more would have to be sacrificed—how much more blood would have to be spilled—before this world would actually be saved?

Connor rose from inspecting the man's pockets. "No key," he said.

"They use fingerprint locks down here," Scarlet squeaked out in a terrified voice. She'd retreated to the corner of the room, and Trinity found she couldn't meet her eyes. "You'll have to cut off his thumb."

The nausea rose to Trinity's throat again. She tried to tell herself he was already dead—he didn't need thumbs anymore anyway—but when Connor knelt down to work, she found she couldn't watch the operation. Instead, she walked over to the door, peering through the window, trying to regulate her breathing.

The room inside was eerily familiar. Cages stacked from floor to ceiling, filled with mostly primates and pigs. Trinity couldn't help but think back to the vision she'd been shown by Caleb long ago, before Emmy had hatched from her shell—of her dragon, locked in a government cage. *This* government cage, she realized, the revulsion rising again. The very same place as the first time around.

Had they managed to change *any* history at all?

She thought about mentioning this little déjà vu to Connor, then bit her tongue instead. He didn't need any more reminders that this rescue mission was all too similar to the last one. Instead, she squinted into the room, focusing on the cage in the very back.

The giant cage. With a giant dragon inside of it.

She gasped. Was that really Emmy? The last time she'd seen her, Emmy had been the size of a Labrador retriever. Now she was the size of an elephant. In fact, the cage she was in could barely contain her massive girth.

"Emmy?" she whispered. "Is that really you?"

"There," Connor announced, rising to his feet. He walked over to the door and pressed the severed digit against the sensor. A moment later, the LED light above the panel blinked green, followed by a loud click as the door unlocked.

Trinity didn't wait for a second invitation. She dove through the door, running toward Emmy as fast as she could—without bothering to check whether there was any more security inside. Her ears caught the cries of the room's other animal occupants, whooping and wailing and rattling their cages in protest of the strangers' presence, but she tuned them all out. At that very moment, nothing else in the world mattered but the dragon in front of her.

When she reached Emmy, her legs gave out from under her, and she dropped to her knees, unable this time to stop the vomit from rising to her throat as she looked at her dragon.

At what remained of her dragon.

Emmy. Beautiful Emmy—the gentlest, sweetest, kindest creature to ever live—now lay listlessly in her cage, her once brilliant-emerald flanks faded to a dull gray, checkerboarded with ugly scars and pus-filled sores. One wing hung oddly at her side, as if it had been broken and not set correctly. And her shorn claws were caked with sinew and blood.

But it was her eyes that were the most troubling. Those beautiful blue eyes that set Emmy apart from the rest of her kind, eyes that had once sparkled like so many sapphires. Now they were colorless, translucent, vacant. Empty eyes drained of all spark and life.

Suddenly Trinity had the urge to go kill that scientist all over again.

"Emmy!" she cried, hating the fact that she was forced to speak out loud in order for the dragon to hear her. "Emmy, it's me! Trinity! We're here to rescue you."

Slowly, Emmy rolled over, a groan escaping her mouth, gagged by a metal binding, as if even this slight movement caused her pain. She stared at Trin dully, with absolutely no recognition in her eyes.

Oh God.

"Emmy, do you hear me? It's Trinity." She turned to Scarlet, grabbing her by the shoulders and shaking her. "Tell her it's me! Tell her we're here to rescue her."

"I can tell her," Scarlet replied, her voice once again filled with her earlier reluctance. "But to be honest, I'm not sure she'll care."

Fury rose inside Trinity like lava from a volcano. "What the hell is that supposed to mean?"

Scarlet looked away, her eyes filled with guilt. "I did try to warn you," she said. "She's…different now. She's changed." She looked back at Trinity. "I mean, don't take it personally. She's hasn't spoken to me for months now."

Trinity's anger combusted into sheer horror. She looked from Scarlet to her dragon and then to Scarlet again. "You were supposed to protect her," she whispered hoarsely, unable to stop the words spilling from her lips. *Oh, Emmy. Poor, poor Emmy.* "That was the whole reason I sent you here. To keep Emmy safe!"

But even as she spoke the words, she realized how useless they were. How could Scarlet have protected Emmy in this place? She'd been a prisoner too.

No. This was all Trin's fault. She was the only one to blame.

I'm so sorry, Emmy. I should have gotten here sooner. Somehow. Someway.

Emmy had chosen her—not Scarlet, not anyone else in the world—to be her Fire Kissed. And long ago, they'd made a dragon/guardian pact to keep one another safe.

Trust me, little one, I'll never let you fall.

Six months ago, Emmy had lived up to her end of the bargain, sacrificing her own happiness, her own safety, her own future, to save the boy Trinity loved—putting her life in jeopardy without a single pause for consideration.

And in return, Trinity had let her down. Allowed her to be captured and taken away. Now, here was her dragon—so filled with life and laughter once—just a shell of her former self. And it was all Trinity's fault.

Her mind swarmed with horrifying visions—of Emmy arriving at the lab, shivering and afraid. Of Scarlet trying her best to comfort her, promising her that the Fire Kissed was certainly on her way. Of Emmy's hopeful face fading to despair as the days passed slowly, with no sign of rescue. Until the dragon was curled up into a ball at the back of her cage, refusing to listen to any more of Scarlet's rescue fairy tales.

"I'm sorry," Trin whispered, her heart breaking into a thousand pieces. "I tried. I really did."

But she hadn't tried hard enough. Emmy had depended on her, and she'd let the dragon down. In some ways, Trin was more to blame for this whole mess than the scientists themselves. And now that she was finally here, was it simply too late?

"Look, there will be time for apologies later," Connor broke in, putting a hand on her shoulder. "Right now, we need to figure out how to get her out of here."

Trinity watched, scarcely able to move, as he ran to the control panel, using the bloody thumb to unlock the cage. When the lock clicked, she grabbed the cell door with both hands, trying with all her strength to pull it open. At first, it didn't budge, and her heart flip-flopped with fear that they might have failed once again. But then Connor and Scarlet joined her efforts, and the three of them were able to widen it enough for Emmy to step through.

But Emmy didn't step through. Not even a glance to the open door to acknowledge her freedom.

"Come on, Emmy!" Trinity begged, yanking off the dragon's gag. "You're free. We need to get you out of here."

But the dragon only blinked dully at her before lowering her head to the ground. Then she closed her eyes. She was so still that only the small twines of smoke drifting from her nostrils gave any clue she was even alive.

This was not good. This was so not good.

"Come on!" Trinity tried again. Desperate. Frightened. Her gaze shot to the back door. Connor had jammed it with a few pieces of heavy equipment, but it wouldn't take long for the guards to break it down if they tried. "They're going to figure out we're in here. We need to leave now. Before it's too late."

Her pulse was skyrocketing now. If Emmy didn't move on her own, what were they going to do? She was too big to carry. She had to weigh at least a couple tons. The only way she was getting out of here was if she walked or flew herself.

And if she refused to do that…

"Emmy, listen to me!" Scarlet broke in. "This is your rescue. Do you understand that? This is the happily ever after I've been promising you."

Emmy opened one eye but made no effort to move.

Suddenly Trinity could feel Connor grabbing her arm, trying to drag her backward. "It's no use," he told her in a tight voice. "They've broken her spirit. I've seen it before, and dragons don't recover from it. It's over, Trin. There's nothing we can do."

"No!" She jerked his hand away, running to Emmy. She dropped to her knees again before the mighty beast, throwing her arms around her neck and squeezing her as tightly as she could. Emmy was so big, so beautiful, even with all her afflictions. And Trin's tears rained down, wetting Emmy's dull scales.

"Emmy, I know you're hurting. And I know you're scared," she whispered to the dragon, her voice so choked at this point she could barely form the words. "And I know you're probably mad at me for taking so long to come. But I'm here now, Emmy. And I'm going to get you out of here. I made a promise to you long ago, and I'm not going to break it now."

She looked up at Connor. "Get Scarlet out of here," she told him. "I'm going to stay with her."

Connor's face paled. "No." He shook his head. "They'll kill you if they find you in here."

"Then they'll kill me," she replied, her resolve firming. "And I'll die with my dragon. I should have never let her go in the first place. And I will never leave her again." She rose, giving him her most defiant look. "Now go."

Connor hedged, looking torn. Trinity opened her mouth to tell him again but was interrupted as Emmy suddenly jerked her head—violently—in her direction. Caught off guard, she lost her balance and went sprawling to the floor, yelping in pain as her ankle jarred from the impact.

What the…? She scrambled back to her feet, turning questioningly to the dragon. Emmy glared back at her. For the first time since they'd arrived in the lab, she thought she saw something in the beast's eyes. And crazy hope stirred within her.

"You don't want me to stay, do you?" she challenged the dragon. "You want me to leave you here and save myself." She crossed her arms over her chest and stared the beast down. "Well, sorry, Ems, that's not going to happen. I'm your Fire Kissed—I don't care if we've been de-bonded. You stay here, I'm staying here. End of story."

Emmy's eyes narrowed. Steam hissed from her nostrils.

"Come on, Trin," Connor begged. "She clearly does not want to go."

"Then neither do I," Trin replied flatly. She planted her feet firmly on the floor, directly in front of the dragon. "You want to die in here, Emmy? No problem. But we'll die together. Sound like a plan?"

Emmy tossed her head angrily, pawing the ground with her foot. Her mouth was slightly open, and Trin could see the warning sparks of fire dancing on her tongue. The dragon took a couple threatening steps toward her, but she held her ground.

That's right, Emmy. Get mad. Get furious. Just don't let them win.

Suddenly she felt Connor at her side. "You know what?" he asked, shooting Trinity a look. "I think I'm going to stay too."

"Me too," Scarlet added, also crossing her arms over her chest as she stepped into line between the two of them. She flashed the dragon a fierce look that sent a thrill up Trinity's spine.

Yeah, baby. Team Dragon represent.

"Sorry, Ems," Trinity said, forcing back a smug smile. "But it looks like you're stuck with us."

Emmy opened her mouth, probably to protest, but a sudden banging at the entryway interrupted her, followed by angry shouting just behind the door. Trinity's heart jolted in her chest. Crap. They'd been found out. And she knew it wouldn't take them long to break down the doors and through Connor's hastily assembled barricade.

Team Dragon's bluff was about to be called, big time.

She turned back to Emmy, trying not to let her fear show. "Your move," she said to the dragon. "Are you going to let us all die here? You gonna just let them win? Or should we live to fight another day and take down the bastards who did this to you?"

For a moment, Emmy stood perfectly still. Then, out of nowhere, she let out a loud roar. Charging out of her cage, she grabbed Trin in her mouth and tossed her onto her back as if she were a sack of potatoes. Trin landed hard and tears stung her eyes. But the pain was nothing compared to the joy rising within her.

She was going to do it! Emmy was going to break free.

Scarlet and Connor joined her a moment later, scaling Emmy's wings until they were sitting behind her. There was barely room for all three of them, and Trin prayed Emmy—in her wounded state—would have the strength to get airborne with the added weight.

But before she could raise the question, the lab's doors burst open. Guards rushed in, guns locked and loaded, barking orders and preparing to open fire. Chaos erupted as the primates and pigs squealed and screamed and rattled their cages in protest to the invasion, but the guards ignored them, their eyes on Emmy and her team of rescuers.

"Step away from the dragon!" one of them yelled.

"Stand down or we will open fire," another suggested.

"Not on your life!" Trinity shouted back. Then she patted Emmy on the neck. "Your move, girl," she whispered. "Show them what happens when you mess with a dragon."

Emmy didn't hesitate. Her mouth burst open, blasting a river of fire straight at the guards. In an instant, the entire platoon was on the ground, screaming and writhing as the flames consumed them. Trin fought back the nausea rising to her throat at the sudden smell of cooked meat permeating the air.

Emmy turned and gave Trinity a guilty look, probably assuming her Fire Kissed would not approve of the violence. But Trin only shook her head and patted her neck. "You did what you had to do," she assured the dragon, echoing Connor's earlier words. "You very well might have just saved the world."

The dragon seemed to nod before pointing her snout to the sky. More fire shot from her mouth, torpedoing upward.

MARI MANCUSI

The ceiling burst into flames, and Trinity and the others had to cover their heads with their hands to avoid the fiery debris raining down on top of them.

And then suddenly, they were flying, soaring, Emmy's wings crackling in the air like thunder. As they shot through the burning ceiling, the fire singed Trin's hair and skin, but she held on tight, and soon they were flying above the government lab.

Free.

"You did it!" Trinity cried to the dragon, pride and happiness rushing through her like the wind at her ears. "Emmy! You did it! You got free!"

Tears of happiness streamed down her cheeks. It had worked. This time, it had actually worked. She sucked in a shaky breath, not sure she'd been breathing the entire time they were making their escape. Then she turned to Connor and Scarlet with excited eyes.

"Let's go meet up with everyone at the rendezvous point," she declared. "They're going to be so excited!" Her voice was filled with laughter and exhilaration. "Oh, Emmy, you're going to love where we're living now! We've got the best dragon lair ever all set up for you. And—"

To her surprise, Emmy seemed to pause at this, slowing her speed until she was simply hovering in midair, flapping her wings to keep elevation. At first, Trin assumed she was just waiting for the promised directions. But then, to her surprise, the dragon dipped her nose downward and started shooting back to earth. Trin's brow furrowed.

"Emmy, what are you doing?" She turned back to look at Scarlet. "What is she doing?"

36

But Scarlet only shrugged helplessly. And a moment later, they found themselves coming in for a landing. Emmy hit the ground hard, stumbling a bit before regaining her balance. Then she turned and looked at them.

"Did you need to take a rest?" Trin asked, fear and confusion mixing in her veins. "I mean, that's fine if you—"

She oomphed as the dragon reared up on her heels, unceremoniously knocking them from her back. As Trin hit the ground hard, she looked up, trying to figure out what Emmy was doing. The dragon gave her an apologetic look. Then, before Trin could speak, she pointed her nose back to the sky. A moment later, she was shooting up into the air, leaving the three of them behind.

"No!" Trin cried. She scrambled to her feet, running after the dragon. "Emmy! Please! No! Come back!"

But the dragon didn't come back. And soon she had disappeared from the sky altogether.

Chapter Three

H ere we are…home sweet home."

Scarlet rubbed her bleary eyes, struggling to regain consciousness. For a moment, she didn't know where she was, the bright light streaming through the truck windows nearly blinding her with its brilliance. Then her eyes fell on Connor, sitting beside her in the backseat of the truck, and it all came rushing back to her.

They had escaped. She was free.

She squinted at the truck's dashboard clock. While it felt as if she'd only dozed off for a minute or two, evidently hours had passed since the truck had picked them up in the desert; she must have slept through most of the trip. And who could blame her, really? It was the first time in forever she could allow herself to close her eyes and not worry about who would be waking her up…and what they'd want to do to her once they did.

She peered out the grimy window, trying to take in her surroundings. They'd pulled off a narrow desert road and had entered the dirt parking lot of what appeared to be an abandoned airfield, tucked away in the middle of nowhere. There was a single runway, a small terminal with boarded-up windows, a few hangars, and a couple of broken-down prop planes that had seen better days.

She gave a low whistle. "Toto, I don't think we're at the old McCormick place anymore."

Connor nodded as the boy he'd introduced as Luke put the truck in park and popped open his door. "Yeah, we've pretty much outgrown anything in the residential market these days," he informed her. "There are at least two dozen of the Potentials living with us now. Plus, the three Dracken kids come by whenever they can get away from school and their families." He counted off on his fingers. "Then there's me, Trinity, Trinity's father…"

He trailed off as Luke pushed his seat forward to allow him to jump out of the truck. Scarlet watched him go, feeling glued to her seat, an icy worry prickling down her spine as she waited for him to finish his roll call. Waited for the one name she hadn't heard yet—the one she was desperate to hear.

In truth, Caleb's name had been on the tip of her tongue since Connor and Trinity had first stepped into her jail cell back at the government lab. But she hadn't managed to muster the courage to speak it out loud, too fearful of what she might learn. She thought back to the last time she'd seen him—lying unconscious in the back of the government truck, his body weak, his face pale, his mind locked in another world—an alternate reality known as the Nether—unable to escape.

Connor held out his hand to help her out of the truck. "Oh, and Caleb too, of course," he added, as if it were an afterthought.

Scarlet's breath let out in a rush of relief. She grabbed Connor's hand and leapt from the vehicle to solid ground.

Then she turned to him anxiously. "So he's…okay?" she asked. "Caleb's okay?"

She waited, heart in her throat, as Connor shot an uneasy glance up at Trinity, who was still sitting in the front passenger seat, her eyes glued to the sky above, looking as if she were barely holding it together.

When Luke had first picked them up, Trinity had insisted they drive around to try to track Emmy with the car. But they'd driven in circles for hours to no avail. Even Scarlet—who still had some connection to Emmy through the blood bond they shared—could not seem to pinpoint the dragon's location. Perhaps it was because she was so drained of spark after all she'd suffered. Or perhaps Emmy was purposely blocking her—there was no clear way to tell. In the end, Connor had called off the search, saying they needed to get back and regroup before heading out again. Trinity had argued, then given in. And she hadn't said a word since.

Scarlet sighed. She'd tried to warn them. But she supposed she understood why Trinity hadn't wanted to listen.

Scarlet turned back to Connor. "Well? Is he okay or not?" she demanded, unable to take the suspense any longer. She was worried about Emmy too. But Caleb… Her pulse quickened.

Connor sighed. "He's alive, if that's what you mean," he said. "But he's been a total vegetable for the last six months. He can eat and drink—and sometimes he even opens his eyes and seems to look at you. But it's all on autopilot. He can't talk. He can't react to anything. His mind is locked in the Nether." He gave a helpless shrug. "I've seen it before. Back home and with Trinity's mother too. People—well, they get to the breaking point—where the Nether is more real to them than their real lives. Their conscious selves fuse to the other reality, and what's left behind is just an empty shell."

Scarlet cringed. She thought back to the last time she'd seen Caleb, deep in this other world. The words they'd spoken, the kiss they'd shared. It was true that Caleb had been helpless, that he had been lost. But, she told herself, he hadn't been broken. He was more than just a shell.

He was a fighter. A survivor. Just as she herself was. She hadn't let the government break her. And she knew Caleb would fight just as hard. Her words came rushing back to her.

Will you stand with me, Caleb? Will you help me fight the monsters?
I want to. God, I want to.

"He'll come back," she stated fiercely, as if she could make it happen by sheer force of words. "I know he will."

Connor gave her a pitying look but, to his credit, didn't try to argue. Instead he turned back to the airfield, making a sweeping gesture with his arm.

"Anyway, this place used to be a small regional airport, mostly private planes coming in for the big desert racetrack a few miles from here," he explained as they walked toward the terminal. "But the track got abandoned after they built a new one north of Vegas about five years ago and there was no use having an airfield this far from any towns. So they closed it down and left it to us." He gave her a half smile. "Wait till you see. It's a pretty cool setup, actually. Trin's father hooked up a couple of generators for electricity, and there are plenty of rooms for people to sleep in. There's even an old restaurant where we meet up to eat meals. And it's so far off the beaten path, we really don't have to worry about being found."

"Nice," Scarlet said, and she meant it. "And that hangar will make for a perfect dragon cave if we get Emmy back, right?" she added, gesturing to the large building a few yards from the main terminal.

"You mean *when*."

Scarlet whirled around at the sudden voice slicing through the air. She found Trinity standing too close behind her, arms crossed over her chest, her eyes red and burning. She must have gotten out of the truck when Scarlet and Connor were talking—so silently neither of them had heard her do it.

Scarlet nodded, feeling her face flush. "Yes, of course. When," she corrected hastily. "I meant when." But Trinity only glared at her harder, as if she blamed Scarlet for everything. And maybe she did.

Scarlet sighed. The two girls admittedly hadn't gotten off to the best start—which Scarlet knew was mostly her fault, even though she'd had the best of intentions. She'd thought she was doing a good thing, breaking in and freeing Emmy from the dark, lonely barn back in her hometown. Instead, she'd inadvertently set all of this in motion. Because of her, their hideaway had been compromised, Trinity's grandfather had been killed, and they'd been forced back on the run. Not exactly the best way to inspire a beautiful friendship.

That said, hadn't Scarlet more than made up for it since then? After all, she'd rescued Caleb from the Dracken, not to mention willingly walked into a six-month prison sentence to save Emmy. Shouldn't all that pain and suffering count for something?

Not judging by the way Trinity was staring at her now. And suddenly Scarlet wondered if the girl would have even bothered rescuing her if she hadn't needed her to find Emmy.

"Easy, tiger," Connor interjected, stepping between them. He reached out to Trin, his face filled with sympathy as he tried to put a comforting arm around her waist. But she only jerked away, turning on her heel and retreating back to the truck, slamming the door behind her. Connor watched her go with a troubled expression. Then he turned back to Scarlet.

"Sorry," he said. "This whole thing has been so hard on her. I mean…" He gave an apologetic shrug. "Not as hard as it's been on you, I know. But God, she loves that dragon so much. And to get this close only to have Emmy take off on her…" He shook his head slowly. "Flecking hell," he muttered. "I don't know what that stupid creature was thinking!"

"I told you," she said slowly. "Emmy's changed. The things they did to her…" She trailed off, shuddering. She could feel Connor's blue eyes boring into her, and she turned away. "Hell, if I were her, I'd never trust another human being again. *Any* human being."

Connor opened his mouth as if he wanted to argue that point, but at that moment, the doors of the terminal burst open, and a rowdy group of teens poured out, rushing them as they all tried to speak at once. The Potentials, Scarlet recognized with a little uneasiness, led by Rashida—the same group of kids with the weird psychic powers who had once tricked her into helping them, only to turn her and Caleb over to the enemy. What were they doing here? Were they now fighting for the home team? She remembered how, just before being taken away, she'd done a little psychic push of her own, sending Rashida a vision of the Dracken's true mission. Had that worked to change their minds—and loyalties? Helped them realize who the bad guys really were?

Connor put his fingers to his mouth and whistled loudly. The group fell silent. "I'm sorry. There's been a slight…complication," he told them. "But I assure you, we're not giving up." He began to give a rundown of the day's events.

Scarlet took the opportunity to slip away from the crowd, unnoticed. After all, she'd already lived the story firsthand, and now she had other priorities. Heading over to the terminal, she pushed open the front doors and stepped inside.

The place was sparse and had certainly seen better days, but it was clean and well kept, and she could tell some effort had been made to bring it to a livable level. There were several tables and chairs spread out across the main room, covered with puzzles and board games and computer tablets, and a foosball table was set up at one end. To her right was the restaurant Connor had mentioned, and Scarlet breathed in deeply, rejoicing in the smell of pizza being baked in a brick oven. It'd been a long, long time since she'd had a slice of pepperoni, and her mouth was watering.

"Well, hello there."

She looked up to see a middle-aged man step out from the restaurant. He was tall and thin, with wild salt-and-pepper hair and dark eyes that crinkled at the corners. He came around the counter, walking with a pronounced limp.

"Hi," Scarlet replied, feeling shy all of a sudden.

"You must be Scarlet," the man said. "I'm Cameron, Trinity's father." He gave her a kind smile. "Are you hungry? Can I make you something?"

The offer was more than tempting. The pizza smelled ridiculously good. But she knew she wouldn't be able to relax and enjoy it. Not yet.

"Do you know where Caleb is?" she asked instead, her heart thumping in her chest.

Trinity's father gave her a curious look. Then he shrugged. "He's down the corridor," he told her. "Third door from the left."

Scarlet nodded wordlessly, then forced her feet to move, one after another, in the direction he pointed. As she walked down the hall, her heart started beating faster and faster in her chest. By the time she reached the third door, she could barely breathe.

She paused for a moment, sucked in a breath, then pushed open the door and stepped inside.

The room was sterile. Cold, almost, with no furnishings save for a hospital-style bed in the center and a metal folding chair set up beside it. The walls were white and blank, and the windows were boarded up. It was bleak. Depressing. *But what did it matter?* she asked herself. *Caleb's body might be here, but his mind is elsewhere. He could be in the most luxurious palace right now, and he wouldn't even know.*

She turned to the figure on the bed, and her breath caught in her throat. He looked so still, his eyes closed, his skin pale. Like a sleeping angel. Her heart squeezed.

"Oh, Bad Seed," she whispered, using her old nickname for him. She stepped forward until she reached the bed, dropping to the chair by his side. Reaching out, she took his hand in hers, horrified at how clammy and cold it felt, how translucent the skin. She stroked his fingers, trying to warm them, while peering down at his face, searching for some sign of life. Some hidden spark, deep down, that told her he was still in there, still holding out, waiting for her to return.

But she saw nothing. Just a deathly pallor that chilled her to the bone. She bit her lower lip, feeling the tears leak from her eyes. Could Connor be right? Was he really gone? Was this only the shell of the boy who had held her in his arms and kissed her as she'd begged him to help her save the world?

No. She frowned, brushing the tears away with an angry swipe. She refused to believe that. Let the others think what they would—she knew he was still in there somewhere, still fighting to get free.

"I'm here now, Caleb," she whispered, still holding his hand. "I'm back and I'm not going to leave. I know you're in there somewhere, and I'm not going to give up on you."

On impulse, she leaned down. As her lips brushed across his cheek, she heard the clearing of a throat behind her. She jumped out of her seat, startled, dropping Caleb's hand like a hot potato. When she turned around, she saw Trinity, silhouetted in the doorway.

"Oh. You scared me," Scarlet said with an uneasy laugh. Her heart pattered nervously in her chest. How long had she been standing there? How much had she heard?

Trinity didn't smile back. "What are you doing in here?" she asked instead.

"Nothing." Scarlet felt her face heat. "I was just… Your father said he was here…and…"

"And…?" Trinity raised an eyebrow.

"And I wanted to—see him," she stammered, now feeling completely flustered. "That's all."

It was then that she remembered that Trinity would have no idea what had gone down between her and Caleb in the Nether. Of course she would be questioning—for all she knew, Scarlet barely knew the guy. She wondered if she should come clean, inform Trinity that she and Caleb were basically a couple now. But something in the girl's black eyes caused the words to stick in her throat.

"Well, here he is, the great and powerful Caleb Jacks, in the flesh," Trinity said wryly as she walked over to the chair Scarlet had been sitting in, plopping down on it like it was an old friend, grabbing a book from underneath the bed. *The Fellowship of the Ring*, Scarlet noted from the spine. She watched awkwardly as Trin opened it to a dog-eared page three-quarters of the way in, then paused, looking up at Scarlet. "Did you… want to…stay?" she asked, sounding as if she really hoped Scarlet didn't.

"No. No, I'm…I'm good," Scarlet said, taking a step backward. "I'm actually—well, I need to figure out where I'm going to sleep and all. And maybe get some of that pizza your dad was cooking. Man, it's been forever since I've had any pizza."

The relief on Trinity's face was palpable. "Try the feta cheese and pineapple," she suggested. "It's really good."

"I will. Thank you," Scarlet replied. "And…well, thanks for the rescue too. It's really, really nice to be here. I owe you everything. And I'm sorry about what I said about Emmy outside. I'm sure she'll come back when she's ready. She loves you, you know. Back at the government lab, you were all she ever talked about. I mean, when she was still talking…"

She trailed off, realizing Trinity wasn't really listening. Just staring down at the book as if waiting for Scarlet to leave. Scarlet sighed. Would things ever be less awkward between them? "Anyway, I'll…catch you later."

With that, she turned, exiting the room as quickly as she could, leaving Caleb to his story time. As she stepped through the doorway, she couldn't help but turn around to give him one last look. To her surprise, Trinity had abandoned the book and was now leaning on Caleb's chest, head buried in her arms.

And she was crying.

Chapter Four

Two Months Later...

"Die, dragon, die!"

As the mighty dragon reared in front of her, Trinity mashed the hot keys on her laptop computer, determined to take the *Fields of Fantasy* boss down. As a Fury Warrior, she needed to deliver enough damage per second to fell the mighty beast before it rained its fire down on her party and destroyed them all. Beside her, the tank warrior took the brunt of the damage while the mage and priest were casting spells behind her. It was an extremely precarious operation—and everyone had to do their jobs just right—or it would be game over for sure.

But just as the dragon was down to its very last hit points, it began to turn orange, signaling the beginning of its annihilation cast. Trin tried to disrupt it, but her sword missed its mark, and the dragon was able to get its spell off. A moment later, the entire party was swept away in a fiery inferno, falling to the ground in one fell swoop. Defeated.

"Stupid game!" Trinity cried, shoving the laptop across the table in disgust. It was all she could do not to grab it and smash it on the floor. "Why do I even play this stupid, stupid game?"

She rose to her feet, accidentally knocking over her chair. It crashed to the floor, causing everyone else in the room to look up. She could feel their eyes on her, questioning her, which only made her angrier.

"Hey, hey!" Connor protested, grabbing her by the arm and dragging her out of the terminal's waiting room, where they'd all been playing on a LAN line. Hooking his hand at her waist, he led her down the hall and into the old employee break room, shutting the door behind him. He sat her down in a chair, then dropped to his knees in front of her, taking both of her hands in his and bringing them to his lips. He kissed her knuckles, one after another, as tears streamed down her cheeks, unchecked.

"You know, I'd tell you it's just a game," he said, "but that's not why you're really upset, is it?"

She shook her head, at first unable to speak. He squeezed her hands harder and looked up into her eyes, his own filled with sympathy. For a moment, they just crouched there silently. Until she found her voice at last.

"She's never coming back, is she?" she whispered. "She's gone forever."

"You don't know that," Connor said automatically. But something in his voice betrayed him. And for good reason too.

It'd been two months since they'd freed Emmy from the government lab. And no one had heard from her since. Every day the Dracken kids scoured the Internet for clues and rumors, and every day the Potentials followed up on those clues, searching the country for signs of the dragon. But in the end, they all returned empty-handed. It was as if Emmy had disappeared off the face of the earth.

"She could find us if she wanted to," Trinity said. "I know she could."

Connor gave her another sympathetic look. "Maybe she just needs some time alone. You know, like how sometimes animals go into their burrows to heal?"

"They go into their burrows to die, Connor," she corrected bitterly. "And for all we know, that's what's happened to Emmy. That's why no one's seen her. She's crawled into some deep, smelly cave to die all alone." She broke out into a fresh set of tears as her mind replayed the nightmares she'd been having for weeks now—of Emmy, weak and helpless and starving. Unable to fly. Unable to eat. Fading away until there was nothing left of her—only accusatory eyes, locked on her former Fire Kissed.

You promised to keep me safe. You promised not to let me fall.

Connor closed his eyes, then pulled her into his arms. His body was warm, and against her better judgment, she melted into him, allowing him to absorb her pain.

"I don't think she's dead," he told her. "I think…" He paused, then pushed forward. "I think Scarlet would know if she was."

Trinity clenched her teeth. "Right," she said bitterly. "Well, maybe if Scarlet would start helping us out a little, we'd have some real leads."

Connor pulled away from the embrace. "Scarlet *has* been helping. She's been searching every day for a sign of Emmy—you know that. She does have to sleep sometimes, you know."

"Hover over Caleb's bedside, you mean?" Trinity retorted before she could help herself.

Connor's expression darkened. "Is that what you're really angry about?" he asked quietly. "Scarlet spending time with Caleb?"

She felt her face heat. "No, of course not," she said quickly. But even as she said the words, she wondered. Until they'd rescued Scarlet and brought her back with them, *she'd* been the one to sit by Caleb's comatose side. The one who fed him and washed him and tried to keep him as comfortable as possible as he went in and out of his Nether-induced coma. At first, it had seemed a burden, but eventually she'd fallen into a routine. There was something comforting about having something so simple and practical to do each day. Always knowing he was there, waiting for her every morning when she awoke. It gave her a sense of purpose to take care of him. To sit at his side, tell him stories, read him books.

Now she could barely get a moment alone with him, what with Scarlet constantly butting in to help. The girl had even pulled in her sleeping mat and laid it out at the edge of his bed so she could be there if he were to wake up in the dead of night. It was as if she thought they were some kind of couple, shared some kind of bond, when in reality, Scarlet barely knew Caleb. Not like Trinity knew him anyway.

She sighed. She was turning seventeen in a few days, and most times, she felt more like seventy.

"Come on, Trin, it's not that bad," Connor cajoled, interrupting her troubled thoughts. "I mean, think of it this way. Emmy may not be with us, but she's not with them either. She's not being abused or mistreated anymore. For the first

time in her life, she's totally free. And it's all because of you."
He gave her a pointed look. "You should feel proud."

"Proud? It's my fault she was captured in the first place,"
Trinity shot back. "If she's just going to die now, after all she's
suffered. I should have just let you…"

She trailed off, unable to continue. It didn't matter anyway.
Connor knew all too well what she should have let him do.
If she'd let him kill Emmy at the Walmart before the government took her away, then the dragon's pain would have ended
instantly. She would have never had to suffer.

If Trin had let Connor do his thing, it would have all been
over forever. One precise shot to the soft scale on her arm,
killing her instantly without a moment of pain. No more
threat of dragon apocalypse. No more running for their lives.
And Emmy could have lived out eternity in the embrace of
the Nether, flying free with her fellow dragons. Wouldn't that
have been better for everyone in the end?

But Trinity had been too weak, too selfish—unable to bear
the finality of death. Unable to accept the loss of the dragon
she loved. So she'd stopped Connor. And she'd sent Scarlet
into the hands of the enemy. At the time, she'd been so over-
confident, thinking it would be no problem to get Emmy and
Scarlet back. God, had she been a fool.

And Connor was so loyal. So loving. She knew he would
stand by her side till the end of time—and never question her decisions out loud. But deep down, he had to be
disappointed in her, right? Furious even. He was a man of
action, after all. A soldier, trained to be decisive and strong.
But instead, he'd listened to her. He'd followed his heart
rather than his head. It was probably all he could do at

this moment not to scream, "I told you so!" at the top of his lungs.

Bitterness wormed its way inside of her. She pulled away from his embrace.

"Well, hey, if she is dead, at least you've accomplished your mission," she stated flatly. "I mean, no more Emmy means no more threat of apocalypse, right?"

"Trinity…" He looked at her, a pained expression on his face, but she turned stubbornly away. "That's not—"

"You know, it's just a shame you can't go home now," she added sarcastically. "Back to the future, I mean. Hell, I bet you'd return as some kind of conquering hero—the greatest Dragon Hunter to ever live."

"I was already a hero," he said quietly. "Trust me, the gig is vastly overrated." He rose to his feet. "And, Trinity, if you really think I'd be celebrating Emmy's death, well, then you don't know me as well as I thought you did. In fact," he added, "you don't know me at all."

He gave her a look filled with such disappointment it made her want to cry. Why was she being so hateful to him? Why couldn't she just accept his comfort? Why did she feel the need to push everyone who cared about her away?

He turned to the door, headed for the exit. Her heart panged painfully in her chest.

"Connor?" she cried out, unable to just let him walk away.

He turned stiffly, meeting her eyes with his own tortured blue ones. "What, Trinity?" he asked in a strained voice.

"I—"

But she never got a chance to finish her apology. Because at that moment, Luke burst through the door. He stopped short, as if he could sense the tension in the room. "I'm sorry," he stammered. "I didn't mean to interrupt. But—"

Connor was at his side in a second. "What is it?" he demanded, the soldier back in his voice. "Did they find something?"

Trin rose to her feet, her heart pounding in her chest, unable to speak as she approached Luke. "Did they..." she managed to say. "Find...Emmy?"

Please don't let her be dead. Please don't let her be dead.

"Look, we got some weird sighting reports earlier today from the website," Luke explained, looking a little guilty. "I didn't want to say anything until we were sure they were legit—you know, we've had so many leads fall through over the last two months. But you told us to check out everything, no matter how small. So I sent out a team."

"And?" Trin managed to spit out, hope soaring and sinking inside of her at a ridiculous rate. "Did they find anything? Some sign that Emmy was there?"

Luke's eyes flashed with excitement. "Not just a sign. Emmy herself. Your girl is alive, Trin. And we're bringing her home."

Chapter Five

L ook! There they are! There they are!"
Trinity burst out the back doors of the terminal,
Connor and Luke hot on her heels. She could hear the
Potentials shouting and screaming down by the runway, all
chanting Emmy's name. Her knees buckled, and she was
forced to stop, clutching an electricity pole for support, her
heart hammering furiously against her rib cage as she watched
the truck approach. She was almost too afraid to look.

"Emmy?" she whispered. "Is it really you?"

What if it was only a dream? What if she woke and found
all of this to be nothing more than a cruel joke played by
her masochistic imagination? Her fingers dug into the pole's
wood, and she could barely stand she was trembling so hard.

"Please…" It was all she could say.

She felt movement at her back and realized Connor had
come up behind her. Connor who, in her frustration, she'd
lashed out at. But he didn't look reproachful now. Instead, he
reached out, cupping her chin in his hand and gently guiding
her face, turning her eyes to meet the vehicle. One of the
Potentials—an Aussie named Trevor—had hopped out of
the passenger side and was walking around to the rear. In one

single movement, he lifted the latch, and the back door rolled up with a loud, long groan.

And then Trin saw for herself. Saw what she thought she'd never see again. A mighty black shadow, crammed into the back of the truck. A shadow she would recognize anywhere.

"Oh, Emmy," she whispered, tears leaking out the sides of her eyes. "It's really you."

She tried to will her feet to move, to run to her dragon, to welcome her home at last. Instead, she found herself frozen in place, staring at the truck with desperate, longing eyes.

She felt Connor at her arm again. "Come on," he urged, taking her hand and pulling her down to the runway to join the reunion. "Don't you want to see her?"

She nodded, scarcely able to breathe. Of course she did. If she never saw anything else in her life again, of course she would want to see Emmy.

And so she allowed Connor to lead her to the truck; then slowly, she stepped forward, heart in her throat, as if she were afraid Emmy would disappear if she moved too fast.

"Emmy?" she called in scarcely more than a whisper. "It's me. Trin."

She peered inside. Emmy was hunched in the very back of the truck, curled up around herself, her massive tail wrapped protectively around her body, her neck arched and posture rigid. Trinity frowned as she realized the dragon was shivering, her eyes white and wild. Drool dripped from the corner of her mouth, and her sides heaved heavily up and down.

"Emmy?" she repeated. "Are you okay? It's just me. Trin. Your Fire Kissed."

Okay, so she wasn't exactly Emmy's Fire Kissed anymore. But she wasn't about to let that little technicality stop her from making a move to enter the van, putting one leg up on the truck bed and—

Emmy let out a loud cry, shrinking back, pressing her body against the rear of the truck so hard the metal groaned in protest. Trin frowned, stopping in her tracks and retreating, her hands up in the air to show Emmy she meant her no harm. When she tried to meet the dragon's eyes with her own, Emmy seemed to deliberately twist her neck to face the wall instead.

Trin let out a small moan of dismay, turning back to Connor.

"What's wrong with her?"

"She's terrified."

Trinity whirled around to see Scarlet come up behind her. With slow, careful movements, Scarlet climbed up into the truck bed, putting out an open hand. "It's okay, Emmy," she whispered. "It's me, Scarlet. No one's going to hurt you, okay?"

Emmy seemed to relax—just a little bit—allowing Scarlet to approach. When Scarlet reached the dragon, she put out her hand again, stroking her nose and cooing at her with a soft voice. Trinity watched, feeling helpless and horrified. When she tried to make a move of her own, Emmy startled again. Scarlet glanced back at Trin, a warning look in her eyes.

"I think she needs some time," she said apologetically. "She's obviously been through a lot."

"Time. Right." Trinity somehow managed a nod, the tears springing to the corners of her eyes again. She forced herself to step back, giving her dragon space.

No, not my *dragon*, she reminded herself, *Scarlet's dragon*.

And then it hit her with all the force of a ten-ton truck.

Everything she'd known to be true from the very start but hadn't really comprehended up until now. After all, it was one thing to know something in theory. Quite another to see it play out before your eyes. And as Trin watched Emmy nudge Scarlet's arm with her snout—a gesture the dragon had done to Trin a thousand times before—something broke inside her, allowing the cold, hard truth to rush in.

Emmy was no longer hers. Emmy would never be hers again.

But she's safe, she reminded herself angrily, swiping at the tears with her sleeve. *She's alive. She's here. She's safe. That's all that matters in the end.*

Now, if only she could convince her heart that this was true.

Chapter Six

How does that feel, Emmy? Does that feel any better?"
Scarlet paused from rubbing oil into the creases
between Emmy's neck scales, her eyes roving over the dragon,
assessing her handiwork. Emmy was still pale and painfully
thin compared to her former self, but Scarlet thought she
could see a slight blush of color coming back to her scales,
and it gave her a small bit of hope.

It had been three days since Emmy had been brought
back to Team Dragon, and Scarlet and the others had worked
around the clock to make sure the dragon felt safe—if not
happy—in her new home. The former airline hangar had
indeed turned out to be the perfect dragon cave—large
enough for Emmy to stretch her wings and fly if she felt the
urge, without the risk of being spotted by anyone from the
outside world. Sure, it wouldn't be the best flying ever—more
like swimming laps in a pool, back and forth, rinse and repeat.
But it was better than anything she'd had back at the government lab and certainly better than the old McCormick barn.

But Emmy hadn't seemed interested in flying. Instead,
she'd retreated to the sleeping nook they'd constructed at the
far end of the hangar. Connor had found and hung some old,

moth-eaten red curtains from the terminal to give her privacy, and Trin had painstakingly decorated, collecting some of the shinier pieces of plane fuselage and placing them around the nest as stand-ins for actual dragon treasure.

But Emmy hadn't seemed to notice their efforts. Nor had she asked to turn on the TV/DVD combo that Trinity's dad had picked up at a garage sale a few towns over. Even Scarlet's suggestion of watching the last season of the BBC show *Merlin*—Emmy's favorite program—had been dismissed with a shrug. All of which worried Scarlet more than she wanted to admit. As did the fact that Emmy was barely eating or drinking. The others chalked it up to posttraumatic stress, which did seem a logical conclusion, but to Scarlet it seemed more than that. Through their bond, she could feel Emmy's nervous energy, bouncing around her head. She wasn't just depressed—she was agitated. Worried about something. But when Scarlet tried to ask her what it was, her words fell on deaf ears.

"How's she doing?"

Scarlet looked up from rubbing to see Trinity hovering hesitantly between the two curtains, shuffling from foot to foot. She sighed and waved her inside. Trinity obliged, still looking a bit nervous as she approached the two of them, and Scarlet could feel Emmy stiffen under her hands.

It was weird. While the dragon was certainly wary of anyone and everyone who approached since she'd returned, she seemed to get particularly fearful when Trinity showed up, which didn't make any sense. After all, Scarlet knew more than anyone how much Emmy loved and cared for Trinity—it was all she would talk about back before she'd stopped talking in the government lab. Yet now that they were reunited? The dragon seemed to go out of her way to avoid her.

"She's clean at least," Scarlet said with forced brightness after pushing a reassuring thought in the dragon's direction. "I scrubbed each scale individually, and now I'm moisturizing. She seems to like that, even if she doesn't want to admit it."

"She always did," Trinity said sadly, sitting down in the chair across from Scarlet and the dragon, giving them space. She, along with several of the others, had attempted to help with grooming when Emmy first arrived. But Emmy refused to let any of them touch her. Only Scarlet. Which wasn't exactly helping Scarlet's already shaky relationship with Trin—as if the girl needed any more reasons to hate her. In fact, Scarlet was pretty sure Trinity wouldn't be talking to her at all if it wasn't the only way to reach her dragon.

"Has she said anything else to you?" Trinity asked. "Like where she was all this time after we broke her out of the lab?"

Scarlet shook her head. "I asked her," she said. "Repeatedly. But she won't answer. She hasn't said anything since she's been back. It's like she's forgotten how to talk."

Trinity gave the dragon a heartbreaking look. "What happened to you, Emmy?" she asked, her voice quavering a little. "Whatever it is, you can tell us. We won't be mad."

Scarlet could practically see the waves of frustration radiating off Trin. She turned to Emmy. *Come on, Ems*, she tried. *She only wants to help you.*

The dragon shifted, turning her face to the wall. But not before Scarlet caught a guilty look crossing her face. And was that…a tear leaking from her eye? She frowned. Something must have happened. Something Emmy didn't want to admit to Trinity or anyone else. But what could it be?

She turned back to Trinity. "I'm sorry," she said apologetically. "When she's ready to talk, I'm sure she will."

"Yeah," Trinity said dully. "I'm sure."

Scarlet watched as the girl rose slowly to her feet, giving Emmy one last look, then sighed heavily before heading back to the curtain. When she reached it, she stopped.

"Maybe I'm not your Fire Kissed anymore," she said in a soft voice, not turning around. "Maybe we're no longer destined. But I still love you, Emmy. I will always love you and I will always protect you. That will never change."

And with that, she stepped through the curtain and disappeared. Scarlet said nothing, listening as her footsteps faded and the exterior door to the hangar clanged shut behind her. Then she turned back to Emmy. The dragon was staring at the closed curtain, a tortured look on her reptilian face.

Oh, Fire Kissed. Why couldn't you have just let me die?

Scarlet startled as Emmy's words echoed through her head. It'd been so long since she'd heard the dragon speak, she'd almost forgotten the sound of her voice. But there it was, clear and unmistakable and unbearably sad.

"Emmy, what are you talking about?" she scolded. "Of course we weren't going to just let you die. That's crazy! Why would you even say something like that?"

The dragon lowered her head to the ground, releasing a long, slow sigh. Scarlet waited, wondering if she should say something else. But then, Emmy spoke again.

She tried to send me away, you know, she told Scarlet mournfully. *To a happy place filled with other dragons. But I didn't go. I thought I could help her. Instead, I ruined everything. And now, because of me, the world will burn all over again.*

Scarlet stared at her, not having a clue as to what the dragon was talking about. A happy place filled with other dragons? The world burning all over again? Had Emmy gone mad from her time in captivity? Was she having delusions? She wondered if she should try to call Trin back—maybe she would know what Emmy was going on about—but she didn't want to upset the dragon further.

"Look, Emmy. I don't know what you're talking about. But I do know that you haven't ruined anything," she insisted instead. "In fact, you've done a lot of good since you've been around, not the least of which was saving my life."

She thought back to the first time she'd encountered Emmy in the cave. She'd been bleeding badly after a fight with her mother's boyfriend and thought she was going to die. But then Emmy appeared—like an angel from heaven—giving her blood from her one soft scale to help seal up the wound. This particular pocket of dragon's blood, it was said, could perform medical miracles if given voluntarily by the creature in question. And without that miracle, Scarlet was pretty sure it would have been game over for her.

Suddenly, a thought struck her. Maybe Emmy's blood could heal Caleb too, bring him back from the Nether once and for all. And maybe healing Caleb would give Emmy more confidence, make her see how valuable she really was. Scarlet's heart pounded in her chest. It was the perfect plan! Something to give Emmy a purpose, and as a bonus, she'd get Caleb back too. Why hadn't she thought of it sooner?

"Emmy, do you think you could maybe…"

She trailed off, realizing the dragon was already shaking her head. Evidently she could still hear Scarlet's thoughts before she voiced them, through their blood bond.

I'm sorry, Emmy said, sounding wistful. *I wish I could. But it seems I am useless in this now, as in everything else.*

"What do you—?" Scarlet started to ask, then broke off as she watched Emmy lower her gaze to her arm. Scarlet followed the look, then gasped as she saw it.

"Emmy!" she cried, horrified. She dropped to her knees, taking Emmy's paw in her hands. So many scales had been broken, she hadn't noticed this one in particular. But there it was—her healing scale, ripped away. Only an ugly scar remained in its place.

The poor dragon. The poor, poor dragon!

"Oh, Emmy!" she cried, looking up at the creature, her eyes blurred with tears. "I'm so sorry. I didn't realize. If I had known, I never would have asked. I'm such an idiot. Please forgive me." Here she thought she was going to make the dragon feel better. Instead, she'd only made things worse.

Emmy regarded her sadly. *It's all right*, she assured Scarlet. *You couldn't have known.*

Scarlet's heart panged at the suffering she could hear clearly in Emmy's voice. She couldn't imagine how much pain the poor beast was going through each and every day. Not just the physical pain that would eventually heal with her wounds. But the mental anguish to know she was no longer whole.

She stepped up to the dragon, opening her arms wide to embrace her fully. Emmy was so big now she could barely manage to get her arms around her head. For a moment, the dragon was stiff, unyielding, But as Scarlet continued to hold her and whisper in her ear, she eventually softened, snuggling her head against her chest, her soft breath tickling the hairs on Scarlet's arms. For a moment, they just stood there, holding one another, pulling strength from one another—no words necessary.

Finally, Emmy pulled away. Scarlet looked at her questioningly. "What is it?" she asked.

While I cannot cure Caleb, there may be another way.

Scarlet's eyes widened. "Really?" she asked, hope rising within her. "What other way? Whatever it is, I'll do it!"

The dragon looked hesitant. *If I help you, will you agree to help me in return?*

"Yes, of course," Scarlet said a little doubtfully, not sure what she was agreeing to. But if Emmy could help Caleb… "I would help you no matter what. You know that, Ems. What do you need me to do?"

The dragon gave her a stern look. *First, you must promise never to speak of this. Not to anyone. Especially not to Trinity.*

Now Scarlet's heart was really pounding in her chest. Was she about to learn what Emmy had been hiding at long last? What had made her so estranged from her former Fire Kissed?

"Of course, Emmy," she assured the dragon. "You know you can trust me."

Emmy seemed to consider this for a moment, then snorted, puffs of smoke billowing from her nose. *Very well,* she said. *Open the door and get on my back. We need to take a little ride.*

Chapter Seven

Thirty minutes later, Scarlet was high in the clouds, Emmy tearing through white mist at breakneck speed. As they dipped and wove through the atmosphere, she couldn't help the small thrill tingling from her fingers to her toes, despite the somber circumstances. Besides the one brief flight after Emmy's rescue from the government lab, the only other time she'd ridden a dragon was in the Nether—when Emmy's future children, Zoe and Zavier, had taken her to Caleb. She remembered then thinking the whole thing was pretty thrilling—like some kind of crazy Six Flags Over Texas roller coaster or the like. But in real life, it was even better.

But she forced back her enthusiasm, knowing Emmy probably wouldn't appreciate it. After all, this wasn't a pleasure ride. And the dragon wasn't having any fun.

Whatever she needs you to do, she told herself, *you need to do it without question. No matter what it is. After all she's been through, she deserves that at least.*

And maybe, as a bonus, it would lead to her getting Caleb back. Her heart warmed as she imagined his blue eyes opening, meeting her own, his trademark smirk spreading across his face.

Oh, Buttercup, she imagined him saying. *I knew I could count on you.*

Finally, after what seemed an eternity (though was perhaps no more than twenty to thirty minutes), Emmy seemed to slow. Scarlet opened her eyes. They were out of the clouds and into the open sky again, and she willed herself to look down. The arid desert landscape seemed to roll out before them like a blood-red carpet in all directions. But straight ahead, a gigantic rock structure, the remains of some kind of long ago volcanic ash, rose to the sky like the Dark Tower of Mordor.

"Where are we?" Scarlet questioned aloud. She had no way of estimating Emmy's average miles per hour and had no sense of whether they were only a few miles or a few hundred from their home base.

Where we need to be, Emmy replied simply. *Now hold on. I am going in for a landing.*

Scarlet gripped the dragon's scales tighter as the beast lowered her head and raised her wings, coming in for a landing on an uneven ledge near the top of the rock structure. A moment later, they touched down—perhaps not as elegantly as Emmy would have done before they'd broken her wings and not set them straight, but Scarlet managed to hold on and bite back an *oomph* as pain ricocheted through her.

Once they were settled, Emmy lowered her wing, allowing Scarlet to leap down to the rocky surface. Now on solid earth again, she looked around, trying to determine where they were and what they were doing there.

Emmy made her move before she could inquire, walking around a towering rock structure and disappearing from view.

Scarlet scrambled after her, curious. Her eyes widened as she turned the corner to find a small, dark cave cut into the side of the cliff. Emmy made a gesture to the cave. *I am too large to enter*, she told her. *But go inside and tell me what you see.*

Now Scarlet was feeling truly freaked out. The last thing she wanted to do was enter some strange, dark cave on the top of a random mountain without any light source. After all, who knew what kind of creature might make this den his or her home?

Stop being such a coward, she berated herself. *Emmy needs you. This is your chance to prove yourself to her, not to mention help poor Caleb.*

Mind made up, she sucked in a breath and pulled out her cell phone, switching it to flashlight mode. Then she willed her feet to step forward, ducking down to enter the cave.

It was small, cramped, not even large enough for Scarlet to stand in, and so she was forced to hunch over and crouch down to walk through it. She wondered, as she made her way inside, how Emmy had even fit inside this small of a burrow in the first place. She'd been told that dragons liked to jam themselves into tight spaces—it made them feel more secure—but this was ridiculous.

It's no different than your pirate cave back home, she tried to tell herself. *You and Mac spent hours in there as kids. It was the safest place in the world.*

The thought made her feel a little better, and she waved the phone/flashlight around, trying to figure out what she was supposed to be looking for. Something Emmy had left behind and was now too big to retrieve?

A sudden thought struck her. What if Emmy's soft scale had fallen off in here back when the dragon was holed up inside? What if that was why Emmy had brought her here—so Scarlet could retrieve it? Maybe it couldn't be reattached to the dragon herself but had enough blood left inside to heal Caleb.

There may be another way, Emmy had said. Could this be what she meant?

Scarlet's heart rate picked up as hope started pumping through her. Yes. That had to be it. She would find the scale, and they'd bring it back to Caleb, and everything would be okay. Turning her flashlight to the ground, she started looking for—

"Ow!" she cried, practically jumping out of her skin as she felt something sharp pierce her ankle. Startled, she leapt away, managing only to slam the back of her head against the cave's low ceiling. Losing her balance, she tumbled to the ground, dropping her phone in the process.

Are you okay? Emmy's voice came through, sounding anxious.

"Yeah, I guess," Scarlet said, reaching up to rub her head. She could feel a large lump already forming. Then she scrambled for her cell phone. "But I think something bit me." Visions of copperheads and scorpions danced uncomfortably through her mind as she felt around for the hard plastic and glass of her phone.

Instead, her fingers made contact with something soft. Leathery.

Something moving.

"What the—?" She scrambled backward, heart in her throat now. "There's something in here, Emmy!" she cried. "Give me a little light!"

The dragon obliged, blowing a small fireball into the cave. The flames bounced off the walls, providing a moment of illumination. Scarlet took advantage, scanning the cave quickly, looking for her phone—looking for what she had touched instead of her phone.

And then she saw it. Or make that *them*. Two tiny birdlike creatures huddled together, peering back at her with large, frightened eyes. One was black as night with sparks of gold dancing off his skin. The other was pink with delicate purple-veined wings.

Scarlet stifled a gasp of surprise, her heart now slamming against her rib cage. It couldn't be. It was impossible. And yet…

There was no other explanation.

Summoning all her willpower, Scarlet's hands closed around her cell phone, and she switched it back on. Then, with shaky fingers, she raised it slowly, back in the direction of the two creatures.

The two baby dragons, to be precise.

"Uh, Emmy?" Scarlet cried out to the entrance of the cave. "Did you forget to tell me something?"

I thought it would be better for you to see for yourself, came the dragon's voice, sounding a little sheepish.

"Not better for my freaking heart, that's for sure," Scarlet managed to reply, trying to breathe normally again. She looked at the baby dragons. They looked back at her. Then the pink one took a tentative step forward, sniffing the air. On instinct, Scarlet held out a hand, like she would do to a strange dog, inviting it to sniff her. The dragon stared at her for a moment as if nervous, then took another cautious step, craning her long neck until she touched the tip of Scarlet's finger with her snout. Then she backed away skittishly to the protection of her slightly larger brother.

"It's okay," Scarlet whispered. "I won't hurt you." She bit her lower lip. "Are you… Do they call you Zoe?" she asked.

Of course it's Zoe, something inside of her insisted. Who else could it be? Zoe and her brother, Zavier, the same dragons she had met in the Nether who had told her they were Emmy's children, waiting to be born. At the time, they hadn't known when this would happen—or if it would even happen at all. But now here they were. Like an impossible dream come true.

How on earth had Emmy, the world's last dragon, been able to have babies? Did those scientists back at the lab have something to do with it? Scarlet had read about scientists cloning a sheep and a dog. Could they have figured out how to clone a dragon as well? Though if they had, wouldn't the baby dragon clones look exactly like their mother? She frowned, wishing she'd paid more attention in science class.

However it had happened, it had obviously happened. And recently too, judging from the remnants of cracked shells she now observed littering the cave. No wonder Emmy hadn't returned to them for two months after being freed. She'd obviously had other things on her plate. And no wonder she'd been so agitated when they'd dragged her back to the airfield; she must have been frantic to get back to her babies.

Drawing in a breath, Scarlet held out both hands this time, petting the creatures' tiny, scaled feet with gentle fingers. The baby dragons looked at one another, blinked their big eyes, then turned back to her. Taking turns, they each crawled up her arms and settled on her shoulders. Scarlet could feel their sharp little claws tickling her skin and couldn't help but laugh. Zoe flapped her wings and squawked with alarm at the sudden noise.

"Sorry!" Scarlet soothed her, reaching up to stroke her gently. "I didn't mean to startle you."

Zoe flapped her wings reproachfully a couple more times, as if to make her point, then grudgingly settled back on Scarlet's shoulder, small throaty noises that sounded like purring escaping her mouth. Scarlet smiled, forcing herself not giggle this time. "That's a good girl," she cooed to the dragon. "That's a very good girl."

She heard a shuffling at the mouth of the cave and remembered Emmy was still waiting for her outside—probably dying to be reunited with her precious offspring. Scarlet felt her heart melting a little as she imagined the impending reunion between mother and babies, proud that Emmy had trusted her with the task. Moving slowly, so as not to startle them again, she crawled out of the cave and back to the mother dragon.

As she emerged, her eyes fell on Emmy, who was pacing the cliff side with obvious agitation, puffs of smoke billowing from her nostrils. *She's worried about them*, Scarlet thought. *How sweet is that?*

"Look, guys!" she said aloud to the baby dragons. "It's your mommy!" She stepped toward Emmy to allow the babies to get closer. Seriously, this had to be the cutest thing ever. Two baby dragons. A worried mom. And she was the one who would reunite them. The one who would—

Emmy let out a low growl from deep in her throat and backed away. Scarlet stopped, confused.

"What's wrong, Emmy?" she asked, squinting her eyes at the dragon.

But Emmy wouldn't look at her. And she wouldn't look at the babies on her shoulders either. Scarlet's heart started pounding uncomfortably in her chest.

"These are your babies, aren't they?" she tried.

Emmy was still for a moment, then nodded reluctantly.

"Well then, don't you want to see them?"

To her surprise, Emmy snorted again, shaking her head violently from side to side. Scarlet took a hesitant step backward, confused as anything. This didn't make any sense.

"I don't understand. Didn't you want me to rescue your babies? Why else would you have brought me here?"

Emmy turned to look at her. *You wanted blood for Caleb*, she said. *I can't give it to you. But they can.*

Scarlet stared at the dragon in shock. In her excitement at finding Emmy's children, she'd almost forgotten their original purpose for coming here.

"Right, I mean, that's great," she stammered. "That's a good idea, in fact. But, Emmy, these are your children, right? Don't you want to—?"

After you take their blood, I need you to kill them, Emmy said suddenly. *Then we will leave this place and not return.*

"What?" Scarlet cried, now completely shocked. She switched to mind speak, worried the baby dragons would sense something was wrong. The poor little things. The poor, helpless little babies! *Emmy, what are you talking about?*

You agreed to help me, the dragon reminded her, giving her a worried look. *You said, whatever it was…*

Yeah, but I didn't mean… Emmy, why on earth would you want me to kill your children?

Because they will not die on their own.

She said it so casually, so matter-of-fact. Scarlet suddenly felt as if she might throw up. *I wasn't asking why you needed me to do it*, she corrected, hardly able to believe she had to clarify this point, *but why would you want your own children dead?*

For a moment, the dragon didn't answer, choosing instead to stare silently out over the horizon. Finally, Emmy turned and leveled her gaze on Scarlet. Her usually warm blue eyes were now icy cold.

Because if they live, they will burn down the world.

Scarlet swallowed hard, frightened at the conviction she saw written on Emmy's face. The revulsion as she gazed on her own two children. She had warned Trinity and Connor that Emmy wasn't the same dragon she once was. But this... this was too much. Was she crazy? Delusional? Paranoid? Or did she know something that Scarlet didn't? She wondered, again, if Trinity would know. But then, she'd promised Emmy she wouldn't tell Trinity.

Her gut wrenched. *Emmy...*

Zoe hopped off her shoulder, flapping her way to the ground and cautiously approaching her mother, a heartbreakingly hopeful look on her tiny face. She stared up at the giant dragon, batting her eyes and giving her what looked a lot like a cautious smile.

Instead of smiling back, Emmy jerked away, looking horrified and disgusted. Then she turned her head, refusing to look down at her daughter. Scarlet watched, her heart breaking as Zoe's face crumbled and she retreated back to the safety of her shoulder. She could hear the dragon making little whimpers in her ear, and it made her want to cry. She reached up, stroking her gently.

"I'm sorry," she whispered. "Trust me, I know what it feels like. It's not you, okay? It's her."

Her mind flashed to countless nights growing up, when her brother, Mac, would whisper the same kinds of things in her own ears. She knew all too well the pain of being rejected by one's mother. And it killed her to see Zoe going through it now.

She turned back to Emmy, fury building up inside of her like an active volcano. *What the hell is wrong with you?* she demanded, all her earlier pity for the dragon evaporating in an instant. *These are your children, Emmy. Not some evil monsters. I mean, just look at them! They're sweet and helpless, and they deserve a chance to live. Just like Trinity gave you when you were their size. Should she have just killed you when she had the chance as well?*

Yes, Emmy replied in a flat voice. *If she had, these monsters would have never been born.*

Scarlet shook her head, giving up. There was obviously no use trying to argue with the dragon; she had made up her mind. Just more proof that she had changed in her time in captivity, whether the others wanted to believe it or not. The old Emmy would have embraced her children. She would have done anything to save them. The new Emmy—the one who had been abused and broken in the government cage—well, with her, all bets were off.

And in a way, Scarlet did grudgingly understand. Emmy had been impregnated against her will—maybe even without her knowledge. And these babies were the result of that crime. It was understandable that she would have a hard time accepting them as her own, seeing as they represented everything she was trying to forget.

But these babies weren't to blame for the government's actions. And they shouldn't be forced to give up their lives to pay for someone else's crimes.

She drew in a breath. *Emmy, why don't you go home?* she told the dragon. *You don't need to be here to see this.*

The dragon looked at her hesitantly. *And you'll take care of them?* she asked. *And then come back home? Will you be able to find your way?*

Yes. I have my phone and it has GPS. I'll be fine. Don't worry.

At first, Emmy looked as if she might argue. But then, to Scarlet's relief, she nodded her head. *Okay,* she said. *I'll let you get started. But remember your promise. You can use the blood to heal Caleb, but you are not to speak of this to anyone. No one can know these creatures ever existed in the first place.*

"Sure, no problem," Scarlet agreed quickly, wanting to get the dragon out of there before Emmy started second-guessing herself and wanted to stay. "I won't say a word. Now go on. Before Trinity realizes you're gone and gets worried."

Emmy flinched at the mention of her former Fire Kissed, which Scarlet had been hoping for. She wondered again why it was so important to the dragon for Trinity not to know about her offspring. What would Trinity do if she found out they existed? Would she want to save them like she'd saved Emmy? Or would she believe, as the dragon did, that they had some crazy apocalyptic destiny?

Emmy bowed her head. *Thank you,* she said. *You are a good friend, Scarlet. I will not forget this.*

Nor will I, Emmy, Scarlet replied, though her meaning was a little different. *Now go. I'll see you back at the hangar.*

And with that, Emmy raised her head and pushed off on her back feet, launching herself into the sky. Scarlet watched her go, a sick feeling worming through her stomach.

"Someday you'll thank me for this," she muttered under her breath. "And if not, well, it'll be your loss."

She turned to the two baby dragons who'd hopped off her shoulders and flown to the edge of the cliff, watching their mother's silhouette fade into the distance. Zoe sank to the ground first, letting out a small, mournful cry. Zavier landed next to her, putting a wing around her little body in comfort, making grunting noises in her ear.

Scarlet watched the two of them, trying to swallow the huge lump that had formed in her throat. It was like she and her brother all over again. Two lost souls against the bitter world.

Except this time she was here too.

She cleared her throat. "Are you guys hungry?" she asked with forced brightness. "You must be, right? Do you want to come with me so we can find some food?"

The two dragons turned to look up at her inquisitively. Scarlet patted her shoulders, inviting them back up. They flew up to her, then settled down, croaking softly under their breath. She reached up with both hands to stroke them.

"Don't worry about her," she said. "She'll come around. In the meantime, I'll be your mother. I'll keep you safe. No matter what I have to do."

Chapter Eight

I t was done.

Emmy's heart ached as she dropped from the clouds and the airfield came into view. Her mind spun with visions of the little baby dragons, chirping sadly, and it was hard not to think of when she'd been one of those dragons herself, left on the side of the cliff to die, by her own mother. At the time, Emmy hadn't understood how her mother could just fly away like that, without even a last look back. Now she understood. That last look would have broken her.

As it had almost broken Emmy.

But her mother had done what had to be done. As Emmy now had herself. Thank goodness Scarlet had been willing to do the job—Emmy had tried three times to smother the baby dragons and each time had stopped at the last minute after seeing the looks in their eyes.

Because you're weak, she scolded herself. *A coward.*

But now the job would be done. The monsters would be destroyed, and the world would be safe. And her beloved Fire Kissed would never need to know.

She thought back to Trinity, how she'd risked her life to save Emmy's pathetic hide. At the time, Emmy couldn't even bear to look her in the eye, so ashamed she was of what she'd let them do to her. She imagined the disappointment she'd see in the eyes of her Fire Kissed when she learned that Emmy had—after all her promises—let her down after all.

And Emmy would be so ashamed.

But now things would be all right. The threat was gone. Trinity would never need to know. The world would be safe, and Emmy could start working to rebuild her bond with her Fire Kissed. To make sure Trinity had that happily ever after she deserved.

Emmy dropped down, making her final decent to the airfield. Yes. This was how it had to be. It was the only way to make things right—the one way to keep the world safe.

So why did it make her so incredibly sad?

Chapter Nine

"Okay, everyone. The meeting will come to order."

Trinity rapped the gavel against the small podium she'd found in one of the office's storage closets. The sound echoed through the terminal, causing everyone to turn in her direction, their chatter fading into silence as they looked up at her expectantly.

Her gaze roved over the group; sometimes it was still hard to believe there were so many of them now. The so-called Potentials—orphan teens from around the world who had once been under the thumb of Darius and Mara—now working on their side. Luke, Nate, and Natasha, the gamer geeks from New Mexico who ran the FreeEmmy.com website and took care of all their high-tech needs. Her father, who she'd once thought dead, and Connor, who she'd once thought an enemy. And now Scarlet, though Trinity didn't see her in the crowd at the moment. Probably hovering over Caleb's bedside, as per usual.

What had once been a couple of kids and a dragon on the run had now turned into a real, full-on operation. *Which is a good thing*, she reminded herself. *We need all the help we can get.*

Feeling the stares on her, Trin cleared her throat. "So obviously I wanted to start off by thanking each and every one of you for your help in rescuing Emmy and getting her adjusted in her new home," she said. "We couldn't have done it without you. It wasn't easy, and you should all feel very proud of yourselves."

The group erupted into excited chatter and a spattering of applause and high fives. Trinity let it go for a moment, then banged the gavel again.

"But as you know, our problems are far from over," she reminded them sternly. "In fact, in some ways, we're back to where we started. The government is presumably still looking for Emmy. Much of the world wants her dead. We've got a good setup here now, to be sure. But we can't expect to stay here undiscovered forever."

"And then there's the issue of feeding her," Trin's father piped in. "The more she grows, the more she's going to need to eat. We have a stockpile for her that we built up over the last two months. But once that's gone, it's going to be difficult to replenish our supply to keep up with her appetite."

"What we need is, like, a ranch!" cried one of the younger Potentials. "We could grow cows and other livestock for her to eat. Then we wouldn't have to be hunting all the time and gathering roadkill."

A few of the others voiced approval at this idea, but Trinity's father only shook his head. "We don't have the funds to purchase a ranch," he reminded them. "And it's not like anyone here would be approved for a bank loan."

"What about…like, an abandoned tropical island?" asked another of the Potentials. "There wouldn't be any people there, so Emmy could fly around to her heart's content, hunting wild boar and whatever else might be native."

Trinity sighed. "Even assuming such an island exists outside of *Jurassic Park* movies and *Lost* reruns, we'd have no way to get there. Unless someone here has a dragon-sized yacht they haven't bothered to mention?"

She watched as their eager faces fell. Sometimes it was hard to remember how young they all were. How young *she* still was herself. In a normal world, they'd be dealing with homework and homecoming, parents, teachers, and friends. They shouldn't have to have the world's weight on their shoulders like this.

"Look," she said. "We can stay here as long as possible, try to get Emmy's strength up at least, and, of course, her spirits. In the meantime, I want some of you to be scouting out possible future home bases. Preferably places with lots of game. When we need to make another move, whether it's because we've run out of food or we've been spotted by the government, I want to be ready."

She pulled out her list of assignments, preparing to dole them out. But a voice broke out from the crowd before she could speak again.

"So, what, you just want us to keep running forever then? Is that your big master plan?"

Trinity frowned as she caught sight of Rashida, now standing in the back of the room, arms crossed over her chest. "Excuse me?" she asked, irritation washing over her. Seriously, she did not need this, today of all days.

She knew Connor liked Rashida. He thought she was smart and resourceful. And he was constantly reminding Trin that if it weren't for Rashida and her team of Potentials, they never would have gotten Emmy back. Still, sometimes it was hard to get over the fact that the girl had once tried to kill her, not to mention turned Caleb and Scarlet over to the enemy. If it wasn't for Rashida, Emmy never would have been caught by the Dracken. And Caleb would be with them now in mind instead of just body. Sure, the girl had switched sides, and Trin was pretty sure she was Team Dragon all the way. But the constant asserting of her opinion in every situation was wearing on her nerves.

"We want to know your long-term plan here," Rashida called out. "I mean, you've tried hiding out before. Didn't exactly go all that well if I remember right."

Trinity felt a blush rise to her cheeks. "No. It didn't. But there were some extenuating circumstances if you remember." After all, who could have predicted Emmy sneaking away to heal Scarlet and Scarlet putting it on the Internet?

Rashida gave her a smug look. "Face it, Trinity Foxx. There's always the threat of an extenuating circumstance. Especially now. After all, Emmy's not exactly the world's best-kept secret at this point. We've all seen the FreeEmmy.com website. Like it or not, she's now an Internet sensation. Everyone's talking about her."

"That'll die down," Trinity protested, furious at having to defend herself like this. "Like it did before. People are only riled up because of the recent sightings. It'll calm down again."

"Which is exactly what the government wants," Rashida argued, like a pit bull who didn't want to give up her bone. "I mean, right now they're probably just sitting back and waiting until it gets quiet again, so they can swoop in and take Emmy away without worrying about any public outcry."

Trinity watched in dismay as Team Dragon all nodded their heads in assent. She was losing them, she realized. Stupid Rashida. Her mind scrambled for something reassuring to say. Which wasn't easy, considering she wasn't entirely sure they were wrong. But still! What alternatives did they have?

"Come on, people," Connor broke in to her relief. "What do you want Trin to do? Sign Emmy up to play Carnegie Hall? You do remember the last time she showed her face in public, don't you? At the Vista football stadium?" He crossed his arms over his chest. "Face it. The world is not ready for dragons."

"Maybe not real-life dragons," Luke said slowly. "But what about online?"

Trinity shot him a puzzled look. "What do you mean?"

The Dracken kid rose from his seat and turned to face the crowd. "Look, it's clear from our FreeEmmy.com website numbers that our girl has a large fan base. Sure, some people think she's some kind of threat, but a lot more think she's pretty cool. Why not exploit that? Work to build her brand? Make her the most famous endangered species in the world?" His eyes glowed with excitement. "We could take photos, make music videos, live stream Q and As…"

Trinity stared at him, incredulous. "You want my dragon to have her own YouTube channel?"

Luke shrugged. "YouTube would be just the beginning. I'm talking about a full-on social media campaign here— Instagram, Tumblr, Facebook." He grinned. "Hell, we can even launch a Kickstarter to help pay for her food."

"But—"

"Trust me," his partner-in-website-crime, Natasha, broke in, also rising from her seat. "We've been online from the start. We've seen people's reactions. They *want* to love her. I mean, of course they do. People think dragons are awesome—even the made-up kind. And now, the idea that's there's a real-life one out there, just like they always fantasied about when they were kids? It's going to blow their freaking minds."

Trinity somehow found her voice. "But wouldn't we get caught?" she asked. "I mean all the stuff we upload, couldn't it be traced back to where we're hiding out?"

"Please," Natasha's brother, Nate, interjected. "Do not even think of insulting me like that. I can jump through a thousand international proxies to hide our web trail. For all anyone will be able to tell, we're broadcasting live from Singapore." He beamed. "It'll be like hiding in plain sight."

Now everyone was talking at once, all seeming completely excited about the idea. Even Trinity had to admit, it was growing on her. "But then what?" she asked. "I mean, that all sounds good and all, but what's our endgame here?"

"Easy," Luke pronounced. "Once we've gotten everyone to fall in love with Emmy, there's no way the government can just swoop in and take her away. Her profile will be too high—they'd take too much heat. And once everyone sees how sweet and gentle she is and all the things she can do to help us as a species, they'll want to protect her. I'm not saying we should be aiming for a presidential pardon or anything. But maybe we could get legislation passed to put her on the endangered species list somehow? So no one can harm her?"

"And she'll finally get to fly free!" Rashida pronounced. "No more hiding."

Connor frowned. "Bengal tigers are protected. That doesn't mean they get to hang out in villages as house cats. I'm sorry, but I can't imagine a world where people are cool with a fire-breathing dragon roaming around their master-planned community."

"Okay, fine. Maybe flying free is stretching it," Luke amended. "But maybe they'd allow her to live on some game preserve? The kind where Hunters are forbidden? Or maybe some billionaire would actually give us that island or ranch we're looking for."

"Look, you said it yourself," Natasha added. "We're basically on borrowed time here. We can't just waste it. Otherwise we'll be no better than when we started out."

"It may not work," Rashida added. "But I think Emmy deserves for us to try."

Everyone broke out into conversations among themselves. Trinity banged the gavel. It took a while this time for everyone to quiet. She looked out over the crowd at the faces that, for the first time, shone with a small light of hope. She let out a resigned sigh.

"Okay," she said. "If you're all in agreement, let's try to put this plan into motion. I'm not convinced it's going to work. But, like you said, at least we'll be doing something."

She just hoped Emmy would be up for this particular *something*...

Chapter Ten

Y ou're quiet. Is everything okay?"

Connor looked up at Trinity, who was sitting across from him on the picnic blanket, staring at him with worried eyes. She'd changed into a thin, flowered sundress for their date and had let loose her hair so it fell forward, a cascade of dark curls framing her heart-shaped face. She looked so stunning, silhouetted in the moonlight, like a fairy princess from a storybook. But Connor couldn't concentrate on her beauty—not tonight.

He'd planned this romantic picnic for the two of them weeks ago, to commemorate the eight-month anniversary of the two of them being together. But after having sat through the Team Dragon group meeting earlier that day, he no longer felt much like celebrating.

"Sorry," he said, poking at his uneaten food with his fork. "I'm just…thinking, I guess."

"About what went down at the meeting?"

He nodded.

"You don't think it's a good idea, do you?" Trin asked, peering at him with concern in her eyes.

"No." He looked up, surprised she'd even phrase it as a question. "I don't. Of course I don't. How could I? I've told you a thousand times I don't want those Dracken kids involved in any of this. It was bad enough they were along for the rescue, though I understand it was the only way to make it happen. But now…" He shook his head. "You've just basically given them carte blanche to start running the show around here—literally. From now on, they'll be controlling the message. We'll be totally at their mercy."

"Connor, don't you think you're overstating things a bit?" Trin argued gently. "I mean, they're just trying to help. To get people to see that dragons aren't these evil creatures out to destroy the world."

"That's exactly my point!" Connor cried. "I don't want people thinking that dragons are just some kind of overgrown lap dogs. Hell, that's what got us in trouble the first time around. And when the dragons did turn on us, we weren't ready."

"But there are no dragons plural this time," Trin protested. "There's only Emmy. And even you have to agree that Emmy isn't a threat to anyone."

"Don't forget—even Emmy has killed her fair share. Though I guess, to her credit, they were mostly the so-called bad guys. She does seem to want to do the right thing. But…" He trailed off but held up his hand to stop her from interjecting. "It would be naive to assume she'll always be the world's last dragon."

Trinity frowned. "What?"

"Think about it," Connor said. "She was in that government lab for six months. Plenty of time for them for take DNA samples and whatever else they might need. Sure, they might not have the technology to clone a dragon yet, but we know for a fact that in ten short years, they will."

He drew in a breath. "For all we know, they're working on it now, as we speak, figuring out a way to clone and breed these weapons of mass destruction. If we go ahead with our 'Dragons are awesome' PR campaign, everyone will start assuming all dragons are just like Emmy. Next thing you know, we'll have some radical animal rights group breaking into the government lab and setting these hybrid monsters on the world."

"That's quite a lot of conjecture, Connor."

"No." He shook his head angrily. "It's not. Don't you see? It's not conjecture at all. It's history. *My* world's history." He raked a hand through his hair, frustrated. "God, sometimes I feel like flecking Cassandra from one of those Greek myths. I keep telling you all what's going to happen from my own personal experience, and yet somehow you all continue to exist in this fantasy world where dragons are cuddly puppy dogs, not world-destroying monsters."

"Connor…" Her eyes were pleading, making his heart ache. He hated to upset her like this. But what choice did he have? Someone here had to speak the uncomfortable truth. And it seemed that he was the only one who could recognize it.

"I'm sorry, Trin," he tried. "I know you guys are all excited about this plan. And maybe…maybe it'll be fine…"

She sighed. "It's obvious you don't think that."

He groaned. "Honestly, I don't know. Maybe things have changed enough. But every day, I feel like I'm living in this crazy déjà vu. Every time I turn around, I see these warning signs that things might not be as different as they first appear." He shrugged. "We've changed the ripples of time, sure. But have we really stopped the tsunami on approach?"

He bit his lower lip. "I know you don't want to hear this, but I still believe that as long as dragons are on the earth, there's always going to be a threat."

"Which is why you're here to stop it," Trinity reminded him. "Don't you see, Connor? That's the real difference this time around. Back then, when the dragon hybrids rose up, we didn't have any way to stop them." She gave him a shy smile. "This time we have you to blast those monsters into smithereens." She mimed locking and loading a pistol, a teasing look in her eyes. "What was that catchphrase again? *Hasta la vista, evil dragon spawn!*"

Anger exploded inside of him. "You think this is funny? That this is all some kind of big joke?" He rose to his feet, looking down at her with furious eyes. "Well, let me tell you, it's not a joke to me. My world was destroyed. My father was killed. And if you think I'm going to just sit around and watch it happen all over again, well, you've all got another thing coming." He turned on his heel.

"Connor!" she cried, scrambling to her feet. "I'm sorry! I didn't mean—" She made a move to stop him, but he shrugged her off.

"Just leave me alone. Go check on your little web star or something. It's obvious she's all you care about anyway."

"That's not true." Trin voice was pleading now. "I care about *you*. I *love* you."

Connor stiffened, his heart squeezing. He'd been waiting so long to hear those words come from her mouth.

But now, as they spilled from her lips, he couldn't allow himself to believe them.

✦ ✦ ✦

From her hiding spot behind the hangar, Scarlet watched as Connor stormed off into the night, leaving Trinity to pick up the remnants of their picnic, her stomach knotted in disappointment and fear. She hadn't been able to hear everything spoken between the two of them, but she was pretty sure she got the idea.

As long as dragons are on the earth, there's always going to be a threat.

It had taken her all day to climb down from that mountain and walk the baby dragons back to the airfield. When she'd finally arrived, she'd stashed them in a maintenance shed at the far end of the runway, then headed back to camp to score them some dinner. The whole time, she'd been debating in her head whether or not to come clean to Trinity, to break her promise to Emmy for the dragons' sake. But now, after overhearing their argument…

Blast those monsters into smithereens…

The fury clawed up her throat, threatening to choke her. All this time, she'd tried to give Trinity the benefit of the doubt. They might not have always seen eye to eye, but at least they were on the same team. Or so Scarlet had thought. But now, she realized with sickening dread, Trinity was no better than the rest of them, assuming, without any evidence whatsoever, that any dragons besides her precious Emmy were monsters.

When really it was Emmy herself who was the biggest monster.

With effort, Scarlet pushed down her anger and squared her shoulders, firming her resolve. They could think what they wanted…for now. She would prove them wrong. She would raise these baby dragons out of sight, giving them the love and respect they deserved. And when they were grown, she would show them.

She would show them all.

Chapter Eleven

H ey, honey, everything okay?"

Trinity shut the door to her father's work shack behind her, then wandered over to the nearby bench, plopping down onto it and scrubbing her face with her hands. Her father set down the piece of metal he'd been welding and walked over, taking a seat beside her. He reached out, giving her a hand a comforting squeeze.

"What happened?" he asked.

She sighed, giving him a brief rundown of her fight with Connor. "What do you think?" she asked when she'd finished. "Do you think the whole social media campaign is a bad idea? Are we setting ourselves up for disaster?"

Her father was silent for a moment. "Honestly, I don't know," he said at last. "I mean, certainly propaganda campaigns have worked, historically speaking. But they can be tricky beasts. And the public can turn on you just as quickly as they once fell in love with you. If you're going to go through with this, you'll have to keep Emmy on a tight leash and really control the message. If she were to be caught on camera, let's say, doing something she wasn't supposed to—like the time she landed in the football field—well, suddenly you'd have another witch hunt on your hands."

Trinity sighed. "I don't even know if Emmy will go for any of this. I mean, back in the old days, I'm sure she would have loved the attention, you know? But she's so different now, so scared and depressed. It's almost as if she doesn't even want to be alive."

"Maybe she doesn't," her father said gently. "Remember, sweetie, she didn't want to be rescued in the first place. And the only reason she's here now is because you dragged her back against her will."

Trinity scowled. "What were we supposed to do?" she demanded, rising to her feet, her stomach twisting in angry knots. "Just leave her out there, unprotected and alone?"

"Unprotected. Alone. But free." He gave her a sympathetic look. "Sweetie, I know you've bent over backward to make this place nice. But to her, well, it might feel like just another cage."

Trinity fell back to the bench, craning her neck to stare up at the ceiling. She sucked in a breath. As much as she didn't want to admit it, she knew her father had a point. But still, what choice did they have?

"Maybe the group's right," she said with a sigh. "If we can get the public's approval, maybe we can get Emmy some kind of protected status, so she can finally be free." She made a face. "It just seems like such a long shot."

"It *is* a long shot," her dad agreed. "No doubt about that."

She groaned. "If only Emmy had just stepped through that stupid time machine you and Virgil made for her when she had the chance. She could be a million years away from the mess, hanging out with other dragons, not a care in the world…"

Her mind flashed back to that fateful day in her father and Virgil's lab. She'd been so sad to say good-bye yet so happy that the dragon would finally find the peace she deserved. One step through the time machine and it would have all been over.

But Emmy had refused to take that step, willingly sacrific- ing her own happiness to save the boy Trin loved. Trinity had wondered many times since then if Emmy regretted making that decision. In fact, maybe that was the reason she refused to look at Trin now, thinking her a walking, talking reminder of her biggest mistake.

"God, I wish I could just go back to that night when I found her in the egg," she lamented. "I'd do everything differently."

Her father was quiet for a moment. Then he spoke. "What if you could?"

"What?" Trinity looked over at him, startled. "What do you mean?" Her pulse quickened. "Have you…figured something out with the machine?"

Since they'd set up shop here at the airfield, her father had been working overtime, trying to piece Virgil's machine back together. But as far as she knew, he hadn't made much progress. Emmy had melted much of the circuitry when she'd attacked Virgil, and the boards had had to be rebuilt from scratch—without the futuristic tools they'd had the first time around.

Sure enough, her father shook his head. "I'm still miles from where we need to be," he told her. "But I'm not giving up either. If we can get this machine back in operation, it'll give us options. We could go back to the original plan—of sending Emmy back in time. Or…" He paused, then added, "Maybe we could reset the clock."

"Reset the clock?"

"Connor and Caleb went back in time to stop the apocalypse. What if I could send you back this time instead?" he said slowly. "Perhaps to a certain Christmas Eve to make sure you received the music box I sent this time?"

Trinity stared at him, mouth agape. "Could you really do that?" she whispered.

If she went back in time, she could stop the Dracken from kidnapping her mother. She could get the egg out of the museum before the government showed up. She could save her grandfather's life. She could keep Emmy out of the Dracken's hands.

She could be her Fire Kissed again.

"I don't know," her father said. "In truth, I may never be able to get this thing working again. But I promise you this, baby girl—I'm going to give it my best try."

PART 2:

EMBER

Chapter Twelve

The Surface Lands—Year 190 Post-Scorch

*W*hat *a waste. What a horrible waste.*

Caleb grimaced as the 'vator's doors slid open, and he stepped out into the middle of the carnage. The grounds that had once housed a small, experimental garden had now been mutilated into nothing more than a blood-soaked grave-yard. The Council had, once again, done its worst, stealing the lives of five magnificent dragons and abandoning their corpses to rot out in the hot sun.

Stomach roiling, he forced himself to pull out his tran-scriber in order to properly catalog each beast. One of his jobs as a member of the Dracken was to keep a ledger of Council kills. This ledger was then compared to the roster of known dragons some of the other Dracken had been compil-ing. Ultimately, Darius hoped to complete a sort of dragon census to help him study the habits and family trees of the mighty beasts.

Caleb leaned down to examine the foot of one of the saffron-colored corpses nearby. He groaned as he recog-nized the Dracken brand, burned into the dragon's right paw. Bastards. He sighed, releasing the leg and then turning back to his transcriber, looking up the dragon's number on his list.

He found it almost immediately. Daisy. It had been Daisy. One of the study dragons and a Pureblood to boot, now nothing more than a black, bloody stain on the landscape. Caleb scowled, now angrier than ever. Killing hybrids he could understand. But this indiscriminate slaughter without even doing a blood check first—this was too much.

He'd always liked Daisy. She was silly, greedy, goofy—like his own dragon, Trinity, had been before she'd needlessly been slaughtered as well. He remembered watching Daisy flip through the sky, as fond of barrel rolls as she was of barrels of food. Darius was not going to be pleased that the Council had gotten one of his own this time.

God, what a flecking waste. It made him sick to his stomach. How could these Dragon Hunters live with themselves? How could everyone laud them as heroes? They were clearly nothing more than mass murderers.

"Better to murder than *be* murdered, don't you think?"

Caleb jerked his head at the sound of the voice. Lost in his revulsion, he hadn't realized someone had come up behind him. No, not just someone. Connor himself. The biggest murderer of them all. Having the nerve to jack into his thoughts without even asking permission.

"Is that your new catchphrase?" he sneered, turning around to take in his brother's crisp Academy uniform, glistening with a multitude of medals. One medal for each murder. He wondered, not for the first time, which shiny pin Connor had received for killing his dragon. His stomach clenched again.

"It's just a fact," Connor said simply. "The dragons know they're not allowed to come within five miles of the Sector. If we hadn't killed them, who knows the damage they could have done?"

"They were probably coming for the cows," Caleb protested. "They're starving. There's not a lot left to eat on the Surface."

"Yeah, well, whose fault is that?" Connor shot back. "They burned all the life off the earth. What did they expect would happen?"

Caleb rolled his eyes. *Here we go again.* "Seriously, Connor, do you ever have even a single original thought in your head?" he demanded. "Or is too stuffed with Council propaganda?"

"I should ask you the same thing about your little Dracken cult," his twin shot back without missing a beat. "I mean, really, Caleb. Why on earth would anyone want to save these hideous beasts?" He kicked Daisy's helpless corpse with his heavy boot. "They've destroyed our world. They've made us prisoners underground." He paused, pursing his lips. "They killed our own father, Caleb."

"Yeah, well, who could blame them?" Caleb ground out, the fury rising inside of him. "They didn't ask to be brought back here. They didn't ask to be genetically manipulated and cloned and made into Frankenstein monster dragons." He looked down at poor, pitiful Daisy, his heart aching. "Maybe if we had respected them. Maybe if we hadn't been so greedy. Maybe if we had been nice to them—maybe things would have turned out a lot differently."

Connor sighed. "Look, I know it's a bad situation," he said. "And hell, if I could go back two hundred years and stop the scientists from creating those first hybrids, I would. But that's impossible. Which means we have no choice but to live in the world as it is. And these dragons? They're violent and cruel. And they're out to destroy mankind." He looked at Caleb and gave a small shrug. "And if it's kill or be killed? Well, I know what choice I'll make every time."

Caleb opened his mouth to answer, then sighed, staring down at the ground. As much as he didn't want to admit it, his brother did have a point. The Dracken had been working to try to tame dragons and bring them into the fold for years now. And while the pure-blooded dragons—the ones directly descended from Emberlyn herself—gladly bonded with guardians and accepted man's hospitality, those with genetically altered genes—the hybrids, as they were called—always ended up turning on them by the time they hit puberty. No matter what the Dracken tried to do.

To make matters worse, the hybrids matured faster. They laid more eggs. They grew stronger and larger than their pure dragon brothers and sisters. And according to the Dracken census, if something wasn't done soon, they would rise to dominance. And the true dragons—the ones with the powers to save mankind—would die out all together.

Which would happen even quicker if the Council kept refusing to differentiate when it came to their kill orders. Despite what the Dracken had tried to show with their research studies, the Council—and most of the stupid sheep below—insisted that the only good dragon was a dead dragon.

And now, here were five more dead dragons.

Connor was right about one thing. This couldn't go on much longer. Something had to be done.

But what?

Chapter Thirteen

Present Day—One Month Later

Scarlet slipped out of bed quietly, so as not to wake the others, then headed out of the dorm and through the terminal, making her way to Caleb's sickroom. Stepping inside, she closed the door behind her, then approached his bed. For a moment, she just stood, watching him lie there, as if he were a corpse. His pallor was still deathly pale. His eyes had rolled to the back of his head. She looked down at the small vial she clutched in her hands.

Would this really work?

She'd been biding her time for nearly a month now, waiting for one of the baby dragons to grow large enough to harvest the healing blood from their soft scale. Each day, she'd wake up petrified that someone had discovered the maintenance shack at the far end of the property where she'd stashed her brood. But no one ever had. Nor had anyone voiced concern about how much food she was "eating" each night for dinner or where she disappeared to afterward. She supposed they were all too wrapped up in their great dragon social media experiment to pay her any mind.

From what she could tell, Emmy was becoming quite a superstar online, with thousands of fans flocking to her daily broadcasts. Scarlet wondered what the dragon herself thought of the show—was she enjoying her newfound fame, or was she still depressed? She'd considered checking up on her once but then decided against it. After all, the last thing she needed was for Emmy to overhear a stray thought in her head and learn she hadn't exactly followed orders.

At times, she'd wondered if she should leave the camp, taking Zoe and Zavier with her. But where would she go? How would she find food? And most importantly, how could she walk away and leave Caleb behind?

She looked down at him now. It was funny; she'd only known him a few short days before he'd entered this Nether coma, yet she felt closer to him than anyone else here. Maybe it was from the time she'd spent as a prisoner in the government lab. She'd thought a lot about Caleb back then, while stuck in her dark cell for endless hours with nothing to do. In fact, some days, when things got really bad, the memory of his lips brushing against her own, his hands tangled in her hair, was all she had left to help her get out of bed. To keep surviving—to not let them break her. Somehow, just knowing he was out there, waiting for her to come back to him—needing her to come back—gave her the strength to keep holding on until she could.

And now, here she was—the only person on Earth with the power to wake the sleeping prince.

On impulse, she leaned over his bedside, pressing her lips softly against his mouth, a silly attempt to wake him on her own. But of course, that was just a fairy tale. And thanks to Emmy's children, she had a much more realistic remedy.

She looked down at the vial. Even after a month, Zavier's scale was still tiny, and it didn't contain much blood. Hopefully it was enough to do the job. Otherwise, she'd have to wait until the dragon grew even bigger for her to try again. And she didn't know how much time Caleb had left...if he had any left at all.

With trembling hands, she pried open his mouth, then put the vial to his lips. The blood dripped down, coating his tongue in a black oil-like substance. She waited for a moment, not exactly sure how this was all supposed to work, then pulled the vial away and closed his mouth, her pulse skittering madly as she waited for a reaction. Any reaction.

At first, there was nothing. Caleb's eyes remained closed. His skin still white as snow. His arms limp at his side. Only his chest, slowly rising and falling in silent rhythm, gave her any indication he was even alive at all.

Still, she waited, trying to ignore the ache of doubt that began to creep into her bones. Was she too late? Was there just not enough blood? Was dragon's blood unable to cure this kind of thing after all?

"Please, Bad Seed," she begged. She laid a hand over his. "Come back to me."

Caleb didn't move.

She slumped into the folding chair next to him, scrubbing her face with her hands, her stomach wrenching with frustration. *Come on*, she begged him silently. *Please wake up. You have to wake up.*

And then, suddenly, his mouth twitched.

Scarlet leapt to her feet, pulse skyrocketing. Had that really just happened? Or had her desperate mind only imagined it?

But no. He was still moving. His eyes were fluttering. His nose was wiggling. And finally, a small, wet burp escaped his mouth—the most disgustingly beautiful sound Scarlet had ever heard in her life. She dropped back down to the chair, grabbing his hand in hers and squeezing it tight, her eyes glued to his face.

"Come on!" she whispered. "Come back to me! You can do it! I know you can!"

She watched, breathless, as his eyes lifted to half-mast, the pupils rolling around underneath, still unfocused and weak. But then they somehow managed to lock onto her face. His mouth quirked to a weak, cocky smile. The very same smile whose memory had kept her alive on those darkest days was now blasting fully on her in real life. It felt like the very sun.

"Buttercup," he gurgled, his voice hoarse. "Where have you been all my life?"

Oh my God. She'd done it. She'd really done it!

She squealed, then bit her lip to quiet herself, not wanting to wake the others. They could find out soon enough that Caleb was back among the living. Right now, she wanted him all to herself. In fact, it was all she could do not to hug the life out of him and cover his face with kisses.

But he was weak. Disoriented. She didn't want to overwhelm him. So she kept herself firmly glued to her chair, though she didn't let go of his hand.

"How are you feeling?" she asked, peering down at him more critically now.

"Like I've been run over by a grumpy dragon," he admitted, reaching up to rub his forehead with his free hand. "How long have I been out?"

"Just over nine months."

His blue eyes clouded with horror. "Nine months?" He shook his head, and she could see his hard swallow. "Why, I've missed the whole party."

"You do have a bit of catching up to do," she admitted. "But it's okay. Everything's okay. We're all back together. We've rescued Emmy from the government lab. She's growing stronger every day. In fact, it's pretty much happily ever after around here these days." She smiled down at him. "Even more so now that we have you back."

As she spoke the words, her mind flashed to the baby dragons, and she wondered if she should tell him about them. He of all people would understand, right? He would want to protect them too, despite what the others thought. A thrill spun down her spine. Finally, she'd have a partner in crime. She'd no longer have to bear the burden on her own. And maybe, with him on her side, they could convince the others that these dragons weren't something to fear.

"Oh, Caleb," she breathed. "I've really—"

"And Trinity?" he broke in before she could finish. "Is she here too? Did she find her father? Was he able to help?"

Scarlet frowned. "Uh, yeah. She's here. And her father's here too. I'm not sure what you mean about him helping though. I mean, he helps out in the restaurant a lot. And he's always tinkering in his lab, though I don't really know what he's up to with—"

"Has she been by to see me?" he interrupted. His hopeful look sent worry fluttering through her stomach. She watched as he glanced around the room, as if he expected Trinity to be hovering somewhere in the shadows.

What about me? she wanted to ask. *Didn't you miss me like I missed you?* But the words seemed to stick in her throat.

"Sure, she's come by," she managed to say, trying to push down the hurt welling in her throat. "She's been pretty busy though. They've got this whole social media campaign they're working on to let people know about Emmy." She forced a laugh. "You know Trinity when it comes to that dragon. Nothing else seems to matter."

She swallowed hard, distressed by the disappointment she saw clearly in Caleb's eyes. Suddenly, a horrible thought struck her. What if he didn't remember his time in the Nether? What if the dragon's blood had wiped out the whole trip in his mind? What if he didn't remember their kiss—her confessions—all the promises they'd made to one another? What if all of that lived in Scarlet's memory alone?

She let out a small moan. All this time, she'd been holding on. The idea of their reunion keeping her going through the darkest days. What if it was nothing more than a fantasy?

"Can I ask you a favor?" Caleb broke in, interrupting her tormented thoughts.

Hope rose inside of her again. "Of course! Anything! Anything at all!"

He gave her a weak smile. "Would you go find Trinity and ask her to come see me? I don't think I can master the whole getting out of bed thing quite yet."

For a moment, Scarlet couldn't speak, the lump in her throat so large it threatened to choke her. Instead, she managed a small nod of her head. "Of course," she said. "I'll... go find her now."

Caleb smiled at her—the very same smile that had, only

110

minutes before, warmed her like the sun. Now it made her blood run cold.

"Thanks, Buttercup," he said, resting his head back on the pillow. "I appreciate it. It's good to see you again, by the way. I'm glad you're still Team Dragon."

She rose to her feet so quickly she knocked over the folding chair. It crashed to the ground with a large bang, and her face burned as she reached down to right it again.

When she rose, she found Caleb peering at her intently. "Are you okay?"

"I'm fine," she spit out with more venom than she'd meant to. She was biting her lower lip so hard at this point she was certain she would draw blood. "You rest. I'll get…Trinity… for you." The name tasted like sawdust in her mouth.

Tell him you cured him! a voice inside of her begged. *Tell him it was all you! That he owes you his life!*

But she kept her mouth closed, her lips sealed. Because, she realized, it didn't matter in the end. After all, she wasn't in need of his gratitude; she wanted much more than that. And if he didn't feel about her how she felt about him, well, she wasn't about to guilt-trip him into doing so.

Besides, that would be compromising her dragons' safety. After all, what if she told him and he went and told Trinity? Trinity would probably go tell Connor and maybe even Emmy. And then they'd all want to make double sure that the sweet baby dragons "destined to destroy the world" had been destroyed themselves.

She couldn't let that happen. She'd made a promise to keep them safe, and nothing—not even Caleb's approval—could make her break that promise.

After all, who needed a boyfriend when you had your very own dragons?

Chapter Fourteen

W hoo-hoo, Ems! Way to go!"
Trinity whooped and cheered as Emmy shot across the hangar, body outstretched and wings close to her side. The dragon tucked her head, executing a perfect barrel roll, then dropped back down to the ground, sticking the landing like a pro. Turning back to Trinity—and Luke, who was filming the whole thing—she did a showy little bow.

"That's my girl!" Trinity cried, clapping her hands together.

"That's definitely going in tomorrow's show," Luke added, giving her a fist bump. "Now, should we do some fan mail before we go to bed?"

Emmy nodded, padding over to the small studio they'd set up at the end of the hangar, on the opposite side of her bedroom. Trinity gathered up the computer printouts off the table and walked over to sit down beside her.

The social media campaign had gotten off to a slow start. But viewership had skyrocketed about a week ago, after BuzzFeed had done a "13 Things to Love about Emberlyn" feature that had gone viral. Now the dragon was well on her way to becoming an Internet sensation, just as they'd hoped. Natasha had even set up an official Team Dragon fan club, and applications were coming in by the hundreds each day.

And Emmy did seem to enjoy the attention. She especially liked showing off when the cameras rolled. Unfortunately, when they went dark, so did her mood. She'd retreat back to her little burrow where she'd binge-watch TV for hours on end, with little interest in doing anything else—not that there was, admittedly, much else to do. Trinity would sit with the dragon during these times, trying to keep her company at least. But all the while, her father's words would ring in her head.

To her, it might be just another cage.

"Just hang in there, girl," she muttered, watching Emmy nose through the printouts as Luke set up the camera. "Once Dad gets the time machine back up, I'm going to fix this, once and for all."

She sighed, a draft of loneliness seeming to roll over her. While Emmy no longer seemed to actively object to her presence as she had when she'd first arrived, they were still miles apart from where they used to be. Emmy could understand her, but Trinity could still not hear the dragon's thoughts. And the one-way conversations were driving them both a little insane.

Suddenly, Emmy lifted her head, a low growl rumbling from her throat as she stared straight ahead, neck tense, ears pricked. Trinity frowned, turning in the direction of the dragon's stare just in time to see a lone figure stepping through the hangar door. *Scarlet*, she realized in surprise. *What was she doing here?*

Scarlet never came into the hangar anymore. In fact, the girl who had once been so dedicated to the dragon—who had shared a blood bond and acted as Fire Kissed—now seemed to go out of her way to avoid Emmy altogether. In turn, Emmy seemed to have no desire to interact with Scarlet either. But when Trinity tried to ask the girl if something had happened between them, Scarlet had turned red in the face and became extremely evasive.

To be honest, Trinity didn't push too hard; deep down, she was relieved to have the competition out of the way, giving her a better chance of someday restoring her and Emmy's bond. Still, she had to admit, it was strange to say the least.

"Um, is everything okay?" she asked now, setting down the printouts and putting a comforting hand on Emmy's arm.

Scarlet nodded, though Trinity thought she caught a dark shadow cross her face before she spoke. "Yeah," she said. "It's just…Caleb asked me to find you."

"What?" Trinity's eyes bulged. Her heart hammered in her chest. "He's awake? Caleb's awake? When…? How…?" The questions flew from her mouth even as she realized how little they mattered. If Caleb were truly awake…

Trinity turned to Luke. "We'll have to finish this in the morning," she told him. "Emmy, I'll be back in a bit, okay?"

The dragon nodded, not taking her eyes off Scarlet. Trinity gave Emmy a small squeeze, then dove across the hangar, launching through the door, toward the main terminal's entrance. Toward Caleb's sickroom, heart in her throat.

Caleb was awake. He was *awake*!

"Caleb!" she cried as she burst into the room, swinging around the corner so quickly she lost her balance and almost ate it completely.

"Watch it, Princess. Wouldn't want to mess up that pretty face of yours."

And there he was. Sitting there, propped up by two pillows, as if he'd just woken from a normal night's sleep.. He was pale, thin, and looked malnourished. His blue eyes were watery, and his hair was mussed. But he was there. Awake. Smiling.

She dove for him, throwing her arms around him, letting loose a floodgate of tears as the emotions swarmed her brain too fast and furious to catalog. For a moment, she couldn't speak. Couldn't move. Couldn't do anything but hold him in her arms, feeling his warmth.

So solid. So real. So alive.

So Caleb.

She managed to pull herself away, meeting his eyes with her own. His beautiful, storm-tossed eyes, wide-open and looking right at her. "They told me you'd never wake up," she rasped. "That you'd be locked in the Nether forever, just like Mom."

"Please. Underestimating me as always," he said with a snort. "As if a little Nether coma could keep me away from all the fun."

She swallowed hard, past the huge lump that had formed in her throat. It had been so long since she'd heard his voice, and yet at the same time, it felt like yesterday. "I never gave up on you," she assured him. "I watched over you, day and night." She didn't know why she was telling him this, only that she felt like she had to.

"Oh yeah? I bet my brother loved that," he said dryly.

Her smile faded. It had been so long since the two brothers had had their fight back at the hotel room in Colorado that she'd almost forgotten how things had left off between them. But evidently Caleb hadn't. And why should he? While

116

so much had happened to the rest of them since then—making the whole thing seem petty and stupid at this point—he'd been stuck in the Nether the whole time with nothing to do but stew over that horrible afternoon. And from the look on his face, she could tell the anger was still raw in his mind.

"Look, Caleb, about Connor," she tried gently. "He's really sorry about what happened between the two of you. And he's been really devoted to your recovery too—he's pretty much come by every day you've been here to make sure you're okay." Sure, that was partially due to her guilt-laden encouragement, but Caleb didn't need to know those pesky details. "Trust me, he's devastated about what happened to you."

"Yeah, I'm sure he's been terribly broken up about it," Caleb sneered. "Probably as broken as my nose after he sucker punched me the last time we hung out. Which reminds me," he added, "do you have a mirror? I'm dying to see the aftereffects of such brotherly devotion."

Trinity sighed. "You look fine."

"*Fine?* Just *fine*?" His mouth quirked. "Not so irresistibly hot that you can barely restrain yourself from jumping my bones and kissing me senseless?" He gave her a mock horrified look that made her want to laugh despite herself. "Then seriously, get me a mirror, woman! My nose must be simply hideous."

She rolled her eyes. "Your nose is perfect. Though I'm thinking your ego may still be a bit bulbous."

"Aw, Princess. Your flattery never fails to get me. It's one of the things I've missed most about being alive." He glanced down at his arms and legs. "Well, that and the food. Mother of mercy, look at me! I'm nothing but skin and bones." He looked up. "Nurse, get me to an all-you-can-eat buffet, stat."

"That I may be able to arrange," she told him with a small smile. "My father is a terrific cook. He'll fatten you up in no time."

Caleb's teasing grin fled from his face. He stared at her with excited eyes. "So you really did find your father," he said. "And he's actually here? Now? Does that mean Virgil is here too? Do they have a plan to save Emmy? God, I've missed a lot while I've been out, haven't I?"

"A few minor things," she agreed with a small snort. "And yes, my father's here. But Virgil is no longer with us. It's a long story, but let's just say their plan to save Emmy didn't exactly pan out. I mean, it would have, probably, if Emmy hadn't decided to bail at the last minute to play superdragon."

"Oh, Hot Wings. Always making it so hard on your poor Fire Kissed," Caleb said with an overexaggerated sigh. Then his expression turned serious. "Look, Trinity. All joking aside, I owe you a huge apology. The way I walked out on you that night at the hotel—after all you'd suffered, after all I had promised." He cringed. "I was so messed up at the time. So confused and angry and scared. And…addicted, I guess. Not that that excuses what I did but…" He paused for a moment, then added, "Let's just say I've had a lot of time to think about things while stuck in the Nether. And about what's really important to me." His blue eyes glowed as he spoke, broadcasting his earnestness. "And now that I've been given a second chance? Well, I'm not about to waste it. I'm here for you, Trinity. Whatever you need, I'm here for you."

Trinity smiled back at him, feeling both ridiculously happy and incredibly sad all at the same time. She'd missed him so much. More than she'd even realized. "We've all made mistakes," she assured him. "But the important thing is we're together now. And we can be a team again."

"I appreciate that," Caleb said sincerely. Then his mouth twisted. "I just hope my brother is as excited about my rising from the dead as you are. After all, I imagine the two of you have gotten pretty cozy over the last months, what with none of my irresistible charm to get in the way."

Trinity rolled her eyes. "Yeah, don't you know? We're totally married with kids at this point. Grandkids any day now."

In truth, her and Connor's so-called relationship had been strained at best after their argument over the Dracken's continued involvement in Emmy's life. Sure, they'd both officially apologized since then, but things had remained a bit awkward. Every time Trinity headed over to film one of Emmy's broadcasts, she could feel the disapproval in Connor's eyes. Which in turn made her defensive and quick to lash out.

Caleb sighed, shaking his head. "My brother, ladies and gentleman, the original pimp."

"Besides," Trinity scoffed, "from what I understand, you've been blasting that so-called irresistible charm of yours all over the Nether." When Caleb raised an eyebrow, she gave him a pointed look. "The name Scarlet ring any bells?"

Caleb blushed, turning away, but not before she caught a sheepish grin cross his face. So there *was* something going on between him and Scarlet. She felt her teasing smile falter a little as something uncomfortable wormed through her stomach. All this time, she realized, she'd been holding out hope that this

so-called romance between the two of them had all been a fig-
ment of Scarlet's overactive imagination. Evidently not so much.

And why shouldn't he, she scolded herself. *You pushed him
away. You told him nothing could happen between you. What did you
expect—that he would just sit and pine over you for all eternity?*

"Sorry," she said, feeling stupid. "I shouldn't have said
that. It's none of my business who you choose to date."

Now it was Caleb's turn to frown. "Date? Trin, you do realize
I've been a flecking vegetable for the last nine months, right?"

Her face burned. God, how deep a hole was she trying to
dig herself into anyway? "Right. I know. I mean… I'm just
saying, like, it's cool if you like her. Uh…not that you need my
permission, of course. But I'm just…"

Seriously, close your mouth and stop talking, Trin!

She felt Caleb staring at her, his eyes so piercing they
could probably burn through dragon scale, but she found she
couldn't look up—couldn't bear to see what she feared she'd
see on his face. Finally he spoke.

"Look," he said in a calm voice. "I'm not going to lie.
Scarlet and I—well, we got close when she came to me in the
Nether. I was dealing with a lot. Feeling like crap. Pretty much
ready to give up on it all. And then she walked in and…"

He trailed off, and Trinity finally dared take a peek at his
face. She could practically see the emotional conflict raging
inside of him. *He likes her*, she realized, a sinking feeling settling into her gut. He didn't want to admit it to her, but he
liked Scarlet a lot.

He caught her looking and masked his face. "Hell, what is
it they say?" he asked brightly. Too brightly. "What happens in
the Nether stays in the Nether?"

"I'm pretty sure that's Vegas," she muttered, trying to shove down the bile rising in her throat as her mind treated her to an all-too-detailed picture of Caleb making out with Scarlet in the Nether—his hands tangling in her hair, his mouth burning against Scarlet's lips.

Just as it had once burned against hers.

I've never taken anyone to the Nether, he'd told her. *No one but you.*

And now Scarlet. But hey, who's counting?

Frustration rose inside of her. At him for moving on. At herself for not wanting him to do so. The tears welled in her eyes, and she angrily swiped them away. Squaring her shoulders, she summoned up all the hardness she could muster. "Well, anyway, it's good to have you back," she said in a clipped tone. "I may need to call on you in a few days to help me with Emmy. You're the only real dragon guardian in this place, and I'm going to need all the help I can get to continue her rehab."

"Sure," he replied. "I can do that. I told you, whatever you need, I'm here for you. All you have to do is ask."

He made it seem so simple when, in truth, it was anything but.

"Okay. Great. Awesome," she mumbled, starting to back out of the room, unable to stay a moment longer. "Then I guess I'll…let you rest. I'll come by and check on you in the morning, okay?"

"I'll be counting the milliseconds."

She nodded, forcing herself to turn, to walk out the door, and to close it behind her before her mouth betrayed her any further. God, what was wrong with her? She'd been waiting all this time for Caleb to wake up. And now he had. She should be singing and dancing and telling everyone, "I told you so."

Instead, all she wanted to do was cry.

Lost in her thoughts, she turned the corner too fast, slamming into something hard and solid.

Make that some*one*.

She looked up, her cheeks flaming as she realized it was none other than Connor himself. He looked down at her, taking his hands and placing them on her shoulders to steady her, his beautiful blue eyes filled with concern.

"Are you okay?" he asked. "You're shaking. And you look like you've seen a ghost."

The weight of his hands on her shoulders felt unbearably heavy. As if he were purposely holding her down. "I'm fine," she assured him, hating how shaky her voice sounded as she said the words. "It's just…Caleb. Caleb's finally awake."

For a split second, his grip on her tightened, nails digging into her flesh so hard she had to stifle a cry of pain. Then he dropped his hands altogether. She could feel him staring down at her but found she couldn't meet his gaze.

"That's…great news," he said at last. "Really great."

Guilt washed over Trinity in waves, and it was all she could do to keep standing upright. "Yeah," she said, forcing her voice to stay steady. "I guess an 'I told you so' is in order?" she joked, desperate to lighten the mood.

"I suppose so," Connor replied vaguely, as if he didn't get the joke. Awkward silence fell over the two of them. He looked at her. She looked at the ground. Then she heard his sad-sounding sigh.

"I guess I should go talk to him," he said. "Do you want to come with me?"

"No!" She shook her head violently. Then she blushed.

"I mean, you guys have a lot to talk about. You shouldn't be distracted by me."

"You're never a distraction, sweetheart," he said, giving her a sad look.

She forced a thin smile. "We can talk later," she told him. "Right now, you should go see your brother. It's late. I've got to get to bed."

Before she could turn away, he reached up, cupping her chin in his hands and peering at her worriedly. His eyes were so blue. So damned blue. "I do love you, you know," he told her, his voice filled with earnest.

She smiled weakly. "I know."

Chapter Fifteen

Go talk to her, you coward!

Caleb hovered at the back of the restaurant, tray in hand, watching Scarlet pile yet another mountain of barbecue ribs on her plate. It was hard to believe someone as small as she was could put away so much food. The girl ate like a trucker. He supposed she was probably trying to make up for lost time—she couldn't have gotten much to eat in the government lab, judging by how skinny she was now.

He involuntarily thought back to how she'd felt when he'd held her in the Nether—soft curves in all the right places. Now she was all hard angles and sharp bones jutting out. Kind of like he himself, he supposed, glancing down at his own scrawny, pasty white body. These days it was hard to believe he and His Buffness—the great and powerful Connor—were identical twins.

The miracle Nether diet! Guaranteed to help you lose all your body fat in just one long sleep.

He watched as Scarlet thanked Trinity's father, then turned, her eyes scanning the restaurant where some of the Potentials were eating. No one made eye contact, he noticed, or waved her over to sit with them. But Scarlet didn't seem too broken up about this—if anything, he thought she looked relieved. She seemed to like to fly under the radar these days. He wondered at times why she even stuck around, since she didn't seem to have any friends in Team Dragon. Once upon a time, he would have assumed it was out of loyalty to Emmy. But Scarlet seemed to be avoiding the dragon these days as much as she avoided the others.

Go and talk to her. Now!

He sighed. He'd been trying to work up the nerve to approach her since that first night, when he'd been so eager to get caught up on their mission that he'd basically kicked her out of the room to talk to Trinity. And ever since then, she'd barely spoken a word to him, going out of her way to avoid him. Every day, he told himself he would pull her aside and talk to her about what happened between them in the Nether, yet every day, he ended up chickening out. And now it was like there was this big elephant in the room, and he didn't know what to do about it.

If only he hadn't kissed her. If only he'd stayed strong and resisted the urge. But she'd been so sweet, so passionate, so earnest in her attempts to save his worthless hide after everyone else had given up on him. He'd been so lonely, trapped in his icy cold prison, so desperate for the warm touch of another human being. And she'd been more than willing to give it to him.

Scarlet was beautiful. She was sweet and kind and thoughtful. Not to mention smart and resourceful. He hadn't forgotten the determined look she'd gotten in her eyes when she'd agreed to his crazy plan to go on the suicide mission. To take out armed guards and escape in the truck. To go warn Trinity and Connor the Dracken were on their way. Trinity, whether she wanted to admit it or not, owed this girl everything. And yet, how had she repaid this bravery and selflessness? By coercing Scarlet to hand herself over to the bad guys and spend the next six months being tortured and starved.

All because of me. If I hadn't been so weak. So pathetic. So addicted…

He felt a familiar rumble in his stomach, a prickling on the surface of his skin. He'd love to have blamed it on being hungry for lunch, but he knew that wasn't the case. This rumble, this prickle, this itch that could never be scratched—it was the pull of the Nether, creeping up on him again. A pull that would always be there, just beneath the surface, probably for the rest of his life.

He still had no idea how he'd escaped the Nether. He'd been there so damn long—there was no way he should have been able to come back to the real world unscathed like he had. Sure, maybe if Emmy had donated blood from her soft scale—maybe that would have done the trick—but Trinity had told him that the scale had been destroyed by the government, and the blood was all gone. Still, something must have been done to bring him back. So what was it? No one seemed to have any idea.

What about Scarlet? Could she possibly know something?

Caleb's gaze shifted back to the girl who was now walking her tray out of the restaurant, her eyes downcast and her shoulders slumped, as if she were trying hard not to be noticed. It seemed unlikely that she would have any clue as to why he'd recovered—she didn't even know that he was a time traveler, for goodness' sake. But still, it was she who had been there when he'd first opened his eyes. Maybe if she were able to give him a kind of play-by-play of what had happened just beforehand, maybe there would be some kind of clue.

And as a bonus, he could apologize to her—or at least make things less weird between them.

Making up his mind, he left the dinner line, ignoring his stomach's protest as he set his tray down on an empty table. Then, slipping back into the terminal's waiting room, he looked left and right, trying to figure out the direction she'd gone. Finally he located her at the end of the hall, silhouetted by the light streaming in through the doorway, dumping her dinner into a large sack. He watched, an uneasy feeling gnawing at his stomach—and this time it wasn't from hunger or any kind of addiction. What was she doing? Was she bringing the food to Emmy in the hangar? Once upon a time, that might have made sense, but these days, thanks to the donation box the Dracken kids had installed on the FreeEmmy.com website, the dragon had more than her share to eat. And besides, from what Caleb could tell, Scarlet and Emmy weren't really speaking anymore—as if something had gone down between them.

But if not for Emmy, then who? Some stray dog? A secret cat with kittens?

He watched as she slipped through the side door, closing it behind her. Then he followed, making sure to keep a safe distance. She crossed the runway and went past Emmy's hangar, seemingly headed to the very back of the property. Caleb trailed along behind her, ducking behind a broken-down plane when, at one point, she turned around. He held his breath as her eyes darted around the field, as if sensing she was being followed. He wondered if he should just show himself now; this was as good a place as any to have their talk, away from prying eyes. But something told him to wait, to see where she was going…and why.

Seemingly satisfied, she took off again, continuing down the field until she reached a dilapidated old shack at the far end of the runway, the kind that had probably been used to store lawn-mowers and other tools when this place was still operational. Caleb watched as Scarlet gave one last tentative look around, then slipped inside, pulling the door shut behind her.

What did she have in there? Now he was dying to find out. Heart in his throat, he tiptoed over to the shack and placed an ear to the door. He could hear Scarlet's soft murmuring coming from inside. And some kind of…cooing noises?

He pulled away, his eyes roving over the shack until he spotted a small crack in the left side. He ran over to it, cupping his hands over his eyes and peering inside.

And then he saw it. Or make that…them. He gasped.

"Oh my God," he whispered. "Those aren't… They couldn't be."

But of course they were.

Chapter Sixteen

Caleb stumbled backward as if he'd been shot, the shock of what he'd just seen more powerful than any lightning strike. Tripping over a rock, he lost his balance and hit the ground with a loud *oomph*.

So much for stealth maneuvering.

"Who's there?" demanded Scarlet from inside the shack, her voice filled with fear. Her head popped through the doorway, her wide eyes scanning the grounds. Caleb scrambled back to his feet, approaching her sheepishly.

"Hey, Buttercup," he said. "Sorry, guess I should have knocked first."

She stared at him, her face pure white. It would have been funny if it wasn't so bizarre. *Dragons*. Scarlet had baby dragons stashed in the maintenance shed. Dragons she'd evidently been feeding for weeks.

Where had they come from? Did the others have any clue they were here? No, of course they didn't. They couldn't.

He heard the dragons squawk with annoyance inside the shack. Probably anxious to get on with their dinners. Scarlet gave Caleb another stressed look then poked her head back into the shack. "What did I tell you about being quiet?" she scolded them.

The dragons fell silent instantly. Scarlet turned back to him. "I don't suppose asking you to walk away and forget you ever saw anything is an option, is it?" she asked.

He shook his head slowly. "I think we're probably beyond that point now."

She sighed then opened the door wider to allow him entrance. "Then welcome to the Dragon's Lair, I guess," she said reluctantly, gesturing for him to come in.

Caleb obliged, his whole body shaking as he stepped into the darkened shack. Once his eyes adjusted to the dim lighting, he examined each dragon closely. One was black as night with gold-flecked scales. The other was a rare pink color with purple-veined wings. Both were still very small—about the size of a couple of puppies.

He reached a tentative hand out to the pink dragon. She chirped nervously then skittered back behind her brother. The black dragon huffed at Caleb, putting a protective wing around his sister as he puffed out the tiniest cloud of smoke from his little nose, as if to say "Just try it, duffer."

Caleb let out a small laugh despite himself. It'd been a long time since he'd been around any baby dragons besides Emmy. He'd almost forgotten how cute they could be when they tried to act all fierce.

He turned back to Scarlet, who was watching him with a strained expression on her face—as if she was *this close* to grabbing the two dragons and trying to make a run for it.

"Well…?" he asked.

"Please don't tell the others," she managed to squeak.

"That's all you have to say?" He stared at her for a moment, then back at the dragons, who were now tussling over a small overcooked rib. "Come on, Scarlet. How about a little back-story here? Where on earth did you find them? How long have you had them? Why are you hiding them here, and why don't you want anyone else to know?"

She bit her lower lip then sank to her knees, continuing to dole out the food. For a moment, he thought she might not answer him at all. Then she spoke. "They're Emmy's children," she said quietly. "The pink one is Zoe and the black is Zavier. They were living in a cave about ten miles from here. From what I can figure, Emmy must have gone there to lay her eggs after we broke her out of the government lab. That's why she was MIA for two months."

Caleb drew in a breath. Unbelievable. Yet, at the same time, undeniable. "So you just decided to bring them here?" he asked. "And you've been hiding them here ever since?"

She shrugged, dropping her gaze to the floor. "I didn't know what else to do."

Suddenly Caleb could feel sharp eyes upon him, and he turned back to the dragons. Zavier had stopped eating and was now peering up at him curiously with a wise, old gaze that belied his young years. There was a heartbeat pause, then Caleb heard it—a voice, whispering across his consciousness. The type of voice he'd believed he'd never hear again.

Are you my Guardian?

His eyes widened. He stared at the dragon. Then at Scarlet. And just like that, all the puzzle pieces slid into perfect place.

"You gave me his blood," he realized aloud. "Emmy couldn't do it, but her babies could. The blood from his scale was what broke me out of the Nether."

Scarlet nodded slowly, still looking a little frightened. "I'm sorry—I didn't know what else to do," she confessed. "They told me it'd take a miracle to wake you. And that made me think of *my* miracle, when Emmy healed me back at the cave. I didn't know if it would work, if it was even the same kind of thing. But I had to try."

Caleb looked down at her, everything inside of him softening. Pretty much the entire Team Dragon—besides Trinity maybe—had given up on the idea of him ever gaining consciousness. Except for Scarlet. And Scarlet had not only not given up, but she'd made sure it actually happened. Why hadn't she told him what she'd done for him? God, now he *really* felt like an ungrateful bastard.

"Well, I'm very glad you did," he said softly, reaching down to touch her shoulder. Scarlet winced as his hand brushed against her bare skin, and she quickly scooted forward, out of his reach, with the pretense of gathering up Zoe into her arms.

"It was no big deal," she muttered. "I'm sure *Trinity* would have done the same."

The hurt in her voice as she spoke Trinity's name was sharp and bleak. Caleb closed his eyes for a moment, hating himself all over again.

"Well, she didn't," he reminded her hoarsely. "You did. And for that, I owe you a great debt of thanks."

"I don't need your thanks," she replied. "I just need you to keep my secret. I can't have anyone knowing the dragons are here."

"What about Emmy?" he asked, glancing around the shack as if the mother dragon could be lurking in the shadows. "Are they a secret from her as well?"

"*Especially* her!" Scarlet cried, turning to him, her eyes wide with what could only be described as pure terror. "She can never know I brought them here. If she found out…"

"I don't understand," he protested. This didn't make any sense. "If they're her children… Scarlet, why would you want to keep her children from her?"

Scarlet drew in a breath. "Because the last time she saw her children, she asked me to kill them." She paused, then added, "And…well, it's possible she might be under the impression that I already did."

"What?" Caleb swallowed hard, not sure what to say. "Why would she want you to do that? That doesn't make any sense."

"You're right," Scarlet said gloomily. "It doesn't make any sense at all. The only thing I can figure is that Emmy's not really right in the head these days, not after what they did to her in the government lab. She was abused, probably impregnated against her will—maybe even without her knowledge. And, well, now she has this crazy idea that these sweet little baby dragons are going to grow up and destroy the world." She frowned, reaching out to chuck Zoe under her chin. "Which is completely ridiculous, of course. Isn't it, baby girl?"

Caleb stared at Scarlet, then at the dragon, a cold chill suddenly spinning down his spine.

Oh God.

That actually wasn't ridiculous at all.

In fact, it made perfect sense.

He watched as Zoe leapt from Scarlet's arms to playfully tackle her brother, who had managed to find another half-eaten rib. Sure, they looked innocent now. But would they stay that way? If Emmy had really been impregnated by the government—and he didn't see how else it could have happened—could these two dragons be the same genetically engineered hybrids that were destined to set the world on fire once they hit puberty?

Scarlet wouldn't know about this, of course. No one would have mentioned the pesky little time-travel details of their mission to her—or of the dragon apocalypse that was forever looming. All she had to go on when it came to dragons was Emmy herself. She had absolutely no idea the possible ramifications of keeping these two creatures alive.

His heart pounded uncomfortably in his chest. "So, what, then?" he asked, trying to keep his voice steady. "You're just planning to raise these guys on your own?"

"What choice do I have?" she shot back, the fear in her voice retreating, replaced by anger. "I mean, just look at the poor little things. Abandoned by their mother for no good reason. Just like…" She trailed off, looking from dragon to dragon, her eyes misting. "Anyway, I don't care what Emmy thinks. Zoe and Zavier are not evil. I know they're not."

The fierceness in her voice made Caleb's heart squeeze. His mind involuntarily flashed to Fred, his own dragon. Sweet, goofy Fred, whose only crime had been devouring too many ham bones at dinner. Connor had assumed Fred evil too. And he'd mercilessly slaughtered her without bothering to find out if this assumption was true.

But still… Caleb set his lips together. "No offense, Scarlet," he said. "But how can you be sure? I mean, if their own mother believes them to be bad…"

She looked up at him, her eyes beseeching. "Because the cave wasn't the first place I'd seen them," she admitted. "I met them before—in the Nether—when I was coming to look for you." Her face heated in a blush, and Caleb swallowed heavily.

"They picked me up and flew me to your sky house," she explained. "They told me they were Emmy's children, waiting to be born. Without their help, I never would have found you. Which means I never would have been able to break out of that truck to go find Trinity and Connor either. Which means," she continued, her voice rising, "Trinity would have let Connor shoot Emmy, and she would be dead now." Her voice broke with frustration. "Emmy owes these baby dragons her very life…whether she wants to admit it or not. And now…so do you," she added, gesturing to Zavier.

Caleb forced a nod, his mind whirling with indecision. These dragons could be hybrids. By all rights, they *should* be hybrids—with history replicating itself in the government lab. And if they were hybrids? Well, Emmy wouldn't be wrong in wanting them dead.

But then again, what if they weren't?

He considered this for a moment. After all, this wasn't like the last time. Not exactly, anyway. This time, the Dracken were in the picture. Mara was working side by side with the government scientists. She was a dragon expert. She could have saved some DNA or sperm from the dragons they'd brought back from the future. Sure, those dragons had been mutated and deformed because of the time travel. But they were still purebloods. And if Zoe and Zavier really were the progeny of that particular type of pairing? Well, that would make them purebloods too.

He knew what he should have been doing. He should have been marching out of the shack right then and reporting everything he'd seen to Trinity and Connor and the rest of Team Dragon. Then, once everyone knew the facts, they could discuss it like rational people and figure out what to do about this little…wrinkle in their plans.

And yet, his feet stayed glued to the floor. Mostly because he knew already, without even taking a step, exactly what his brother would say. What the rest of them would say. No one was going to want to risk rearing these babies to puberty just to find out for sure—it was too dangerous, they'd argue. There was far too much risk. They'd worked so hard to try to save the world. They weren't about to let two scaled, ticking time bombs have the opportunity to go off now.

But what if they were wrong and Scarlet was right? What if these two dragons were the first purebloods to be naturally born into this new world? What if, with the right care and respect, they'd grow into law-abiding dragons like Emmy, instead of monsters ready to burn down the world? All the gifts they could bring mankind. Unlike Emmy, they still had their soft scales. Their blood could be studied, made into medicine—possibly bring about the cure for cancer.

He thought of his mother, how dragon's blood had saved her life. How many more potential lives could be saved by allowing these two dragons to live? It was the very reason he'd agreed to come back in time in the first place. He'd wanted to save the world.

Could these dragons be the key to doing it?

Caleb felt movement against his leg and opened his eyes. Zavier had approached him and was pushing his little snout against his knee. Against his better judgment, he found himself dropping to the creature's level, putting out his hand, an ache rising inside of him as he felt the warm dragon breath tickling his palm. Then he reached out, stroking Zavier behind the ear, in the very same spot Fred had always liked best.

Zavier looked up at him with happy puppy-dog eyes, and pleasurable noises gurgled from his throat. Caleb's heart panged with a mixture of sorrow and joy, a new thought whispering across his mind. If this actually worked... If the dragons truly were pure...

He could have his own dragon again.

He could have a second chance.

Once upon a time, he'd failed to save Fred. He'd watched helplessly as his brother struck her down. But this time—this time, it could be different. He could be in control. He could keep Scarlet's secret, and the two of them could observe the dragons until they hit puberty. He knew what to look for; the Dracken had taught him well. And if they did start to show signs of hybridity, he knew how to take them down.

He realized Scarlet was still watching him, a worried look on her face. Her hands wringing together in front of her as she waited for what he was going to say.

"Come on," he said. "These two guys are filthy. Let me show you the proper way to clean their scales. And then," he added, giving Zavier a knowing look, "we'll work on some proper food gathering. The way they're growing, there's no way they'll be content living off cafeteria scraps for long."

Scarlet's face broke out into a look of pure joy. She threw her arms around Caleb, squeezing him tightly. "Thank you!" she cried, the tears raining down her cheeks and onto his shoulders. "Thank you so much. I was so scared to tell anyone after the way Emmy acted. But it's been so much work—I'm so glad to not have to do it on my own anymore."

"I know," he assured her. "And I'm happy to help. But you're right not to mention anything to the others. At least not right now. They might not understand."

"I won't say a word," she promised, her eyes shining. She left him to reach down for Zoe again, cuddling the dragon in her arms. "Come on, baby girl. We're going to give you a bath."

Zoe cooed and nipped playfully at her ear, causing Scarlet to giggle. The sound was like a ray of light bouncing happily around the room. And Caleb couldn't help a small smile of his own as a warmth settled in his stomach.

Yes, this was the right thing to do. The only thing to do.

He looked down at Zavier, then held out his arm. The dragon flapped his little black wings, fluttering up and perching himself on Caleb's shoulder, his sharp nails digging into his skin. Caleb gave him a small pat on his feet.

"I guess it's me and you, Sparky," he said. "Just don't make me sorry I saved your ass, okay?"

Zavier croaked in response, burping a small ball of fire and singeing the hairs on Caleb's neck.

He groaned and shook his head. *Dragons.* Then he laughed. "Fine. I'll take that as a yes."

PART 3:

SMOLDER

Chapter Seventeen

The Council Chambers—Year 190 Post-Scorch

T he Council will see you now."
Connor looked up from his reader, meeting the eyes
of the assistant who was leaning in the doorway to the inner
sanctum. She smiled and made a gesture for him to follow
her. Rising from his seat, he walked through the doorway and
into the smooth, circular hallway that glowed with phosphorescent light. A few feet ahead of him, the assistant used her
remote to open airlock door after airlock door as they passed
through. The Council chambers were not only more than
a mile underground, but they were also completely disaster
proof. Rumor had it they had enough food, water, and beds
inside for the entire council to sit out a nuclear winter if the
situation demanded it.

"Have you ever been here before?" the assistant asked,
keeping a brisk pace. Connor had to practically jog to keep
up with her.

"No," he admitted. "I'm more of an in-the-trenches kind
of guy," he added with a sheepish grin. "Politics really isn't
my thing."

"Mine either," the girl confessed, giving him a sly sideways glance. He hadn't realized at first how young she was. Tall, slender, pretty, with stick-straight brown hair that hung long down her back. "But it's a job and it puts food on the table. Also, there's the scholarship."

"Scholarship?"

"To the Academy, of course," she said as if it were obvious. "So someday I can train to be a Hunter just like you."

He masked a cringe as he caught sight of her shining eyes, her face glowing with ambition. It took everything he had not to grab her and shake her and tell her what a bad idea that was. That if she were smart, she'd stay here, deep below the surface of the world, where she was safe as a person could be. She had a job—a good one at that. She probably even qualified for Council housing, which was usually located in the best stratas. Why would anyone want to give that up for a dangerous, dirty surface job like his?

Because she doesn't know what it's really like, he reminded himself. *She only knows what the Council tells her.*

"This is a little embarrassing to admit," the girl added, her cheeks coloring prettily. "But I still have your rookie card. My father won it playing Jongu down in Shanty Town a couple years ago. It's pretty torn up, and my mom thinks it's probably a fake. But I don't care. I still like looking at it, imagining you boys up there, fighting with everything you have to save our world." She giggled. "Anyway, like I said, if I'm lucky, maybe someday I'll get to join you up there."

"That would be stellar," Connor replied, mostly because that was what she expected him to say. What the Council insisted on being said. And hey, far be it from him to dissuade people from joining their ranks—they could use all the Hunters they could get. Still, something deep down wished he could persuade her to take another path—*any* other path than his.

"Here we are!" she chirped brightly, stopping in front of a pair of ornately carved, gold-trimmed doors. "The Inner Circle." She grinned conspiratorially at him. "Good luck in there. I'll be here waiting to escort you back when you're finished. And maybe…" She paused, fidgeting a little. "We could go get a drink or something afterward? I'd love to hear about all your adventures on the Surface Lands. I've never been, myself, of course. But it seems so *interesting*."

He sighed. "Sure, I guess, maybe," he said. "Let me get through this first, okay?"

She nodded, then reached up and pressed a hand to his shoulder. It was a simple gesture, and it should have felt friendly. But to Connor, it only felt invasive.

You belong to the people, his sergeant had scolded numerous times. *You gave up private life the second you donned the Academy uniform.*

It was true. But that didn't mean he had to like it.

He gave her a farewell nod, then turned to the doorway and stepped through. The Council chamber was cavernous—with at least a fifty-foot ceiling. Tall ceilings were a rare luxury in a world that had had to be carved out of solid rock. He wondered if this had been some sort of cave they'd found and finished off or if they'd built it from scratch.

He looked around, taking in all the ornate decorations, the wooden benches and chairs. Wood was almost impossible to gather these days, what with the dragons having decimated the world's trees. Only a few heavily guarded forests grew in special greenhouse glass structures, and many had lost their lives protecting the Glades. The Council had justified this by claiming wood was necessary in certain medicines and weapons. But here, in this room, it just seemed like a waste.

And then there was the food. Mountains of it, piled high on almost every available surface. And not just the genetically engineered rations that everyone else ate on a daily basis, but real, unprocessed meats and cheeses and breads and sweets. Just looking at them made his mouth water—and his stomach churn. There was enough food here to feed half the Dragon Hunter army. Was it really just meant for these twelve people?

"There he is! Our man of the hour!"

Connor reluctantly turned away from the feast to focus on the front of the room. There, behind a long, carved wooden table set high on a dais, sat all twelve members of the Council, looming above like giant gods, ready to deliver blessings or curses to any who dared step into their inner sanctum. Connor swallowed heavily.

They're just people, he tried to remind himself. *No different than me or anyone else.*

But that wasn't true. Not exactly. These were people with power.

He sucked in a breath and cleared his throat. "Thank you for seeing me," he said, hating how nervous and hoarse his voice sounded.

"Please. It is *us* who should be thanking *you*," declared the councilman at the center of the table. His name plaque read "Solomon." "I hear you saved us from quite a potential disaster this week, while the rest of your comrades were across the strata at the Peace Parade."

Connor had wondered if they were going to reprimand him for skipping out on the so-called Peace Parade as he had. But evidently they were willing to overlook the infraction, due to his eventual heroics.

"I was just doing my job," he replied stiffly. "I was fortunate enough to be able to sing the five into stasis until the others could arrive to finish them off."

"So modest too," cooed the woman to Solomon's left—Frederica, according to her nameplate. "A rare quality for a Dragon Hunter." She laughed, and the fat under her chin jiggled. Then she raised her fist in the air. "What is it you say again? *Hasta la vista*—?" She looked at him expectantly, and he blushed.

"Hasta la vista, dragon spawn," he muttered.

The Council laughed and cheered at this. Connor contemplated crawling under the table in embarrassment. But he forced himself to stand strong. He was a soldier. He'd come here on a mission. And he wouldn't let these people intimidate him.

"So, Dragon Hunter," Solomon said after the room had quieted. "I'm sure you didn't come all this way to listen to a bunch of old men and women sing your praises. What can we do for you?"

Connor cleared his throat. This was it. "I wanted to report a violation of the Flame Shelter Act of PS One Fifty-Three."

Solomon glanced at his fellow councilmembers, then back to Connor. "And what might this violation be?"

"As you know, the rules state no one should be turned away from a shelter unless they're at full capacity, regardless of race or religion or economic status," Connor continued, his voice growing stronger and more confident as he spoke. "But when I tried to bring a little girl to Negative twenty-three during the attack, the guards at the door attempted to turn us away, even though they were clearly not at capacity."

"The guards tried to turn *you* away?" the man to Frederica's left broke in, raising an eyebrow.

"They didn't know who I was," Connor admitted. "But that's not the point. According to the law, they shouldn't have turned me away regardless of my rank." He drew in a breath. "It is my belief they are accepting bribes as payment for entrance to keep the crowds down. Which, I think you'll agree, is a clear violation of the statute."

He scanned their faces, searching for some sign of horror or offense that people could be doing such a thing to their fellow man. But the Council remained impassive, their expressions unreadable.

"Thank you for your report, soldier," Solomon said at last. "We shall look into it, and I assure you, justice will be served."

"Thank you," Connor said, shuffling from foot to foot. "That's all I ask." He bit his lower lip. "Except…"

"Yes, soldier?"

"The little girl I told you about. Salla. She couldn't find her parents, which is why I brought her down to Neg twenty-three in the first place. But when I came back after the fight, I couldn't find her among the others. And when I asked around, no one seemed to remember her ever being there to begin with." He frowned. "I wanted to make sure she got back to her family all right."

And that the bastards didn't kick her out the second I walked away, he wanted to add but didn't.

Frederica reached for her transcriber and dragged her long, painted fingernail across its side to wake it. Then she pressed at the screen a few times before looking back up. "Is this the girl you're talking about?" she asked, holding up the device for Connor to see.

He took a step forward, squinting at the hologram. "Yes," he replied eagerly. "That's her. That's Salla. Is she…?"

Frederica gave him an apologetic look. "I'm sorry, Connor. It appears she didn't make it."

"What?" he asked, ice spinning down his back. "What do you mean, didn't make it?"

Frederica looked down at the transcriber again. "From what this says, she was found near the Surface Lands after the strike. It looks like she was one of several casualties that day."

"But that's impossible! She should have been a mile underground!" Connor protested, fury warring with fear.

Solomon shrugged. "Perhaps she left."

"Or *perhaps* those guards forced her out once I turned my back," he returned, the fury gaining dominance. "God, she was only a little girl." He scanned the Council, desperate for an ounce of sympathy. Compassion. Humanity. But all he saw were blank, expressionless faces.

And why not? he thought with sickening dread. She *was* only a little girl, as he himself had just pointed out. People died every day. Dozens. Sometimes hundreds. The Council couldn't possibly allow itself to care too much for just one more dead little girl.

But Connor could. And he would.

He squeezed his eyes shut, remembering her grubby face, the way she'd held up her trading card and stared at him with wide, worshipping eyes. He'd been her hero. And despite his best efforts, he'd let her down.

"Those guards—they should be arrested. Punished. Stripped of their posts," he cried, squeezing his hands into fists and taking a step forward.

"Now, now, calm down, Mr. Jacks," Solomon said sternly, holding up a hand to stop him. "There's no need to get upset. We appreciate you making your report and are very sorry about your friend. I know it must be devastating news to hear. But I promise you, we have taken down all of your information, and we will take appropriate measures."

Connor wanted to believe them. He really, really did. "Okay," he said limply, feeling the fight drain from him. "That's all I can ask. I appreciate you taking the time to hear me."

"And *we* appreciate you taking the time to come here and tell us," cooed Frederica in a saccharine-sweet voice. "Now go, Dragon Hunter, and continue to fight the good fight. And know that we at the Council are watching and applauding you from afar."

"Right. Thank you," he muttered, forcing himself to turn toward the door. It was all he could do not to run from the room, frustrated tears cascading down his face. Instead, he pushed his shoulders back and puffed out his chest. He was a soldier, after all. A goddamned hero. "Good-bye," he managed to say.

He'd almost made it to the door when he heard the whisper.

"Yes, he will be perfect. Just perfect."

But perfect for what, he had no idea. And he had too much pride to turn around to ask.

Chapter Eighteen

Present Day—Five Months Later

S o you're sure this won't hurt them?" Scarlet asked, giving Zoe a doubtful look. "You're sure they're big enough now?"

"Are you kidding me?" Caleb grinned. "They're practically the size of Clydesdales." He slapped Zavier affectionately on his front flank. "And trust me, they're ready. Just look at how excited they are."

Zavier puffed two twin balls of smoke from his nostrils as if to confirm his guardian's words. And Zoe pranced around, barely able to keep all four feet on the ground as Scarlet attached the makeshift saddle to her back.

"Poor Zoe! Is the mean man calling you fat?" she cooed. "That's no way to speak to a lady!" She shot Caleb a mock offended look. "You go on and tell him, you're just big boned!"

Caleb snorted, turning back to his own big-boned beast and slapping a hand against his left flank. All joking aside, it was hard to believe how fast the two dragons had grown in the last five months. When Emmy had been their age, she'd only been the size of a large dog. Zoe and Zavier were probably double that size now—growing strong and sleek and tall.

At first, the rapid growth had worried him a bit; according to Dracken research, a quick growth spurt could be a sign of hybridity. At the same time, some subspecies of dragons were just quicker to mature than others, so it could have just been something they'd inherited from their unknown father.

Besides, he thought as he secured the saddle to Zavier, if they really were hybrids, they'd be showing other signs by now. Instead, the two dragons were gentle, friendly, with none of the food aggression or antisocial behavior one would expect from hybrids, and they took orders without question. Zoe was a lover, not a fighter, always doting on her brother and making sure he had everything he needed. And Zavier, while fiercely protective of his sister, was a total marshmallow under his tough, ebony scales. In fact, when Caleb had gone and killed a mouse in front of him the other day, the dragon had been so horrified that Caleb had been forced to laughingly apologize for his unprovoked violence against rodents. He was pretty sure if Zavier ever found out where meat truly came from, he might end up becoming the first dragon vegetarian.

Caleb tugged on the saddle, making sure it was secure. Then he turned to Scarlet, who was struggling to climb aboard Zoe without much luck, her feet slipping on the dragon's sleek scales.

"Watch and learn, young grasshopper," he teased, then turned back to Zavier, requesting the dragon lower his wing as they'd practiced. The beast obliged, and Caleb scrambled up the wing on all fours, then swung his leg over to straddle the dragon's back, settling down into the saddle between Zavier's neck and wings. As he shifted in his seat to find the sweet spot, he couldn't help a small smile. God, it felt good to

SMOKED

be on the back of a dragon again. He glanced over at Scarlet, catching her admiring eyes. He felt his face heat.

"I know, I know. It's hard to even watch such supreme dragon mastery, isn't it?"

She rolled her eyes. "Actually, it's your supreme humility that gets me every time."

Caleb laughed, watching her as she followed his lead and successfully mounted her own dragon. The two of them had fallen into a comfortable pattern over the last five months, and the awkwardness had all but faded between them. In fact, at times, it almost felt as if they had their own little secret family, and he found himself looking forward to waking up in the morning to sneak out of the terminal to meet her. They'd go hunting at the crack of dawn, before the others awoke, and return to the maintenance shack to deliver breakfast to their hungry brood. Then they'd head back to the terminal to try to sneak in midmorning naps before tackling the daily Team Dragon chores. Sometimes at night, they'd sneak out again while the others worked to put together the evening Emmy broadcast, to allow the dragons a supervised fly in a large crater they'd found about a mile away from the airfield, far from any prying eyes.

"How was that, oh great Dragon Master?" Scarlet teased.

He smiled. "Like you were born to be a guardian."

A flush of pride colored her cheeks, and it made him happy to see it. When they'd first started this adventure, she'd been so nervous and stressed, always worried she wasn't doing something right, that they'd be discovered by the others—or worse, by the government. But as the dragons had grown, so had her confidence, and the haunted look had lifted from

151

her eyes. In fact, these days, she was more likely to be laughing and smiling at something Zoe did or said than crying in a corner.

And she wasn't the only one. Caleb had to admit good clean living had done wonders for his own physical and mental health. Being outside had brought the color back to his skin, and while he might never be quite as buff as his brother, he'd filled out nicely from all the physical labor dragon guardianship entailed. More importantly, he could barely remember the last time he felt the pull of the Nether. Real life was too interesting these days, he supposed.

He looked down at Zavier. *Are you ready for this, Big Boy?*

Please. Zavier puffed out his chest and belched up a few sparks. *I was born ready!*

You were born a scrawny little pipsqueak, Caleb teased. *But we'll let you live with the fantasy.* He glanced over at Scarlet. "On your mark, Buttercup."

She grinned, looking both nervous and excited. "Get set..."

"GO!" they both cried in unison.

The dragons burst from the shack, launching off their back feet and leaping into the night sky, their leathery wings claiming the air currents and beating them into submission. It was zero to sixty faster than any sports car, and though Caleb tried his best to look cool, calm, and collected—as if this were just another Tuesday—inside, his pulse was racing and his stomach was flip-flopping madly. It'd been so long since he'd been on the back of a dragon in real life. He'd almost forgotten how exhilarating it could be.

The night was dark, with heavy cloud cover over the moon and stars. Caleb had insisted they wait for a night like this, to make sure they were able to fly unseen. It was a bit colder than he would have preferred, however, and the icy wind whipped at his face without mercy. But he didn't care. He was flying a dragon again. *His* dragon. Talk about a dream come true.

"Oh my God, this is AH-MAZ-ING!" Scarlet squealed from somewhere nearby, though he couldn't see her through the clouds. His heart warmed at the joy he heard in her voice. Like him, she'd suffered so much. And now, like him, she was finally free.

How does it feel? he asked, switching to mind speak to be better heard over the rush of wind.

Like I've died and gone to heaven, she replied blissfully. *I thought I'd be scared, but I just feel so good. Like…I don't know…I was born to do this or something.*

Caleb smiled. *Maybe you were.*

They cut across the sky, dipping and soaring and weaving in and out of the clouds, Zoe and Zavier teasing one another as they danced their dragon dance. Caleb was pretty sure the two dragons were having as much fun as he and Scarlet were, which meant they were having quite a lot of fun indeed.

In case I didn't tell you lately, you're pretty awesome, he told Zavier, slapping him playfully on the neck. The dragon turned to him, lifting a skeptical eyelid.

As awesome as the legendary Fred?

Caleb gave him a scolding look. *Now, now, let's not get crazy here.*

But even as he teased the dragon, he knew the truth. While Fred would always have a special place in his heart, Zavier had already proven himself a worthy successor. For the first time since he could remember, Caleb felt a strange sort of peace about his first dragon's death, and he liked to imagine that Fred was looking down from the Nether, smiling at him (while chomping down on a huge steak bone, of course!), happy to see her guardian moving forward with his life.

They found a rocky campsite a few miles away, atop a small desert mountain. Once on the ground, they dismounted their dragons and found a few boulders to sit on while Zoe and Zavier curled up around one another, tails entwined as they set out to clean each other's scales with their long, black tongues. *Silly creatures*, Caleb thought, *really not much different than overgrown house cats.*

He sighed contentedly, stretching out his legs in front of him and his hands above his head. "If only we were in the Nether now," he remarked. "I could conjure us up a nice fire and roast us some marshmallows—really make this night perfect."

But Scarlet only shook her head, lying down on her back and staring up at the sky. "It already is perfect, Caleb," she said.

He looked down at her, at her simple unguarded face. At the contentedness sparkling in her dark eyes. Warmth flooded his stomach again. She was right. This was perfect.

And so was she.

He closed his eyes. How easy it would be for him to just crawl over there now, to take her into his arms and pull her to him, their mouths and bodies coming together in mutual heat. Scarlet, he knew, would never push him away. She'd never call him a distraction. She would never make him feel even the tiniest bit unworthy of her love.

He stifled a groan. Was this how Trinity had felt when he'd gone and kissed her in the Nether? At the time, he couldn't fathom how she could just pull away like she had—deny all that was so obvious between them. Now he was beginning to understand how it felt to be conflicted.

He could kiss Scarlet now. He could kiss her for hours and hours, never bothering to come up for air. And she would sigh under his mouth, and she would pull him to her, and they would tangle up in one another until they lost track of where one of them ended and the other began.

He had no doubt it would be wonderful.

But it wouldn't be fair.

He could kiss Scarlet. He could probably allow himself to love Scarlet. But he couldn't give her everything. That small part of his heart that still belonged to Trinity and always would—he couldn't surrender that. Even to someone as wonderful as her. He'd made Trinity a promise to always be there for her. Which meant he couldn't afford to be distracted.

And if he couldn't give Scarlet everything, was it fair to offer her anything at all? Or would he only end up hurting her more than he could bear? He thought back to the second time he'd met Trinity in the Nether—how distraught he'd been, how hopeless he'd felt. She'd gone to kiss him, and he'd pushed her away. Because he knew she would never be able to truly feel for him what he felt for her.

You'll just make it harder, he had told her. *And it's so hard already.*

Scarlet had been through so much. So many people in her life had betrayed her trust. He couldn't be one of those people, couldn't bear to see hurt in her eyes and know he was to blame.

You think you want me, he thought bitterly. *But I'm the last person to deserve someone like you.*

"Earth to Caleb. Come in, Caleb!"

He startled, looking up to find her hovering over him, her

face drawn in concern. God, she really was beautiful though. In another life. In another world…

"Yeah, sorry." He sat up, shaking himself. "Sometimes I still get a little spacy. Side effects of all that Nether time." The night air bit at him, and he shivered involuntarily.

Scarlet gave him a sympathetic look. She pulled her sweater over her head and held it out to him before he could stop her. "Take it," she urged. "It probably won't fit you, but you could put it over you like a blanket or something."

"Are you calling me fat?" His mouth quirked.

"Nah, you're just big boned."

He took the jacket, laughing. "Won't you be cold?"

"I'm never cold. My grandmother always used to say I was born with fire in my blood."

"Hm. Maybe that's why you're so good with the dragons."

Even in the dim light, he could see her blush. "Do you think I'm good with them?" she asked hopefully. "I'm always afraid I'm going to do the wrong thing and screw them up for life or something."

He shook his head. "Are you kidding me? Just look at them. They're strong; they're healthy; they're happy. What more could you want in a dragon?"

She nodded, watching them with affection. "I guess you're right. And they have each other too. That's the most important thing. Emmy always seems so lonely." She gave the dragons a wistful look. "Though I guess it's her fault. I mean, if she had just given them a chance, then she could have seen how kind and gentle they are. There's no way these two softies could ever burn down the world. Zoe barely manages to burn her food before eating it."

Caleb laughed. "I agree," he said. He paused, then added gently, "Which brings me to something I wanted to talk to you about."

Chapter Nineteen

W hat is it?" Scarlet asked, trying to ignore the sudden flip-flopping of her stomach at Caleb's unexpected words. She didn't know why, but for some reason, she had a distinct feeling she wasn't going to like what he was about to say.

For a moment, he didn't answer, which only served to heighten her nerves. Finally, he cleared his throat. "I think it might be time for these guys to become acquainted with Team Dragon."

"What?" she cried before she could stop herself. Then she shook her head, staring at him incredulously. Tell Team Dragon about Zoe and Zavier? How could he even suggest such a thing?

"Absolutely not," she declared. "I mean, there's no way. After all, Emmy thinks I killed them months ago. What is she going to say when she learns they're still alive?"

And more importantly, she thought but didn't say aloud, *what would she do?*

She thought back to Emmy's cold eyes as her gaze rested on her children. How Zoe's hopeful face had crumbled as the mother dragon turned her back on them. The sound of

Zavier's dismayed whine as his mother flew off, leaving them essentially orphans. Scarlet squared her shoulders. No way was she about to put her dragons through that kind of rejection again. After all, she knew far too well what it felt like.

Caleb gave her a sympathetic look. "Don't get me wrong," he said. "You've done an amazing job raising them up until this point. But even you have to admit it's getting to be too much. We need help. They're eating more than the two of us can hunt for each day. Soon they'll have outgrown the maintenance shack. Where are we going to hide them then?"

"I know…but…"

"It takes a village to raise a dragon, Buttercup," he said in a gentle voice. "We should be thankful we have a village to fall back on. With all the people donating to Emmy's cause these days, they have, like, unlimited funds. Zoe and Zavier could eat like kings and queens—versus the pitiful scraps we're able to scrounge for them now."

She squeezed her hands into fists. "But Emmy—"

"Emmy is their mother. Once she sees that they're good dragons, that they're not a threat to anyone, she's going to have to accept them as her own. I know she will." Caleb smiled. "I mean, look at them. Who could not love these big fire-breathing dorks once they got to know them?"

Scarlet shot a glance over at Zoe and Zavier, her heart panging in her chest. Zoe was doing a goofy little show-off dance as Zavier chirped his approval, flapping his wings in time to her steps. She sighed. She wanted so badly for Caleb to be right. But still… "You're sure?" she asked, turning back to him. "You're absolutely sure? It would kill me if something were to happen to them."

"I know. But I've already figured this out. As you know, tomorrow is the anniversary party—to celebrate six months of Emmy being on air. They're doing this huge celebration and live streaming it across the world. From what Luke was telling me, they sold over four million subscriptions to the online event."

"And...?"

"And so everyone will be tuning in. They'll get to see the joyous mother and baby reunion, broadcasted live." He grinned, looking proud of himself. "Don't you see? There's no way Emmy will be able to just turn her back on her babies then. Not with everyone watching. She'll have to give them a chance—at least for the cameras. And then, once she actually interacts with them, she's going to realize how awesome they are."

"And if she doesn't?"

"Then the rest of the world will," Caleb pointed out. "And Trinity and Team Dragon will have to accept them too or risk having their fans turn on them." His eyes sparkled his excitement; he'd obviously been conjuring up this idea for some time now. "And again, once they get to know them and realize they're no more a threat than Emmy is, they'll welcome them into the fold."

"I guess that makes sense," she said slowly, still feeling a nervousness crawling through her stomach. "Still, why now? I mean five months ago, you were just as concerned as I was about keeping them a secret. What's changed your mind?"

He gave her a sheepish look. "I wanted to wait until they hit puberty," he explained in a slow voice. "Some dragons— well, they don't always stay tame. When they hit a certain age, they become violent and wild and destructive—the kind of dragons that could very well want to break away and destroy the world—like Emmy feared. We call them hybrids. And since we didn't know these guys' full parentage, we didn't know for sure whether they were hybrids or not."

Scarlet stared at him, realization washing over her like a tidal wave. She scrunched up her face, trying to ignore the feeling of betrayal stabbing her in the gut. "So you've been waiting this whole time," she whispered. "You believed from the start that Emmy could be right, that they could grow up and turn on us."

"Yes," Caleb said simply. "But," he added, "I wouldn't have let that happen. I was fully prepared to...take care of things if they suddenly went south."

"Take care of things? What are you, suddenly Connor?" Scarlet cried, horror coursing through her now. She found herself stepping in front of the dragons protectively. "And here I thought you were on our side!"

Caleb let out a frustrated breath. "I *am* on your side. God, Scarlet, don't you see? That's the whole reason I agreed to help you in the first place—to give the dragons the benefit of the doubt. Not everyone would have done that. But I figured if there was even the slightest possibility that they were purebloods, they deserved a chance to prove it. To me, it was worth the risk." He paused, then added, his eyes leveling on hers, "*You* were worth the risk."

Scarlet's heart fluttered involuntarily at his words. Damn it. He always did know exactly what to say to stop her in her tracks. To make her consider even his craziest ideas.

And was this even crazy? Was it a bad thing that he gave the dragons a chance to prove that they were good and peaceful? He'd done everything she'd asked over these last five months. And though he'd never said it aloud, she was pretty sure he loved Zavier and Zoe almost as much as she did. There was no way he would just willingly put them in danger now.

"Look, Buttercup," he said, his voice softening. "Don't be mad at me. I was trying to do the right thing. Yes, I probably should have told you the whole story, but I was afraid it would scare you—or stress you out. I didn't want you all worried until I knew whether there was anything to be worried about. And now we know there's not. Zoe and Zavier are clearly not hybrids. And everyone back at the base is going to love them as much as we do." He shrugged. "Still, if you don't think it's the right time, we can keep going on as we have. Or try to find another way."

She opened her mouth to speak, then closed it again, unsure of what she'd been planning to say. She knew Caleb was making sense. But a strong ache still crawled through her gut all the same. It took her a moment to identify the feeling. And when she did, she realized uncomfortably that it had nothing to do with the care and feeding of dragons.

And everything to do with Caleb himself.

She sighed. Over the last five months, they'd grown so close, as if they had a secret family, just the four of them. A special bond between them. Would that still be there if they rejoined the rest of the group? Or would Trin charge in, taking over as she always tried to do?

No more hunting expeditions. No more sneaking out for nighttime flying. No more chances that somehow she and Caleb would become more than they were.

Don't be stupid, she scolded herself. *Caleb doesn't think of you in that way. All this time spent just the two of you, and he's never even tried to make a move.*

Well, not since that one night in the Nether, anyway. But they never talked about that night. To be honest, she still wasn't positive he remembered it had happened at all. Which made her wish it actually *hadn't* happened, because there was no way she could forget that it did.

Stop thinking of yourself, she scolded. *It's Zavier and Zoe you should be thinking of now. And Caleb's right. We can't keep doing this on our own. We need help. They need help.*

"You're right," she found herself saying before she could change her mind again. "You're absolutely right. There's no way to continue on as we have been. We need to get the others on board if we want to keep everyone happy and safe." The words tasted like sawdust in her mouth, but she knew they had to be said.

She felt Caleb's eyes on her, curious and searching. She turned to face him, and he gave her a sad smile. "You should be proud, you know?" he said softly. "All you've done for them? They couldn't have asked for a better mother."

She blushed, suddenly embarrassed. "Yeah, well, turns out you're not such a bad baby daddy yourself," she managed to quip.

He shook his head slowly, his glowing blue eyes never leaving her face. "God, Scarlet," he whispered, "why do you have to be so sweet?"

Her breath caught in her throat. His words. The look in his eyes. Was he really going to kiss her? She found herself taking a step toward him, wanting him to know she was willing—that if he took the risk, he wouldn't be turned away. Her heart pounded in her chest. *Kiss me*, she wanted to beg. *Just for once, let go of whatever is holding you back and kiss me like you mean it.*

But instead of stepping toward her, instead of grabbing her face in his hands and pressing his lips against hers—he stepped away. Retreating, putting distance between them. Yet not before she caught a shadow of guilt cross his otherwise beautiful face.

Desperate, she reached out with her gift—to try to glean what he was thinking. She knew it was beyond rude to jack into people's thoughts without permission. But at the moment, she couldn't help herself. She swallowed hard, straining to hear.

I can't, he was thinking. *I made a promise to Trinity…*

Scarlet's shoulders stiffened. Her mind darkened. She squeezed her hands into fists as she stared at him with fury. Was he really still holding on to that fantasy after all this time?

Trinity has Connor, she wanted to scream. *She doesn't get to have you both.*

But what good would it do? You could rationalize till the dragons came home, but you couldn't change someone's heart. No matter what she did, no matter how "sweet" she was, she could never be Trinity Foxx, Caleb's manic pixie dream girl.

He liked Scarlet. That was obvious. But he loved Trinity. And if she allowed herself to fall for him, she would end up falling alone.

Oh God, what if she already had?

She forced herself to turn around, trying to hold back the tears pricking at the corners of her eyes. She tried to tell herself this was for the best. She knew for certain now, which meant no more wondering how he felt—no more hoping he was pining for her as much as she was pining for him. She knew where he stood now. And that meant she could move on.

"We need to go," she ground out. "It'll be morning soon, and we can't be flying in the daytime."

She tried desperately to keep the hurt from her voice, but from the look on his face, she could tell he heard it anyway. He opened his mouth to speak, but she waved him off.

"Don't," she said. "Just don't."

He closed his mouth, his face reflecting his guilt…and pity. Anger rose within her. How dare he feel sorry for her? When he was the one who made her feel this way to begin with?

Are you okay?

She whirled around. Zoe was peering at her with worried eyes. Scarlet forced a smile to her lips, then reached over to scratch the dragon under the chin.

I'm fine, she assured her. *I'm excited actually. Tomorrow you're going to get to see your mother.*

Zoe's eyes widened into saucers. *My mother?* she repeated in amazement. *You mean Emberlyn? I'm really going to get to see Emberlyn?*

Scarlet couldn't help a small smile as the dragon broke into an excited jig—so fast her feet barely made contact with the ground. *Yes*, she assured the dragon. *You're really going to see her at last.*

Oh, Scarlet-mom. Thank you, Zoe gushed, stopping her dance to give Scarlet a huge slurp on the face. *Thank you so much!*

Don't thank me, Scarlet corrected, glancing over at Caleb, who had busied himself with adjusting Zavier's saddle. *It was Caleb's idea.*

And, she thought but didn't say to the dragon, *I really hope it's a good one.*

Chapter Twenty

*W*ake up, wake up!

Zavier groaned, rolling over and putting a paw over his eyes. The shack was still dark, and only the faintest pink on the horizon glowed from the outline of the doorway. His sister was silhouetted in that light, bouncing up and down excitedly.

Go back to sleep, Zoe, he grunted.

I can't! she cried. *I couldn't sleep all night. I don't know how you could. Today's the day, you know!*

He grunted. *How could I forget, with you reminding me every five seconds?*

She snorted, little puffs of smoke punching from her nostrils. Then she grinned. *Oh come on!* she cajoled. *You know you're just as excited as I am.*

He gave up, rolling over and playfully shoving her backward. She teetered for a moment, then regained her balance, leaping on top of him and wrestling him to the ground. He laughed, only half fighting back.

Maybe I am a little curious, he admitted. Then he sobered. *But, Zoe, I don't want you to get your hopes up. We don't know how she's going to react to seeing us again.*

Zoe stopped her bouncing, giving him an offended look. *She's our mother, Zavier. How could she not be as excited as we are? I mean, once she sees us and gets to know us? After all, we're awesome, right? That's what Scarlet-mom always says. How could she not like dragons as awesome as we are?*

Zavier laughed despite himself. *It's true we are awesome,* he admitted.

And she's awesome too! Zoe added dreamily. *She's the prophesized savior of all dragons! Remember how they used to talk about her in the Nether? Our mother is legendary. Amazing! She's going to singlehandedly save our entire race!*

Zavier sighed. Typical Zoe, always so hopeful and optimistic. Seeing the best in everyone and everything. If only he could be like that.

But someone had to be the responsible one. The one who sniffed for danger around every corner and didn't give trust away easily. Scarlet-mom was constantly telling them that the world was a dangerous place for dragons. And one misplaced friendship could lead to their extinction. He trusted Scarlet-mom. He was pretty sure he trusted Caleb-dad too—they shared a blood bond, after all. But as for the rest of this so-called "Team Dragon" they were supposed to be meeting? He preferred to reserve judgment.

And as far as their bio mother? Well, Zoe might have managed to block out those early memories of Emberlyn turning her back on them and flying away. But Zavier hadn't. And he didn't see why anything would be different this time around.

Not that he cared, he reminded himself. It made no difference to him the opinion of some random dragon who just happened to share the same gene pool. But it would be devastating to Zoe. It would hurt her more than she could bear.

And no one hurt Zavier's sister. No one.

Chapter Twenty-One

Right this way, Ems. It's almost time for your surprise."
Trinity motioned for the dragon to follow her, out of
the hangar and down the runway, where everyone had gathered
for the live broadcast. The place had been decorated within an
inch of its life with every shiny party decoration they could find
at the closest Walmart, and the effect was so blinding in the blazing sunlight that Trinity hoped it wouldn't mess with the cameras.
The Potentials had arranged all the folding chairs they could
find in the terminal, placing them in a circle around the pièce
de résistance—Emmy's anniversary present, which lay under a
huge tarp. Trin's father and Connor had even rolled out the gas
grill and were busy preparing some awesome-smelling barbecue.

She waved to Nate and Natasha, who were hard at work
setting up the feed. When they'd first suggested going live,
she'd thought they were insane. Would people really pay to
attend an online dragon party? But then the subscriptions
started pouring in. Over four million in the past week. They'd
already made enough money to feed Emmy for the next five
years and then some.

She had to admit, the social media campaign had vastly
exceeded any of her expectations. Not only had it brought in

enough money for the care and feeding of the dragon herself, but they had also succeeded in building something more important: a real-life community of dragon lovers coming together to support Emmy. Where once Team Dragon had been made up of four members—then about forty with the addition of the Potentials—today they were more than four million strong. People from all over the country, all over the world, were celebrating Emmy's existence on the planet. No matter what Connor said, that couldn't be a bad thing.

Trinity scanned the crowd, realizing two people were missing from the festivities. Caleb and Scarlet, surprise, surprise.

She frowned. It was hard to believe Caleb's continual denial that something was going on between he and Scarlet when they were constantly disappearing together. In fact, whenever Caleb wasn't occupied helping Trin with Emmy, he was usually MIA with Scarlet. And while she knew she had no right to be jealous of their secret dalliances—whatever they might be—she couldn't help, at times, feeling a little resentful. They were supposed to be working as a team, after all, not breaking off into their own little groups.

Can you blame them though? a voice inside of her nagged. *You didn't exactly roll out the red carpet for Scarlet.*

She shook her head. Okay, fine. That was probably true. But still—couldn't they have made an exception for today of all days? It was Emmy's big party. And the live broadcast was the biggest thing they'd attempted to pull yet. They needed all the support they could get. Couldn't the two of them pry themselves off of one another for just one day?

"Everyone ready?" Luke's voice broke out, amplified by a microphone. "We're live in three, two, one..." He grinned.

"Hello, Team Dragon! I'm your host, Luke Skyflyer, and you're watching FreeEmmy.com TV. Thank you for tuning in and for all your support for your favorite dragon, Emberlyn. This is a monumental day for Team Dragon, and we're glad that you're here to share it with us. PernDancer, do you want to go over the rules for us?"

"Sure, Luke," Natasha agreed, taking the mic. "As always, if you have any questions about Emmy or for Emmy, please type them into the chat window below your screen, hashtag question mark. We can't promise we'll get to all of them— there are four million of you, after all. But we'll do what we can." She paused, then added, "If for some reason you have to leave the broadcast early, you can return in twenty-four hours to watch the entire upload of the event. Lastly, if you haven't made your contribution to Emmy's gift, please click on the DONATE NOW button on the right-hand side of your screen. All donations go directly to our girl here and her dragon-sized appetite."

"And now, here's the moment you have all been waiting for," Luke cried, taking back the microphone. "*Heeeeere's EMMY!*"

Nate turned the camera toward Trinity and the dragon. Trinity gave a shy smile and wave. She still felt odd about being turned into some kind of Internet web star. Emmy, on the other hand, tossed her head with pride, prancing around, totally ready for her close-up. She loved being on TV almost as much as she loved watching it.

"And in three, two, one!" Trin's father cried to the group.

The Potentials in the audience all burst into song, singing "Happy anniversary" at the top of their lungs. Emmy grinned, rising up onto her haunches to do a little jig. Everyone cheered. From over in the broadcast booth, Luke gave Trinity a thumbs-up. This was going better than they could have hoped for.

"That was great!" he cried when they had finished. "I hope all of you at home were singing along as well. Remember, you still have about ten minutes left to upload your own messages to Emmy on Vine or Instagram. We'll be playing some of the videos later in the broadcast, and the most creative will win one of Emmy's beautiful watercolor originals."

Trin stifled a smile at this. It had been Natasha's idea to put a paintbrush in Emmy's mouth a few months back during one of their slower webcasts, thus producing a few masterpieces that wouldn't exactly rival a three-year-old's artistic prowess. And yet, the interwebs had exploded over these dragon scribbles with artists all over the world theorizing the implied meaning behind each and every brushstroke. It had gotten so crazy that Trin had finally had the idea to upload the designs to a CafePress store and sell them as prints and T-shirts.

Luke turned to Trinity. "But now, is Emmy ready for her surprise?"

"Actually," Trinity said, walking over to Luke and taking the microphone from him as they had practiced. "I have something of my own to give her first." She walked back over to Emmy, pulling out a small box tied with a red ribbon. She held it out to the dragon. Emmy looked at it, then turned to her, cocking her head in question.

"Go ahead," Trin urged. "Open it."

The dragon obliged, snuffing at the box with her enormous nose until she finally managed to nibble off the ribbon and nudge off the lid. Her eyes widened as she realized what was inside. There, nestled in a white silk handkerchief, was the necklace Trinity had bought her in Walmart before she'd been taken away by the government.

Trinity grinned, then turned back to the cameras. "Once upon a time, Emmy returned this necklace to me. We thought we were about to be separated forever." She glanced up at the dragon, tears misting her eyes. "Emmy loved this necklace, but she gave it up, wanting me to have something to remember her by." She smiled. "Because that's the kind of dragon she is."

Emmy looked down on her, and Trin realized the dragon's own eyes were wet at the corners. She reached out and hugged Emmy before turning back to the cameras. "But now," she added, "thanks to all of you out there on Team Dragon, I don't need anything to remember her by. Because we're together every day—and nothing can break us apart!"

Behind her, she could hear the Potentials cheer. Reaching into the box, she pulled out the necklace, then looked at Emmy a little doubtfully. "Though I'm not sure it's going to work as a necklace anymore," she teased, noting the circumference of the dragon's neck. "Maybe a bracelet?"

Everyone laughed at this. Emmy snorted, nodding her massive head eagerly. Then she lifted a paw up to Trinity. It took a little effort, but Trin finally managed to work the piece of jewelry over the dragon's claws and down to an approximation of where her wrist would be. Just seeing Emmy's face as she stared down reverentially at the red-paste jewels made Trinity want to both laugh and cry.

"You deserve this, Emmy," she whispered, softly so the microphone couldn't pick it up. Some things were still just between her and her dragon. "I only wish I could give you more."

You've given me everything, Fire Kissed. So much more than I deserve.

Trinity's mouth dropped open. Had Emmy just...

"Did you just say something?" she whispered, suddenly wishing they weren't live on TV.

Emmy looked a little sheepish. *Caleb's been helping me*, she confessed. *Turns out a bond between dragon and Fire Kissed can be broken—but never severed completely. And with the right exercises...*

Trinity's heart leapt in her chest. "Why didn't you tell me?"

I didn't know if it would work. And I didn't want to disappoint you if it didn't. I've already disappointed you so many times...

"Oh, Emmy!" Trinity cried, throwing her arms around the dragon. "You have never disappointed me. Never ever, ever!" She buried her face in the dragon's neck, unable to stop the happy sobs. And when Emmy nuzzled her back with her snout, her heart felt so full, she was half-convinced it would burst from her chest.

"Uh, Trinity?" Luke broke in. "Not to interrupt this happy moment, but..."

Trinity blushed, pulling away from Emmy and giving him an apologetic look. After all, to the rest of them and everyone watching, she might as well have been talking to herself. There would be all the time in the world to talk to Emmy later. Right now, the dragon's public awaited.

"Sorry," she said, turning to the cameras with a laugh. "It's time for Emmy's real present. The one you all helped us make for her." She turned to Rashida. "I think she's ready! Let's do this!"

The camera panned over to the large tarp, and Rashida and Trevor walked over, grabbing the ends and yanking it away.

Trin watched, laughing, as Emmy's eyes grew wide as saucers as she stared down at the most massive pile of raw meat any of them had ever seen. It was a mountain of meat.

"Well, what are you waiting for?" Trin teased. "*Bon appétit!*"

She watched Emmy start over to the pile, drool dripping from her massive jaws. Her heart swelled in her chest. That was her dragon. Her beautiful dragon.

They were still destined, she and Emmy. And nothing could tear them apart.

She turned back to the broadcast. "Thank you all for tuning in to help us celebrate Emmy's online anniversary. As always your support is—"

"Excuse me, everyone? May we have your attention please?"

What? Trinity turned, surprised at the sudden interruption. She'd been about to introduce the fan videos so that Emmy could eat in peace. That's what they'd rehearsed anyway. So who was that, speaking over a bullhorn now? It sounded almost like—

"Caleb?" she called out. Her heart pounded uneasily in her chest, though she wasn't sure why.

"Before Emmy digs in, we have another surprise for her," Caleb continued from wherever he was hiding.

Trinity watched as Emmy paused from her meal, looking up with uneasy eyes. The scales on the back of her neck seemed to rise, giving her the look of a threatened dog. A low warning growl emerged from the back of her throat as she nervously began to scan the skies.

Trinity shot a look to Luke. He started to shrug, then stopped short, his eyes focusing on something above her. Concerned, Trin followed his gaze, heart in her throat, looking up at the sky and…

"Oh my God!" she cried. "Are those…dragons?"

Chapter Twenty-Two

What the…?

Trinity watched, along with everyone else, as two young dragons the size of small horses swooped down from the sky, weaving in and out of each other's flight paths as if showing off for the cameras. One was pink with purple wings and the other as black as Trinity's eyes with golden sparks that seemed to dance over the ebony scales.

Dragons. How could there possibly be dragons?

And if that wasn't crazy enough… She did a double take. *Was that really Caleb and Scarlet, riding on their freaking backs?*

Guess they weren't about to miss the party after all.

Trinity's first thought was she must be dreaming. Because what other rational possibility could there be? Certainly not actual dragons coming in for a landing a few feet in front of her. She tried to pinch herself, to wake herself up somehow. But as Caleb and Scarlet slid off their dragons and approached the cameras, she realized this was no dream.

No. This was a real-life nightmare.

"What the hell is going on here, Caleb?" Connor demanded, stepping up to Trinity's side as his twin strode toward them with a distinct swagger in his steps. Connor sounded angry, but Trinity could also hear the fear winding through his voice. Not surprising, she supposed. This was everything he'd been warning her against—everything she'd refused to listen to.

"Come on, Bro," Caleb cried with a self-satisfied smirk on his face. Trin could tell he was enjoying his brother's distress a little too much. "Haven't you ever seen a dragon before?"

Connor stared at him, apparently rendered speechless. As the moment stretched out, Trin caught Nate waving wildly at her, then gesturing to the camera. The still-rolling camera, she realized with a start. Crap. They were still live—in front of four million people, no less. If they showed any fear—if they made the world think this was anything more than a planned part of their regularly scheduled program, everything they'd been working toward all this time could end up being for nothing.

Damn you, Caleb! What are you thinking?

"Of course he's seen dragons," she rushed in, beaming at the cameras as she took what she hoped looked like a confident step forward. "We were just expecting you a little earlier. But hey—fashionably late dragons are fashionably late. It's not a big thing." She swallowed hard, stepping up to the two dragons and daring to reach out, giving each a pat on the nose, praying they wouldn't see fit to bite her hand off for doing so. "It's great to see you," she told them cheerfully, as if they were long-lost friends. "Make yourselves at home."

"Uh, we've got a question from the audience," Luke broke in, in a hesitant voice. When they all turned to him questioningly, he glanced down at his laptop. "Um, Marie Krakowski in Kansas City asks, 'We thought Emmy was the world's last dragon. So where did these two come from?'"

It was the question of the century. Trinity held her breath, waiting for Caleb or Scarlet to answer. Her mind flashed back to Connor's warning five months before.

It would be naive to assume she'll always be the world's last dragon.

Had these two dragons been cloned in the government lab? Had Scarlet and Caleb broke them out somehow? Had they been keeping them a secret this entire time? Suddenly, their frequent disappearances started to make a lot more sickening sense. What a fool she'd been, assuming they just had some kind of bad romance going on.

"Oh, Marie," Caleb replied, turning to look right into the camera, his eyes twinkling. "Are you really asking us where baby dragons come from?" He made an exaggerated wink. Then he turned to Emmy, doing a big *ta-da* gesture with his hands. "Zoe and Zavier here are Emmy's dear children, of course!"

Everyone gasped. Emmy let out a low, horrified whine. Trinity turned to look at her, wishing to God she still had the two-way psychic link they once shared so she could ask one of the million questions swirling through her brain without it being broadcast to the world.

In any case, Emmy wasn't looking at her. She was staring straight at Scarlet. And the betrayed look in her eyes told Trinity everything she wanted to know and then some.

You promised me, Scarlet, she overheard the dragon cry. *You said you'd taken care of them!*

Oh God. Trinity shrank backward, fear now rioting through her insides. *Emmy knew.* She'd known all along.

Of course she knew, you idiot, she scolded herself. *It's not like you could just accidentally give birth and not know it.*

Suddenly everything seemed to slide into a stomach-turning place. Emmy must have been pregnant when they'd freed her. *That's* where she'd gone the two months before they'd brought her back home. She had to go lay her eggs. And that's why she'd been so evasive when Trin tried to grill her about what she'd been up to during that time.

She frowned. But then what? Had Emmy asked Scarlet to raise these dragons? No. Trinity shook her head. It was clear Emmy was just as shocked to see them as everyone else.

Had she asked Scarlet to kill them?

God. If only the cameras weren't rolling. But, Trin supposed, that was probably no coincidence. Leave it to Caleb to concoct a plan that rendered everyone helpless when he introduced the new members of the dragon race to the world. Caleb would have known his brother would flip out—maybe even try to kill the dragons on sight without bothering for explanations. But he couldn't do anything while they were live on the Internet.

Trinity felt Emmy nudging her hard with her snout. She turned to look at the mother dragon. "You okay?" she whispered.

Emmy gave her a tormented look, her eyes wide and frightened and filled with guilt. *I'm sorry*, she whispered in Trinity's mind. *I'm so sorry. I should have told you. I should have—*

Trinity shook her head. There would be time to talk this through later. Right now, she had to figure out how to salvage this broadcast before it went viral.

She turned, only to find that the pink dragon—Zoe, Caleb had called her—quietly approaching her mother, looking up at the larger dragon with wide, purple eyes. Despite herself,

Trinity felt her heart squeeze a little as she recognized the apprehension mixed with hope written on the dragon's face. She was reminded, suddenly, of her own mother. They'd had a...complicated...relationship to say the least. But at the end of the day...

Maybe this will be okay, she tried to tell herself. *Maybe it'll be no big deal.*

But just as she'd almost managed to convince herself of this, Emmy let out a low, threatening growl, taking a quick, aggressive step toward her daughter, as if trying to scare her away. Trin watched uneasily as Zoe whimpered and retreated a few steps, the hope fading from her eyes, replaced by a horrible sadness.

Trinity turned to her dragon. If looks could kill, Zoe would currently be nothing more than a messy puddle on the floor. She bit her lower lip. "Easy, Ems," she tried in a slow, overly calm voice. "She's okay. She's just saying hi. She doesn't want to hurt you."

The tension in the air was now so thick you could cut it with a knife. Trin glanced back at Nate, trying to push the idea of shutting down the webcast into his head. Sure, it was too late to just pretend this never happened, but maybe they could cut it off before things got more volatile. But Nate was just staring dumbstruck at the scene unfolding before him, and she couldn't seem to get his attention.

Desperate, she turned back to Caleb. "Maybe this isn't the best time?" she suggested, looking at him with pleading eyes. *Come on, Caleb. Show some common sense for once in your life...* "After all, Emmy's just about to have her big feast. Maybe we could let her eat in peace and schedule this whole family reunion for

SMOKED

later this afternoon?" *You know, once we're not broadcasting live to the world?* she pushed.

At first Caleb looked as if he wanted to argue. Then his shoulders slumped, and he gave her an apologetic shrug. *All right*, he agreed. *Let me just—*

He broke off, his gaze darting behind her, his face draining of color. Trin turned slowly, not sure she really wanted to know what he was looking at. For a moment, she couldn't figure out what was going on. Then she saw it. While Zoe and Emmy had been facing off, Zavier had broken away and was now wandering dangerously close to Emmy's mountain of meat. His mouth was open in an excited pant, and his eyes were sparking with greed.

Trinity frowned. "Caleb! Get your dragon away from—"

Zavier dove into the meat, mouth open wide, bathing himself in blood as he practically vacuumed up the food. Gristle and bone flew from his mouth as he chomped happily before letting out a loud burp that seemed to echo across the airfield.

For a moment, Emmy just watched him, a horrified look on her face as her precious meal began to disappear at an alarming rate. Then another growl wound up her throat, and steam began to shoot from her nose.

"Stop it!" Trin cried to Zavier. "Get away from Emmy's food!" She whirled around, no longer caring about the cameras. "Caleb, call off your stupid dragon—now!"

To his credit, Caleb didn't argue. "Come, you overgrown garbage disposal," he scolded. "That's your mother's dinner. You'll get yours later."

But Zavier ignored him, continuing to suck up large pieces

183

of meat and swallowing them without even bothering to chew. Caleb groaned.

"Hang on. I'll get him out of there."

He ran to his dragon, attempting to grab him by his saddle and drag him away from the meat. But Zavier refused to budge. And when Caleb made a second, more concentrated effort, the beast flicked his wing, shooing him away like an irritating fly. The force of the blow sent Caleb flying, and he arced several feet into the air before hitting the ground with a sickening thud.

"Caleb!" Scarlet was at his side in an instant. "Oh God, Caleb! Are you okay?"

Trin found herself running to him as well. Dropping to her knees before him, taking in his white face. His leg was twisted, definitely broken. She glanced back at the group. "Turn off the cameras and freaking help us!" she cried.

But no one was paying attention; instead, their eyes were all locked on Emmy. The dragon had reared onto her haunches, letting out a deafening roar. Trin watched; it was as if the scene were playing out in slow motion, as the dragon's mouth creaked open and a cannonball of flames shot out, blasting Zavier full on. The raw meat sizzled and smoked under the sudden heat, but Zavier only looked up at her, his black eyes flashing something cold and hard.

The once-joyous celebration had now become a disaster film—people running, people screaming. The air was thick with smoke, making it difficult to see or breathe. Trin watched as Zavier rose to his feet, a scraggly roar rasping from his throat. A moment later, he was charging at Emmy, slashing at her with sharp claws.

Emmy leapt away, barely in time to dodge the attack, the whites in her eyes flashing and sparks dancing on her tongue. Summoning heat for round two?

"Emmy, no!" Trin cried. But even as she made the command, she wasn't a hundred percent sure she wanted the dragon to listen. After all, Emmy had to defend herself, right? What if this creature hurt her? What if his sister joined the fray and Emmy found herself outnumbered?

The two dragons met head-on, slashing with their claws, biting with their teeth, rolling around on the ground until it was tough to determine where one ended and the other began. Trin looked at Scarlet, who looked back at her with an equal amount of horror in her eyes. "We have to do something!" she cried.

But what? They couldn't jump into the middle of the fight. That would be suicide.

Then Trin heard it. A wailing song, both beautiful and terrible, bursting through the air. She whirled around to see Connor, standing behind her, singing at the top of his lungs. He was in full-on Hunter mode, trying to lull the beasts into submission with his song.

Emmy and Zavier both stopped in their tracks, a haze crossing over their eyes as they stared at Connor, their fight all but forgotten. Trinity watched, unable to even breathe as Zavier took a hesitant step toward the Hunter. His tongue was lolling from his mouth and his scales were wet with blood.

"No!"

Caleb shoved Trinity and Scarlet out of the way as he stumbled toward his brother. He shouldn't have been able to stand, never mind run, but the adrenaline was coursing through him, and he seemed to feel no pain. Trinity watched helplessly as he dove for his twin, knocking him to the ground and interrupting his song. His fist rose, slamming down on Connor's face—once, twice, three times. "Don't you even think about singing to my dragon, you flecking bastard!" he screamed.

Trin found her voice. "Caleb, stop it! He's just trying to calm him down!"

But Caleb didn't stop, and Trinity wasn't surprised. After all, the last time his brother had sung his Hunter's song, it had ended in Fred's murder; there was no way Caleb was going to risk this a second time with a second dragon.

"Help me!" she cried to Scarlet. "Get them off each other." They may have not been able to stop a dragon fight—but with the brothers, they'd take their chances. Together they dove at the boys, using all their strength to try to pull them apart. Connor had regained some control, rolling on top of Caleb, so Trin worked on him first, throwing her arms around his neck and yanking as hard as she could.

"Stop it!" she begged. "You're going to kill each other!"

She felt Connor startle at her words, reality breaking into his fury-induced haze. He started to back off, releasing Caleb, allowing her to pull him away. Unfortunately, this only gave Caleb opportunity to tackle him all over again. And worse, he'd somehow found a rock, cradling it his hand and slamming it down on Connor's head. In an instant, Connor fell into her arms, dead weight. Trinity screamed as Caleb raised his arm for a second blow.

"Stop it, Caleb!" Scarlet cried. "That's your brother!"

"He was trying to kill my dragon!" Caleb protested. But even as he argued, Trin could see the horror ghosting his face as he looked down at his unconscious twin. He hadn't meant this to go so far, she realized.

Not that good intentions meant much at this point.

Caleb staggered backward, the rock falling from his hand as he collapsed into Scarlet's arms, all the fight having drained from him. Trinity looked down at Connor, heart in her throat. His breathing was shallow, and there was a huge egg-sized lump on his forehead. Had Caleb given him a concussion?

"He needs help!" she cried. "Please!"

But there was no help. And it wasn't like they could summon any either. All she could do was cradle him in her arms and pray that he was just knocked out and would be okay. But even as she tried to convince herself, she wasn't sure. He looked so pale. So still. Her heart wrenched.

Connor. My sweet, brave Connor.

She thought of all the arguments they'd had over the last year, all the times he'd tried to warn her something like this could happen—that history could repeat itself. That dragons could turn wild.

He'd tried to tell her. Again and again. But she hadn't listened. No, not only had she not listened, but she'd fought him over it as well. And now...

Connor, please! Don't leave me.

Suddenly Trin felt someone behind her. She turned to see her father had approached. His face was grave. "Caleb and Scarlet, go round up your dragons," he commanded. "I want them in the hangar, chained up and gagged, within the hour. Once they are secured, we will talk this over and figure out what to do."

"But Zoe didn't do anything!" Scarlet protested. "She shouldn't be—"

MARI MANCUSI

"Do it," her father said. "Or I will kill them both myself."

Caleb opened his mouth as if wanting to protest, then glanced over at his unconscious brother and seemed to think the better of it. He slunk over to Zavier. The dragon gave him a bloody-mouthed smile, and Trin couldn't help but notice how extended his belly was from his recent feast. Caleb sighed, gave the dragon a rueful look, then climbed on his back, and together they flew toward the hangar's entrance. Scarlet watched them go, then turned to Trinity.

"Zavier didn't mean it," she insisted, her eyes filled with tears. "I'm telling you, he's really gentle and sweet. You would like him, I swear, if you got to know him." She paused, then cried, "It wasn't supposed to be like this!"

"No," Trinity agreed in a tight voice. "It wasn't supposed to be like this at all."

But it was. And now the entire world knew what happened when you couldn't control your dragons.

Chapter Twenty-Three

W hat the hell were you two idiots thinking?"

Trinity slammed the door to the office shut, whirling around to face Caleb and Scarlet. She looked from one to the other, trying to quell the fury that burned through her like a fire. Raking a hand through her hair, she stormed over to a chair, pulled it out, and sat down on it backward. Then she gestured for the two of them to take a seat on the nearby couch.

"I want to know everything. From the very beginning. And don't even think of leaving anything out."

And so they told her the tale, everything that had been going on behind her back the whole time. When they had finished, she shook her head in disbelief. "Why couldn't you have just come to me?" Trin asked. "I mean, from the very beginning?"

She could hear the hurt creeping into her voice, despite her best efforts. But who could blame her? While sure, there was no love lost between her and Scarlet, she had thought at least Caleb was on her side. They'd been so close. And yet he hadn't trusted her to keep this secret.

And neither had Emmy, she realized, suddenly feeling a little nauseous. What kind of person did they think she was—that they couldn't trust her with their secrets?

"Come on, Trin," Caleb interjected. She noticed his face was still bruised from where his brother had struck him. But his leg looked better—Zavier must have shared some of his blood to help it heal. "You know as well as I do that if we brought the dragons to you as babies, everyone would have assumed, like Emmy did, that they were hybrids and a threat to the world. Sure, you may not have gone and actually sentenced them to death, but you would have at least locked them up until you could determine the risk for sure." He gave her a half-cocked grin. "Hell, you should be grateful we saved you the trouble!"

"Saved me the trouble?" she repeated incredulously. "Are you even on this planet? We just freaking live streamed Dragon World War Three to four million people. I mean, maybe you haven't noticed, but we've been working our asses off to sway public opinion when it comes to dragons. And now everything's ruined. You think anyone's going to be Team Emmy now? Do you think we're going to get people writing their congressmen in favor of dragons being allowed to roam free after seeing that firestorm?"

"A firestorm created by *your* dragon," Scarlet broke in. "May I remind you that Zavier was only trying to defend himself after your stupid dragon viciously attacked him for no reason. Hell, she's admitted she's wanted them dead from day one. So who's really the bad guy here?"

Trin closed her eyes, trying to reset her sanity. She didn't even know what to say at this point or if it was even worth saying anything at all. After all, what good would it do? The most she could hope for was an apology. And that apology would change nothing in the end. What had happened had happened. It couldn't be changed. They could only figure out a way to best move forward from here.

Caleb groaned. "Look, I'm sorry, Trin," he said. "I admit, it wasn't my brightest idea ever. But trust me, we were trying to do the right thing. I thought if Emmy just saw them again, realized they weren't the monsters she believes them to be…" He gave her a helpless look. "What do want us to do?"

"I don't know," she snapped. "I just don't know. The group is freaking out. Connor's still unconscious. Emmy's shut herself away." She shook her head slowly. "Look, can you guys just hang tight for now? I promise we won't take any action until we have a chance to talk things over as a group."

"Uh, are you really suggesting that we leave the fate of our dragons up to a committee?" Scarlet broke in. "'Cause I'm definitely not cool with that." She made a move to rise to her feet. "Our dragons have done nothing wrong. Emmy should be the one being punished, not them!"

Trinity shot a look at Caleb. *You need to calm her down*, she pushed.

"Scarlet…" Caleb said in a warning voice, reaching out to try to pull her back down beside him.

She shook off his hand, looking down at him with angry eyes. "Oh, of course. Let me guess. You're just going to take her side, right?"

Seriously, Caleb, Trinity pushed again.

What am I supposed to do? he pushed back, looking from one girl to the next.

Whatever you have to. Do not let this get any worse than it already is.

"Look, Buttercup," Caleb said, after drawing in a breath. "No one's taking sides here. It's just a simple chat between friends. And I do agree with you—Emmy's as much to blame as anyone else if not more so. And I'm sure Trinity is on her way to talk to her now. She's not going to just get a pass. Right, Trin?"

Trinity gave a grudging nod. "Though to be fair, you did blindside the poor dragon. And during her big party too."

Caleb shot her a look. *You're not helping.*

Trinity sighed. "Look, we just need to keep clear heads, okay? We've been in tight situations before, and we've always managed to work things through. We'll regroup in the morning and assess the situation. You guys can properly introduce your dragons to the group, and I will do what I can to talk Emmy down. Does that sound fair?"

Scarlet opened her mouth to speak, then glanced guiltily to Caleb. Trinity noted he was squeezing her hand very hard. "Fine," she spit out instead. "We'll wait until morning. But we'd better get our fair say, Trinity Foxx. Zoe and Zavier deserve another chance."

"And they will get one," Trinity assured her, dropping her shoulders in relief. "I promise." She rose to her feet. "Now if this is all settled, I'm going to go talk to Emmy."

She glanced over at Scarlet, still not liking the dark look in her eyes. She turned back to Caleb.

You told me once—whatever I needed—you would be here for me. That all I had to do was ask.

Caleb bit his lower lip. *Yes. Of course. But…*

Then keep her away from those dragons tonight. No matter what you have to do.

Chapter Twenty-Four

E mmy? Are you awake?"

Trin stepped quietly into the hangar, blinking her eyes to adjust them to the darkness. From the far end, she could hear the hum of the television set and see the faint, blue glow seeping under the red curtains.

Her shoulders relaxed. Emmy was watching TV. That had to be a good sign, right?

Crossing the hangar, she pulled back the curtains, peering in to find Emmy curled up in front of the set, her long tail wrapped securely around her body and her head resting on her paw.

Trin cleared her throat to make her presence known. "Did you start watching the fourth Harry Potter without me?" she started to tease. "I thought we were…"

She trailed off as she caught sight of the TV screen and frowned. No, not Harry Potter. Something much darker.

FOX News. And, it appeared, the subject of the day was none other than the once-dubbed Touchdown of Terror herself.

Crap.

"Watch this," one of the commentators was saying as the video rolled on the other half of the screen. A disturbing, slow-motion replay of Emmy blasting fire at Zavier. "Does this look like America's next top house pet to you?" he asked gleefully.

"I don't know. I'm pretty sure I couldn't afford the fire insurance premiums," joked his cohost.

Oh God.

"Emmy..." Trin tried. But the dragon's eyes stayed glued on the TV.

"As you know, over the last few months, the liberal media has been all over themselves trying to convince us that this creature should be part of some kind of animal-rights campaign," added the third commentator. "And PETA has been actively petitioning to get this fire-breathing beast on the endangered species list." He turned to face the cameras. "We have social media expert Ike Sudukus with us via satellite. Ike, is this the kind, cuddly creature we should be embracing as a society?"

"I know I'm not embracing anything with claws like that," the first commentator interrupted with a snort. "I mean, give that poor beast a mani-pedi, why don't you?"

Trinity cringed as she caught Emmy stealing a peek at her actually very beautiful, shiny claws. The dragon had spent months growing them back after the government had shorn them and had been so proud of their length, showing them off to everyone who came to visit. Now she looked down at them sorrowfully and tucked them under her belly, hiding them from view. It was all Trin could do not to take a bat to the TV set.

The video switched to the social media expert. "It's clear this creature has a fan base. There are thousands of websites dedicated to the dragon, and its weekly web show has drawn viewers from all over the world. The question is will those fans stay loyal now that this video has surfaced? Now that it's obvious that this is, indeed, a wild animal and clearly dangerous."

"Not your grandma's Puff the Magic Dragon, kiddos," chimed in the female commentator. And Trinity's heart broke at the shame she saw in Emmy's eyes.

"In the last twenty-four hours, we've started to see an anti-Emmy backlash—with websites popping up all over. And the hashtag *Kill Emmy* is currently trending on Twitter," added the social media expert helpfully.

Emmy's eyes widened as the graphical representation of the hateful hashtag flashed across the screen. Trin grimaced. This was so not good.

"And yet this dragon has been so popular for months now. Why do you think people are so angry?" asked the host.

"Basically, they believe they've been lied to. Manipulated. Played for cash. For example, since the beginning, the Free Emmy group has been touting this creature as 'the last of its kind,' and yet now you clearly see on the video, there are at least two more in existence."

"And they don't appear to be besties either," joked the female host as the video looped and Emmy shot fire at Zavier all over again. "I mean *ouch!* Take a look at the blast radius."

"Right? Maybe the military needs to start recruiting dragons," added her cohost. "Talk about a weapon of mass destruction! I mean, can you picture the look on a terrorist's face when they suddenly find themselves up against a real-life dragon?"

Trinity stalked over to the TV and switched it off. Emmy whined, looking angry, then guilty—then just plain sad.

"Talk to me, Emmy," Trinity commanded, sitting down in the chair across from the dragon. "Tell me everything that went down."

Emmy didn't reply. Instead, she dropped her head to the floor and stared off into space. Trinity's heart wrenched to see the anguish on the dragon's face. But she couldn't let her get off that easily. She thought back to her talk with Scarlet. If she didn't make good, the girl was going to do something rash. And things were bad enough already.

"You thought they were dead, didn't you?" she pushed. "You told Scarlet to kill them, and you thought she had."

Emmy gave a small huff. Trinity decided to take that as a yes.

"Why didn't you come to me from the start?" she demanded, her voice rising in frustration. "I could have helped you. We could have dealt with this together. Instead, you went and hid it from me!"

I didn't want you to know.

"But why?" Trinity cried. "I thought we were a team. I thought we shared a bond. And yet, over and over, you've chosen to go behind my back. How am I supposed to help you, Emmy, if you never tell me what you need?"

I don't deserve your help. Not when I can't help you in return.

Trinity sighed. "What are you talking about, Emmy? You've done so much. Hell, you sacrificed your one chance at true happiness to save the boy I loved."

And now all you do is fight with him—because of me.

Trinity cringed. She hadn't realized the dragon had picked up on the tension between her and Connor. "That's not your fault," she tried to protest.

But Emmy wasn't listening. *Because of me, you have lost everything. Your mother, your grandfather, your normal life.* She closed her eyes, letting out a soft groan. *If I had just done what you asked. If I had gone to the place with all the dragons, none of this would be happening now. The world would not be doomed.*

Trinity cringed at the self-loathing she saw clear on the dragon's face. Poor Emmy. No wonder she'd been so miserable this whole time. The guilt she'd been living under must have been suffocating.

When I saw you walk into that lab, I could barely look at you. I was so ashamed. After what I let them do to me…

"You didn't *let* them do anything," Trinity corrected, her voice cracking with frustration. "Emmy, you were captured. You were tortured. You were experimented on and impregnated against your will. How can any of that be your fault?"

Emmy didn't answer, and the silence stretched out between them. Finally, she looked up at Trinity, her eyes unbearably sad.

You said there might be a way to turn back the clock? she asked. *A way to undo all that's been done?*

"Maybe," Trinity said hesitantly. "I mean, my dad's still trying to work that out, to see if it's even possible. I don't know how much progress he's made though. Maybe someday. But in the meantime, Emmy, we have to deal with what's happening now. You have two children, whether you like it or not. And how we deal with them now will make all the difference for the future."

Emmy regarded her with solemn eyes. *You want me to give them a chance, don't you? Even knowing what we know?*

Trinity bit her lower lip. "We don't know anything," she corrected. "Not anymore. Connor and Caleb's future, as far as I'm concerned, has already been eradicated. We're on a new path now. And each step on that path can lead to a new destiny."

But is it worth the risk?

"You were a risk once," Trinity reminded her. "If Connor had had his way, you'd have been dropped into a volcano when you were still in your egg. But Caleb convinced me that we should give you a chance to prove yourself. And you did, Emmy. Ten times over. Don't these dragons deserve the same opportunity? They are your children after all."

She rose to her feet, giving the dragon a sympathetic look. "I'll let you think it over, okay?" she told her. "But, Emmy, really think about it. Think about what it could be like for you to have children. For your children to have a real mother—like you never had. Imagine what you could do if the three of you were on the same team." She gave the dragon a wistful smile. "Imagine what it'd be like…to never be alone again."

Chapter Twenty-Five

I think he's in here.

Zoe peeked her head through the window, squinting to see inside. Zavier stepped up beside her, shoving her snout away so he could get a better look for himself. From this vantage point, he could just make out Caleb-dad's brother, lying very still on the bed.

Yes, he agreed. *That's definitely him.* He frowned, glancing at the door they'd come through from the outside. *Are you sure you want to do this?*

It's our fault he's in there, isn't it? Zoe reminded him stubbornly. *I'm not going to just let him die on us. He's Caleb's brother, after all. Just like you're my brother.*

Zavier opened his mouth to remind her that it had been Caleb who had done this to his brother in the first place, then gave up before speaking. He knew better than anyone that there was no way to change his sister's mind once she got something in her head. Besides, if it would make her feel better about everything that had gone down, how could he deny her that? Anything to get off the hook for his earlier actions.

Zoe had been so furious at him. And he supposed he'd deserved it in a way. But still, what choice had he had really?

Just stand back and let that bitch dragon threaten his poor sister for no good reason? All poor Zoe wanted was to be acknowledged. To be loved by her mother as any dragon deserved to be loved. But instead, she'd been scorned. Dismissed. As if she were nothing more than last night's soup bones, already gnawed clean.

No one treated Zoe that way. Not with Zavier around.

Emberlyn had looked so angry—as if she were only seconds away from attacking Zoe where she stood—and the ice in her eyes had made his blood run cold. He knew he had to do something to distract her away from his sister before she made a move, and going after her food was the only thing he could come up with on short notice.

Sure, he knew it was wrong; Caleb and Scarlet had taught them both that touching food that didn't belong to you was disrespectful and rude. But how much ruder had Emberlyn been to Zoe? The dragon deserved to have her dinner devoured—and so much more.

He spit, remembering. The food hadn't even tasted good—it was raw and bloody and disgusting.

But it had gotten Emberlyn's attention, that was for sure.

He groaned. He hadn't meant for anyone to get hurt. And the last thing he wanted was for Zoe to be angry with him. So when she had brought up the idea of going and healing Caleb's brother, he'd agreed to it, despite thinking it completely insane.

And so they'd broken through their chains—which were nothing more than a joke really—and headed to the main building after everyone went to sleep. They'd snuck through the back door and were now ready to prove to the gang that they really were good dragons, despite public opinion.

You wait out here, Zoe instructed him. *Make sure no one's coming.*

What am I supposed to do if someone comes?

Something nonviolent. Something a nice dragon would do.

Should I offer to make them tea and crumpets?

I'll settle for you not burning them to a crisp.

Fine, Zavier replied, his eyes dancing. *But hurry up. We don't want to get caught out here.*

Zoe nodded, clamping her teeth over the door handle and twisting it open. The door creaked loudly, and for a moment, both dragons froze, wondering if the sound would wake someone up. But the building remained silent and still, so Zoe carefully pulled the door open a little more, then slipped inside to do what she had come there to do.

Zavier peered through the window, watching her lean down to bite at the soft scale on her arm. The scale that, according to Scarlet-mom, could heal people who were sick or hurt. Just as his own blood had healed Caleb-dad, both back when he was a baby and earlier today. It was a pretty cool superpower, he had to admit, though the blood was in limited supply. He, himself, was currently all tapped out and would be for the next couple weeks. As Zoe would be once she was done giving her blood to Connor.

The blood transfusion only took a moment, and before he knew it, Zoe was bursting back through the door, her eyes shining with excitement. *I did it!* she announced proudly. Then she turned, peering through the window. She paused for a moment, then bounced up and down in glee. *He's waking up!* she cried. *He's okay!* She turned to Zavier. *I did it! I healed him!*

Good work, Sis, Zavier said, softening. Zoe'd been so upset earlier; it warmed his heart to see her happy again, no matter what the reason. *Now let's get out of here before they find out we broke through our chains.*

Zoe nodded. *And then tomorrow, we can tell Scarlet-mom what we did! And she'll tell everyone else. They'll call us heroes. Good dragons who save people*, she added with much bravado. *And then they'll have to let us stay.*

They walked out the back door and into the open air. The night was cool but not cold, and a full moon shone down on them, illuminating the landscape and casting dark shadows on the field. Zavier found himself looking out into the distance, wondering what the world was like beyond this place.

Are you sure you want to stay? he surprised himself by asking.

Zoe gave him a sharp look. *What do you mean?*

I mean… He raised his paw, sweeping it across the landscape. *There's nothing forcing us to stay. We could leave tonight, just the two of us. Never look back.*

Zoe's face twisted in horror. *Leave?* she repeated. *Leave Scarlet-mom? Caleb-dad? Where would we go? What would we do? How would we eat?*

We're dragons, Zavier reminded her. *We can go, do, and eat anything we want to. We're kind of top of the food chain, if you didn't notice.*

But Zoe only shook her head. *Then they really would believe we are bad dragons*, she told him. *We've already messed everything up. Now's our chance to show them that they're wrong about us, that we're good dragons and we deserve to be part of the team.*

Zavier let out a frustrated breath. *Why do you even care what some humans think?*

Zoe dropped her gaze, shuffling her feet against the sand.

She looked so dejected Zavier felt bad for his harsh tone. *I'm sorry*, he amended. *I know you want them to like you. It's not that I don't. It's just, I'm just worried that you're hoping for something that can never happen. We have no idea whether they'll ever accept us after today. And what if they decide to do something worse?*

Worse…?

You know. Like hurt us. Or…worse, he amended lamely. A moment ago, she'd been so happy, and he was the bad guy dragging her back to earth.

But Zoe only shook her head. *Scarlet-mom would never let that happen*, she told her brother. *She promised to protect us, and she never breaks her promises.*

Zavier sighed. As with everything else, he knew it was impossible to make her see what he saw. And while he could easily go off by himself, leave her to the human world she loved, at the end of the day, he knew it wasn't really an option. They were a pair. They'd been together since they were eggs. The world held nothing of value to him besides his sister.

Okay, he said, putting a wing around her. *Let's go back to the hangar.*

Chapter Twenty-Six

T his is not good. This is so not good."

Scarlet paced the small bathroom she and Caleb had retreated to after their talk with Trinity, her steps quickly eating up the distance between walls. Caleb watched from the doorway, wanting desperately to reach out to her, to pull her into his arms. But he wasn't sure she'd appreciate the gesture.

"It's going to be okay," he tried to tell her for what felt like the thousandth time. The lie rolled more easily off his tongue now but still knotted in his stomach. "You heard Trinity. She's not going to let anything happen to them."

Scarlet whirled around, her face radiating her distress. "And you just believe her? What, because she's the great and powerful Trinity Foxx? You're just going to sit back and let her decide the fate of your poor dragon instead of standing up and fighting for him?"

Caleb raked a frustrated hand through his hair. "Look, I know you don't believe this, but Trinity is on our side, okay? I mean, sure, she's a little pissed off at us right now. But that doesn't mean she won't make every effort to do the right thing." He took a step forward. "After all, she's dedicated her entire life to protecting the dragon race."

"After walking on water, right? Saving the world before breakfast?"

Caleb groaned. "Look, I know you don't like her, okay? And I'm not saying you should either. But, Scarlet, what choice do we have?"

"We could leave," she said flatly, staring him down. "We could walk out that door and take Zoe and Zavier with us."

Panic rose inside of him. She was serious. Trinity's voice seemed to echo through his head.

Do not let this get any worse than it already is.

"No." He shook his head. "There's no way."

Scarlet scowled. "Why not?"

"Because that would basically prove we have something to hide. Don't you see? We have to show them we're cooperating. If we break them out and take off—that's basically handing my brother permission to come after us."

"Well, he won't need permission if we're just hanging out here, our dragons nice and neatly chained up and ready for the slaughterhouse."

His gut sank as he saw the look on her face. She meant everything she said, and she was going to do it. Which left him, in his best estimation, with three options. He could help her. He could try to stop her. Or he could simply let her go. None of them sounded very promising.

"Please, Scarlet. Just give it one night," he tried at last. "My brother's unconscious, locked up, and stuffed to the gills with painkillers. He can't do any harm tonight. And in the morning, we'll go and talk to the others as we promised. We'll make them understand. And if for some reason they don't? Well, then we can leave." He met her eyes with his own pleading ones. "But at least let's try to give them the benefit of the doubt first. Okay?"

Scarlet let out a small moan, and Caleb could see the fight slipping from her shoulders. With her bravado gone, she looked small and scared. He found himself stepping closer to her, then, after a moment's hesitation, taking her in his arms.

"I'm sorry," she murmured into his shoulder. "It's just… I'm so frightened. The idea that something could happen to them…" She cringed. "They're all I have in the world, you know."

Caleb swallowed hard. "That's not actually true," he told her, remembering something she had said to him in the Nether, back when he had been the one to feel all alone in the world. "You have me."

She froze, looking up at him with wide, fearful eyes. "No," she said, her voice shaky. "Don't say that if you don't mean it. It's not fair. It's not—"

He silenced her with a kiss, his heart squeezing in his chest as their lips came together, hungry, desperate, seeking something solid and real in a world gone mad. Her lips were soft, so impossibly soft, and as his mouth moved against hers, his hands took on a mind of their own, pulling her to him, tangling himself around her, their breath coming hard and heavy and fast. She tasted like mint gum. She felt like heaven. And for a moment, he wanted her more than he'd ever wanted his precious Nether. Which was quite a lot indeed.

How long had he been holding back, scared of letting go? And now that he had, he never wanted it to end. He wanted to kiss her until there was no breath left in his lungs. And then to kiss her some more.

But she was already pulling away, meeting his eyes with her own. Such desperate eyes, such pleading eyes. It was all he could do not to say yes, no matter what her next request.

But he was pretty sure he was going to have to say no.

"Please, Caleb," she begged. "Let's get out of here. Let's take the dragons and go. We can be a family—just like we were. We don't need the rest of them. You don't need her."

Don't need her.

Caleb jerked as reality crashed down, shattering the fantasy world. Suddenly, his mind flashed to their earlier meeting with Trinity. To her imploring eyes. To her voice, whispering across his subconscious.

You told me once—whatever I needed—you would be here for me.

He'd dedicated his whole life to her, given everything to help her in her quest. And yet time and time again, when she'd needed him most, he'd failed her. He'd made stupid decisions, given in to temptation, proven himself weak.

Keep her away from those dragons tonight. No matter what you have to do.

"What's wrong?" Scarlet asked, staring at him with a devastated look on her face. "Why are you looking at me like that?"

He hung his head. "I'm sorry," he said quietly. "I'm really, really sorry. But it's for the best."

Before she could reply, he stepped back, through the door and into the hallway. As she made a move to follow, he closed the door in her face. Then he clicked the lock.

"What are you doing?" she cried, banging her fist from the inside. "Let me out!"

"I'm sorry. I can't," he said again, his heart breaking into a thousand pieces as he turned and walked away.

Chapter Twenty-Seven

Connor opened his eyes. It was dark. The middle of the night. Quiet. Everyone must have still been asleep. For a moment, he couldn't remember where he was, what had happened. Then he reached up and touched his forehead, and it all came rushing back to him. The dragons. His attempt to sing them down. His brother attacking him, slamming a rock into his temple. Blackness crashing around him.

The dragons. His heart pounded in his chest. *What had happened to the dragons?*

He slid out from under his blanket, stifling a groan as his bare feet connected with icy-cold floor. He paused for a moment as the room spun. God, he felt as if he'd been run over by a truck. He glanced at the bed, tempted to lie back down. To close his eyes. To sleep away the pain.

Instead, he slipped out the door and into the hallway. When he passed Trinity's room, he stopped for a moment, staring at it wistfully. Things had been so strained between them, and now it would only get worse. In fact, he wouldn't be surprised if, after tonight, she never spoke to him again. A heavy remorse blanketed his shoulders.

The soft spot you have for that girl will be the death of you…and the rest of the world, his father's voice jeered in his head.

And for once, the old man was right.

His mind flashed to little Salla back in his world, sucking on a messy pigtail as she looked up at him with awestruck eyes. She was counting on him. The world was counting on him, whether they knew it or not, and he was the only one who could save them now. He'd warned Trinity of the potential dangers time and time again. He'd begged her to take precautions. But she'd refused to believe him. Now things had come to the boiling point. And the time for hesitation was through.

He'd traveled two hundred years back in time to stop the dragon apocalypse, only to be thwarted at every turn. Now here was his chance, once and for all, to make things right.

For you, Salla, he thought. *And for you, Trinity, even if you'll never understand why.*

He slipped outside. Closing his eyes, he drew in a breath, focusing his Hunter's gift on his prey. They were still alive. Nearby. Most likely holed up in that second hangar. But quiet—maybe asleep. Good. If all went well, perhaps they'd never even wake up. Walking around to the storage locker at the back of the terminal, he spun the combination dial and opened it. Then he reached for his gun-blade.

"What are you doing?"

He froze at the sound of the voice piercing the otherwise still air. Whirling around, he recognized none other than Rashida, dressed all in black, slipping through the darkness like a thief in the night.

"I thought you were, like, in a coma and locked up or something," she said, giving him a skeptical look.

He swallowed hard. "I…had to go to the bathroom."

Rashida raised an eyebrow. "Funny. And here I thought the bathrooms were inside."

Fleck. What was he supposed to say now? "Yeah," he stammered. "I just… I wanted some fresh air, I guess." He started to back away, trying to conceal the gun-blade behind his back.

"Please. You expect me to believe that? After all we've been through? Come on, Connor. You know I'm not stupid. And I know you don't give a crap about fresh air. Admit it, Hunter. You're out here for one reason and one reason only."

He pursed his lips, his pulse thrumming at his wrists. "Which is…?"

She met his gaze. "The same reason I am. To kill the dragons."

Connor stared at her, for a moment rendered speechless. Then he grabbed her and dragged her under the shadow of the storage locker so as not to be caught by anyone else. His hands found her shoulders, and he shook her hard. "No," he said, his voice leaving no room for argument. "You can't kill the dragons."

"Well, I'm certainly not going to let them live," Rashida shot back, grabbing his hands and wrenching them from her body. "I mean, did you see the black one? It almost killed poor Emmy. How can we just stand around and risk it happening again?" She scowled. "Besides, you're the one always going on and on about the looming dragon apocalypse. I actually thought you'd approve."

Connor groaned. This was so not how he'd wanted this to go down. "Look, just go back to bed, okay?" he pleaded. "I'll take it from here. Trust me. This is what I trained for, after all. This is what I do."

"Yeah, well, this is what *I* do when a dragon threatens my friend. Sorry, Connor, but you're not getting rid of me that easily."

Connor let out a frustrated breath, shooting a look at the dark and quiet hangar. They were wasting precious time. And who knew how long it would take for someone else to wake up and start nosing around? Besides, he told himself, it was never a bad thing to have backup along. Rashida understood the dangers, and he wouldn't mind having her along to help.

"Fine," he said, reaching back into the storage locker and tossing her his laser pistol. "Then let's do this. Let's end this— once and for all."

Chapter Twenty-Eight

A loud creak echoed through the hangar, startling Zavier awake. He opened one sleepy eye, then another, trying to focus on the crack of light that had appeared across the room. Was someone coming? He reached out, trying to feel for the sudden presence. Was it Scarlet-mom, returning for them at last? But no, it wasn't her. It wasn't Caleb-dad either. But there was definitely someone there.

A cold chill seemed to sweep over him, and the scales on his back bristled, though he wasn't sure why. Forcing himself to lie totally still, he watched the sliver of light widen. He wondered if he should wake his sister, who was sleeping soundly beside him. She was exhausted and weak from giving Caleb's brother her blood. *Poor thing*, Zavier thought, his nostrils flaring a little. *He'd better appreciate her sacrifice.*

He strained to listen again as a song began to weave through the air. No, not just any song, he considered, but perhaps the most beautiful song he'd ever heard. Against his better judgment, he found himself craning his neck forward, his ears pricking, desperate to catch each and every note. Beside him, he could feel his sister stirring; she must have heard it too.

He realized he'd risen to his feet without even being aware of doing so—as if his body had somehow taken over his conscious mind. He took a step forward, feeling himself drawn to the song. The hauntingly beautiful song.

He wanted to roll around in it, bathe in it, drown in it if he could. It was that good.

What is that? he heard Zoe breathe softly beside him. *It's so...beautiful.*

He glanced over; her eyes were open but had a glazed look to them, as if under a spell, and her mouth had curved into one of her sweet smiles. Not surprising—Zoe had always loved music. In fact, when Scarlet-mom had first moved them into the maintenance shack, she'd brought them this amazing device that would play thousands of songs at the touch of a pane of glass. Sometimes, he'd wake in the middle of the night to find Zoe lying on her back, staring up at the ceiling, lost in the music.

But none of those songs sounded quite like this one. This song—well, it was almost as if all the dragons in the Nether were lifting their voices into a single chorus.

It's him, Zoe exclaimed suddenly. *I can feel him! I can hear him!*

Zavier frowned, the spell broken at her words. *Who?* he asked, confused.

The boy I healed! Caleb-dad's brother. Zoe turned to him, her eyes alive and dancing with delight. *He's awake! He's come to see me! Do you think he knows I cured him? Is this his way of thanking me? By singing me this beautiful song?* She sighed dreamily, taking another step forward. *I'm here, my blood brother. I'm right here.*

Zavier frowned, her words seemed to itch at the back of his brain, though he couldn't pinpoint why. But something was wrong. Something was very, very wrong.

He looked back to Zoe only to realize she was no longer standing beside him. She had broken her chains again and was already halfway across the hangar, bounding happily toward the source of song. He frowned.

Zoe! he tried, worry winding through his voice. *Come back here!*

He's calling me, Zavier! He wants me to come to him! He wants to thank me for—

A shot rang out, the recoil of the rifle cutting through the song like a knife through hot butter. Dazed, it took Zavier a moment to understand what was going on.

Then he heard his sister's scream—a scream that blasted his ears with such force, he wondered if he would go deaf from it. Horrified, his eyes locked on her a few yards away, terror pounding at his insides. He could see Zoe standing perfectly still, staring off into the distance, a confused look on her face.

The bullet missed her, he told himself, trying desperately to quell his fear. *It just freaked her out. But it didn't get her. She's okay. She's totally okay.*

Zoe, we have to get out of here. Before—

His sister let out another scream, this one louder and more piercing—so piercing it could probably break glass. Then she fell, hitting the ground with a loud crash. Zavier watched her for a moment, frozen in place, as she writhed and kicked her feet in the air. Then somehow, he found his feet and raced to her, heart in his throat, steam shooting from his nose. When he reached her, he let out a horrified gasp.

No. Zoe, no!

Blood, black as night, gushed from his sister's soft scale as her chest heaved up and down with effort. The very same scale she'd used to bring a boy back to consciousness only hours before, now the instrument in her death. Helpless, Zavier let out an alarmed wail, desperately pawing her exposed flank with his foot. His sister looked up at him with glassy eyes filled with hurt and betrayal.

I thought he wanted to thank me, she whispered.

Zavier dropped to the ground, trying to lick her wound clean. But the blood was gushing, too fast, too furious. Try as he might, he couldn't stop the flow.

Please, Zoe. Don't leave me! he begged, the tears rolling down his cheeks, splashing onto his sister and soaking her scales. Even as the words spilled from his mind, he knew it was a selfish request. But the idea of living a life without her…

Another shot rang out. Zavier grunted as it nicked one of his scales and ricocheted off, bouncing across the hangar before dropping to the ground. He turned to glare at it, hating how harmless it looked, just lying there now. A tiny piece of metal with the power to destroy his world. Suddenly, his sorrow turned to anger, and his blood boiled as he let out a loud, angry roar.

For a moment, Zoe's cloudy eyes cleared. *Go*, she told him. *You must get of here!*

No! he cried, shaking his head furiously. *I'm not going to just leave you here! To this…this…butcher.*

His sister—his beautiful, sweet, gentle sister—looked up at him with her wide, pleading, purple eyes. *Please*, she begged. *I can't leave this world without knowing you're safe. Go find Scarlet-mom. She will protect you.*

He bristled, anger threatening to throttle him. *I don't need anyone's protection.*

215

But she may need yours.

And with that, her body failed her, her neck going limp, her head crashing to the floor. Zavier let out a horrified cry, nudging her with his snout, pleading for her to get up. But he knew, in his heart, she would never get up again. And as another bullet rang out, this time missing him by a hair, he stretched back to full height, unfurling his wings and pushing back on his hind legs, rising to the rooftop—free.

The song came again. But this time it only sounded like a funeral requiem, and he put his paws over his ears to block it out. At the same time, his eyes sought out the singer, prepared to seek his revenge.

It was then that he saw them—two humans at the edge of the hangar, hiding cowardly behind a blue plane. One had a gun with a long blade at the end. The ugly weapon that had stolen the life of his sister.

In a rage, Zavier opened his mouth, releasing the fireball that had been building up inside of him, torpedoing it straight toward his attackers. Then, not waiting to see if he'd hit his mark, he shot down toward them, flames still streaming as he flew. One of the humans dove out of the way, but the other fell, the fire consuming her as she writhed in agony. He grabbed her in his mouth—her screams nothing more than a lullaby as his teeth dug into her flesh. He shook her violently until she went limp. Then he spit her onto the ground, disgusted. He didn't have time to eat her, even if she deserved it.

Besides, the fire was burning inside of him again, and so he turned to seek out the other killer, his gaze darting around the room but coming up empty. He was gone. But Zavier would find him again. And he would make him pay.

He swallowed the fire back down—for now—not wanting to waste the heat. Then he turned again for one last look at his sister. His sweet, sweet sister, who only wanted to love and be loved in return. And yet instead…

They will not get away with this, he vowed. *I will stay alive for you, Zoe. I will avenge you. I will kill them all.*

Chapter Twenty-Nine

*B*e brave! You've got be brave! Don't let him see how much it hurts! Connor jerked back into consciousness. His eyes darted around the dark room, assessing quickly as the horror rose inside of him at an alarming rate. He must have hit his head when he'd dived behind the plane to avoid the dragon's fire and managed to knock himself out.

Now the hangar was ablaze, flames greedily licking at the walls as all around him, smoke twisted and danced a devilish jig. A few yards away, the pink dragon lay where he'd shot it, its mighty flanks heaving up and down with great effort. The other... He scanned the perimeter but came up empty—until his eyes rose and he saw the giant, dragon-sized hole in the ceiling.

He'd gotten away. Fleck.

I can't breathe... It hurts. It hurts so much!

Connor frowned at the sudden, high-pitched cry piercing through him like a bullet. Confused, he looked around again, his lungs seizing as his gaze fell upon a charred lump nearby. A human-shaped lump, black and bloody and torn.

Rashida. Oh no.

He leaned over just in time to empty his stomach, yellow bile spewing from his mouth and onto the floor. As tears sprung uninvited to his eyes, he forced himself to straighten and wipe his mouth with his sleeve. He should have never let her come. It was his mission, not hers. She should have never been involved.

But she had insisted. And in doing so, she'd saved his life. He squeezed his eyes shut, then opened them again, trying to reset his sanity as they'd taught him to do in the Academy.

"Don't worry. I'll get him, Rashida," he swore under his breath. "I promise you, you won't have died in vain."

Please, Mr. Hunter. Don't hurt him. He's a good dragon. Really he is.

What was that? Connor clapped his hands over his ears, frustrated, but the gesture did nothing to dampen the sound. Because, he realized suddenly, he wasn't hearing it through his ears. It was coming from inside his head.

What the actual hell…?

Cold dread clawed at his stomach as his eyes slowly turned back to the dragon he'd shot. It was clearly dying, blood pooling around it in a blackened halo as it struggled to take in its last shallow breaths. But while that should have made him happy—overjoyed, in fact, mission accomplished and all that—for some reason, all he could feel was an inexplicable grief washing over him like a tidal wave. So much anguish pounding at his insides that, for a moment, he could barely breathe. In fact, it was all he could do to stop himself from running over to the monster and trying to staunch its wounds. To save its life. Even though moments before, he'd want nothing more than to kill it dead.

He's a good dragon, Mr. Hunter. He's sorry for what he did. Please don't kill him.

Connor's heart lurched, realization seizing him with a clammy grip. His trembling hand rose involuntarily to his forehead. The same spot his brother had struck him with a rock earlier that day. The spot that should have been badly bruised—a huge goose egg at the very least. Instead, the skin was completely smooth, unmarred—healed in a way that should taken weeks.

He staggered backward. They couldn't have. They wouldn't have. They knew how he felt about dragons. There's no way they would…

You were dying. I helped you. I thought it would make you understand. No!

It took everything he had to force himself to turn away from the beast, running toward the exit and pushing through the double doors to burst out onto the empty runway. Once outside, he turned his eyes to the night sky, scanning for some sight of the other dragon. Where was it? It couldn't have gone far.

He had to end this. Now.

The Hunter song ripped from his lungs, burning as it burst from his scorched throat. But he ignored the pain. He had to get the dragon back here—before it got out of range and could no longer hear the song.

Before it was too late.

Come on, you damn dragon, he swore. *Come back to me!*

God. He squeezed his hands into fists. He'd had them. He'd had both dragons caught in his song. Both well within his line of sight. All he'd had to do was raise his gun and shoot one after another—bang, bang—and it would all be over.

But then he'd heard that voice. The high-pitch whisper across his consciousness, paralyzing him where he stood and staying his hand. Forcing Rashida to take the shot instead. And as her bullet sang true, the pain punched him in the gut, and he'd dropped to the ground, his gun-blade clattering uselessly to his side.

At first he'd thought he'd been shot somehow too. He'd even pulled up his shirt expecting to see a bloody mess. But his skin was untouched. And yet the pain was so bad, he felt as if he would pass out. And so he'd dove behind the plane for safety and allowed the second dragon to escape.

Allowed Rashida to be killed.

A screwup to the end, his father mocked. *I should be ashamed to call you my son.*

Suddenly, Connor caught a flicker of movement from the corner of his eye. His heart leapt to his throat as he watched the black dragon, shooting up from behind the back of the terminal and speeding across the sky.

There you are, you bastard!

He dove into action, running as fast his legs would allow, screaming his Hunter song at the top of his lungs. In the back of his mind, he realized how stupid he was being. Going out into the open sky without cover or proper backup. But what choice did he have? He couldn't let the beast get away.

Please, Mr. Hunter. I'm begging you! Spare my brother's life!

"Shut up!" Connor screamed. "Get the fleck out of my head!"

The black dragon turned on a dime, its beady eyes locking onto him as if he'd heard Connor's scream. For a moment, it did nothing—just stared at him with an expression of vile hatred that made his blood run cold. Then, it opened its mouth, and fire shot from its throat, raining down on the pavement, the tar sizzling and melting under the sudden heat.

Connor threw himself to the side, his bad ankle jarring as he rolled out of the fire's path. Leaping back to his feet, he searched the sky again, seeking and finding his target. He was still singing, he realized vaguely. But the dragon didn't seem interested. It was too busy setting everything on fire.

"Good dragon, my ass," he muttered.

He lifted his gun, his hands trembling so hard he could barely manage to line up the shot.

"Hasta la vista, dragon spawn," he spit out. And this time, he meant it.

But just as he was about to pull the trigger, the dragon turned, pointing its snout to the sky and shooting upward, disappearing into the clouds. Connor tried to run after it, to get a better angle, but found his path blocked by a lake of fire.

And then, there was nothing he could do. Only stand there, helpless, watching everything around him burn as the dragon flew away, free. He'd failed. Once again, he'd failed. And now there was a dragon on the loose. A vengeful, angry dragon, ready to tear up the world, once more with feeling. His eyes lifted again, praying for that one last chance that he knew in his heart he wouldn't get.

"Come back," he whispered. "Oh God, please come back."

He felt a presence behind him and whirled around. Trinity stood there, staring at him, mouth agape. Her eyes dropped to the gun he still held in his hands, a look of horrified recognition on her face.

"What have you done?" she whispered hoarsely.

Chapter Thirty

*M*other! *Wake up, Mother. Please!*

Scarlet groaned, plugging her ears with her fingers to drown out the loud rapping noise breaking through her deep sleep. Ugh. Was it morning already? She felt as if she'd been run over by a truck. "Five more minutes, Mac," she begged.

Please! Mother! You have to get up now. You have to come with me—before it's too late.

What? Scarlet jerked to a sitting position, confusion swirling through her as she suddenly recognized the voice through her sleep-induced haze. "Zavier?" she whispered, puzzled. "Is that you?"

The rapping came again, and she leapt to her feet, flying to the tiny bathroom window as the events of the last twelve hours came rushing back to her. *Oh God. Has something happened?* Her eyes fell to Zavier outside her window, pacing back and forth, blowing billows of smoke through his flared nostrils. What was he doing out there? How had he gotten out of the hangar? And what—she swallowed heavily—what was that black oily stuff coating his legs?

"What are you doing out there?" she demanded, wishing the window was the kind that opened. Even if she smashed it, it was too small to crawl through. "Why aren't you in the hangar? Where's Zoe?"

Zavier gave her a tortured look. *Mother, something's happened. We must leave this place. Now.*

Oh God. Scarlet's heart was now in her throat. "Zavier, you're not making any sense. Where's Zoe? Is she still in the hangar? We can't just take off on her and…" She trailed off, seeing the flash of pain cross Zavier's face. "Oh no," she whispered hoarsely. "No."

Reaching out with her mind, she searched for her dragon through their shared link. Her precious baby girl. Where was she? Why wasn't she with Zavier? Zoe was always with Zavier.

Zoe? she called. *Are you okay? Talk to me, girl. Tell me you're okay!*

But there was no answer. Only silence. A horrible, deafening silence.

Come on, Mother, Zavier urged, a small, worried whine escaping his mouth. *Please! You must come now! We must fly from here before he finds me.*

Scarlet abandoned the window, running to the door, her fingers grasping for the handle. Of course it was still locked. She took a few steps back, then slammed her body against it, hitting it hard and practically seeing stars from the impact. But the door did not budge.

Because the boy she had loved, the boy she had trusted, had locked her in.

Panic seizing her, she looked around the room, desperate for something to use. Her eyes fell upon the ceramic toilet bowl and the lid to its tank. She grabbed it, then backed up, preparing to use it as a makeshift battering ram. Sucking in a breath, she charged, slamming it into the door. It took three tries before the door cracked and gave way.

She dropped the lid to the ground, then pushed her way through the hole in the door. She took off down the hall, her heart slamming against her ribs and her breath coming in short gasps.

As she took a sharp right into the main waiting room, she dug in her heels, stopping short as she took in the sight. The air was thick with smoke, and everyone was running around, desperate and wide-eyed, filling buckets of water and running them out the front doors, trying to put out the fire. Scarlet watched, horrified. What was going on here?

Somehow she forced her feet to move, one after the other, pushing through the doors and running toward the hangar where Zoe and Zavier had been taken. Where she had taken them. Where Caleb had forced her to leave them—unprotected and alone.

Oh, Zoe. Please, Zoe.

She pushed her way into the hangar. The smoke was even thicker here, and several of the abandoned airplanes had caught fire. A few of the Potentials were running in and out with their pitiful buckets of water, attempting to douse the flames, but she ignored them, scanning the area, trying to squint through the smoke.

And then she saw it. The large, pink lump at the far end of the room, swimming in a pool of black.

Oh no.

No, no, NO!

"Scarlet!" She felt a presence behind her, but the voice sounded muffled and far away. She could vaguely feel hands grabbing at her arms, but she shook them off impatiently, her eyes locked on the horrible sight in front of her.

"Zoe!" she screamed, rushing toward her dragon. "No, oh God, please no! Zoe!"

The dragon was lying on her side, soaked in blood, the single scale on her arm—the one with the lifesaving blood—pierced and drained. Zoe's eyes were open, and for a moment, Scarlet held out hope for a miracle. But as she got closer, she saw they were glassy, unseeing. And her tongue, that silly black tongue that had given Scarlet a thousand playful kisses over the last months, now lolled from her gaping mouth. Cracked. Dry. Dead.

Dead like the dragon herself.

"Oh, Zoe," Scarlet sobbed, throwing herself on top of the dragon and holding her as best she could as the tears fell like rain from her eyes. "My poor baby. My poor, poor baby! Who did this to you?"

But the dragon, of course, didn't answer. And Scarlet knew in her heart that the dragon would never answer her again. Burying her face in her scales, she sobbed pitifully, her heart feeling as if it were being ripped apart, piece by agonizing piece.

Everything she'd suffered up until now: her stepfather's abuse, her mother's neglect, the government's experiments—nothing had felt as bad as this. Maybe it was because, in all of those situations, there was still underlying hope. Hope of rescue. Hope of escape. Hope of starting a life anew. But now, as she held the dead dragon to her, she realized there was no longer any hope left at all. And there never would be, ever again.

They'd killed her dragon. Despite all Caleb had said, despite what Trinity had promised. They'd gone and done it anyway. And she'd been helpless to stop them.

"Scarlet!"

She looked up, so blinded from the mixture of tears and smoke she couldn't recognize the figure who stood above her for a moment. But when he crouched down and tried to put his arms around her, she realized it was Caleb.

She shoved him back with as much force as she could muster. "Get the hell away from me!" she growled.

"Scarlet, the fire's spreading. We have to get out of here."

She stared at him, rage burning through her like wildfire. "That's all you can say?" she screamed, her voice raspy from the smoke. "She's dead, Caleb! They killed her! Just like I said they would."

His face twisted in anguish. "I know, baby. I know." He tried to reach for her again. She leapt back, staring at him with hatred.

"I could have done something. I could have gotten them away." she cried, her words spilling from her lips. Angry. Afraid. And so, so sad. "I counted on you. *They* counted on you. But you didn't care about that, did you? You only cared about her. And now Zoe is dead, and they're probably after Zavier too!"

Suddenly she remembered him standing outside her window. He was waiting for her. Even now, with his sister dead and his life in danger, he was waiting to take her to safety.

She slowly rose to her feet, taking one last pained look at her dead dragon, then turned to face Caleb. "I hope you and your precious Fire Kissed rot in hell," she growled.

She pushed past him before he could reply, out of the hangar, her lungs now burning from smoke inhalation. But she didn't care. She ran across the airfield, her bare feet hitting the cement one painful step after another. Finally, she made it back to the window, where Zavier had been waiting, praying the dragon hadn't given up on her and flown away.

But no. It was *people* who gave up on you. *People* who betrayed you. Dragons were loyal. They would be there for you. They would not let you down.

And as she turned the corner, there was Zavier, proving her right. Pawing the ground with marked agitation and impatience, but still there. Still waiting to take her away. Scarlet ran to him, throwing her arms around him and holding him close, unleashing yet another round of tears. Zavier whined nervously, his scales bristling, his nose steaming smoke. She could feel him shaking with fear and upset.

"I know, baby," she murmured, her voice choking on the words. "I know."

It was me, not her, the dragon protested. *She didn't do anything wrong. She didn't do anything, but they killed her anyway. Why would they do that? Why would they kill my sister?*

Scarlet bit her lower lip to keep from sobbing. Sometimes it was hard to remember, since Zavier was so big, that he was actually still so very young. He could be physically strong for her, but at the end of the day, she had to be his rock.

She was his mother, after all.

"Because people are monsters," she said simply. "And from this point on, we are done with monsters."

Chapter Thirty-One

O h, Connor, what have you done?"

Trinity stared at Connor, his silhouette illuminated by the flames raging behind him. Her hands curled into fists as frustration and fury threatened to consume her. It was all she could do not to tackle him to the ground. To punch him in the face.

To break out into tears.

How could he do this? They were supposed to be a team. They were supposed to be working together. How could he just go and act—commit such an atrocity without even consulting her first?

Because it was his mission all along, a voice inside of her nagged.

"Trinity." He turned to her, his face a mask of anguish and pain that sucked the breath from her lungs. He looked as devastated as she felt, but she forced down the pity she told herself he didn't deserve. Instead, she squared her shoulders and tightened her fists until her nails cut into her palms, drawing blood. She wouldn't back down. She wouldn't alleviate his guilt or assure him it was okay.

Because it wasn't okay. He'd killed a dragon. He'd killed Emmy's daughter.

"How could you?" she repeated, her voice shrieking. "How could you just go and do something like this? After all we talked about!"

She closed her eyes, unable to even look at him as the feeling of betrayal warred with her grief. They'd been together so long, shared so much. But deep down, she now realized, she'd been lying to herself from the start, telling herself that he had changed. How many times had he told her, after all, that he could never truly rest until dragons were gone? And yet still, she'd held on, all this time, to this vain hope that there would someday come a time when he would abandon his quest for vengeance. When he would set down his weapons and accept what was—and what she believed could be.

What a fool she'd been.

"I don't know why I'm even surprised," she growled. "After all, it's why you came to our godforsaken world in the first place, right?" She stared at him, her eyes flashing fire. "Well, congratulations, Hunter, mission accomplished. Too bad you can't go back home. They'd probably give you a medal of honor."

"A pin."

"What?"

"They give pins," he said softly, his eyes dull and defeated. "If you kill a dragon, you get a pin."

Trinity scowled. Oh she'd like to pin him all right—pin him to the ground and punch him in the face. To make him feel even half the pain he had inflicted on her. On Caleb. On Scarlet. On Emmy's poor, poor daughter.

Connor wrung his hands together. "Look, Trin. I think I—"

His words were interrupted as Luke and Nate ran up to

them, their faces white with fear. Nate dropped an iPad into Trinity's hands. "Look!" he cried. "This just came in."

Trinity stared down at the tablet. A news report from a town a few miles away, the one with the Walmart they'd frequented. The Walmart that, according to this report, was now on fire.

After being attacked by a dragon.

"Is this what you wanted?" Trinity roared at Connor, shoving the iPad in his face. "They were penned up. They were calm. They were peaceful. And now we have one dead and the other ready to take down the world in revenge. Was this your big fat plan for saving our world? 'Cause it's pretty crappy if you ask me."

Connor stared down at the iPad, then back up at her. "Trin…"

She held up her hand to stop him; she didn't need to hear any of his excuses now. None of them could possibly make a difference anyway. Instead, she turned to Nate and Luke, forcing her anguish at bay and summoning all her remaining bravado. She couldn't let her personal feelings stop her from doing what had to be done. Team Dragon was counting on her now more than ever—not to mention the rest of the world. She didn't have time to fall apart.

"We need to do some serious triage. Go set up the studio to do a quick broadcast assuring people we're going to take care of this. In the meantime, Emmy and I will head out to find him. Keep logging every sighting you get; we're going to need them if we want to track him down before he does too much damage."

Nate and Luke nodded and ran off. Trinity turned back to Connor. He closed his eyes and sighed.

"Look, Trinity," he said after a heavy pause. "This wasn't a decision I made lightly. Time and time again, I've held back. I've kept my finger off the trigger, even as I saw things getting worse and worse. And you know why?" he asked, looking up at her with cold blue eyes that made her shiver.

"Because of me," she whispered, feeling her heart squeeze till it hurt. "You did it for me."

"And this was for you as well," he said, his voice rising with urgency. "Whether you choose to see it or not."

"No." She shook her head. "Don't pin this on me. You did it for your father. You did it for yourself. For your world, maybe—fine. But don't you dare say you did it for me."

His face crumbled as her words struck him harder than any blow. It killed her to see him look like this, but she forced herself to stay strong. He had to understand. This was unforgivable.

"Fine," he said at last. "Think what you want. It doesn't change anything anyway." And with that, he turned his back on her, starting to walk away. Fury rose inside of her, mixed with overwhelming grief.

"Where are you going?" she demanded.

He paused, not turning around. "To finish this once and for all."

A cold chill spun down her back. "Connor Jacks," she found herself shouting. "You walk away from me now and you can't come back. You'll no longer be a part of this team. And we'll…we'll…" She trailed off helplessly, unable to make a threat she wasn't sure she could follow through with.

But he didn't need to hear her say it out loud. He knew her heart. Better than anyone, he knew her heart.

He turned back to her slowly, shoulders stiff, head held high. He looked so beautiful—so strong and angry and fierce, it took what remained of her breath away. At that moment, it was all she could do not to throw herself into his arms, soak up his strength as her own as she'd done so many times before. But she couldn't. And she never would—ever again.

"You'll thank me one day," he told her. "And if you don't, well, at least I'll know you're safe. That's all that matters to me in the end."

Chapter Thirty-Two

E mmy!"
Trinity burst into the hangar, her eyes searching until they fell on the dragon. Emmy was awake, pacing back and forth, her ears pricked and her nostrils flared. She turned to look at Trinity with wide, frightened eyes.

What's happening? she demanded. *I smell smoke.*

Trinity gave her a grim look. "It's not good. I'll explain on the way. But we have to go, Emmy. Before it's too late." She made a move to get on the dragon's back.

The dragon gave her a terrified look, backing away before she could mount her. *Something's happened to them. To Zoe and Zavier. Is that right?*

Trinity sucked in a breath. "Yes," she admitted. "I'm sorry, Emmy. But Zoe's dead. And Zavier's on a rampage." She gave a brief rundown of what had gone down best she knew. "We have to go after him and talk him down, before he does too much damage."

Emmy moaned, her face mirroring her obvious distress. Trinity wondered what the dragon was thinking—after all, she had been the first to want them dead. Would she refuse to help save Zavier now? Trin waited, breath in her throat.

Finally Emmy seemed to come to a decision. She lowered her wing, nodding for Trinity to climb aboard. Trin did, relief rushing through her as she scrambled up the dragon's back, settling between her neck and shoulders. "Okay," she said. "Let's go."

"Wait!"

Emmy paused. Trinity turned to see Caleb burst through the hangar door. He was out of breath and covered in ash. When he reached them, he leaned over, putting his hands on his knees, gasping for breath.

"There you are," he managed to spit out. "I've been looking everywhere."

Trin bit her lower lip, waiting for the accusations to spill from his lips, guilt gnawing at her stomach. After all, she was the one who had begged him and Scarlet to wait. To trust that the group would do the right thing.

She still had no idea how it had all happened. When she'd last checked on Connor, he'd been out cold, doped up on painkillers. Not to mention they'd locked his sickroom door, just as a precaution. So how had he managed to wake up? To stroll out a locked door like it was no big thing? Sure, someone else could have broken him out. But he should have been weak, exhausted, barely able to stand, let alone take on two dragons and survive.

She shook her head. In the end, the how made no difference. What they did next was all that mattered.

"Look, Caleb, Emmy and I are going after Zavier. I'll report back in when I have some—"

"I'm coming with you," he interrupted.

"No, Caleb. I don't think—"

"You don't understand," he argued, and she could hear the strain in his voice, still raspy from smoke inhalation. "Scarlet's with Zavier. She took off on his back. If my brother finds him… If he shoots Zavier down…" He trailed off, his face a mask of devastation.

He really cares about her, Trin thought suddenly. *More than he even wants to admit to himself.*

"I don't know," she hedged. "It'll be quicker if I just—"

"Please! I can help you!" Caleb begged. "Zavier and I share a bond thanks to the blood Scarlet gave me. Maybe I can help talk him down—at least talk Scarlet into talking him down." He gave Trinity a tortured look. "Please, Trin. If anything were to happen to her…"

"Fine," she relented. What else could she say? Besides, she could admittedly use all the help she could get. "But we have to leave now. Before that dragon of yours proves your brother right."

PART 4:

FLARE

Chapter Thirty-Three

Council Lab—Year 190 Post-Scorch

I ntruder. Intruder alert."

Caleb swore under his breath as his foot accidentally brushed against a thin red beam of light as he made his way into the Council lab, succeeding in tripping the alarm. *Damn it.* He kicked the wall furiously. He'd almost had it—had almost been through. Now, angry lights flashed above, and a piercing siren scolded his ears. He was busted. Big time.

He rose to his feet. No need to be stealthy anymore. Time to dine and dash. Grab and go. Get what he came here for and get the hell out. Darius was counting on him, after all, and he wasn't about to let the Dracken Master down.

He scanned the lab quickly, looking for some sign of his objective. Darius had told him it would be bright purple, a powder derived from crushing up amethysts. But everything he could see in the vicinity now was dull, muted, gray—a few beakers, still bubbling on their Bunsen burners; a few uncut gems, weighing on a scale; glass jars, stacked from floor to ceiling. Nothing with the telltale purple hue he was looking for. For a moment, he wondered if he was in the right place or if their intelligence had been wrong.

But then…

His eyes locked onto a small, opaque canister behind a wall of glass—the only canister in the place made of metal instead of glass. Why? He squinted at it for a moment, studying every inch of it. Until his eyes caught the faintest smudge of purple around its rim. As if someone had screwed the cover on too quickly and a tiny bit had spilled—so faint that the casual onlooker would have missed it. The scientist who put it away definitely had.

He smirked. Careless fools. Maybe this would work out after all.

Diving for the case, he wondered if he should bother with his lock-picking tools; he'd come here with a full thief's arsenal, and it was almost a shame not to put them to good use. But the sirens kept wailing, and he knew, in his heart, there was no time—or need—to be elegant here. Instead, he pulled out his pistol and slammed the butt end against the case, causing the glass to shatter on impact. Carefully, he reached in, making sure not to cut himself as he retrieved his prize.

With trembling hands, he unscrewed the lid, praying his hunch had been right. He sucked in a breath as the cover fell away, his eyes brightening with excitement.

There it was. Unmistakable. The Council's secret experimental weapon against dragons. Now in his hands.

"Sorry, folks," he muttered under his breath. "But I think I'll be taking this."

After screwing the lid back on, careful not to let even a drop spill, he shoved the canister in his satchel and dove out the door. He'd known, even before taking on this mission, that if he were caught, it would be game over for sure. He'd be sent to the mines for good. And his life would all but be over.

But so what? In truth, his life already had been over—before the Dracken had pulled him from his pit of despair. Before they gave him a job and a dragon. Darius had chosen him—the one everyone else had forgotten about—to play a role in saving the world. And Caleb wasn't about to let him down.

He glanced down at the map he'd scribbled on his hand. Just two more turns and he'd be at the exit where his Dracken partner was waiting with the getaway bike. Picking up the pace, he propelled himself forward around corner number one, his feet skidding across the floor. So far so good. He just prayed there was no one manning the doors as he headed for corner number two.

But before he could turn, a lone figure stepped out from behind the corner, his gun raised and ready. Caleb stopped short, digging in his heels as his heart thudded in his chest. He looked up, taking in the crisp Academy uniform. The multiple shiny pins that adorned it.

The face above those pins that mirrored his own.

"Caleb?"

God. It had to be him, didn't it? Of all the people who could have caught him, it had to be his hero brother. Seriously, he thought, *when did the world become so unfair?*

"What are you doing here?" Connor demanded. "Are you stealing from the Council now? Is that what your little Dracken cult has you doing?"

Caleb felt his face flush involuntarily at his brother's jabs. It was crazy—a moment ago, he'd been so proud of this mission. Proud of who he'd become. But one look at his twin's disappointed face, and suddenly he was no longer a member in good standing in the largest dragon sympathizer group in the world—just a no-good Shanty Town rat, as he'd always been. Still thieving, still running from the law, still nothing and nobody and pathetic as hell.

He scowled, straightening his shoulders and firming his resolve. "Get out of my way, Connor," he growled. "Or shoot me if that's what you're planning to do. But make it count. I have zero interest in spending the next thirty to fifty in the mines."

His brother's face flickered with something he couldn't decipher. A moment later, he spoke. "You don't have to do this, you know," he said, his once-steady voice now taking on a pleading tone. "I can talk to the Council. They owe me a favor. I could get you a reprieve. Maybe even a job. You have information about the Dracken. Maybe we could make some kind of...deal."

"A deal to rat out the only friends I've ever had?" Caleb barked out a laugh. "Not bloody likely, oh brother of mine. Don't you get it? I don't want your help. I never have and I never will."

Connor closed his eyes, as if resigning himself to his fate. "Fine," he said. "But please don't make me kill you. I couldn't do that—not to Mom. Just, please, put down your bag and walk away. I'll pretend I never saw you."

Caleb hedged, shuffling from foot to foot. It was a tempting offer—certainly more than he deserved. And for a split second, he tried to imagine a life where he and brother actually got along. But then his mind flashed to his dragon. The dragon his brother had killed in cold blood for no reason at all.

No. Caleb would never accept his brother's help. Not when other dragons were now counting on him. He couldn't save his dragon. But the dust in his satchel would save countless more.

Sorry, Connor. No deal.

Slowly, he made a move, as if reaching for his bag. Then, with lightning speed, he turned his gun on his brother, blasting him where he stood. Connor screamed in pain as he fell to the ground, electrical shocks sparking off his skin. For a moment, Caleb just watched, his mouth set in a thin line.

"From now on, stay away from me," he told him. "Because next time? My gun won't be set to stun."

Chapter Thirty-Four

Present Day

C aleb put a hand over his eyes, attempting to squint into the blazing sun, swearing under his breath as Emmy flew him and Trinity through the skies. They'd been traveling all night, trying to puzzle out the sightings reports Luke was calling in over the walkie-talkies and match them with the signals Trinity was getting from Scarlet through her gift.

Problem was, while at first it seemed as if both dragon and rider were traveling the same path, as the sun began to rise, the reports started to conflict with one another—Scarlet still in the location they'd been heading and the dragon flying in the opposite direction. A fact that set Caleb's nerves on edge. Had Zavier dumped Scarlet? Had she fallen off his back? Was she hurt? Was she…?

"We're closer to Scarlet," he told Trinity. "Let's find her first."

"No," Trinity said. "We can't waste time. We have to get to Zavier before Connor does."

Caleb gritted his teeth. "Come on, Trin. We've been flying around in circles, playing catch-up all night. Scarlet might know where he's headed. She could save us time in the long run and give us a better chance of catching up to him."

And I can make sure she's okay, he added to himself.

Trinity turned, giving him a pointed look. "What makes you think she'll tell us, even if she does know?"

Caleb sighed. He didn't want to admit she had a point. Scarlet had been so angry before she'd taken off on him. The things she'd said… Things he totally deserved for her to say.

He'd spent the entire flight wracked by guilt, trying to figure out a way to get Scarlet to forgive him—and so far he'd come up empty. And who could blame her? He'd basically tricked her—kissed her, then locked her up, taking away her free will. Taking away her chance to protect her dragons. She'd warned him they weren't safe, but he'd refused to listen.

And now Zoe was dead. It couldn't have been more Caleb's fault if he'd struck her down with his own hand.

"I'll make her see," he declared with a bravado he didn't feel. "Whatever she thinks of us personally, she's going to need help to keep Zavier safe. And we're the only ones who can do that."

Trinity frowned, not looking happy about the plan. But to her credit, she didn't argue, only directed Emmy to turn west, skimming an old desert road until a rocky mountainside rose up to greet them. Caleb squinted down at it, heart in his throat. Was she there? Was she alive?

Please be okay. Please be okay.

"Hurry," he urged Emmy.

Emmy complied, swooping in for a landing on the largest of the mountain's ledges. At first, it appeared empty, just jagged, barren rocks mocking them in all directions. But then, his eyes locked onto something moving. A small, dark shadow peeking out from behind a stalagmite.

His heart leapt to his throat. It was her. She was alive.

He dove off the dragon, ignoring the jarring in his ankle as he hit the ground too hard and at a bad angle. Running to her, he could feel the tears brimming in his eyes, his heart lurching in his chest. "Buttercup!" he cried. "Oh my God, Buttercup."

She stared at him warily, taking a step back as he approached, anger and confusion warring on her face. Her eyes went from him to Trinity and Emmy before returning to him. "What are you doing here?" she demanded in a tight voice.

Caleb forced himself to stop short. Even though all he wanted to do was to put his arms around her and squeeze her tight—to throw himself at her feet and beg for a forgiveness he didn't deserve.

"I…just…I wanted to make sure you were okay," he stammered.

She frowned. "I was until you showed up."

"Scarlet…"

"Look, Caleb," she interrupted, cutting him off with a wave of her hand. "Zavier will be back any minute now, and trust me, you don't want to be here when he comes. Let's just say the merciless slaughter of his innocent sister hasn't exactly put him in the cheeriest of moods."

"Where is Zavier now?" Trinity demanded, slipping off Emmy and stepping forward. "Where did he go? And why did he leave you here?"

Caleb frowned, shooting her a warning look. *Let me handle this*, he begged. *You're only going to make it worse.*

Sure enough, Scarlet's face twisted. "Why would I tell you?" she sneered. "So you and your little boyfriend can finish the job?" She shot a look at Caleb, her eyes burning fire. "Or is *he* your boyfriend now? I never can seem to keep track."

Caleb's gut wrenched. "Scarlet, that's not fair."

"No! This isn't fair!" she screeched. "You promised me they'd be safe! You promised no harm would come to them! I trusted you! And you repaid that trust by locking me up so I couldn't protect them!"

He closed his eyes as he felt her fury rain down on him, knowing he deserved it all and more. "I know," he said when she was finished. "And I'm not expecting you to forgive me for what I did. But Zavier's still alive, Scarlet. And my brother is after him. We have to work together if we want to save his life."

Scarlet's face paled. She opened her mouth, then closed it again, looking devastated.

"Where is he?" Caleb pressed, deciding to go for it. "Where is Zavier now?"

"I…I don't know," she blurted out, bursting into tears.

He stared at her. "What?"

She dropped her gaze to the ground. "He dropped me off here. Told me to wait—that he'd be right back. But that was hours ago, and I haven't seen him since." Her expression tightened. She shot a look at Trinity. "I mean, he's probably just out hunting or something," she added quickly. A little too quickly. "He'll be back any minute now, I'm sure."

But she wasn't sure, Caleb realized with sickening dread, as he caught the shadow of doubt flickering across her face. She wasn't sure at all.

"Come with us," he said gently. "We can find him together."

"No." Scarlet shook her head. "He's coming back. I need to be here when he does."

Caleb sighed. "Okay," he said. "If that's what you want, then that's what we'll do." He forced himself to calmly walk over to a pile of dead brush, grabbing a few larger pieces and tossing them into a small pile.

"What?" Scarlet cried, looking horrified. "No way. You can't stay here!"

"Why not?" Caleb forced an innocent shrug. "We're looking for Zavier. You claim he's on his way back. Why shouldn't we stay?"

He felt Trinity's stare burning a hole into his back but forced himself to ignore it. Instead, he turned to her dragon. "Emmy, do a guy a solid and light us a little fire, won't you? It's getting pretty chilly up here, and I forgot my coat."

Emmy widened her eyes, looking as doubtful as her Fire Kissed beside her, but in the end obliged, blowing a short burst of flame onto Caleb's makeshift fire pit. Caleb thanked the dragon, then settled onto the ground in front of the blaze, kicking out his legs and propping his head behind his hands. Now both girls—all three if you counted Emmy—were staring at him in disbelief.

"What?" he asked innocently. "Can't a guy get comfy while waiting for his dragon to return?"

"You can't be here," Scarlet repeated. "He'll kill you if he sees you here."

"Maybe. But I doubt it," Caleb replied. "He and I are blood brothers, remember?"

Scarlet scrunched up her face, glaring at Trinity. "Yeah, well, what about *her*?"

"Admittedly, he's probably less fond of her," Caleb agreed. "In fact, I wouldn't be surprised if he'd enjoy dining on her raw." He paused, then added, "Or maybe he'd flambé her first. For an old school carnivore, he's oddly fond of over-cooked meat."

Trinity rolled her eyes.

"Caleb, can I talk to you for a second, please?"

"Of course." Caleb scrambled back to his feet. "Be right back, Buttercup. Don't eat all of my imaginary marshmallows while I'm gone."

Scarlet groaned, shaking her head as she sat in front of the fire. Encouraged, Caleb followed Trinity. Once they were out of earshot, she turned to him.

"What the hell do you think you're doing, Caleb?" she demanded.

"I think it's pretty obvious."

"No. What's obvious is that Zavier is gone. And let's face it, he's probably not coming back."

"Maybe so. But she's not going to just give up that easily. You know Scarlet."

"I don't care about Scarlet. She's made her choice. It's you I'm concerned about here," Trin argued, pacing back and forth, raking a hand through her tousled curls. "You can't just stay here. I mean, you can joke all you want, but you know as well as anyone Zavier could still be dangerous. And he might want to kill you."

Her voice broke on the words, and he watched as she bit her lower lip, tears welling in her large black eyes.

"Trin…" he tried.

"Don't you see, Caleb?" she pleaded. "I almost lost you once. I can't bear to lose you—all over again."

He met her eyes with his own, a sadness falling over him. It was funny; for so long he had wanted her—had been so desperately in love with her. And now, he realized, with Connor out of the way, he might finally have his chance. The way she looked at him now, he knew she wouldn't refuse him. He could take her into his arms, tell her how he felt about her once and for all.

Except… He frowned. He wasn't sure he felt that way anymore. Sure, he loved her. He would always love Trinity Foxx. But it was a different sort of love now—almost a nostalgic love for a time gone by. When he had been a different boy. And she had been a different girl.

"Please, Trin," he said gently. "Don't ask me to go with you. Because if you ask, I'm probably going to say yes. After all, I dedicated my entire life to you long ago and promised to do anything to keep you safe. And I will keep that promise if you ask me. But right now, it's Scarlet who needs me, and I want to be there for her."

Trinity was quiet for a moment, and Caleb's heart ached as silence stretched out between them. Half of him couldn't believe he'd just said that. The other half felt an overwhelming relief that it had finally been said.

"You really like her, don't you?" Trinity said at last.

He gave her a helpless look. "I think I love her," he admitted. "I'm sorry, Trinity. God, even saying that makes me feel like a disloyal bastard. I'll always love you, you know. That'll never change. But Scarlet…"

Trinity waved him off before he could finish. Which was for the best, since he had no idea what he'd been planning to say.

"Of course I won't make you leave," she said roughly. "But, Caleb, be careful, okay? If you guys run into trouble— any trouble—just call me and I'll come for you. And Scarlet too, of course. Just promise me you'll stay alive. I've lost too many people in my life. I cannot lose you too."

"Please," he said, his voice as shaky as it was sarcastic. "You should know better than anyone, I'm not that easy to kill."

Chapter Thirty-Five

So Trinity and Emmy headed out, back on the quest to find dragon and Hunter. It felt very strange to be on her own again, Trinity thought, without Connor or Caleb by her side. Even stranger to realize it hadn't been her choice this time. Once upon a time, both boys had dedicated their lives to her; now they both had other priorities. Connor had chosen his mission. Caleb had chosen Scarlet. And Trinity was, once again, on her own.

Come on. Aren't I enough for you, Fire Kissed?

Trinity startled at the sudden voice teasing through her head. "Emmy?" she cried, her pulse kicking up in surprise. "Did you just read my mind?"

The dragon also seemed to startle. She turned to look at Trin, her blue eyes sparkling with excitement. *I guess I did!* she exclaimed. *Quick! Think something else to see if I can hear it.*

I love you, Emmy.

The dragon sighed. *I love you too.*

Trinity reached down, wrapping her arms around her and squeezing her tight. *Are you okay?* she asked her when she'd released her. *We took off so quickly, I didn't really get a chance to ask you how you felt about everything.*

I don't know. I guess I'm...sad, Emmy admitted after a pause. *It's so strange. For so long now, I thought they were already dead. And I was okay with that. At least I thought I was. But last night, after we talked, I got to thinking about what it would be like to be their mother for real. To nurture them, to teach them, to show them how to be dragons—something I never had from my own mother. And I guess, well, I guess I kind of got excited. When I finally allowed myself to think about would it could be like*—she closed her eyes for a moment, her wings still steadily flapping in the air—*I thought it could be good. Really good. Not just for them...but for me as well.*

Trinity's heart ached at the pain she heard in the dragon's voice. "It would have been," she agreed. "And maybe it still can be. Zoe might be dead. But Zavier's still alive. If we can reach him... If we can make him see—"

Her words were cut off as her walkie-talkie burst to life. "Trinity! Come in, Trinity!" She grabbed it from her pocket and put it to her mouth.

"What is it?" she asked.

"A sudden surge of 911 calls, coming from the town of Callaway. Fire trucks have been dispatched. We're not sure if it's related—no one's emailed us yet. But..."

In a juggling act, Trinity stuffed the walkie in her pocket, then reached for her cell phone, wishing dragons came with integrated GPS. After checking the map, she swapped devices again. "We're really close," she told him. "We'll go check it out now." She stuffed the walkie-talkie back in her pocket and turned to her dragon. "Emmy, head north, okay?"

Emmy obeyed, shifting slightly to change trajectories, flying toward the town. As they grew nearer, they saw it: a cloud of thick smoke billowing in the air. Trinity scanned the skies, searching for Zavier, adrenaline surging in her blood.

It could be just a brush fire, she reminded herself. *Or an oil fire. Or someone could have dropped a cigarette in a bale of hay.* But deep down, she knew there was no way they'd be so lucky.

Oh, Zavier, she thought miserably. *Please don't force us to take you down.*

It was the last thing she wanted, but she knew, in the end, that they would do what had to be done. If the dragon couldn't be controlled. If people had been hurt. Or worse… She and Emmy would do what they had to, to keep the world safe. Connor wasn't the only one with a mission after all.

But hopefully it wouldn't come to that.

As they got closer, she could hear the fire engines wailing below, but there was still no sign of a dragon. She frowned. Where was he? Had he done a drive-by and already headed to the next town?

"Go ahead and land," she told Emmy. "Let's see if we can find out what's going on here. But be careful. If things seem hairy, we might have to take off quickly. After all, if these people have just been attacked by a dragon, chances are they're going to assume you're an enemy too."

Understood. Emmy gave a quick nod, then dipped her head, flying in large circles as she dropped elevation. Finally they landed in the middle of a small park in the town's square. Trinity cringed a little as she took in the all-too-familiar scene—smoking buildings, burning trees, shell-shocked citizens wandering around aimlessly, covered in soot and ash.

"Look!" cried a voice behind them. "There's another one!"

Oh crap. Trinity whirled around to find a bearded man wearing a vintage Aerosmith T-shirt, probably in his late twenties, pointing at her, a terrified look on his face. In an instant, everyone was looking at them. Someone screamed. A little girl a few feet away burst into tears. Trinity bit her lower lip, panic rising inside of her. Maybe this had been a bad idea.

"It's okay!" she cried. "Emmy and I are here to help you!"

"Oh my God! It's her! It's really her!"

A girl with black-rimmed glasses shoved her way through the crowd, waving something in her hand. Trinity squinted; from where she was, she could just make out the sprawling gold script. What was…?

Then it dawned on her. It was one of the printable Team Dragon membership cards that Natasha had created as a thank-you for those who had donated to the FreeEmmy.com website.

She let out a breath of relief. Team Dragon was in the house. Thank goodness.

The girl stopped in front of Emmy, dropping to her knees as if in worship. Her eyes were wide and bloodshot from the smoke, but her face had lit up like a Christmas tree. "Thank God you've come!" she said in a voice filled with reverence and respect. "We need your help."

Trinity looked around, assessing the rest of the crowd, who had huddled around them now. Some looked suspicious still, others more cautiously hopeful. She supposed they must realize that if Emmy was going to hurt them, she probably would have gotten started already.

"When did this happen?" Trinity asked the girl.

"A half hour ago," she replied, rising back to her feet.

Her eyes never left Emmy. "He just swooped down out of nowhere and started tearing things up."

"He was huge!" added a woman to her left. "All black and as big as a house!"

Trinity frowned. In truth, Zavier wasn't much larger than a good-sized Clydesdale, but she supposed it was hard to accurately estimate something's size while you were running for your life.

She squared her shoulders. "Was anyone hurt?" she asked, fear thrumming through her veins. "Did anyone get burned? Or…" She trailed off, not wanting to voice the worst.

"We don't think so," the bearded man said to her relief. "Everyone seems accounted for. Though we can't be sure."

"Right." Trinity nodded. That was something at least. "Okay," she said. "Here's what we're going to—"

"Look!" screamed a young boy, pointing his finger to the sky. "He's back!"

Everyone screamed, their eyes shifting to the nightmare above. Trinity followed their gazes, her own eyes locking on the black shadow swimming across the sun. She had to admit, he really did look pretty large from this vantage point—not to mention extremely angry.

"Everyone, take cover!" she cried, attempting to be heard over all the screaming. "He may have summoned up enough fire by now for another big blast."

"What are you going to do?" asked the little boy, staring up at her with awestruck eyes.

"Whatever I have to," she replied grimly. "Now go!"

The crowd dispersed, though Trinity noticed some dragged their feet, now appearing more curious than afraid. And there were more than a few who had their phones pointed to the sky. They wanted to see the dragons fight, she realized, feeling a little sick at the thought. But who could blame them, really? It was a Michael Bay flick come to life.

Hopefully it would leave less destruction in its wake…

"Emmy? Are you ready for this?"

The dragon gave her a rueful look. *As I'll ever be, I suppose.*

"Then let's do it!"

She leapt onto Emmy, grabbing on tight as the dragon pushed off on her back legs, springing into the sky, her wings beating the air in rapid pulses to gain elevation. As the ground fell away, Trin forced herself not to look down, half wondering if she should have taken cover with the rest of the townspeople and let Emmy go at it solo. But she'd promised the dragon they were a team, and maybe some of her power to push minds could be used on Zavier too.

She closed her eyes and gave it try.

Zavier. You don't want to do this, Zavier.

Out of nowhere, the dragon rose up before them, popping out from a cloud of lingering black smoke. His eyes locked onto them, and his mouth opened to an angry growl, baring glistening, sharp teeth. Trin sucked in a breath, taking him in. He looked so different now than he had back at the airfield. Sure his scales were still midnight black with the same flecks of gold intermixed. But his eyes had changed. The gentle black eyes had hardened, filled with hatred and rage.

Zavier, please stop this! she tried again with no assurance that he could hear her. *I know you're angry. And you have every right to be. But these people did not kill your sister. They're innocent.*

But Zavier didn't answer—only opened his mouth and let loose a cannonball of fire straight in their direction.

Emmy! Trin cried, horrified.

Her dragon darted right, narrowly dodging the flames. The fire shot past them, nicking Emmy's wing before slamming into a church steeple, setting it ablaze. Emmy turned on a dime, diving toward the church and wrapping a wing around the steeple, effectively smothering the fire before it could spread.

The heat was so intense now that Trinity was drenched in sweat, and she was half-afraid her clothes would end up simply disintegrating from her body. Of course, being naked was about the least of her worries at this point.

Come on, Emmy. Stop him!

Emmy turned back to Zavier, her neck jutting out, followed by her body—a dragon-shaped torpedo shooting through the skies. Trin had to hang on for dear life as they cannonballed through the air, Emmy's claws outstretched and her teeth bared.

The dragons met head-on, claws raking at scales, teeth biting into necks, wrestling through the air, snarling and screaming as they went. Through it all, Trin held on for dear life, pretty sure, at any moment, she would fall and careen to her death. She struggled to take in shaky breaths, repeating her mantra over and over in her head.

She's not going to let me fall. She's not going to let me fall.

Emmy roared and attacked again, this time gouging Zavier's side with her sharp teeth. But he retaliated quickly—slashing at her neck and drawing blood. To a casual observer, they would seem evenly matched—able to fight on and on forever. But as the battle continued, Trinity realized that Emmy was tiring while Zavier didn't even appear winded.

Come on, Ems, she urged worriedly. *Don't give up now.*

To her credit, Emmy kept fighting like a champ, but Trin knew it was only a matter of time. Emmy's sides were bruised and her mouth bloody. All that time spent in the government lab was catching up to her, and though her will was strong, her body was proving too weak to take the other dragon down. If the fight continued much longer, Trinity was pretty sure they were going to lose. Emmy would fall, and they would both be killed.

But just as Trin was about to give up—to beg Emmy to retreat to live to fight another day—she heard something else in the distance. A strangely familiar sound, permeating the air. Her eyes bulged from her head as she recognized it.

A Hunter's song. Could it really be?

For a moment, both dragons froze, hovering motionless in the air, caught by the song's powerful spell. Trinity waited, hardly able to breathe as the moment stretched out in front of them. Then, without warning, Emmy broke free of the trance, charging toward the other dragon, whipping her tail around until it collided with his head. For a moment, Zavier stared at her, stunned. But Emmy didn't pause, grabbing his wing between her teeth and ripping it clean from his body.

Now the dragon was falling, careening to the ground at a frightening speed. Emmy spit out the bloody wing, sending it on after him, then dove down, not willing, evidently, to let him get away. He hit the ground with a thunderous crash, and a moment later, Emmy was on top of him, wrestling him into submission.

His scale! she screamed at Trinity.

Trinity rolled off her dragon, slamming hard into the pavement and seeing stars. Once she'd recovered, she scrambled to her feet, looking around for a weapon. At first, she came up empty. Then her eyes lighted on a street sign that had been uprooted, its metal end jutting out. She ran over to it, grabbed it, and dragged it back to the two dragons. It was heavy and awkward, but she forced herself to keep going. This was their one chance to end this.

Her eyes roved over Zavier, looking for the mark. Locating it, she pulled back on the sign and plunged it into the dragon's one soft scale.

I'm sorry, Scarlet. There's nothing else I can do.

Zavier screamed, black blood exploding from his body, splashing onto Trinity and Emmy like a tidal wave. Trin wiped the blood from her eyes, watching, praying it had done the trick. Zavier was writhing now, still screaming, a look of pain and anguish on his face. Then, at last, he fell silent, collapsing for the final time.

Trinity leaned over and emptied the contents of her stomach onto the pavement. Then she staggered over to Emmy. The dragon was breathing hard and still bleeding in several spots. "Are you okay?" Trinity asked her, her voice choked with tears. She reached out to the dragon, holding her in her arms. They were both soaked in black blood, but at the moment, neither one of them cared.

I'm okay, Emmy assured her. *Most of the blood is his.*

Oh, Emmy. Trinity buried her face in the dragon's scales. *I'm so sorry.*

She looked up, realizing they were surrounded. All the townspeople were coming out from hiding, rushing over to see the aftereffects of the battle. Some hung back, as if they still weren't sure they could trust Emmy, even though she clearly had just saved their lives. Others were jubilant, cheering loudly and literally dancing in the streets. Still others were busy uploading photos and videos to their various social media accounts, as you did, Trin supposed, in times like these.

"You saved us!" cried the girl with the FreeEmmy.com badge. "I knew you would!"

Trinity gave her a rueful smile; she knew she should be just as happy as the rest of them. But instead, a heaviness seemed to weigh on her shoulders. Caleb and Scarlet were going to be so upset.

And Emmy—well, now both her children were dead. Before she'd ever gotten a chance to get to know them. A choking sound escaped her throat.

She turned to the townspeople. "Burn the body," she instructed. "And bury the ashes deep in the ground." She didn't need the government swooping in and helping themselves to any more dragon DNA.

As the townspeople moved to obey, she turned back to Emmy. The dragon was pawing the ground nervously, looking at Zavier's corpse with puzzled eyes.

I'm so sorry, Emmy, Trin whispered again. *You know I didn't want it to come to this.*

It didn't, Emmy said suddenly, looking up at her.

Huh? Trinity cocked her head in question. *What do you mean?*

"That's not Zavier."

Trinity whirled around, heart in her throat at the sound of the sudden voice. There behind her stood none other than Connor himself. The Hunter looked drained and tired and filthy. But the sight of him caused her heart to flutter despite herself.

He must have arrived just in time, seen the fight, and stepped in to help with his Hunter song when they needed him most. Saved their lives, just as he'd promised to do.

"What do you mean it's not Zavier?" she demanded. She stared down at the dragon's corpse, confusion creasing her brow. Now that she had time to better look at him, she realized Connor was right. This dragon was not only bigger than Zavier, but it had a strange coloring under its wings that Emmy's son didn't have.

She looked up. "But...who else could it be?"

"I don't know," Connor said grimly. "But I have a feeling things are about to get a whole lot worse."

Chapter Thirty-Six

This was bad. This was so very bad.

Three hours later, Connor was pacing the desert floor, his eyes returning, over and over again, to the scorched ruins that had once served as a government lab. It was hard to believe, looking at it now, that he and Trinity had been there only months before, preparing to break in and steal back her dragon. At the time, it had seemed an impenetrable fortress. Now it was nothing more than a burnt-out husk.

Once they'd realized the dead dragon wasn't Zavier, it hadn't taken much to put two and two together. After that, they'd acted decisively, putting aside their personal feelings and jumping on Emmy's back to fly to the lab, hoping they wouldn't find what they both knew in their hearts had to be true. Connor had never wanted to be wrong more.

But of course, he wasn't.

He swore under his breath. He should have predicted this, he told himself. How many times, after all, had he read the original story of Trinity and her Dracken friends breaking into the lab to free Emmy only to find sixteen more baby dragons waiting for them inside. Sixteen hybrids that had been genetically altered into monsters. Sixteen hybrids that would rise up against their rescuers and decimate the world.

But they hadn't seen any baby dragons when they'd staged Emmy's rescue. And so he'd tried to convince himself that it hadn't happened that way this time—that because it was ten years earlier, the government wouldn't have had the technology to clone. That because it was only six months versus years, they wouldn't have had the time.

But they did have one thing they didn't have the first time around, he reminded himself. They had Mara, the Dracken's Chief Birthing Maiden, working with them. Perhaps she had futuristic technology at her disposal to help them create these fiends.

And now they'd been set on the world once again.

"Guess with his sister gone, he needed some backup," Trinity remarked, not bothering to keep the bitterness from her voice. Connor sighed, stepping closer to her, laying a hand on her shoulder, not sure she would accept his gesture of comfort. His heart ached as he watched her trying to be brave, trying to keep it together.

"Go ahead and say it," she spit out, not turning around. "You told me so. You told me so, and I refused to listen."

He gave her a rueful look. "It's okay," he said. "I didn't want it to be true either. Believe me, Trinity, I wanted so badly to be wrong."

She opened her mouth to speak, but at that moment, her phone rang. Frowning, she glanced at the screen and saw Luke's name pop up on the caller ID.

"We've got problems," Luke said before she could say hello. "The Internet has been blowing up. There have been so many dragon sightings in the last hour that they crashed my email server. It's all over the news too. I don't know how the hell Zavier's getting to so many places so quickly. We've been trying to pin them on the map, to come up with some kind of flight pattern to follow. But they don't make any sense. As far as I can see, there's no way he could be in so many places at once."

"He's not," Trinity said flatly. "He's got thirteen pissed off brothers and sisters to help him."

"What?" Luke's voice was incredulous. "Since when?"

"Just keep charting the sightings, okay?" she told him. "And send them to my email. Try to get as detailed a description as you can for each dragon, so we know what we're dealing with here."

"And if any of them sound like Zavier," Connor added, "alert us immediately. He's probably acting as the leader, and if we take him out first, it may confuse the others long enough for us to track them down."

"Roger that."

Trinity said good-bye to Luke and stuffed the phone in her pocket, turning back to Connor. "This is not good," she said, the understatement of the century. Behind her, Emmy gave a worried whine.

"No," he agreed. "It's not."

She moaned softly. "If only I had—"

Connor held up a hand. "There's no time for 'if onlys' right now," he reminded her. "We have an apocalypse to stop. And we're running out of time." He gave her a stern look. "I know we've had our differences, Trinity. But...are you with me? Will you help me now?"

She nodded. "Of course. What do we do?"

"We need to get into the lab," he told her. "I need to find out what I can about these other dragons—how many there are, what their genetic makeup is. If we can figure out what their DNA is spliced with, maybe we can determine a weakness." He shrugged. "It's a long shot, I know. But it may be the only one we have."

Chapter Thirty-Seven

The dragons had done their worst, and the lab was pretty much in shambles, all the entrances, including the loading dock, now blocked by rubble. In the end, they'd been forced to turn to Emmy for flyover help.

At first, the dragon had balked at the idea of willingly entering her prison all over again but eventually obliged, allowing the two of them to climb onto her back. She took flight, and together they flew over the building, looking for some kind of hole they could drop down into. The dragons had to have exited somehow, Trin surmised, meaning there had to be something to use as an entrance.

At last they saw it, at the far corner of the building: a black gaping pit, like a monster's mouth, ready to swallow them whole. Trinity glanced nervously at Connor, then instructed Emmy to check it out. Connor pulled his weapon from its holster. They needed to be ready for anything.

As they dropped down into the building, Trin blinked, trying to adjust her eyes to the sudden darkness. Connor, who, of course, had much better vision, gave an excited cry. "This is it," he told her. "This is where we rescued Emmy."

Trinity squinted, her eyes finally coming into focus. Sure

enough, from the dim light above, she could just make out a tangle of cages and wreckage. The place looked like a scene from one of the *Fallout* video games, she thought. And she wondered uneasily if there would be anything left to search for.

Emmy let out a low whine, pawing the air nervously as her gaze darted around the room. Trinity didn't blame her; so much had happened here, and now they were back at the scene of the crime. She reached out, pressing a comforting hand against the dragon's back.

It's okay, girl. Nothing here can hurt you now.

Emmy seemed somewhat comforted by this, dropping down for a graceful landing. Once she was securely earthbound, Trin and Connor slid off her back, turning on their cell phone flashlights and looking around. The first thought Trin had was how quiet it was. All the primates and pigs and other animals that had shared a prison with Emmy were long gone.

"Do you see any—?" she started.

Her words were cut short as a jolt of terror rang through her. *Emmy's* terror, she realized with dread. She whirled around, heart in her throat, to make sure the dragon was okay. Emmy was white eyed and panting and staring into space.

"What's wrong?" Trinity asked, rushing back to her. "Are you—"

Suddenly her own skin prickled, her gift picking up the presence of another—and not far away either. She bit her lower lip, concentrating on the source. She could feel it, just beyond her line of sight. Whoever it was, they were strong in the gift, she realized. Which meant it wasn't just some janitor come to clean up the mess.

"Over here," she whispered to Connor, gesturing for him to follow. To his credit, he didn't ask for an explanation, just stepped in behind her as she attempted to navigate the maze of broken cages. Meanwhile, Emmy stayed put; she was too big to get through the tangle of wires and seemed to have little desire to go exploring even if she could.

It didn't take long to get to the source: a large cage in the very center of the room. The only cage that hadn't been destroyed beyond repair.

The only cage that wasn't empty.

Trinity's mouth gaped as she stared at the cage's occupant. "It's you…" she breathed, horrified and fascinated all at the same time.

Mara looked up at her. The Dracken Chief Birthing Maiden, who had once been so beautiful and elegant and poised, had been reduced to a hot mess. Her normally smooth blond hair was snarled and ratted, and her face was covered with scratches and ash. Her clothes were ripped, and there was a long, ugly gash on her left arm that looked infected.

She leveled her gaze on Trinity and Connor. "I was wondering when you'd show up."

What had happened to her? Had she been here when the dragons were freed? Had she helped Zavier set them on the world? After all, the Dracken's true mission had been to cause chaos and burn the planet down so they could eventually take over. They had to be pretty pleased at how things were turning out.

But for some reason, Mara didn't look pleased. In fact, she looked downright defeated as she collapsed onto the cage's filthy floor. For a split second, Trinity was tempted to move to help her but forced herself to stand back. This was the woman who had kidnapped her dragon. The one who had tortured Scarlet. The one who had set this whole nightmare in motion. She didn't deserve a scrap of pity.

But she might be able to give us some answers, Connor reminded her silently. *If we push her right.*

Trinity nodded. In fact, looking around at the state of things here, Mara might be their only hope in ever learning for sure what these dragons were made of.

"What happened here?" she asked, trying to keep her voice cool and calm. "Why are you in that cage?"

The Dracken's eyes darkened. "Isn't it obvious?" she snapped. "I locked myself in here for protection when they were destroying everything in sight. And now they're gone. The dragons are loose. Everything I've worked for is ruined."

"Ruined?" Trinity repeated. "And here I thought you'd be thrilled. That was your endgame, was it not? To reload the apocalypse? Pretty mission accomplished, if you ask me."

Mara's eyes dropped to the ground. Her hands wrung around one another. "You're thinking of Darius," she said in a voice so low Trinity could barely hear her. "He was the one who wanted to destroy the world."

"And you didn't?" Trinity asked, raising a skeptical eyebrow.

"Of course not!" Mara snapped. "What rational person would want to burn down the world? It was madness, of course!"

"And yet you went along with it anyway."

"I had no choice," she informed her sadly. "I didn't know of his true plan until it was too late. His gift is strong. He held us all in thrall. Me, the Potentials…" She looked up. "Even your little pal Caleb there."

Trinity stiffened at the mention of Caleb's name. "You better start talking."

Mara sighed, suddenly looking very old. "I was on the streets when he found me, having been fired from my job as chief scientist by the Council after someone sold me out as a dragon sympathizer, citing some of the research I'd been doing on the side on how to tame hybrids." She made a face. "At the time, I thought he was my savior, picking me up off the streets and giving me a job and a home and a new lab to continue my research. It wasn't until much later that I suspected he was the one who had turned me in to begin with. He needed my expertise, but he knew I'd never work with him unless I had nowhere else to go." She shrugged. "That's how he does it. That's how he gets everyone. They're either already hopeless, or he makes them become so."

Trinity thought about how Darius had tried to trick her much the same way—telling her that her grandfather was dead, then sending assassins to make it true. But she'd had no idea that this was his typical MO. She glanced over at Connor, realizing his face had paled.

"What is it?" she asked.

He ignored her, his eyes locked on Mara. "Caleb," he said. "You said he did this to Caleb too?"

Mara smiled wanly. "Who do you think gave you that anonymous tip?"

"What tip? What are you talking about?" Trinity demanded, looking from one to the other, her pulse kicking up in alarm.

Connor turned to her, a sober expression on his face. "I'd just gotten back from seeing my mother," he said slowly. "She'd told me Caleb had a dragon, and I was looking everywhere for him to find out if it was true. At the time, I'd planned to just lecture him—to try to talk him into giving it up. But then I got this strange call—the caller told me that the Council had learned about my brother's dragon. That they were sending a team. That if I didn't get there first and take care of things, Caleb would be killed along with her." He grimaced. "I thought I was helping him. I thought I was saving his life…" He trailed off, looking devastated.

"It was the only way for Darius to ensure your brother's loyalty," Mara broke in. "Give him the ultimate gift, then have someone he loves steal it away. Follow up by feeding him bread crumbs—or in this case, Nether gems—to allow him to see his dead dragon. And he's putty in Darius's hands."

"Oh God." Connor cringed. "I was so concerned with doing the right thing, I never questioned—"

"None of us did," Mara interrupted. "Darius played us all like fiddles. And when he offered me the chance to come back in time—to stop the government from creating hybrids in the first place, of course I jumped at the opportunity. I thought if I could infiltrate their ranks and show them how to breed pure-blooded dragons this time, I'd not only be saving the world, but I'd be saving the dragon race as well." She sank back onto her knees. "It was only after you broke into the mall to rescue Trinity that I learned his true plan.

"And so I sold him out," she continued. "I testified against him so they'd send him to federal prison, and I joined the government scientists to continue my work. I had stolen some sperm samples from the dragons we had brought back in time with us, but I needed more. I needed a host…a mother." She gave Trinity a rueful smile. "And there was only one dragon that fit the bill."

Trinity bristled. "So you kidnapped Emmy. And you tortured her."

"I saved her life," Mara shot back angrily. "The rest of them had no idea how to take care of a dragon. Without me, Emmy wouldn't have survived a week. I made sure she was properly fed, and I insisted on her receiving daily visits from the girl who surrendered as her Fire Kissed so she'd have some emotional support as well. But in the end, there was only so much I could do without risking my position and losing her forever." She gave Trinity a pleading look. "You have to understand. The fate of the world depended on me being there, making sure things didn't go the way they had the first time around. So yes, I'm sorry to say your dragon suffered collateral damage," she added flatly. "And the girl did too. But we all must make sacrifices to save the world. No one is immune."

Trinity sucked in a breath, forcing her anger at bay. Then she closed her eyes, using her gift to push into Mara's head, searching, seeking for some kind of clue as to whether she was lying or telling the truth. But try as she might, she could find no traces of deceit, only tumultuous feelings of regret mixed with frustration.

She opened her eyes, stealing a glance at Connor. *What do you think?* she asked him silently.

From what I can tell, she's sincere, he replied with a shrug. *She was a victim, just like the rest of us.*

Trinity nodded, turning back to Mara. "So the dragons you created," she managed to ask, wanting to be clear once and for all, "what are they mixed with? What's in their DNA?"

"Nothing."

"What?" Trinity cocked her head in question. "What do you mean nothing?"

"I mean, they're pure-blooded dragons," Mara clarified, looking a little offended. "The true sons and daughters of Emberlyn and a dragon named Gabriel that we brought back from the future. I mean, come on! Do you think I'd really create hybrids after what happened the first time around?"

Trinity stared at her, then turned to Connor. His face had gone stark white. "They're pure-blooded?" he whispered. "All of them? Even Zoe and Zavier?"

"Of course. They're all from the same litter, after all. We had put Emmy to sleep right before you staged your little rescue and had harvested most of the eggs by that point. Unfortunately, we were still working when all that craziness happened with the flash mob you staged, and we were told to finish up later. But of course, then you all barged in and set her free. I always wondered if the last two eggs had survived. From the state she was in when she left, I was pretty certain she would have just killed them herself." She sighed. "But evidently not. And now, thanks to your massive screwups, everything I've worked for is ruined. The dragons are loose in the world, just like the first time around. Congratulations. Darius, in whatever prison he's rotting away in, must be thrilled."

"But wait—you just said yourself they're not hybrids this time," Trinity cried. "Doesn't that make a difference?"

Mara gave her a rueful look. "Nature can only make so much of a difference. In the end, I believe nurture plays the largest role. Think of a dog: some breeds tend to be more prone to violence, but any dog can turn if it's mistreated enough. Dragons are no different. With more time, we could have raised them to respect and value humans. Now it's too late."

Trinity heard Connor's low moan beside her. She reached out to squeeze his hand, knowing what must be going through his mind. If he hadn't acted, if he hadn't killed Zoe—basically proving mankind to be the bad guys—would everything be different now?

After all he'd done to try to stop the apocalypse, had he been the one to start it all?

She turned back to Mara, squaring her shoulders and firming her resolve. This wasn't over yet. Not by a long shot. "There's got to be a way to prove to them that we're not the enemy," she argued. "If we could just gather them up some-how, talk to them, tell them what happened and apologize…" She trailed off. "I know that's probably impossible."

Mara was silent for a moment. Then she slowly nodded her head. "There may be one way," she said at last. "It's a long shot…but…"

"What is it?"

"If we could get our hands on some of the Nether dust."

"Nether dust? What's that?"

"It's something the Council was working on," Connor broke in. "To help control the hybrids. They crush up Nether gems into microscopic particles and put them through a vaporizer."

"Right," Mara agreed. "It produces a highly concentrated dose that can put even the largest of dragons into a Nether state. If we could use it and bring them all to the Nether at one time, we may be able to force them to listen, without the dangers of doing so in real life."

"But if it's something from your future—"

"It was stolen," Connor interrupted, his voice hoarse. "The Dracken stole it from the Council." He turned to Mara. "Did they bring it here? Do you know where it is now?"

Mara shrugged. "I assume it's still at the mall where we once had our headquarters. Safe and sound, deep in my lab. I don't know if we'll be able to reach it—the mall is in pretty bad shape these days—after the fire and all. But if we could, it could give us a chance."

"If we're going to do this," Connor said, "we need all the chances we can get."

Chapter Thirty-Eight

W here is he? He should be back by now!"

Scarlet scanned the skies for what felt like the thousandth time, a shiver escaping her body. The temperature had dropped, and the chill was beginning to creep into her bones. Still, she refused to give up, pacing the area and watching the sky, waiting for Zavier to return.

Suddenly, she felt a presence behind her. She turned to find Caleb standing there, a distraught look on his face. A shiver ran down her back.

"What is it?" she managed to ask, though she was already pretty sure she didn't want to know the answer. *Please don't let Zavier be dead.*

Wordlessly, he held out his cell. She took it with trembling hands, holding it for a moment before daring to look down at the screen. It was a news report. About dragons.

Not *dragon* singular. *Dragons.*

And they were tearing up the state.

"How in the hell…?" she whispered, sinking to her knees as the report played on, showing building after building aflame. The president had declared martial law, the reporter was saying. The military had been dispatched. People were on the streets. Looting had begun.

Scarlet swallowed hard as Emmy's long-ago words raged back to her consciousness.

If they live, they will burn down the world.

She looked up at Caleb. "I don't understand. How...?"

He gave her a grim look. "There must have been more dragons back at the government lab. Zavier must have gone and freed them, recruited them for his revenge."

She nodded, handing the phone back to him with trembling fingers, unable to look down again and watch the devastation. "I should have made him stay here," she said, her voice betraying her barely concealed hysteria. "But he was so restless. So angry. Honestly, I was getting a little scared. So I told him he should go hunting, you know? I thought maybe that would calm him down until I could figure out our next move." She shook her head. "What an idiot I am."

"No." Caleb dropped to his knees before her, taking her hands in his. "You're not," he insisted. "If you had let him stay, he might have hurt you. Not on purpose—I know he loves you. But he's angry and hurt—and he might have lashed out. You did the right thing."

"The right thing," she repeated bitterly. "I'm sick to death of people and their so-called right things. It's how we justify everything we do. And yet, if we're all really trying to do the right thing, how come everything keeps going so wrong?"

Caleb was quiet for a moment. Then he spoke. "Maybe because it was meant to be this way."

"What?" She stared at him, confused.

He sighed. "I know you came late into this whole thing, but it's been like this since the beginning. Every move we've made, everything we've tried to do, it's like it makes no difference.

We still keep charging forward—to the brink of disaster." He dropped her hands, staring down at his phone. "Sometimes I don't know why we even bother to keep trying. No matter what we do, the Scorch keeps looming. And I don't know anymore if there's any way to truly stop it."

She scrunched up her face, trying to interpret his words. "What are you talking about, Caleb?" she asked. "What's the Scorch?"

"I have to tell you something," he said suddenly. "Something I should have told you a long time ago. I warn you, it's going to sound crazy—like really crazy—but I promise you, it's true. And maybe it'll help you see: none of this is your fault. None of this is any of our faults. Or maybe it's all of our faults, I don't know."

"Oh-kay…"

And so he told her. A story too insane to be true yet too insane to be made up. She listened without interrupting, and when he had finished, he gave her an apologetic look.

"I'm sorry, Scarlet. You should have never been dragged into any of this. This should have never been your fight."

She sucked in a breath, her mind racing, trying to sort it all through. "Why didn't you tell me from the beginning?"

"Would you have believed me if I had?"

Of course she wouldn't have. She could barely believe him now.

"But you knew this whole time what could happen," she insisted. "You knew, just like Emmy did, what these dragons were supposed to grow up and do? And yet you decided to help me protect them anyway?"

"I thought they deserved a chance. Just as Trinity gave Emmy."

"Right. Trinity." Scarlet made a face. "I guess that explains why everyone's always kissing her ass too. She's like the Luke Skywalker chosen one in this whole deal, right?"

He nodded grimly. "The girl who would save our world."

"And here I thought you were just in love with her."

Caleb sighed. "I'm not going to lie—at one time, I thought I was. Back home, she's like a celebrity. I worshipped the ground she walked on before I ever even met her in real life." He shrugged sheepishly. "It took me a while to recognize who she really was. Not some goddess—just a girl. I mean, don't get me wrong. She's pretty awesome. But she makes mistakes. She gets mad. She follows her heart instead of her head—"

"It sounds like you still care about her."

"I do. And I always will," he admitted. "But she and I were never meant to be. Not in the way you're thinking anyway. We tried, sure, but we never made each other happy." He paused, then added, "Not like I've been happy with you."

She looked up, her breath caught in her throat. "Have I... really made you happy?"

He met her eyes with his own piercing blue ones. "Trust me, Buttercup," he said with a crooked smile. "If this really is the end of the world? I wouldn't want to spend it with anyone but you."

And then he kissed her. And she knew suddenly from the kiss that he meant every word he'd said. And that if she wanted him, he would be hers, totally hers, forever.

"I'm sorry," he said, his lips against her mouth, causing delicious shivers to run down her spine. "I've put you through so much. I don't deserve another chance. But I promise you, Scarlet, I promise—"

His words were cut off by a loud cry, followed by a shadow crossing over from above. They broke apart, and for a moment, as her eyes flew to the sky, Scarlet thought it was Zavier, come home at last.

But it was Emmy crossing the horizon, coming in for a landing. With Trinity riding on her back. Scarlet and Caleb rose to their feet as they dropped down to the ground, Caleb putting a secure arm around Scarlet's waist, leaving no doubt as to their relationship status.

But Trinity didn't seem to notice as she slid off Emmy's back and approached the two of them. Her expression was grave and her steps purposeful. "Something's happened," she announced.

"We saw the broadcasts," Caleb assured her. "Do you have a plan?"

"Yes," Trinity said. "But I need your help. Both of you."

Scarlet listened as she broke it down.

"What do you think?" Trinity asked when she'd finished. "Will you help us?"

"It's up to Scarlet," Caleb declared, and Scarlet's heart flip-flopped at the earnestness she heard in his voice. "Whatever she wants to do."

Trinity nodded. She turned to Scarlet. "Look, I know I have no business asking for any favors from you," she said. "But if you want to help Zavier, we have to work together. You were right; he is a good dragon. They're all good, pureblood dragons deep down. And we need to get their attention and get them back on our team." She gave a grim smile. "But let's face it, he's not going to listen to me. And he's not going to listen to Emmy. And he's certainly not going to listen to Connor."

Scarlet nodded slowly. "But you think he'll listen to me?"

"I'm betting the fate of the world on it."

Chapter Thirty-Nine

Here we are. Home sweet Dracken home," Caleb announced as Emmy came in for a graceful landing in the parking lot of the abandoned Nevada mall a few hours later. It had been a long flight and mostly quiet—everyone lost in their own thoughts.

Trinity looked around; she thought the place had been decrepit the first time around, when it had served as the Dracken's secret headquarters. Now it looked like something out of a Mad Max movie—half-burned down with frayed police tape clinging to the perimeter and colorful graffiti splashed on every available surface. She wondered why they hadn't just torn it down; it looked like a lawsuit waiting to happen.

"This is where the bad guys lived?" Scarlet asked after giving the place a skeptical once-over. "'Cause as far as secret lairs go, it's kind of weak."

"That's what I thought when I first saw it," Trinity replied, thinking back to the first time she and Caleb had pulled into the parking lot. It seemed like a lifetime ago. "But inside, it was pretty sweet. All the comforts of home."

"I doubt it'll be too comfortable now."

They whirled around. Connor and Mara had stepped up behind them. The two of them had taken the truck and driven directly to the mall to suss the place out while Trinity and Emmy had gone back to retrieve Caleb and Scarlet.

Trinity noted Scarlet giving Connor a dirty look while saving an even dirtier one for Mara. Of course, Trinity couldn't blame her for either. If they pulled this off, maybe someday they could all sit down and have a heart-to-heart about what had happened and who was really to blame. But right now, they needed to put personal feelings aside and concentrate on the mission.

Connor reached into the trunk of the car, pulling out a few flashlights and ropes. "We stopped at a Walmart on the way here," he told them. "Grabbed some supplies. I don't know what we're going to need in there, but it's better to be prepared."

"My unit tore things up pretty good," Caleb explained to Scarlet, "when they raided this place looking for Emmy. And then there was the fire on top of that."

Scarlet nodded. "What about Emmy?" she asked, as she slid off the dragon's back and onto solid ground. "Where's she supposed to go while we're inside? I don't think she should just hang out, out in the open where someone could see her."

"We found an automotive center around back," Mara piped in. "Evidently it used to be some store they called Sears back when the place was open. It's pretty big—Emmy could hang in there until we came back."

"Would that be okay?" Trinity asked the dragon. "Would you feel safe there?"

I guess so, Emmy replied, though she didn't look too sure. Trinity didn't blame her. After all that had happened—what was still happening—it was doubtful Emmy would ever feel entirely safe again.

"I can stay with you, Emmy," Scarlet announced suddenly. The three of them turned to look at her.

"Scarlet, are you sure?" Caleb asked. "You don't have to. She's a big dragon. She can take care of herself."

But Scarlet had clearly made up her mind. "I think the two of us have a few things to talk about anyway," she said. "And to be honest, I'm not so good with the whole closed-in, dark spaces thing—after all those months spent in that cell." She shot a resentful look at Mara when she said this, and the Dracken blushed.

"I can stay too," Caleb suggested.

"No." Trinity shook her head. "We need you. You're the only one who knows this place as well as Mara does."

You need to be there in case she tries to pull some kind of trick, she added silently. *We still don't know if we can completely trust her.*

Caleb nodded, catching her send. "Fine. But we can't just leave Scarlet by herself."

"I'll stay with her," Trinity told him. "You guys go. We'll be fine."

Caleb didn't look thrilled about this either but, to his credit, didn't try to argue. "Fine," he said. "But if you need us, seriously, just call." He turned to Scarlet, his piercing eyes filled with concern. "I'll come for you, okay?"

Trinity watched as Scarlet smiled, leaning forward to kiss him on the forehead. She waited for the familiar strain of jealousy to worm through her insides. But it never came. Instead, she found herself glancing over at Connor. Poor Connor, who hadn't been able to even look her in the eye since finding out the dragons were purebloods. She wanted so badly to pull him aside to let him know she understood why he'd done what he had—that they'd all made mistakes at one point or another. But there was no time for that now. She just hoped the guilt she could see weighing him down wouldn't serve as a distraction to their mission.

Be careful, she sent silently, taking a step toward him. *We don't know what's down there. It could be a trap.*

I'll be fine, he mumbled. *Just take care of yourself and Emmy.*

And with that, they turned to leave, Mara leading the way, her steps a little uneven from the rope handcuffs they'd put on her. Trinity watched them go, her stomach twisting uneasily as the distance increased between them. She found herself reaching out, searching Mara's head again, looking for some tiny nugget she might have missed, to prove that the Dracken was hiding something. But there was nothing—only earnestness and sincere regret for her role in this whole mess.

Perhaps, sometimes, even monsters could be redeemed.

She only hoped it wasn't too late.

✦ ✦ ✦

"I was worried the DNA locks would still be active," Caleb remarked as he, Connor, and Mara approached the front doors of the mall a few moments later. "But it looks like we're past that point now."

In fact, they realized, as they got closer, there were no longer any doors at all, the once nearly impenetrable fortress with its high-tech security system now seeming to rely only on official-looking signs reading "Condemned" and "Unsafe" and "No Trespassing" to ward off any undesirables.

Of course, with the Dracken long gone and their leader, Darius, locked up in prison, well, perhaps they figured the undesirables could have it.

Caleb watched as Connor peered into the darkened hallway first. Then he stuck his head back out. "But we do have another problem," he announced soberly.

"What, Abercrombie had a run on tight black T-shirts?" Caleb couldn't help but tease, trying to lighten the mood. His brother didn't even crack a smile.

"See for yourself."

Caleb obliged, peering through the door. "Um, problem is kind of an understatement, don't you think?" he asked after coming back out. "The mall has no floor."

"No floor?" Mara repeated.

"Not at least for the first twenty feet," Caleb told her. "The fire must have hit this side of the building really hard." He scratched his head, scanning the perimeter. "Maybe we should look for another entrance or something."

"I don't think we need to," Connor replied. "Look. There's a ledge along that side. We could probably walk across that and skirt the pit. It's not that far…"

Caleb peered in a second time to see what his brother was talking about. Sure enough, there was a very narrow support beam crossing the ravine against the far wall. He raised an eyebrow. "I don't know…"

"Trust me, I can do this," Connor assured him. "Just tie the end of the rope to the door, and when I get across, I'll tie up the other end. Then you can hold on to the rope as you cross to keep your balance. It's simple, really."

"You might need a refresher course on the definition of

'simple,'" Caleb grumbled. But he did as his twin requested, pulling the rope from the bag and securing it to the door. Connor grabbed the other end and placed his back against the far wall. Then he inched sideways along the narrow space, step by careful step. Caleb watched, nerves tensing.

"Be careful," he barked as he watched a piece of cement crumble from under his brother's foot and drop down into the darkness below. It seemed a long time before he heard it hit the ground. "I mean, I know you're Supertwin and all. But—"

He was cut off midsentence as the beam crumbled out from under his brother. Caleb gasped as he watched Connor lose his balance, his feet slipping off the wood. For a heart-splitting second, his twin seemed to hover midair like a cartoon character. Then he dropped like a stone into the blackness.

"Connor!" Caleb screamed. He turned to Mara, who was staring down into the open pit, her mouth gaping. "Connor!" he tried again. "Say something! Are you okay?"

For one horrifying moment, there was nothing. Only a deafening silence, seeming to stretch out into infinity. Caleb grabbed the wall for support, feeling as if he was going to throw up. After all that he and his brother had been through, it couldn't just be over like that, could it?

Please, he begged silently. *Please be okay.*

Then…a spark of light flickered in the darkness.

Connor's flashlight!

"I'm okay," he called up.

Caleb shook his head, shooting Mara a look of relief. "Connor Jacks, man of steel, ladies and gentlemen," he muttered. Then he turned back to the pit. "Are you able to pull yourself back up the rope?" he called down. "We could go find that other entrance."

"Actually, I think you'd better climb down here yourself," Connor said, after a small pause. "You're not going to believe what I'm seeing."

Chapter Forty

Emmy watched as Scarlet paced the garage floor, her face drawn with worry. Trinity had gone outside to keep watch ten minutes before, leaving the two of them alone in awkward silence. It was the first time they'd been alone, the dragon realized, since that fateful day on the side of the cliff, where she'd asked Scarlet to do the unthinkable and Scarlet had pretended to agree.

It seemed crazy now, but at the time, Emmy had been so frightened—so guilty over what she'd inadvertently brought into the world. Trinity could say all she wanted that it wasn't Emmy's fault, but the creatures had come from Emmy's body. And without her, they would have never been born.

If only she'd confessed to Trinity from the start. Maybe things would have turned out differently. Instead, she'd acted like a coward, turning to Scarlet to do what she couldn't bring herself to do.

But in the end, maybe it was for the best. Because if Emmy had gone and done the job—crushed those poor babies under her body's weight the moment they'd hatched from their eggs—they would both be gone, their lives snuffed out before they began. Now she still had a chance to redeem herself. To save her son.

She glanced back at Scarlet. *Are you okay?* she asked.

Scarlet looked up at the dragon. She raised an eyebrow. "What do you think?"

Emmy hung her head. Scarlet clearly wasn't going to make it easy on her. Though maybe that was what she deserved. *I think you're sad,* she said. Then she added, *I'm sad too.*

Scarlet's face twisted. "You shouldn't be. You got what you wanted, right? One down, one to go."

Emmy winced. *You're wrong,* she said. *I never wanted it. I thought it was necessary. I thought it was the only choice we had. But I never wanted it. She was my daughter, Scarlet. My flesh and blood. And I never got a chance to know her.* She trailed off, unable to continue.

"Your loss," Scarlet said, not turning around. "She was amazing."

Tell me about her.

"What?" Scarlet half turned this time, her face a mess of anger and sadness.

About Zoe, Emmy clarified. *What was she like?*

Scarlet scowled again, and for a moment, Emmy thought she wouldn't answer. Then, at last, she shrugged. "She was wonderful," she told her, her voice sounding a little rough around the edges. "Really sweet and kind. She loved music too. Any kind of music. I brought her an iPod. She burned that thing out she listened to it so much. She was a big fan of Taylor Swift. And she loved to make up these little dances to all the songs and then perform them for me when I came to visit." She laughed softly. "I'm pretty sure Zavier thought it was all completely ridiculous, but he never let on. He was always so supportive of his sister. Anything she wanted or needed, he was there for her. He was the best brother a girl could have. A lot like my brother, actually, back in the day."

Emmy nodded slowly, feeling the tears well at the corners of her eyes. She thought back to her own brother, the young ruby, who was taken away by their mother before she even learned his name. Would he have protected her like that? Would he have been her best friend? What a wonderful thing—to have someone to share things with, someone to laugh with and cry with. From the beginning, Emmy had always been alone.

Maybe if this all worked out, maybe if they could find a way to bring Zavier and the others home and quench their thirst for revenge—maybe Emmy would get a chance to say she was sorry. To start over and really be a mother this time. She imagined going from being alone to being a mother to fourteen dragons! It sounded incredible.

I wish I could have known her, she said to Scarlet. *But I am so grateful she had you.*

Scarlet's face crumbled. Emmy stretched out her neck, nudging her arm with her snout. For a moment, Scarlet just stood there. Then she turned to Emmy and threw her arms around her head. The dragon nuzzled her face against her chest, her own tears falling as they embraced. For a moment, they just stood there, holding one another, before Emmy pulled away.

I'm so sorry, Scarlet, she said. *I hope someday you can—*

But her words were cut short as Trinity burst back into the garage, a frantic expression on her face. "We've got trouble!" she cried. "Someone's coming. We need to get out of here. Now."

Chapter Forty-One

W hat is this place?"

Connor shone his flashlight up at his brother, who was climbing down the rope behind Mara, a puzzled look on his face. Connor didn't blame him either. He'd been more than a little surprised himself when he'd dropped down into this place. He'd expected more of what they'd seen above—a burned-out shell of a building in grave disrepair. Instead, a smooth, shiny tunnel that looked brand-new stretched out into the darkness. He raked a hand through his hair, puzzled.

"Was this under the mall this entire time?" he asked his brother. He knew that there had been some back passageways that Trinity and he had used to make their escape the first time around. But this seemed way more extensive, not to mention undamaged—as if these corridors had been built after the mall had been burned and abandoned. Which didn't make any sense.

Caleb shook his head. "If it was, I certainly didn't know about it." He glanced over at Mara. "How about you, Blondie?" he asked. "You remember anything like this?"

Mara didn't answer. She just stared down the corridor, wide-eyed and white faced. A chill wound down Connor's spine. This was getting too spooky for him.

"Okay," he said, channeling his inner soldier to stymie his encroaching fear. "We'd better see where this leads. Maybe we can find another place to climb back up, where the floor is in better shape." He turned to Mara. "In the meantime, I apologize, but I have to tie you back up."

Mara nodded wordlessly, holding out her hands. Connor worked to tie them, a little looser this time, pretty sure that even if she wanted to escape at this point, he could shoot her before she got very far. "Which way?" he asked.

"My lab was located in the mall's former Bath & Body Works," she told them. "Our best chance to find the Nether dust is to head there."

"That was pretty much in the dead center of the mall," Caleb remembered. He glanced down at his phone's GPS. "So we need to head this way."

They crept down the corridor, using their flashlights to light the way. Connor kept his gun in his hand, checking around every corner to make sure they were alone. At first, everything seemed okay, and he began to relax a little, telling himself this must have been here all along and Caleb and Mara just hadn't come across it. But then…

"What was that?" he hissed, stopping short. Caleb and Mara slammed into him from behind, almost making him lose his balance. He gestured for them to be silent. Then he closed his eyes, listening carefully.

A moment later, it came again. A loud moaning, from somewhere close by. He glanced over at his companions to see if they'd heard it too. From the looks on their faces, they had.

Without a word, he gestured for them to follow him, flicking off his flashlight and depending on his own night vision to guide them through the darkness. As they crept along, his pulse kicked up, adrenaline igniting in anticipation of whatever lay ahead.

Pushing through a door, they discovered a small spiral staircase leading down into the darkness. As they stared at it, the noise came again. Whatever it was, it was clearly coming from this pit. Taking a deep breath, Connor took the steps, winding down deeper and deeper into the abyss. Where did it lead? And was that a faint light he caught far, far below?

Finally, after what seemed an eternity, the stairs ended, and he found himself on solid rock. He frowned, clicking on his flashlight again. The room burst to life, and he gasped at what he saw.

It was an apartment, carved into stone. A simple apartment: a few chairs, a crude table, a couple of hammocks serving as beds. But it wasn't the furnishings themselves that took his breath away—rather their familiarity.

"The model home," he whispered.

It was a photo straight from his history texts. A humble, underground dwelling that had been advertised as mankind's salvation—a refuge from the Scorch. The powers that be had sold thousands of these apartments back in the day—before the more extensive cities were constructed years later. Those who purchased these studios were promised shelter and safety while the rest of the world lived in terror above.

But what was it doing here, now? He shot a worried look over at Caleb and Mara. Their eyes told him they were thinking the same thing he was.

"Oh my God," Mara breathed. "He did it. He really did it."

"Who?" Connor found himself asking. But deep inside, he realized he already knew, of course. There could be only one—the Dracken leader, Darius himself.

"He must have found a way out of prison," Mara whispered. "He must have been here this whole time, constructing this place to wait out the storm." She rose to her feet. "Come on," she added. "We have to know how far he's taken it."

Connor didn't know exactly what she meant by this, but he followed her anyway, out the apartment front door into a smooth hallway lined with identical doors every few yards. *More apartments*, he realized with growing dread. Darius and his followers must have been quite busy indeed.

Ahead of him, Mara stopped short, her breath now hissing from her throat. They'd reached a large metal door cut into the rock. Unlike the other doors, which were crude and made of wood, this door was constructed out of some kind of shiny, solid metal that looked to be titanium.

Mara glanced back at them, her eyes wide with fear. "This can't be," she whispered. "It just can't."

"What?" Connor demanded, his heart thumping hard in his chest. "What is it?"

"We need to get out of here. Now. Get back to Emberlyn and make sure she's okay."

"No," Caleb interjected. "We can't. Not until we have the Nether dust."

"Fleck the Nether dust," Mara cried. "Don't you see? It doesn't matter now! None of it matters!"

Connor opened his mouth to demand to know what she was talking about. But then, the noise came again. Louder.

Closer. Whatever it was, he realized in terror, it was coming from behind this massive door.

Pushing past Mara, he grabbed the door's handle. He yanked it open.

And he saw for himself.

+ + +

Trinity dove back into the former automotive garage, her heart slamming against her ribs. Scarlet and Emmy watched her, looking confused and scared.

"Get on Emmy's back!" Trinity instructed. "Someone's coming. We need to get out of here. Now!"

To her credit, Scarlet didn't argue, scrambling up Emmy's wing and swinging her leg over her back. Trinity followed suit, joining her a moment later.

"Go, Ems!" she cried. "Fly like the wind!"

"What about the boys?" Scarlet broke in. "We can't just leave them here."

"We'll have to come back for them. Or they can take the car. I'll try to send a message." Trin closed her eyes, concentrating.

We've got trouble, Connor. We're going to have to—

But her send was cut short as something sickly sweet enveloped her senses. She frowned, opening her eyes and turning to Scarlet, wanting to ask if she smelled it too. But the words stuck in her throat, and she found she could only look at Scarlet, who was also now struggling to breathe. Trinity reached out, trying to grab on to her. But her vision swam.

And blackness consumed her.

Connor slammed the door shut, his breath coming in short gasps. "Dragons," he whispered. "Holy hell, where did those dragons come from?"

Mara shook her head, her expression grave. "Darius must have discovered what I'd done at the lab and decided to hedge his bets. And I'm guessing these aren't purebloods either."

Connor paced the corridor, raking a hand through his hair, his steps eating up the distance between the walls as his mind flashed back to what he'd seen in the next room. Dragons. Twenty or more. All at least the size of Emmy—possibly larger. He'd heard hybrids could grow to twice the size of pureblood dragons, which meant they might not have even been full grown.

"They were mutated," he remarked. "At least the ones I could see. Extra legs, eyes where there shouldn't be eyes…" He looked up. "Just like the dragons you brought back from the future that were destroyed in the fire."

"Maybe he managed to rescue a few of them," Mara concluded. "Or at least some of their DNA? But how would he breed them? Sure, he could clone them, but he'd still need a host. Like I needed Emmy. We'd tried to use ceramic eggs under an incubator and even implant embryos into other egg-laying species like ostriches. But it never worked."

"What if he didn't make them at all?" Connor interjected. "I mean, what if he brought back more dragons from the future than we ever knew about? What if they've been down here this whole time, deep under the mall, growing and waiting for the moment when Darius planned to unleash them on the world?"

"Flecking hell," Caleb swore under his breath. "If they get free now—if they're able to breed with Emmy's true children…" He trailed off; he didn't need to finish anyway. Connor knew all too well what could happen—what *would* happen if they didn't figure out a way to stop this and fast.

"Come on," he said. "We need to get Emmy. We'll have her set fire to this place. Raze it to the ground and the hybrids with it. That's the only way we can—"

He broke off as a voice slammed into his consciousness. Trinity's voice.

We've got trouble, Connor. We're going to have to—

It stopped midsentence, as if cut by a knife.

Trinity! he tried to send back. But there was no answer. He turned to his brother and Mara, who were looking at him questioningly. "Something's wrong," he told them. "We have to get back to the surface. Now!"

He bolted down the hall, not waiting for an answer, assuming they'd follow. Sure enough, he could hear them step in behind him as they ran through the apartment, up the stairs, down the corridor. But then, just as they were closing in on the entrance, Connor's ears caught footsteps echoing on the smooth floors, headed their way.

"Someone's coming," he whispered.

And then he heard the voice. He glanced over at his brother. "Darius," Caleb whispered. "It's him."

✦ ✦ ✦

299

Trinity? Scarlet?

Emmy twisted her long neck to look up onto her back, where the girls had suddenly gone silent. Worry churned in her stomach.

Should I go? she asked. *Should I fly?*

No answer. She snuffed her nose at them only to have them slip off her back and onto the garage floor with a sickening thud. She stifled a whine of alarm. What was wrong with them? Why were they so still? And what was that smell? She paused, sniffing.

She turned to the building's exit, not sure what to do. Something was wrong. Very, very wrong. Trinity had been scared. She'd wanted them to leave. *Fly like the wind*, she'd said. The dragon glanced down at the unconscious girls; she could grab them and place them back on her back, but they'd likely just fall off again. Maybe she could take them in her arms instead, cradling them against her chest as she flew. She tried this for a moment, but they were so soft, it was hard to get a good grip on them, and she didn't want them to slip out while in the air.

She moaned again, not sure what to do. The smell was getting more intense, and it was getting harder to breathe. Her wings were feeling heavy—so very heavy—and she was no longer sure she could even get airborne if she tried, with or without the girls. What was going on here? It was all she could do not to curl up into a ball and go to sleep.

But you can't, she scolded herself. *They need you.*

She looked around, desperation rising within her. If she couldn't fly them away, she had to hide them somehow—before whoever was doing this came. But where?

Finally, her eyes locked onto a large rusted bin at the far end of the room. The kind they used back at the airfield to store trash in. Making her decision, Emmy grabbed Trinity in her mouth as gently as she could, then dropped her into the bin. Then she returned and did the same with Scarlet—a little slower this time, her legs feeling like lead, but somehow she managed to get her inside. Then she snuffed the other trash with her nose, burying the girls and closing the lid. They would be safe there. As safe as possible, anyway.

She turned, trying to breathe, trying desperately to clear her head. Now what? Could she try to hide herself? But there was nothing big enough to conceal her entirely. She could try to leave, but she didn't want to stray from the girls, in case they needed her help.

But oh, that smell. That noxious smell—sweet yet at the same time rotten to the core.

You need to run, she told herself. *You need to fly*.

Instead, she could only sink to the ground, her legs collapsing out from under her as her head dropped and her vision spun. A moment later, men stormed in wearing strange gray masks over their faces, shouting and throwing a net over her. She wanted to laugh at that; it was so unnecessary. She couldn't have moved if she'd tried. She could vaguely feel them dragging her onto some kind of flat truck bed, hauling her away. It was all she could do not to glance back, to make sure Trinity and Scarlet were still hidden. But she forced herself to stare straight ahead, not wanting to give their location away.

And a moment later, she too succumbed to the blackness.

✦ ✦ ✦

Darius. The voice was definitely Darius's. And from the sound of it, he was coming this way.

Caleb felt his pulse kick up as nausea rolled through his stomach. The man who had once been his hero, his master, his savior—now nothing more than a devil Caleb wanted to exorcise forever. He imagined, for a moment, rushing him, tackling him to the ground, beating him senseless in retribution for all Darius had let loose on the world. But he knew in his heart that would be a suicide mission. And while he didn't care so much about saving his own hide, he had Scarlet to think of now.

"What are we going to do?" he hissed. "He's blocking the way to the exit."

His brother glanced behind him. Caleb knew what he was thinking. There might be another way out, but would they be able to reach it without running into anyone else? Even if they could, the time it would take to get there would mean leaving the girls and Emmy in more danger.

His brother reached for his gun. But Caleb stopped him. "No," he hissed. "He's probably not alone. If the others hear a gunshot, they'll come running. We need to take care of this quietly."

"Untie me."

The two boys whirled around. Mara held out her hands, her expression grave.

"I'll take care of him. Just untie me and wait for your chance."

Caleb glanced at his brother. Connor shrugged, then moved to undo the Dracken's bonds. Caleb bit his lower lip; he didn't like this—didn't trust Mara to do the right thing. She could easily sell them out to save her own hide and get back on the winning team. What did she owe them, anyway?

But they had no other real alternative, and they both knew it. So they watched and waited, holding their breath, as Mara walked out to face the Dracken Master. Connor clutched his gun with white-knuckled fingers. His eyes focused, his ears cocked and listening.

"Darius!" they heard Mara exclaim a few minutes later. "I can't believe you're actually here!"

There was a pause, then, "Mara," Darius replied, spitting out the name as if expelling poison. "How…lovely to see you."

"What are you doing here? I thought you were in jail."

"I was," Darius replied, evidently choosing not to elaborate further. Caleb wondered if he knew that his former partner had been the one to send him there.

To her credit, Mara pressed on. "I can't tell you how relieved I am to find you here. My lab was attacked, and my dragons escaped. I came here to find some Nether dust to help gather them up and bring them home. I never expected to find all of this." She waved a hand in the air.

"Yes, well, we've been busy. It sounds as if you have been as well."

She nodded. "It's been difficult, going at it on my own. And you should see the primitive technology I've been forced to work with. But I knew I had to press on, to keep our mission alive no matter what." She beamed at him. "But now, I'm home. I can't tell you how happy I am to be home."

Darius gave her a long, slow smile. "And we, of course, are happy to have you back. Especially given the fact you brought such a lovely gift."

"Excuse me?" This time Mara's voice did falter a little. "Gift?"

Caleb shot Connor a worried glance. Connor shook his head.

"I confess," Darius replied slyly. "I've been a very naughty boy. Peeking at my Christmas present early. So sweet of you to bring me exactly what I wanted."

"I'm sorry, Darius. I don't know what you mean. I didn't—"

"Come, Mara, don't play coy," he said, his voice tightening. "We found your little ride, stashed in the automotive shop, nice and tidy. All that was missing was a bright red bow."

Oh God. Caleb exchanged a horrified look with his twin. Darius had Emmy? Did that mean he had Trinity and Scarlet too?

"Look, Darius…" Mara was trying.

"You thought you were so clever, didn't you?" Darius sneered. "Thinking I was locked up, thinking I couldn't escape some pathetic twenty-first-century prison. Please. I walked out the front door the first month, after using my psychic powers on those ridiculous, weak-minded guards." He shook his head. "Imagine my surprise, though, when I went to find you, only to learn that you had been the one to betray me. The one to have me locked up in the first place." Caleb thought he heard a hint of hurt in the Dracken's voice.

Mara burst out a protest, but he raised a hand to wave her off. "Don't even think of denying it," he told her. "I know what you've been up to. And I know you bred purebloods instead of the hybrids I asked for. You've done everything in your power to tear down what we were supposed to be building. And yet"—he smiled widely—"it wasn't enough, was it? The apocalypse is still starting, despite your best efforts. Your dragons are on the rampage, and the earth will burn just as we planned."

"Please, Darius," Mara tried, her voice now more than slightly hysterical. "You don't understand. I only did what I had to, to survive. I never wanted any of it! I only wanted you! And…and…I'll prove it too! I'll show you where the rest of them are! Trinity and her friends. They're here, you know. They're here and I can—"

A shot rang out before she could finish, followed by a sickening thud. Then laughter—Darius's laughter.

"Stupid bitch," Caleb heard the Dracken leader mutter. "What would I want with them? I have their dragon. That's all I need." He paused for a moment and then, "Come up here and clean up this mess," he barked, presumably into a phone.

Caleb waited, heart in his throat. If the cleanup crew came up the back way, he and Connor would be trapped. He glanced at his brother. But there was nothing they could do.

Then, to their relief, they heard footsteps fading in the distance—Darius heading in the opposite direction. Caleb let out a breath of relief.

"Come on," Connor urged. "We need to get to the garage. Now!"

Caleb didn't need a second invitation. They turned the corner, passing Mara's lifeless body swimming in a pool of her own blood. Caleb shook his head. He almost felt bad for her, even if she had tried to sell them out to save her skin. She had been a victim, just as he had. But in the end, she'd made good: sacrificing her life for the cause, whether she meant to or not.

Now all they could do was make sure that sacrifice had not been in vain.

Chapter Forty-Two

Connor followed his brother up the rope and out of the mall, blinking to adjust his eyes to the sudden, bright sunshine. He looked around, trying to pinpoint any movement. Any guards that might be hanging out nearby. Darius had said he didn't care to go after them, but that didn't mean a random guard wouldn't take potshots if he had the chance.

They skirted the mall, keeping their backs against the outer wall to hide in the shadows. When they neared the garage, Caleb grabbed his brother and yanked him down behind a pile of rusted shopping carts.

"Look," he hissed, pointing across the parking lot.

Connor's heart sunk as he followed his brother's finger to the group of men securing an unconscious Emmy onto a flatbed truck. "Damn it," he swore.

"What are we going to do?" Caleb asked.

"There's nothing we can do now," Connor replied. "There's got to be at least twenty of them, and they're all armed. We'd never be able to take them on." He frowned, his thoughts racing. "We just need to see where they're taking her. She's too big to fit through the front door of the mall, which means there's got to be a bulkhead or something nearby to get her underground with the other dragons."

"Right," Caleb agreed. "But what about the girls? Do you think they're still in the garage?"

Connor closed his eyes, focusing his gift to seek them out. A moment later, he opened them and nodded. "They're in there," he assured his brother. "Though…they're really still."

"Of course they're still. They're hiding!" Caleb retorted roughly, obviously not willing to admit any possible alternative. "Look, I'll follow the truck. You go find the girls."

Connor nodded. "Okay," he agreed. "Come back to the garage when you're done, though. If they're hurt, I won't be able to move them both."

Caleb gave him a curt salute, then took off, heading in the direction of the slow-moving truck. Connor watched him go for a moment, then turned back to the garage, continuing to skirt the perimeter of the mall until he reached the open doors.

At first glance, the place seemed deserted, and Connor had a wild thought that maybe they'd been taken along with Emmy after all. But he forced the thought away and closed his eyes again, summoning up additional spark. His stomach roiled with the effort, and he was forced to grab on to a support beam to steady himself. But it was enough.

"Trash bin," he affirmed to himself.

Diving into action, he ran to the back of the garage where the large Dumpster sat, hurtling himself over the edge and starting to dig, tossing random pieces of metal and other trash out of the bin to clear it.

"Come on," he begged. "I know you're in here."

Then, like a miracle, his fingers brushed against something cool, smooth. Skin.

"Trinity!" he cried, clearing the trash off of her, pulling her out of the pile. A few moments later, he was holding her in his arms. "Trinity!" he cried again.

She was so still. Cold as ice. He slapped her across the face, but she didn't respond. Adrenaline skyrocketing, he put his cheek to her lips, desperate to feel some sort of breath, while his fingers found her pulse.

He lifted his head, letting out a shaky breath. She was alive. Unconscious but alive.

Using all his strength, he managed to drag her from the Dumpster, setting her gently onto the floor. Then he went back in, digging deeper until he was able to find Scarlet too. She was in a similar state—cold, pale, but still breathing.

"Did you find them?"

He looked up. His brother had returned. He motioned to the girls. "They're unconscious," he said. "I'm not sure why." Then he added, "What about Emmy?"

"They brought her around back," Caleb informed him. "Drove her down into that parking garage we escaped from last time. There must be a connecting passageway underneath. I couldn't get too close to see. But it looks like she's definitely staying on the premises, for now at least." He dropped to his knees before Scarlet. "What's wrong with her?" he asked, looking up at his twin with horror. Connor started to shrug.

Then he saw it. So faint most people would have missed it. But it was there all the same, a slight purple ring around Trinity's nose. He grabbed his brother's arm, pointing it out. "Nether dust," he whispered. "They've been dosed by Nether dust. The Dracken probably used it to down Emmy, not realizing—or caring—that the girls were here too."

He grabbed Trinity by the shoulders. "Wake up!" he cried. "Trinity, baby, please wake up!" Beside him, Caleb started working on Scarlet, trying to get her awake. Connor could see his brother's face was white with fear. Not surprising; he knew the dangers of the Nether more than anyone.

"How long will it last?" Caleb asked in a trembling voice.

"I don't know. I guess it probably depends on the dosage, right? Though if they used enough to knock out a two-ton dragon…" Connor trailed off, not wanting to voice the obvious.

Come on, Trin, he begged silently. *You're stronger than this. You can fight it. Do not let them win.*

His heart wrenched as his mind flashed back to all the fights they'd had over the last year. They seemed so stupid now. So meaningless. All the time he'd wasted being angry, because she wouldn't listen to him. But had he, at the same time, ever really listened to her? Just like with his brother and the dragon, he'd charged in, assuming he knew what was best. That his knowledge of one possible future made him an expert on them all.

But this future, as she'd told him a thousand times before, was yet unwritten. It might have similarities to his, but it wasn't the same.

Which meant they still had a chance, however small, to make things right.

To not let the Dracken win.

He squared his shoulders and turned to his brother. "Let's get them to the car," he said "We'll drive them back to the airfield. Once they're safe, we'll figure out what to do."

✦ ✦ ✦

Back at the airfield, they unloaded the girls from the truck and, with heavy hearts, carried them into the sickroom, where once upon a time, both Caleb and Connor had lain. Neither of them had stirred the entire ride home, and Caleb's fear was expanding at an alarming rate. He thought back to his own time trapped in the Nether, how lonely he'd been, how long it had seemed to drag on. Now, to think Scarlet was suffering the same fate…and this time, they didn't have any easy access to dragon blood to wake her up.

"What are we going to do?" he asked, looking up at Connor, his stomach swimming with unease. "We can't just leave them like this."

"No," his brother agreed. "I'm going to go in after them. One way or another, I'll get them out." He leveled his gaze on Caleb. "Both of them. I promise."

Caleb nodded slowly, watching his brother reach into his backpack and pull out something small and shiny. He jerked involuntarily as he realized what it was.

"Sorry," Connor said, looking a little guilty. "I didn't mean to…"

"It's okay," Caleb said quickly. "I'm okay." He turned from his brother and concentrated his gaze on Scarlet. Sweet, beautiful Scarlet, who was so much better than any drug. "I'm just sorry I'm such a loser that I can't help you do it."

"You're not a loser," Connor scolded. "You were manipulated, lied to. We all were. Your addiction to the Nether? It wasn't an accident. Nor was the murder of your dragon."

Caleb listened, wide-eyed, as his brother recounted what he'd learned from Mara. When Connor had finished, Caleb whistled softly. "I can't believe it," he said, shaking his head. "All this time, I thought…" He trailed off, not knowing what to say.

"Not that any of this excuses what I did," Connor added, giving him a look of pure regret. "I acted out of fear. I didn't pause to think it through. I wanted to protect you, but I didn't give you the chance to protect yourself. I was so sure I knew, back then, the right thing to do. But I was wrong. I should have trusted you. I should have respected your decisions. I should never have killed your poor dragon." He raked a hand through his hair. "I don't deserve for you to forgive me. But I do want you to know that I'm sorry—and that I know what I did was wrong."

Caleb drew in a breath. He'd been waiting his whole life for his brother to say those words, but he'd never once thought they would actually come from his lips. "Thank you," he said at last. "You don't know how much that means to me." He paused then added, "We've had our differences. But we are brothers. We were born on the same team. Maybe it's time we start acting like it."

"I'd like that," Connor replied. He paused, then added, "What is it they do in this world again? Should we hug it out?"

Caleb found himself laughing. "Uh, yeah. Let's not get carried away." He shook his head at his brother. "Look, Dragon Hunter, how about you go rescue my girlfriend, and we'll call it even?"

Connor nodded. "That I think I can do."

Chapter Forty-Three

"Connor?"

Connor opened one eye then the other, trying to gain his bearings. For a moment, he had no idea where he was—white walls and ceiling and floor, stretching out as far as he could see. He rubbed his eyes, searching his brain for answers. Where was—

Then it all came rushing back to him. "Trinity!" he cried, scrambling to his feet.

And then, there she was.

He ran to her, throwing his arms around her, his heart soaring as he lifted her off her feet and twirled her around, burying his face in her curls. "Trinity," he murmured. "Thank God." He pulled away from the hug and peered down at her with anxious eyes. "Are you okay?"

"I'm fine," she replied. "Just waiting for this stupid Nether overdose to wear off. From what I'm told, it'll take at least another day." She looked at him in concern. "Is my real-life body okay?"

"You're safe," he assured her. "You and Scarlet are both back at the airfield. We took you home after we weren't able to wake you up."

She bit her lower lip. "What about Emmy? She was here, briefly, before the Nether dust wore off on her. She told me that men had come to take her away."

Connor sighed. "I'm sorry, Trin." He gave her a rundown of what had happened at the mall. Trinity listened, her eyes growing wide.

"I should have known," she whispered. "After all, Darius is too smart not to have had a backup plan." She scrunched up her face. "But poor Emmy. Trapped all over again. And this time, it's so much worse." She looked up. "We have to break her out."

"No offense, Trin, but I don't see how we could," Connor replied. He knew it would do no good to sugarcoat things here. "They've got an army of hybrid dragons guarding her. And we don't have any way to take them on."

Trinity stared down at her feet. "There's got to be some way. There just has to be."

"Where's Scarlet?" Connor asked, wanting to change the subject. "I told Caleb I'd check on her too. He's freaking out worried."

"Where do you think?" Trinity snorted, pointing across the white space. Connor followed her finger, his heart lurching as his eyes fell on none other than Zoe herself, goofily dancing through the skies with Scarlet on her back. She was bigger than she'd been on Earth, and her scales were so bright and sparkly it almost hurt to look at them.

"They've been up there for hours. If it weren't for Caleb back home, I'm not sure she'd ever want to leave."

Connor turned away, guilt stabbing him in the gut. Zoe looked so beautiful. So innocent too. Just as Caleb's dragon had been.

He felt Trinity's hand on his arm. He looked up.

"She gave me her blood, you know," he blurted out.

"What?"

"To heal me after Caleb hit me with that rock," he explained. "At first, I thought you did it. Or maybe Caleb or Scarlet. But then I got to thinking. And I realized if you had, you would have been there when I woke up."

Trinity gave a low whistle. "You know, I had been wondering how you got up like you did. We'd doped you up on so many painkillers, there was no way you should have been able to stand, never mind go dragon slaying."

"It's ironic, right?" He shook his head. "She went and saved my life—so I could, in turn, steal hers away."

"Well, if it's any consolation," Trin said, "I'm pretty sure she's loving being back in the Nether. I mean, she misses her brother, of course, but I actually think she prefers it here to Earth. No more being trapped in a small shed. No more hunger. No more fear."

"It's like dragon heaven," Connor concluded. "Literally, I guess." He sighed. "If only we could have gotten that Nether dust, brought Zavier and the rest of them here, had them talk to Scarlet and Zoe. I'm sure they would have been able to convince them to call off their war."

"And save Emmy," Trinity added. "Having an army of dragons at our disposal would certainly make things easier."

Make what easier?

Connor whirled around. Lost in his troubled thoughts, he hadn't noticed the giant green dragon with golden wings step up behind them. He glanced questioningly at Trinity, noting recognition in her eyes.

"Lyria!" she exclaimed before he could inquire. "Emmy's mother," she added in explanation to him.

Yes, the green and golden dragon agreed, sounding a little sad. *Though, in truth, you were always more mother to her than I.*

"Yeah, well, Emmy hasn't exactly been a contender for mother of the year either," Trinity remarked wryly. "Though she regrets it all now. And I'm pretty sure when she's finally reunited with Zoe and the rest of them, she'll be begging for forgiveness."

"If things keep going the way they are, they might not have long to wait," Connor muttered.

Suddenly he felt the dragon's eyes on him. *What do you mean?* Lyria demanded. *Is my Emberlyn in trouble?*

Connor gave a reluctant nod, breaking it down for the dragon. She listened, wide-eyed and worried.

You must help her, she told Connor when he'd finished.

"Believe me, I would love to," he assured her. "But it's not that easy. The Dracken have an army of hybrid dragons at their disposal. They're not going to give her up without a fight."

Lyria ruffled her wings, looking offended. *Well, then we should give them one. Emberlyn has thirteen remaining children on Earth, does she not?*

"Who, thanks to me, are busy with their own apocalyptic crusade," Connor reminded her bitterly. "Maybe if we had gotten the Nether dust, we could have brought them here to talk it through. Zoe could have convinced Zavier, and he could have talked to the rest of them. But now…"

Lyria seemed to consider this for a moment. *It is true you cannot bring Zavier to the Nether. But what if you could bring Zoe to Zavier?*

"How could we do that?" Connor wrinkled his brow. "She's dead. We can't just bring her back to life…" He paused. "Can we?"

There may be a way. But it would require some sacrifice.

Connor's heart started beating fast in his chest. "Whatever it is, I'll do it."

Lyria gave him a solemn look. *You have my granddaughter's blood swimming through your veins. You're not fully bonded to her—but you could be. And if you were, then you would share a life force.*

"And if we did…" Connor bit his lower lip, realizing what the dragon was getting at. "Are you saying we could trade places? Like, I could stay here and she could return to Earth to talk to her brother?"

Yes. It would be possible. If you both agreed to complete the bond.

"Hold on!" Trinity interrupted. "Connor would have to stay here in the Nether so Zoe could be brought back to life on Earth?"

Lyria nodded. *A life for a life.*

"No!" Trinity shook her head. "That's crazy. Connor, there's got to be another way. You can't just stay here forever." Her voice broke. "That's not fair!"

Connor sighed, reaching over to take her hand in his. He stroked it with gentle fingers. "No. What I did to her was not fair," he said slowly. "And it's the reason her brother is on his rampage now. Don't you see, Trin? Once Zavier realizes I've sacrificed my life to give him back his sister, he will have to come around. Then he and Zoe can talk the others into saving their mother too."

"But, Connor—"

He looked up at Lyria. "It's perfect. Tell me what I need to do."

Chapter Forty-Four

A re you okay?"

Trinity looked up. Connor was staring down at her with worried eyes. His face was probably as pale as hers was, though not as tear streaked. Connor was the soldier. He wouldn't cry. Even when he had every reason to.

"How could I be okay?" she blurted out. "In what world could I possibly be okay?"

She turned from him, realizing that this could very well be the last time they were alone together as they waited for Lyria to prepare for the bonding ceremony. And it wasn't even as if they were actually together, not physically anyway.

The implications hit her hard and fast. She'd never get to hold him again. Never get to kiss his lips and trace his face with her fingers. Never get to stare into his beautiful eyes and feel his whisper in her ears.

Connor sat down beside her. "Honestly, I wasn't sure if you'd even care," he said quietly. "After all that's happened…"

His words caused a fresh burst of tears as her mind flashed to all the fights they'd had. All the time they'd spent apart, time wasted on stupid arguments and egos. Time that could have been spent in one another's arms.

"Of course I care," she blurted. "I love you. Even when I was furious with you, I still loved you."

Her voice broke. Connor took her hands in his, finding her eyes with his own steady blue ones. He gave her a wistful look that made her heart shatter.

"I love you too," he said, his voice filled with earnest. Then he gave her a shy grin. "Since I first met you at your grandfather's museum and you blinded me with Mace."

She laughed through her tears. "Yeah, well, you should have known better than to come between a girl and her dragon."

He grabbed her, pulling her close, until her face was smashed against his chest. She could feel his heartbeat against her ear—usually so strong and steady, now beating fast, almost erratically. He was scared too, she realized. He was trying to hide it from her. But he was terrified.

"I don't want you to do this!" she found herself blubbering.

"Oh, Trin," he murmured. "Don't you see? This is why I came here. This was my mission all along. I never expected to come back, you know. When I signed up for this gig, I knew it was a one-way trip. And it's been a far longer, crazier trip than I could have ever imagined. But even so, now it has to end."

"Please," she begged, knowing she sounded pathetic and weak but at the same time not caring that she did. "I can't lose you. You're all I have left." Her mind flashed to all those in her life who had already fallen—her mother, her grandfather, her friends. But Connor—she'd assumed he'd always be there, had taken for granted the fact that he would be. "If you leave, I'll be all alone."

"No," he corrected gently, though his voice sounded strained. "You'll have Emmy back. And you'll have my brother. I know he's infatuated with Scarlet, but he'll take care of you too. I know he will." He gave her a small smile. "He loves you, you know. In his own crazy, messed-up way, he'll always love you. And he'll always keep you safe."

"But it's not the same…"

"You also have your father," Connor continued. "And the other Potentials. And even…" He shrugged. "Those goofy Dracken kids. I have to admit, they're handy in a pinch." He leveled his gaze on her. "Trinity, you have a huge family. A team. You'll never have to be alone again."

Trinity closed her eyes, forcing herself to draw in a shaky breath. He was right, of course. Most of her life, she'd had to navigate on her own. Going from foster home to foster home, changing families like so much underwear. But now, things had changed. She had a big, beautiful, crazy family who had dedicated their lives to her and her crusade to save the world.

But they weren't Connor.

She burst into a fresh set of tears. "I can't take this!" she cried. "I'm sorry! I know you want me to be brave. And I usually am. But I can't… I don't want to…" She broke off, unable to continue.

"Trinity," he groaned, his own voice hoarse. "I'm begging you, sweetheart, please try to stay strong for me. This is killing me. You know that, right? The last thing on earth I want to do is leave you." He pulled away, searching her face with his eyes. His blue, blue eyes, shining at her with an earnestness and desperation that tore her heart in two.

"All I want to do is stay with you," he continued. "I want to marry you. I want to give you babies and create the kind of beautiful family that neither of us had growing up. A stable, normal, boring old family that plays flecking board games on Friday nights and pops popcorn."

He gave her a sad smile. "But I can't be selfish here. You haven't seen what I've seen. You can't even fathom how bad it will get if we don't stop it now. How many people will die. How many normal, boring families will be torn apart. That's why I came here in the first place, you know. To do whatever it took to save the world." He gave her a rueful look. "I just hadn't planned on falling in love before I managed to do it."

Trinity let out a choking sob. "Connor..."

They fell into each other's arms, reaching, grasping as if their very lives depended on it, their mouths finding one another, kiss after desperate kiss—each one closer to the last.

She'd pushed him away for so long. And yet now, at that moment, all Trin wanted was his mouth on hers forever and always, the world outside be damned.

But the world refused to go away, and all too soon, Lyria was stepping up behind them, telling them it was time. They reluctantly broke apart, their fingers still clinging to one another, as if powerless to let go. Connor swiped his face with his sleeve to wipe away the tears she hadn't believed he would shed, and she followed suit, remembering his words.

Stay strong for me, he'd said.

All this time, he'd done everything for her, never asking for anything in return. And now, in the end, this. This was all she could do.

What she had to do.

320

Chapter Forty-Five

Scarlet-mom? Are you here, Scarlet-mom?

Zavier paced the cliff side, smoke hissing from his nose as the panic rose inside him at an alarming rate. Where was she? He was sure this was where he'd left her when he went off to find his brothers and sisters and set them free.

So where had she gone?

Mother! he tried again, pawing the ground in agitation. *Where are you? Answer me. Please!*

But there was nothing.

He could feel the eyes of the others watching him skeptically. They hadn't wanted to come here. They'd only wanted to seek revenge against the humans who had kept them in their cages. But Zavier had talked them into coming to the mountain, to meeting the one human who was worth saving—the dragon mother to them all.

But now she was gone. Had something happened to her? Or… His mind skittered nervously. Had she betrayed them too?

No. Not Scarlet-mom. She would never do that.

The trick, however, he thought as he glanced over at the others, was to convince them.

Zavier!

His ears pricked at the sudden voice echoing through his head. *What was that?*

Turn around, Zavier!

The voice was commanding, and he almost obeyed. But at the last second, he stopped himself, realizing his mistake. The voice was his sister's. And she was gone. Whatever he was hearing, it was only in his imagination. He would never hear her real voice again.

A weight seemed to fall over him like heavy blanket, threatening to smother him, and for a moment, he wasn't sure he cared if it did. He was so exhausted from the day's events. And in the end, what did any of it matter? What good was revenge? It wouldn't get his sister back. And he knew, deep in his heart, she would not approve.

You can't fight violence with violence, he imagined her scolding. *And now you've lost Scarlet-mom too. You promised me you'd protect her. And instead, you left her to fend for herself.*

He hung his head. *Zoe. I'm so sorry, Zoe.*

It's okay, Brother. I forgive you.

He looked up, angry. That stupid voice again—that stupid, impossible voice that sounded just like his sister's, crashing uninvited through his head. He let out a small whimper despite himself, trying to block it from his mind. It was too much, too soon. He couldn't bear it.

You're not real, he found himself crying. *You're dead. You're not coming back.*

Want to make a bet?

He looked up. He couldn't help it. His eyes fell on the other dragons, now shifting and shuffling and turning their snouts to the sky. At first Zavier told himself they'd just spotted some kind of prey—a vulture, perhaps, or another large bird. Or maybe even an airplane flying too low. But then his ears picked up their excited murmurs. This was no bird, he realized. No plane.

It was a dragon. And not just any dragon. It was his sister. And she was coming in for a landing.

At first, he thought he must be hallucinating. But then he realized if he was, the other dragons were seeing the same hallucination. As she dropped down from the sky, they circled around her, snorting and sniffing her over. They all saw her. She was really there.

One of the larger dragons, a ruby red, turned to Zavier, narrowing his eyes at him. *I thought you said they killed her*, he demanded.

Zavier took a hesitant step back, his whole body shaking with fear. What was this? How was this possible? Could it really be her?

They did, he stammered. *I saw her die. I…*

Words abandoned him as Zoe turned, meeting his eyes with her own beautiful purple ones. A slow, goofy smile spread across her face. Then she took a hesitant step toward him. Her face was gaunt. Her soft scale was pierced and drained as it had been when she had died. In short, she looked like hell. But she looked like his sister. His sister whom he thought he'd never see again. She was there. Standing in front of him. Breathing. Living.

He took a step forward, and suddenly they were nose to nose. She laughed and gave him a slurp on his cheek as she'd done so many times before.

Hey, Bro, she said with a grin. *Want to help me save the day?*

PART 5:

CHAR

Chapter Forty-Six

The Council Chambers—Year 190 Post-Scorch

T he Council will see you now."

Connor looked up from his reader, meeting the eyes of the assistant who was leaning in the doorway to the inner sanctum. The same girl who had escorted him the last time he was here, the one who had his rookie card and wanted to be a Dragon Hunter. But this time, she wasn't smiling as she made the gesture for him to follow her.

Rising from his seat, he walked through the doorway and into the same smooth, circular hallway that glowed with phosphorescent light. This time, however, there was no cheerful banter. No flushed cheeks, no talk of rookie cards or Academy scholarships. And when they reached the Council chambers, her voice was cold as she instructed him to go inside. Suffice to say, there was no suggestion of a post-interview rendezvous this time around either.

Not that this surprised him. Ever since he'd woken up in the hospital the week before after being shot by his own brother, he hadn't exactly received a warm reception from the population. But who could blame them? The security cameras had caught it all, and everyone now knew he was to blame. He had let his feelings for his family stand in the way of protecting the people. And now, because of him, the Council was in jeopardy of losing power to the Dracken.

He hadn't known just what his brother had stolen at the time. But it shouldn't have mattered. He had been an intruder in the most highly secured government lab—he should have been shot on sight, no questions asked. But Connor hadn't been able to do it—and had allowed himself to be shot instead. Caleb probably thought he was showing mercy, setting his gun to stun. But instant death would have been far better than the shame and humiliation Connor had suffered since. The knowledge that because of him and his weakness, the secret weapon—the precious Nether dust that the Council had spent the last ten years developing—was now in the hands of the enemy. They would use it to tame dragons and turn them on the Council. They would stage a coup, and the world would soon fall to their whims.

And it was all Connor's fault. In a moment, he'd gone from hero to zero, his Dragon Hunter posters stripped from the walls and set on fire. His status had been revoked, they'd taken his pins and uniforms, and now, today, the Council would decide his ultimate fate.

Drawing in a breath, Connor stepped inside the inner sanctum, this time not bothering to catalog all the luxuries inside. What did it matter? If the Dracken indeed got their way, it would probably all be burned.

"Connor Jacks," the Council leader, Solomon, called out in an austere voice. "Approach the bench."

Connor did what he was told, his head bowed, his eyes to the ground. He wondered if they would sentence him to the mines or just let him loose on the streets. He wouldn't last long in either scenario, he realized. The public wanted him dead; he had no doubt they could make this happen, wherever he ended up.

He didn't care. He deserved that and more. It was his mother whom he was worried about. Would she be kicked out of her apartment? Publically shamed in front of her friends? He winced. His father would have been so disappointed in him.

"Poor dear. He looks as if someone told him there was no Santa Claus," cooed Frederica, the woman sitting next to Solomon. "Don't worry, Connor. Things are not as bad as they seem, I promise."

Connor forced himself to look up, knowing he must look a sight: black shadows under his eyes, skin yellowed from the aftereffects of the stun gun. He hadn't been able to eat anything all week, his stomach tossing and turning, sickened by the public outcry. When once he had ventured out for food, people cursed at him and threw garbage at his head. And the shopkeepers all locked their doors.

"Just get it over with," he muttered. "I'm ready."

The Council members exchanged glances with amused expressions that told him they knew something he didn't. It should have concerned him, but in the end, what did it matter?

"Look," he said. "I know it won't make any difference, and I'm prepared to accept whatever punishment you plan to implement. But let the record show, I am sorry. I know I made a terrible mistake. I fell short on my duties. I let my emotions sway my judgment. And I will live with the guilt of this for the rest of my life."

"We appreciate your honesty," Solomon replied. "And we are glad to know you understand the seriousness of your crime. It is a bad time for all of us, as you might imagine."

"Yes. I understand."

"The law states that your crimes should be punishable by death or a life sentence in the mines," Solomon said. "Do you understand this?"

Connor winced despite himself. "Yes." He held his breath, wondering which they would choose. While he had no real desire to die, it would be over quickly. A lifetime in the mines, he knew, would only drag out the inevitable.

"But what if there was a way to redeem yourself?" interjected Frederica. "What if we offered you a way to atone for your sins? Would you be interested?"

Connor looked up, his eyes wide, his heart panging in his chest. "Of course," he cried before he even bothered to think about what they might mean by this. "I'll do anything. Anything at all. Do you want me to raid a Dracken sky house? Try to get the dust back?"

"No, no," Solomon replied, shaking a hand dismissively. "It's nothing like that. My dear boy, what's done is done. At this point, the powder has probably already been dispersed and dissected. There's no going back from there. But we do have another…proposition. Another…mission, if you will. For a brave Dragon Hunter like yourself."

Connor squared his shoulders. "I'll take it. Whatever it is, I'll do it."

The Council erupted in excited conversation. Solomon banged his gavel. "Don't you want to know what it is first?" he queried, looking at Connor with raised eyebrows.

Connor shrugged, heart thumping in his chest. He knew whatever was to come next would change his life forever—and probably for the worse. But he had no choice. He'd made a mistake. He had to make good. Everything he'd worked for his whole life depended on it.

So he listened as they told him what they wanted him to do. And when they had finished, he found he was barely able to stand, his legs were wobbling so hard.

"So?" Frederica asked with a slow smile. "What do you think? Do you think you're up for such a task? Remember, once you go, there will be no coming back."

He nodded. After all, in the end, what was there to come back to anyway?

He cleared his throat, his heart slamming against his rib cage so hard he was sure he'd break a rib. But somehow he found the voice to speak.

"I'll do it," he declared. "I'll go back in time. I'll destroy the egg. I'll destroy the girl." He sucked in a breath. "I'll stop the apocalypse. And I'll save the world."

Chapter Forty-Seven

Present Day

G ather round, guys! It's dinnertime."

The hangar erupted in cheers and roars as Trinity and Caleb, aided by a few of the other Potentials, lugged large carts of food through the door. A moment later, they found themselves surrounded by thirteen hungry dragons, who were panting and eyeing the meat with much enthusiasm. It was a good thing they'd been stockpiling, Trin considered with a small smile, since they were literally now feeding a dragon army.

Once she'd found her brother again, it hadn't taken Zoe long to convince him to call off his campaign. And the other dragons had eagerly followed suit once they learned there was food to be eaten back at the base. Typical greedy, lazy pure-blooded dragons, Caleb had joked, eager to abandon their quests for vengeance in exchange for belly rubs and roast beef.

And so together, they'd headed back to the airfield where they were greeted enthusiastically by their new guardians—the Potentials—and briefed on their mission.

Of course, things were still bittersweet. Everyone was worried about Emmy. But they were excited to meet the new dragons too. This was, after all, what the Potentials had trained for all that time under Dracken rule. It was ironic, really, that now that same training would be used against their former masters.

Trinity had first assumed they'd assign the dragons to their new guardians, but Caleb had explained that the assignation should come from the dragons themselves. Just as Emmy had chosen her, they would choose their own guardians.

And so they did. The Potentials all standing in line, pulsing with excitement as the dragons looked them over carefully. And then, one by one, they chose. Trevor got a huge ruby dragon he named Burgess, after his favorite rugby player. Aiko was chosen by a sleek golden she named Filia, after a dragon in a beloved anime. Even little Noa was chosen, by a runt of the litter she called Baby. Trinity wasn't sure it was the best idea to send a ten-year-old onto the battlefield, but Caleb reminded her they needed all the help they could get. In the end, it was decided Noa and Baby could serve as medics, delivering lifesaving dragon blood to those who fell.

The week was spent practicing their maneuvers under the mask of night, so they could stay flying under the radar. Things had somewhat calmed down now that the attacks had stopped, but the terror alert remained high, and the government was still presumably looking for them. Luke and Nate and Natasha did what they could, feeding dragon sightings onto the Internet from places far and wide to help scatter the search.

At first, things were admittedly disorganized and chaotic. The dragons had never been ridden before, and the extra weight made them unbalanced and clumsy. A few Potentials suffered some bad falls. But by the end of the week, everyone was starting to feel good.

Trin watched Caleb stroll down the hangar now, talking with each of the Potentials as they rubbed down their dragons after their meals. He spent time with each and every one of them, going over the night's practice and quizzing them on the strengths and weaknesses of each dragon. Trin had never seen Caleb so happy and confident. For the first time in his life, he was the leader, and everyone respected his commands. He'd come a long way since the days of being a shivering Nether Head, and, she noted as she watched Scarlet come over and kiss him happily on the mouth, she was pretty sure she knew the reason. Alone, the two of them had been broken. Together, they had become whole.

Her heart wrenched—not from the old familiar jealousy worming its way through her as it used to. She was happy that they were happy and wouldn't want things any other way. She just wished she could have had the same happiness with Connor. It had only been a week without him, but it already felt like a lifetime. And to think of him trapped in the Nether, just as her mother had been…

She reached into her pocket, fingering the last Nether gem. It would be so easy to palm it now, to find him in his prison and run into his arms and cover his face with kisses. It was funny; she'd never truly understood how someone could get addicted to the Nether. But now she totally got it, all too well.

She pulled her hand from her pocket. She would wait. Going to the Nether now would only drain her spark, and she needed all the spark she could get to face the Dracken— hopefully for the last time.

"Save the dragon, save the world," she muttered. "Let's do this thing once and for all."

Chapter Forty-Eight

O kay, we're on approach. Everyone stand by."

Caleb barked the commands into his headset as he and his fellow dragon riders approached the squat, gray mall that had once served as a shopper's mecca, now transformed into an apocalyptic bunker. As they'd practiced, he laid a hand on Zavier's neck to get the dragon to slow and wait for the others to fall in line behind him. This had to be a synchronized effort if they had any chance of pulling it off.

Okay, he pushed to his dragon. *We'll start the flyover now. Hold your fire until I give the signal. Then, you alert the others.*

He glanced back at the team. They all looked excited but nervous—but mostly excited, he decided, and he couldn't blame them either. He was pretty excited himself. The whole time they'd been training, it all felt so right—as if he'd finally stumbled on what he'd been born to do. What all of them here, now, had been born to do.

He heard a noise and turned to see Scarlet and Zoe had come up to hover beside them. Scarlet grinned, giving him a thumbs-up. Caleb smiled back, returning the gesture. He hadn't wanted her to join in; it was a dangerous mission, and he couldn't bear the idea of her getting hurt. But of course,

Scarlet and Zoe would have none of that "sexist male talk." They were just as capable as the boys and weren't about to sit on the sidelines.

Caleb drew in a breath. "Okay," he said into the headset again. "Let's start our initial flyover. We'll circle the mall clockwise, dropping a few firebombs as we go. Be careful with your aim though. We're just trying to lure them out at this point. We don't want to burn the place down or collapse it before we can get Emmy out."

A chorus of "okays" and "roger thats" came through his earphones as everyone called out their assent. They were ready and raring to go, and there was no time like the present. Caleb dug his heels into Zavier's flanks. "Okay, boy. Let's rock and roll."

His dragon didn't need a second invitation. He spread his wings and dove down, gliding on the air currents as if they were a slippery slide. As they approached the mall, his mouth creaked open, and he belched a small stream of fire in its direction. A moment later, the fire hit an abandoned car below, and it burst into flames. The other dragons followed suit, and soon there were small fires everywhere, lighting up the night sky as the dragons flew together around the mall.

After they completed their circle, they rendezvoused a short distance off, watching. Waiting. Summoning more heat for the next round. It was the Dracken's move now. And Caleb could only hope they took the bait.

At first, they saw nothing. Then…

"Look!" Scarlet cried. He followed her pointing finger to a loading dock at the farside of the mall. It was opening—a dark, gaping maw, like a giant beast yawning.

"Here they come!" he reported over his headset. "Stand tight. Do not break formation."

And then they came, dark shadows torpedoing from their underground lair, filling the air with ear-splitting screams as they shot into the skies.

"Steady," Caleb reminded them, noting a few of the dragons were looking a little too eager. "Let them come to us."

He watched as the hybrids approached, cataloging them quickly. Like their predecessors, they were all malformed in some way—misshapen, ugly, some missing body parts, others with extra to spare. Some didn't even have wings or feet and were grotesquely squirming on their bellies out of the bulkhead like massive worms.

But what they lacked in majesty and beauty, they made up for in sheer size—more than twice the size of Zavier and Zoe and their siblings. And as they grew closer, Caleb recognized the icy coldness in each dragon's eyes. There was no mistaking it; these were true hybrids. And they were out for blood.

Let's do this already! Zavier hissed.

Caleb raised his hand and started the countdown. "In three, two, one…"

The Potentials shouted a victory cry as their dragons let loose their flames, creating a tsunami of fire sweeping toward the other dragons, stopping them in their tracks. Then, at Caleb's command, they directed their beasts to fly up and over the fire, dive-bombing the hybrids before they could figure out what was going on, claws outstretched and mouths ready to bite and tear.

Then it was dragon on dragon, with humans holding on for dear life, using their mental gifts to push at the enemy in an attempt to disorient, confuse, and, if they were lucky, scare them into fleeing. It wasn't something that would work on every dragon, Caleb had warned, but if they could convince even a couple to bow out of the fight, it would be worth the effort. And sure enough, two dragons seemed to succumb almost immediately, taking off in the opposite direction, squawking madly. Caleb gestured for Scarlet and Zoe to go after them and ground them for good.

But just as he was admiring their defeat, Zavier bellowed in pain. A moment later, Caleb felt it too, thanks to the bond he and the dragon shared, and he whirled around, realizing one of the hybrids had somehow gotten behind them and was slashing at Zavier's tail with razor-sharp claws. It was a huge dragon, and whatever deformities it might have, Caleb couldn't see them from his position. He urged Zavier to turn around, to face the beast, but as they pivoted, the dragon made another swipe, this time slashing Zavier's scales, creating a huge gash in his side. Blood fountained from the wound, and Zavier staggered, dazed, for a moment forgetting to fly. Caleb gripped on tight as they started plummeting to earth, his own sides aching with phantom pain from his dragon's injury.

Fly, you overgrown marshmallow burner! he screamed in Zavier's head, desperate to get him back in the game. He was *this close* to passing out from his own agony at this point, so he could only imagine what his dragon was suffering.

Thankfully, Zavier seemed to hear this, his eyes shooting open, his claws slashing out at his enemy. But they'd dropped down too far, and he missed his mark, swiping only at empty air. The other dragon's lips curled, and his mouth opened, and

Caleb winced as he caught sparks igniting from inside. There was no way Zavier was going to be able to dodge this in time.

Zavier seemed to realize this too. He dove toward the ground, landing hard and bucking his rider from his back. Caleb was thrown to the earth, hard, and saw stars seconds before the hybrid let loose his flames on his dragon.

Dragons could usually withstand a great deal of heat, Caleb knew, thanks to their heavy scales, but the open wound on Zavier's side provided no such protection, and the fire from the hybrid seared him hard, knocking him over with its force. As Caleb watched helplessly, his own body feeling as if it had caught fire, the dragon screamed in a mixture of pain and rage, clawing uselessly at the air as he attempted to rise. The hybrid landed in front of him, his beady eyes locking onto Zavier. Steam shot from his nostrils. He opened his mouth to fire again.

"No!" Caleb cried. He leapt to his feet, ignoring the pain, his brother's gun-blade in hand, shooting before he had time to line up the shot properly. The bullet hit the dragon's side, missing the sweet spot. But it did the trick all the same; the dragon left Zavier to turn on Caleb instead.

Fleck. Caleb raised the gun again, but it was useless until it recharged. In the meantime, he was a sitting duck. And there was no place to hide.

But just as the dragon was about to stomp him flat, Zavier jumped back into the fray, wrestling the dragon to the ground and biting him hard on the neck. Over and over, they tussled, each gaining then losing advantage. Caleb's gun was now recharged, but he couldn't get a clean shot. And Zavier was starting to tire.

Scarlet! he cried. *I need you! Now!*

And then, like angels from heaven, Scarlet and Zoe were there, dropping down from the sky, Zoe's claws outstretched. She grabbed the other dragon in her talons, ripping into his flanks, black blood spraying everywhere. Zavier took advantage, diving on top of him. Now, two against one, it didn't take long to finish him.

Once the dragon was down, Zavier staggered backward, dropping heavily to the ground. Zoe let out a worried whine, bounding over to him and nudging him with her nose. His flank was still badly burned, and the skin was still smoking. Caleb ran over to him, reaching into his bag to pull out the burn salve. Grabbing a handful, he spread it liberally over the wound, desperate to cool the burn. But though it seemed to provide Zavier a little pain relief, the dragon was not getting up.

Zavier! No, Zavier! Please!

Tears stung Caleb's eyes as he watched Zoe dance around her brother with marked agitation, her eyes wide and her mouth trembling. But there was nothing she could do. And there was still a battle to be won.

"Caleb, look!" Scarlet cried, pointing upward. He reluctantly turned his attention back to the skies. The other dragons were still fighting, locked in fierce battle. As he watched, two purple hybrids cornered Burgess and Trevor, savagely ripping at Burgess's wings. A moment later, dragon and rider were careening to the ground, Trevor's screams echoing through Caleb's headset at deafening volume. He ripped off the headset and turned to Scarlet.

"I'll stay with Zavier!" he cried. "You get him!"

MARI MANCUSI

Scarlet and Zoe leapt into the sky, diving under Trevor and catching him midair. Burgess, however, was not so lucky, crashing to the ground, writhing in pain. The two purples dropped on top of him, ripping into his flesh, blood pouring out like black water.

Zoe dropped to the earth, and Scarlet and Trevor hopped down. Then Zoe attacked the two dragons violently, biting, spitting, clawing.

"We need help down here!" Scarlet shouted into her headset.

A moment later, Aiko and Filia dove down, accompanied by Noa and Baby—surprising their enemies, taking them by the tails, grabbing them, and dragging them off Burgess. It was all the advantage the red dragon needed. He ripped into the first purple, pulling his head clean from his body. Zoe followed suit.

Caleb watched in awe. Gone was the gentle, sweet dragon they all knew. Now she was a warrior and she was determined to avenge her brother. Opening her mouth, she blasted the second dragon with fire, literally burning its eyes from its head. Now blind, the dragon stumbled around uselessly until Burgess, Zoe, and Filia put it out of its misery.

"Man, that sister of yours..." Caleb swore under his breath. The pain was starting to subside somewhat, and he was feeling a little better. "She's something else, isn't she?"

But Zavier didn't answer. And when Caleb looked down at his dragon, he realized in horror that he would never answer again.

Zavier was gone. And Caleb was dragonless once again.

But, he told himself as the tears sprung uninvited to his eyes, at least this time it wasn't a senseless murder. Zavier had

342

died a hero. Sacrificed his life to the greater good. To save his brothers and sisters. To save the world.

"You did good, Sparky," Caleb said, his voice choking on the words. "Now get some rest. You've earned it."

Chapter Forty-Nine

As the dragon battle raged on outside, Trin crept through the back door of the mall, using the rope to climb down into the Dracken basement. The hallways were eerily dark and deserted, prompting worry to crawl through her gut. She had hoped a good number of the Dracken would be distracted by the fight going on outside, but to have everyone gone—well, that was just too lucky to be a good thing. Her pulse kicked up in concern, and she found her eyes darting to every corner, sensing a trap. But in the end, she had no choice, and she forced her feet to move forward.

She followed the route Caleb had described until she reached the passageway that dead-ended at a large, heavy door. Peering inside, she saw a huge open room: the dragon holding pen. Empty except… Her heart leapt as she spotted Emmy at the far end, penned up in a metal cage.

Emmy! Trin sent. *We're here to rescue you. I'm outside your door.*

The dragon's head jerked up. Her eyes turned to the door, and Trin let out a breath of relief, realizing she'd been heard.

Just hang on, Emmy. I'll be there in a—

Wait! Don't—

But it was too late. Trin had already pushed open the door—just as a dark figure stepped out of the shadows.

It was Darius.

The Dracken looked older than she remembered him. Whereas once his skin had been smooth and unshaven, now he was scarred and burned, and his hair was wild and unkempt. In fact, he looked as crazy on the outside, Trin thought, as he had been on the inside all along.

She squared her shoulders. "Step aside," she told him, hoping to exude a confidence she didn't quite feel. "It's over. You've lost."

He raised an eyebrow but stood his ground. Then, to Trinity's chagrin, he started to laugh. "Over?" he repeated. "Now that's a good one."

She frowned, feeling her semblance of control fleeing, though she had no idea why. "Your dragons are dead," she added. Maybe he didn't know what was happening outside. "Or they soon will be."

"Those dragons were already dead before the fight began," he said dismissively. "Mutated, sterile, insane. Your dragons did me a favor, putting them out of their misery."

Trinity stared at him, her heart pounding in her chest. "But you were going to breed them with Emmy," she blurted before she could stop herself.

"Was I?" he asked. "No, of course I wasn't," he answered quickly. "Why would I want to create an army of hybrids when I can have the real thing?"

"What?"

"They were bait beasts, of course, nothing more," he said with a sick smile. "A means to giving Emberlyn's children their first taste of blood. Now that they have it, they will always thirst for more."

Trinity watched, confused, as he reached into his pocket and pulled out a cell phone. He pressed at the screen and then held it out to her. There, she saw a live stream of the dragon fight going on outside the building.

"In one hour, this video will be uploaded to all the major news outlets around the world, and humanity will see for themselves, once and for all, what dragons are truly capable of," he explained. "Then it's just a matter of time. The government will mobilize. The army will be sent in. The dragons will be forced to defend themselves, and the Scorch will begin all over again, despite your best efforts to the contrary." He smiled smugly. It was all Trin could do not to punch him in the mouth.

"But...they're purebloods," she protested, feeling all her arguments slipping through her fingers like so much sand. Had Mara been lying? Were they really hybrids after all? But no, they couldn't be. They wouldn't have taken to riders so easily...

Darius laughed. "Yes. Mara thought she was so smart, breeding purebloods instead of hybrids. But what she failed to see is that, in the end, it makes no difference. Dragons are dragons. And now these dragons know how to fight as a team when someone does them wrong. And in this world, my dear? There's always someone ready to do them wrong."

Trinity felt her stomach fall. "No," she said, though the fight had fled from her voice. "I don't believe it."

"My dear, it doesn't matter what you believe. It doesn't matter what you try to do. Everything will lead to the same outcome." He paused, a slow smile crossing his whiskered face. "After all, do you really think this is the first time this has happened?"

"What?"

Now his smile was wide as the Cheshire cat's. "I hate to break it to you, but everything you've been told thus far has been a lie. Well, not a lie, exactly. At one time, I suppose, there was a kernel of truth. But that was many cycles ago."

Trinity started to feel faint. "What are you saying?"

"Don't you see? You're not the ones who started this apocalypse. You're the ones who keep it going. Two hundred years from now, we will send a new Connor and Caleb back in time to find you. The three of you will attempt to prevent the apocalypse, and instead, you will be the ones to make it happen." He snorted. "Time and time again."

"No." She shook her head, unwilling to believe it. "It was you. You and your religious campaign to destroy the world."

"You know, you really should learn not to take what people say at face value, Miss Foxx," Darius scolded. "I mean, 'religious campaign'? Come on. How cliché can you get?"

Trinity stared at him, for a moment not able to even speak as her world came crashing down all around her like a house of cards. She tried to tell herself he was lying. But something inside of her told her this was finally the truth.

"So then…why are you here?" she managed to ask, grasping at straws.

"Consider us…insurance. To make sure you and your group screw things up as royally as you always do. Though, to be fair, you never need much help. You're pretty capable of messing things up all by yourselves."

347

Trinity swallowed hard, her stomach swimming with nausea. She thought of Connor. Of Caleb. Of her grandfather and her father and her mother and everyone else who had sacrificed so much to try to change the world. Could they really only be some part of a sick master plan?

"But why?" she choked out. "I mean, if not a religious campaign, why on earth would you want to bring about the apocalypse? Why would anyone want the world destroyed?"

"Because it allows us to live like kings," he replied. "We made a deal with the Council a long time ago. They send their duff back in time, and we send ours, and together they bumble everything up so badly that it starts all over again. Each time we vary the game a bit, just for fun. Like this time we decided to send twins. That was my special added touch," he added with a laugh. "I hope you enjoyed your little love triangle."

Trinity's stomach roiled. She thought about Connor's constant concerns, about how everything was different yet still the basically same. He had no idea how right he'd been all along. She was only glad that he wasn't around to hear this. She imagined his devastation as he realized that his mission had been nothing more than a plot, that the Council he served was as evil and sick as his supposed enemy. She squeezed her hands into fists, the anger inside threatening to boil over. "You sick bastard," she growled. "How can you just sit there and willingly allow the world to be destroyed?"

"Please. It won't be destroyed." Darius snorted. "Well, the surface will take a beating. But we have been building beautiful cities underground for years now, ready to be sold to the highest bidder. Mankind will survive. We will profit. The world will keep spinning on its axis. All ends well."

"But you won't be alive to enjoy it," she growled. "Because this time, I'm not going to let you live. You make one move to escape, and I will gut you where you stand."

Darius nodded, looking unperturbed. "I'm counting on it," he said pleasantly. "If you don't, I'll be forced to do the job myself. And I find that's always far messier."

"You…want to die?" She hated the despair in her voice, but she couldn't prevent it.

"Of course!" he cried. "Do you think I want to live through the Scorch? No. I will die now, and in about a hundred and sixty years, I will be reborn in my proper time line. By then, the Council will have rewarded my efforts with a trust fund of silver and a beautiful sky house. And this time," he added, "was my last go around. I've played the part of the evil Dracken leader for five cycles running. Now I get to retire. In my next life, I can enjoy the fruits of my labor until I die peacefully in my bed." He smiled slowly. "So I suggest you go ahead and do what you came to do."

She stared at him, so sickened she could barely breathe. "No," she said at last. "I'm not going to do it. Because I don't want you to die. I want you to live so you can see for yourself that this time we've foiled your plan, that we've stopped the apocalypse and you won't be getting your cozy little retirement plan when you respawn."

To her chagrin, he only chuckled. "Come, come, my girl. You know that will never happen. As long as there are dragons in the world, the apocalypse will come. It's only a matter of time." He shrugged. "But suit yourself. If you're not going to kill me, then I suggest you get on with rescuing your dragon. She's waiting for you, you know."

And with that, he stepped aside, giving her a gallant bow as he allowed her to pass. She did, her legs feeling as if they were made of lead as she walked across the room to where Emmy was being held. Woodenly, she pulled open the cage door, which, of course, wasn't even locked. Because she was meant to free Emmy—just like she'd been meant to do everything else. Every choice she made, every conscious decision to try to save the world—the whole time, she'd been nothing but a puppet on a string, dancing.

But Emmy didn't know that. She didn't understand. She bounded forward, covering Trinity's face with slurpy kisses as she bounced up and down with glee. It was all Trinity could do not to throw up then and there, so sickened by the whole thing. But somehow she managed to hold herself in check. To smile at Emmy. To hug her back. It wasn't Emmy's fault, after all. She was as innocent a victim as the rest of them.

Oh, Fire Kissed, Emmy cried joyously. *I knew you'd come for me. I never doubted it for a second.*

"Of course I'd come for you," Trin managed to say. "After all, we're destined, right?"

And it was true, she suddenly realized, but not in the way she had ever dreamed.

Chapter Fifty

The after-party back at the airfield was looking as if it would last all night. Dragons and humans together, dancing, eating, celebrating their victory. Some of the dragons were injured, and their new guardians were tending their wounds with great care. Some of the Potentials had also suffered, and the dragons freely gave their blood to help them heal. The bonds were growing between them. It should have been a beautiful thing.

But as Trinity watched from the sidelines, a slow dread rose up inside of her, and her heart felt as if it weighed a ton. Was Darius right? Was this only the calm before the storm? Would the world ever accept dragons—or would it force the dragons to turn on the world, as Darius had predicted?

She had to admit, it wasn't looking good so far. The rest of them didn't know it yet, but the video Darius had shown her had been released, just as he'd promised. In response, the president had gone on record, vowing to protect the country by any means necessary. Now, government soldiers were likely on their way. It was only a matter of time before they were tracked down here. And then what would they do? Would she allow their dragons to be slaughtered? Or should she let them fight for their lives, knowing full well how it would end?

She watched as Caleb and Scarlet worked together by the fire to clean Zoe's scales. Gone was the fierce dragon they'd seen on the battlefield; now she was only a defeated shell of her former self.

When she'd learned of her brother's death, she'd been so distraught that, for a moment, Trinity had feared she would turn violent, as Zavier had done. But then Emmy had come over. She'd taken Zoe under her wing and soothed her. They'd cried together, mourning the brother and son they'd lost. Trinity's heart warmed to see the mother-daughter bond growing between them. But it also made her want to sob like a baby, imagining all the horrors they would be forced to face so soon.

Because in the end, the world was not ready for dragons.

"For someone who just saved the world, you don't look too happy about it."

She whirled around at the voice, realizing her father had come up behind her. He gave her a sympathetic smile. "What's wrong, honey?" he asked. "Why aren't you out there celebrating with the others?"

She sighed deeply. "Because there isn't anything to celebrate," she said, the whole story spilling from her lips.

When she had finished, her father reached out, pulling her into a warm hug. She sobbed into his shoulder.

"My Trinity," he whispered. "The bravest girl in the world."

"No," she said. "I'm the biggest coward. I let my love for Emmy destroy the world. And evidently I've been doing the same thing, life after life, countless times over. And because I never know it until it's too late, I never make the right choices."

Her father pulled away from the hug, meeting her eyes with his own. "What if you *did* know the next time around? What if you were in control of the reload instead of them?"

Trinity cocked her head in question. "What do you…?" She trailed off, then her eyes widened and her heart pounded in her chest. "Did you fix it?" she asked in a whisper. "Oh my God, did you actually fix the time machine?"

He nodded, regarding her with serious eyes. "It's fixed," he told her. "And if you want to go back and do this all again like we talked about before? Well, I think I can make that happen."

Chapter Fifty-One

E mmy? Are you in here?"

Trinity peeked through the doorway of the hangar, looking for her dragon. She hadn't seen her outside at the party and assumed she must have retreated to her lair. Sure enough, the red curtain had been pulled aside, and Emmy had plopped down in front of the TV, a couple of her children curled up beside her. She looked up at Trinity, then gave her a sheepish grin.

Sorry, she said. *I just wanted to show them the first episode of* Merlin. *I've been telling them all about it and—*

Trinity waved her off. "It's fine," she assured the dragon. "But can I talk to you for a moment?"

Of course. Emmy rose to her feet, giving her children a fond look then following Trinity to the opposite end of the hangar. When they stopped, the dragon leaned down to nuzzle Trinity with her snout. Trinity smiled, kissing her nose, then reaching up and scratching her behind the ear.

"Oh, Emmy," she said to the dragon, "I've got the best news ever." Excitedly, she related to the dragon what her father had told her. Emmy listened quietly, without interruption.

"Isn't that amazing?" Trinity asked once she'd finished. "We can fix everything, and the Dracken can't do a thing about it! I can go back in time to when you were still an egg. And I can make sure everything happens right this time around. I can defeat the Dracken. I can protect you from the government. You won't be taken captive this time. You won't be impregnated against your will." She beamed. "It'll be happily ever after, Emmy. Just like we always dreamed about."

She looked up at the dragon, then furrowed her brow. Instead of the excited, happy expression she expected on Emmy's face, the dragon looked concerned. Trin watched, puzzled, as Emmy glanced back to where her children were watching TV. Then she turned back to Trinity, a guilty expression on her face.

"What's wrong?" Trinity asked, her pulse kicking up in concern. "I thought you'd be thrilled. This is what you wanted, right? What we talked about? This was what we've been working toward all this time."

I know. But… Emmy gave her a tortured look.

"What, Emmy…?" Trinity started to say. Then she closed her mouth, realization washing over her. She glanced up at the dragon, then over at her children. "Oh," she said. "Right."

If you turn back the clocks, they will never be born, Emmy said slowly. *They risked their lives to save me. How can I turn around and take theirs away?*

Trinity nodded slowly, realizing what the dragon was saying. "I know, Ems," she said. "But what other option is there? We can't hide you all forever. The government is going to close in on us. If we stay, the apocalypse is going to begin again, no matter what we do. We can't just sit back and let Darius win!"

Emmy considered this for a moment. *What about the place with all the dragons?*

355

Trinity stared at her. In her excitement about the opportunity of the do-over, she'd forgotten the original purpose of the time machine: her father could send all the dragons back in time a million years—and they would all be safe.

But still…

She felt tears well in the corners of her eyes. It took everything inside of her not to scream, "What about me?" She and Emmy were supposed to be destined. And now Emmy was ready to walk away forever.

She drew in a breath. She couldn't be selfish here. Emmy had tried everything to make it work and had suffered so much by doing it. Now she just wanted to be a mother. To save her children.

She had a life now. A life beyond Trinity. And Trinity had to finally learn to let her go.

"Okay," she said. "I think we can do that." Her voice broke on the last bit, and Emmy peered at her, looking concerned.

Will you be okay? she asked. *I won't go if you need me to stay. I made a promise to you. I would never let you fall.*

Trinity forced herself to smile, even as her heart broke in her chest. "I will be fine," she assured the dragon. "Not that I won't miss you like crazy. But I'll be fine."

And, she realized as she said the words, she would be. She had lost so much over the last year—her mother, her grandfather, Connor. Now her dragon. But through it all, she had stood strong. And she would continue to stand strong in whatever was to come. Even if that meant a very un-epic, unexciting existence from this point on.

She watched, swiping away the tears, as Emmy bounded over to her children to share the news. This wasn't a sad thing, she reminded herself. The dragons were going home. To a place where they would be top of the food chain. She tried to imagine them skimming the surface of the world, unfettered and free. Her only regret was she couldn't watch it for herself.

But Emmy's world was not hers. And hers was not her dragon's. They would part. But they would both stand strong. Alone but always, deep down, together.

They were destined after all…

Chapter Fifty-Two

Trinity kept her promise, informing the group the next morning what the dragons had decided to do. The team was sad; they loved Emmy, and in the short time they'd gotten to know the other dragons, they'd grown to love them too. But at the same time, they understood the reasons behind the decision. How could they not want them to be safe?

They spent all morning saying their good-byes. The dragons looked almost as sad as their guardians when at last they shuffled toward the time-travel gate. But Emmy gently urged them forward, nuzzling them and encouraging them as they went. And the way they looked at her—well, it made Trinity's heart melt with pride. She didn't have a single doubt that Emmy was going to take good care of her brood. Be the best dragon mother ever.

Once the dragons were all lined up and the time machine had powered up, Emmy turned to Trinity, giving her a sheepish look.

I don't know what to say. I don't know how to say good-bye.

Trinity bit back her tears. "I've never been good at it," she confessed. "It's hard to let go. But I'm excited for you, Emmy! I'm so excited. You're going to have an amazing life. And your children will be strong and happy and free. That's all that matters in the end."

For a moment, Emmy seemed to smile at this. Then she sobered. *Are you sure you're going to be okay? I hate leaving you alone.*

"I'm not alone," Trinity reminded her, gesturing to the group of people behind her: her father, her teammates, Caleb. Even Scarlet, who stood there with tears streaming down her cheeks as she clutched Caleb's hands. "I'll never be alone, Emmy. And even if I were? Well, I'd be okay."

I know you would, Fire Kissed. That is why I am able to go. But before I do…

The dragon stopped in front of her. She held out her paw. The beautiful, sparkly necklace dazzled at her wrist. Trin looked up at Emmy. The dragon grinned.

To remember me by.

Trin took the necklace with trembling hands, slipping it back over her head. Then she grabbed Emmy and hugged her with a fierceness that took both their breath away. Finally, they parted, and Trin bowed her head to the dragon, forcing back a fresh round of tears. There was nothing to be sad about now, she told herself. This was a joyous moment.

Good-bye, Emberlyn, she whispered in the dragon's head, not trusting herself to speak.

Good-bye, Fire Kissed.

Emmy turned then, breaking their gaze and stepping toward the time machine. Trin watched as she sucked in a breath, then stepped inside. There was a flash of light. Then, just like that, Emmy disappeared.

Everyone gasped. The other dragons whined and pawed the ground nervously. But Burgess stepped up to the gate next, nodding at the others. He was a born leader, Trinity realized. They all looked up to him. So when he stepped through the gate and disappeared like their mother had, they all eagerly clamored to follow suit, one by one by one.

Trinity glanced over at her father. He was counting the dragons as they went, keeping the machine powered and ready. And as the last dragon walked through the gate, Trinity let out a breath. She turned to the others.

"Well," she said. "I guess that's it." A lump formed in her throat.

"Wait," her father said. "I think we're missing one." He ran over his calculations then compared them to the tally on the machine. "One dragon did not go through the gate."

Trinity's heart stuttered. Had one of the dragons changed its mind? None of this would work if they didn't all go through. She looked around wildly as the others did the same. "Who was it?" she demanded. "Did anyone see? Whose dragon did not go through the gate?"

"It was Zoe."

Trinity whirled around, heart in her throat as none other than Connor himself stepped into the hangar. He was white-faced and trembling, looking more like his brother than himself. But he was here. He was alive. He was back on Earth.

"Connor," she whispered, feeling as if she was seeing a ghost. She supposed, in a way, she was. "What…?"

He stepped forward, pulling her into his arms, pressing his whole body against her as he hugged her fiercely. She could feel his heartbeat driving against her chest as he held her close, the slight tremor in his hands. Her heart soared, and the tears began to flow freely all over again.

"What are you doing here?" she whispered in his ear.

"Zoe had a change of heart," he told her. "Without Zavier, she had no desire to stay in this world. She wanted to go back to the Nether and join him and her grandmother. They belonged together, she told me. Just like you and I belong together."

Trinity shook her head, scarcely able to believe it all. But what did it matter anyway? The end was the same. Connor was back. And for the first time ever, there was nothing to keep them apart.

"So, uh, mission accomplished," she chokingly teased as she reached up to brush a lock of hair from his eyes. "Apocalypse averted. Hasta la vista, dragon spawn."

"And bon voyage, Emmy and her family," he added. "I hope they all find peace and happiness at last."

"You know what would probably make Emmy truly happy?" Trin asked, with a wistful smile.

"What's that?"

"If you gave me a happily ever after kiss."

And so he did. A Hollywood-worthy kiss that would make even the most TV-addicted dragon proud.

Epilogue

A warm breeze caressed Trinity's face. She opened her eyes. A lush jungle spread out around her as far as she could see. It was warm. Wet. With large caves at every turn.

Trin's heart thumped in her chest as she looked around, wondering if this would really work. She bit her lower lip, garnering her courage.

Emmy?

For a moment, there was nothing. Then she heard it: the familiar sound of thundering wings above. She remembered once being scared of the sound. Now it was the sweetest music she'd ever heard. A moment later, the giant green dragon landed in front of her, looking at her scoldingly.

What are you doing here? she asked Trinity.

Trinity gave her a sheepish smile. "I wanted to see you," she admitted. "And, well, I guess I wanted to hear the end of your story, how it all turned out for you guys. You're not the only one who appreciates a happily ever after, you know."

Emmy snorted grumpily, but Trin could see the smile tugging at her mouth. Then, to her delight, the giant dragon curled herself around her, allowing Trin to take a cozy seat between her belly and her legs. Once she was settled,

Emmy leaned forward to give her a slurp on the top of her head.

Just this once, she told Trin sternly. *After all, you know more than anyone what can happen if you keep coming back to the Nether.*

"I know," Trin assured her. "And I won't."

The dragon seemed to accept that. She stretched out her neck, rubbing it against a nearby tree trunk to scratch her scales. Looking at her now, it was hard to believe that only one day had passed since they'd said good-bye. One day for Trinity, anyway. But a lifetime for Emmy, who had lived and died a million years in the past and now made her home here in the Nether with the rest of her kind.

The place you sent us was beautiful, the dragon told her. *And we were able to make a home. We met other dragons, and they showed us how things worked. We were terrible dragons at first; we didn't know how to hunt for food or really fly. But they helped us. And soon we were capable of surviving on our own. But we stayed with them anyway. We hunted. We mated. Before I knew it, I had grandchildren, then great-grandchildren.* The dragon smiled. *It was a wonderful life, Trinity. A perfect life. My only regret is I couldn't share it with you.*

Trinity hugged the dragon, feeling tears roll down her cheeks. "I feel the same way," she told her. "Though it's only been one day without you for me, it's been one really long day. I don't know how I'm going to get through the rest of my life."

The dragon gazed down on her kindly. *You'll manage*, she told her. *And you are not alone.*

"No," Trinity agreed. "I'm not, am I?" She rose to her feet. "None of us are."

She opened her mouth, wanting to see if the dragon would conjure up a TV so they could spend some time binge-watching something on BBC, just like they used to. But then she caught Emmy glancing to the side when she thought Trinity wasn't looking. And when she followed her gaze, she saw something moving in the bushes.

"Emmy!" she cried. "Do you have a boyfriend?"

If dragons could have blushed, Emmy would have been purple. She turned away, a goofy grin on her reptilian face.

His name is Ash, the dragon admitted. *We've been…hanging around…for a while now.*

"Oh, Emmy!" Trinity's heart felt as if it were going to burst. "Can I meet him?"

He's very shy, Emmy hedged. *He doesn't like humans much either, no offense.*

"I don't really blame him," Trinity replied, smiling sadly at her dragon. "And it doesn't matter—as long he likes you."

A slow smile crept to Emmy's lips. *I'm pretty sure he does.*

"Well, then," Trinity replied, feeling choked up. "I should head out then."

Emmy looked guilty. *No, I didn't mean to make you leave—*

"It's okay, Ems," Trinity said, standing on her tiptoes to kiss her cheek. "You've got a life to live. And so do I." She met the dragon's beautiful blue eyes with her own. "I'll never forget you, Emberlyn."

Nor I you, Fire Kissed. I have shared your story with all the dragons. You will live in our collective unconsciousness till the end of time. Trinity Foxx. The Fire Kissed. The girl who saved the world.

Trin smiled through her tears. "I like the sound of that."

And with that, she forced herself to turn and walk away—the hardest steps she knew she'd ever have to take. Sure, she could come back. But at the same time, she knew she wouldn't. Because that was how it was supposed to be. Before she exited though, she did take one last peek. Just in time to see a giant ruby-red dragon step out from the jungle and approach Emmy. He was huge, glistening and sparkling under the sunlight. When he reached Emmy, he nudged her with his snout, and she nudged him back. Then they turned and headed back into the jungle together.

"Good-bye, Emmy," Trinity whispered. "I'm glad you got your happily ever after at last."

And with that, she exited. Back to her own life. Her own family. Because she had a happily ever after of her own to get to. And she couldn't wait to get started.

Acknowledgments

It's a bittersweet thing to bring a trilogy to an end. To close the door on a world that you created and lived in for so long. But I hope you readers enjoyed Team Dragon's adventures and I feel privileged that you chose to go on the journey with me. In many acknowledgments, readers are mentioned last—or not at all—but without you, there would be no reason to write. And so first and foremost, thank you for loving Emmy and Trin, Connor and Caleb, and the rest as much as I have. Thank you also to my editor, Aubrey Poole, and her dragon-sized enthusiasm for this project. It's nice to have an editor who truly "gets" my geek. Thank you also to the publicity and marketing team at Sourcebooks for sharing it with the world. And to the sales team for getting the books onto the shelves at bookstores. And to all the librarians and teachers who have shared them with their students.

Thank you also to Scholastic for including Scorched in your book fairs and clubs—I was a big Scholastic reader back when I was a kid, so seeing my book in the flyer feels like a childhood dream come true. Special thanks to Ed Masessa for making it happen. (May you live long and prosper.)

Thank you to Kristin Nelson, who championed and

agented the series. To Leah and Derry, who worked on the earlier books and first ignited the flame. And to my writer friends who offered crazy support and encouragement when I needed it most. It's hard to name everyone without leaving someone out, but the biggest shout-outs to Diana Peterfreund, Cory Putman Oakes, Cynthia Leitich Smith, PJ Hoover, Madeline Smoot, Jo Whittemore, Simone Elkeles, Ally Carter, Heather Brewer, Tracy Deebs, Tera Lynn Childs, and, of course, ALL of #teamberlin.

And, of course, lastly I want to thank my husband, Jacob, who is always encouraging and more supportive than I deserve him to be. Without him, none of this would be possible.

About the Author

Mari Mancusi always wanted a dragon as a pet. Unfortunately, the fire insurance premiums proved a bit too large and her house a bit too small—so she chose to write about them instead. Today she works as an award-winning young adult author and freelance television producer, for which she has won two Emmys. When not writing about fanciful creatures of myth and legend, Mari enjoys traveling, cosplay, watching cheesy (and scary) horror movies, and her favorite guilty pleasure—playing video games. A graduate of Boston University, she lives in Austin, Texas, with her husband Jacob, daughter Avalon, and their dog Mesquite.

SCORCHED

Mari Mancusi

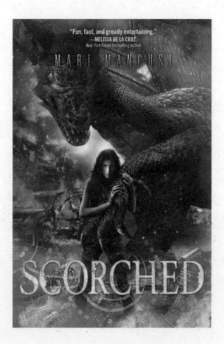

SHATTERED

Mari Mancusi

NIGHT SKY

Suzanne Brockmann and Melanie Brockmann

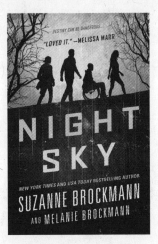

Destiny can be dangerous...

Hunted. Kidnapped. Bled. Someone is snatching girls and draining them for a secret that's in their blood. A hormone that makes them stronger, faster, smarter. A hormone that the makers of a new drug called Destiny will murder to get their hands on. These girls could be anyone. They could be anywhere.

They could be you.

When Skylar discovers she's a Greater-Than, a girl with terrifying power, her life will never be the same. The only way to stay alive is to join the fight against Destiny and become the ultimate weapon.

WILD SKY

Suzanne Brockmann and Melanie Brockmann

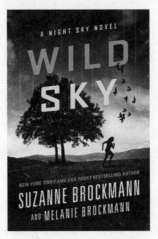

Destiny has chosen Skylar.
Now it might destroy her.

Skylar is a girl with extraordinary power. A girl with a mission to use her Greater-Than gifts to stop the makers of Destiny from getting people hooked on their deadly drug. But Sky is still mastering her new abilities, and her first mission to destroy a Destiny lab leaves her best friend addicted to the drug. For a few days, Cal will be able to walk again—until it kills him. Time is running out for Sky to save the world without sacrificing her friends, to become truly Greater-Than...